The Three Damosels

The Three Damosels

VERA CHAPMAN

VICTOR GOLLANCZ

LONDON

First published in three volumes in Great Britain 1975, 1976
by Rex Collings Ltd
Published in Great Britain 1996
by Victor Gollancz
An imprint of the Cassell Group
Wellington House, 125 Strand, London WC2R OBB

© Vera Chapman 1975, 1976

A catalogue record for this book is
available from the British Library

ISBN 0 575 06340 8

Typeset by CentraCet Ltd, Cambridge
Printed in Great Britain by
St Edmundsbury Press Ltd, Bury St Edmunds, Suffolk

96 97 98   5 4 3 2 1

Contents

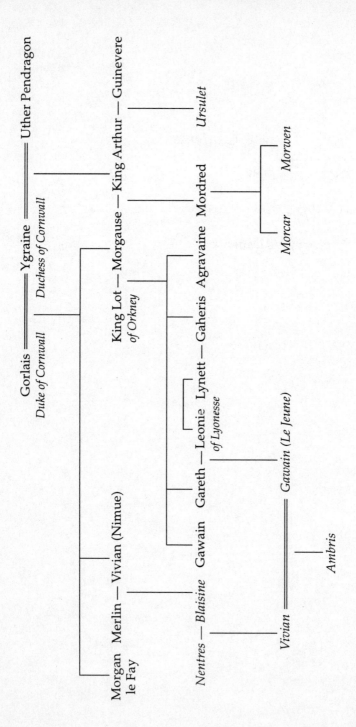

[*Author's note:* Those in italics are my own invention. The rest are according to Malory.]

The Green Knight

Note from the Author

Sir Gawain and the Green Knight is a metrical romance of the fourteenth century, of which the late and honoured Professor J. R. R. Tolkien made a very special study. Several modern versions of it exist, but the Professor's own version is eagerly awaited.

The story is not to be found in Malory, though he has many tales of Sir Gawain of Orkney, a character who does not at all fit the present story, so that I have taken the liberty of supposing a younger Gawain. The story told in the romance seems on the face of it unfinished; and it occurred to me to speculate whether the Green Knight and the Lady of the Castle Haut-Desert might not both have been unwilling accomplices of Morgan le Fay. Thus the rest of the story developed in my mind.

The liberties I have taken with the traditional Arthurian legends are no more than gleeman or romancer would have taken in his day; this is a story and nothing more, and as a story it begs a hearing.

V.C. 1975

1 · Vivian

We turned our horses and rode into that terrible dark wood – the Lady Morgan le Fay, myself, her fifteen-year-old niece, and the four silent serving-men that followed us. I had never been in so dark a wood before.

Indeed, I had never been in any wood before – since up to an hour back, I had lived, as far as I could remember, in the quiet, safe, sunny retreat of the convent at Amesbury; and now I was going into this . . .

The horses' hoofs made no sound on the soft pine-needles. It was so dark that at first I could see nothing at all; then as my sight cleared, the first thing I saw was a little thin yellow snake, hanging head downwards from a branch, right on a level with my eyes – and its head and face were that of a tiny little woman. I cried out and crossed myself.

'Don't do that,' came my aunt's voice, low, level and severe. She pointed a finger at the woman-headed snake and it coiled itself up like a spring above us, and we left it. But the whole wood was full of things, all rustling and stirring and peering with bright eyes – little birds were everywhere, but not only birds – squirrels and stoats, and what else? The wood was all of firs or pines, with no lighter trees or undergrowth – only the endless brown trunks, and the webs of spindly dead twigs that fringe the lower parts of fir-trees where nobody comes. Presently I saw that some of the small animals were not animals but tiny brown men, scuttling among the dead branches. Some were part men and part animals, squirrels with little human heads and arms, or birds with odd beaky human faces. They frightened me, but now I dared not cross myself.

'Why do you concern yourself with those things?' my aunt said, without looking round. 'They are quite normal and natural here – they are even vulgar. If you want marvels I will show you better ones presently.'

She was really my great-aunt, my only living relative as far as I knew. I am Vivian, the daughter of Blaisine, who was the daughter of Vivian called Nimue. This Vivian-Nimue had been the youngest of the three witchy daughters of the beautiful Ygraine of Cornwall – Morgause, the Queen of Orkney, and Morgan le Fay being the other two. But Ygraine was also the mother of King Arthur by Uther Pendragon, so I am some sort of kin to King Arthur. Also I suppose there is witch blood in me, though I thought by the time it came to me it must have run rather thin. But I did not know then who my grandfather was.

My mother had died when I was born, and my father had died fighting for King Arthur, so as far back as I could remember my home had been with the kind nuns at Amesbury. A peaceful place, and still is; our poor Guinevere has found peace there at last, after all she has been through – but this isn't Guinevere's story, thank God, but mine. No one ever came to see me there but the Lady Morgan le Fay, and she was an exciting though rather disturbing relative to have. And then one day – the very day before this story opens – she had descended upon us, and told the Lady Abbess that she had come to take me home with her. She did not say where, nor yet why.

There she was in the Lady Abbess's parlour, glowing and crackling like a fire, and the Lady Abbess, who was an outstanding personality if ever there was one, and twice as alive as any of us, looking like a cold fish beside her. So when she said, 'Well, little Vivian, will you come?' of course I said, 'Oh, yes!' as if I were spellbound.

'We will miss you, Vivian,' the Lady Abbess said gently, and I replied, 'Yes, of course—' in such an airy and offhand way that it wasn't till afterwards that I remembered that I had done less than justice to that kind woman and all the others. When I remembered, a long time afterwards, I cried, but it was too late then.

'When do we start?' I asked eagerly, and when Aunt Morgan said 'Tomorrow early,' I could hardly wait for the Lady Abbess's dismissal before I tore away like a wild bird, to babble the exciting news to my companions, fling my few possessions into a bag, and show off the gown and mantle my aunt had brought me for the journey.

She spent the night in the convent, of course, and never was there such exemplary courtesy, such meek piety, as Morgan le Fay showed at refectory and in chapel – so dignified, so gentle, so circumspect, so devout. That was something I laughed about afterwards. At the time I thought she should have been a Lady Abbess herself. Just two things were odd, and I only remembered them later. She never crossed herself, and she took care not to touch the holy water.

Early in the morning we started off. There was a nice cream-coloured pony for me to ride (of course I was accustomed to a little gentle riding, for we used to take sedate exercise in fine weather, on ponies, donkeys and jennets, through the village and down the safe part of the road) – she herself had a tall white mule, and four serving-men rode with us on cobs, each leading a packhorse. We were quite a cavalcade. All was bustle and excitement, most of the nuns crying at my departure, and some of my companions too – the Lady Abbess looking very grave – the servants all in a flutter. My aunt gave out gold pieces to the servants like pennies, and they cheered her.

All this I recollected as we went through that eerie wood, until at last there was light in front of us.

'Aunt Morgan,' I ventured to ask her, 'where are we going?'

'To the Castle of Haut-Desert,' she replied. 'Sir Bertalik is the castellan.'

'Oh, is he your husband?' I asked, all in my innocence.

She turned right round in her saddle and looked at me.

'My husband? Good God, no. What a silly question to ask. You must learn not to ask silly questions.' And she gave a short, shallow laugh.

I was glad when she turned away from me again. We began

to see daylight now through the fir-trees, and soon we were out on the bare wild heath – such country as I had never seen, treeless as far as the eye could reach, and almost flat – the contours just gently undulating, high and dry under the heavens, sprinkled only with crouching juniper bushes. And there before us – there were the Stones, that great ancient place that the country folk called Stonehenge, or the Dance of the Giants. There it stood on the skyline above us as we came out of the wood – old, old, ever so old, but perfect, a circle of vast hewn pillars with an even row of lintel stones above them, sometimes dark thundery grey, sometimes, as the light changed, startlingly white; and above the circle made by the lintels, five great trilithons towered up from inside, three of them overtopping the rest. There was another circle of stones inside, and from somewhere within there went up a single thread of smoke. And outside, as we approached, one vast pillar of stone stood up alone by the lip of green bank that encircled it all; and between that upright stone and the circle another stone lay recumbent, with a wreath of flowers on it.

I quite thought, seeing that my aunt was at home with all witchy things, that she would approach the Stones as by right; and I dreaded to see her lead the way there, and drag me with her into some unimaginable rite of devils. Perhaps she had brought me here to lay me down on that recumbent stone and slit my throat with the knife at her girdle? But to my surprise and relief, she turned away, and led the cavalcade in a detour as far from the Stones as possible. Yet a shudder ran over me, such as they say happens when a goose runs over one's grave. We turned north, as far as I could guess from the sun, and soon were out of sight of Stonehenge and into another forest.

This forest was of oaks and beeches, lighter and gayer than the fir-wood, and as it was high summer, it was full of life and beauty. Wild-rose bushes and flowering elders stood here and there by the wayside, and the bracken was warm in the sunshine, with the deer showing their antlers above it. Here, instead of the small brown men, there were lovely winged creatures like little girls, fluttering up into our faces and away again; and several times I saw a gang of curly-headed fauns scuttling away together. But my aunt treated all these with contempt, as if they were low forms of life not worth her notice.

It was high noon now, and I began to feel very hungry, so I was glad when she called a halt and we dismounted in a very pleasant grassy glade. We settled ourselves comfortably at the foot of a beech-tree, while the serving-men (who all this time had never said a word) withdrew a little way with the horses.

As we sat under the beech-tree, I looked at her, and wondered. Now, nobody ever knew how old Morgan le Fay was. That was only one of the odd things about her. I have seen her look like a girl in her teens, and I have seen her look like an old crone on the edge of the grave; but mostly she looked like a fine woman of forty-five. She was my grand-mother's sister, I knew that, so she must have been old enough to be my grandmother – yet she had a smooth oval face, with a clear, slightly olive skin; black hair without a thread of grey, and I'd swear it wasn't dyed; a perfect figure, upright and supple as a wand, her waist no bigger than mine. But that gives you no idea of her bold, slightly sinister beauty. She was like a handful of jewels, even when she was wearing none. Men would feel the pull of her like a string, and even women could not remain indifferent to her.

'Now,' said my aunt, 'if you really want to see something surprising—'

She raised her hand and snapped her fingers in a peculiar way.

First came the music – exquisite unearthly music, floating out of nowhere, as from no instruments I had ever heard, and blent with voices that sang a tune but no words. Then there entered through the trees, moving to the music, two tall beautiful women, one in pale green like the beech-leaves with the light through them, and one in silver-grey. They bowed low before us, and then came two more, one in copper-brown and one in the pale pink of the wild roses. All their dresses were most curiously wrought with gold threads and small pearls. Then they four went through a slow and stately dance. But then the music changed, and eight gay and slender little girls, in blues like the late bluebells and the wood violets, danced intricately round and round, and eight boys in brown and gold sprang among them and partnered them. Then came gay little dwarfish mountebanks all in gold from top to toe, dancing a neat, merry, laughable dance. And then came a stately procession of tall black men in gold and white and scarlet, bearing dishes of food, of the rarest and richest I had ever seen. There were dressed capons, and jellied pies, and fruit, and sweetmeats – and oh! I was so hungry – how my mouth watered in anticipation of the feast they were setting before us ... The black men bowed low and offered us the dishes, and, being very young and very hungry, I reached out and took one of the delicious cakes they offered – it was a cream tart, I remember – and put it into my mouth. My lips closed on just nothing. In my bitter disappointment I burst into tears, and instantly the whole pageant was gone.

'Heavens, child,' said my aunt, 'you expect too much.' She didn't seem furious, only mildly annoyed and a little amused.

'But I'm hungry !' I cried.

'Well, well! But of course.' She produced a saddlebag that lay against her knees, and took from it bread and cheese, pasties, apples and a flagon of ale; good homely food, and I was glad of it, but it wasn't like the feast I had seen spread before me. It was a long time before I got over the disappointment.

'I thought my shows might amuse you,' my aunt said. 'But of course – you prefer something more – shall we say? – material. Of course.'

Later on I ventured to ask her why the serving-men did not eat too.

'Oh, them!' she said. 'They never eat. They are just shapes, like the others. Look!' She beckoned one of them over – he stood dully before us, looking out at nothing with expressionless eyes. She snapped her fingers in front of his face, and suddenly he wasn't there at all; then she snapped her fingers again, and there he was once more, without one ripple of expression on his stupid face. She sent him back to the others with a wave of her hand as if steering him.

'Very useful,' she said. 'They put up a good show, in case of attack from men or beasts, and if necessary I could make them fight; but they never eat, drink or sleep, and I can get rid of them whenever I wish.'

We journeyed on through the afternoon, with the sun declining on our left, and when it grew dark the uncanny serving-men pitched a tent for us – 'pight our pavilion' as those court-poets would say – and there we spent the night, with those four ghostly servitors keeping watch, like statues, all through the night at the four corners of the tent, unsleeping. I can't say I slept much; I knew we were quite safe with those inhuman watchers, nonetheless it gave me the creeps to think of them.

So we travelled on for two days more, always going northwards, through country ever becoming wilder and more desolate. Never before had I seen forests growing in regions of sheer rocks, the roots of trees denuded and hanging in the air above precipitous falls, where we picked our way sideways along paths cut out of the face of the cliffs. The creatures we met grew stranger too – little brown or black earth-men, round and rolling and muddy; or big brown gnarled satyrs (the look of them terrified me) – and once in the distance a towering bearded centaur. But these were not at all friendly creatures, though they seemed, I thought, to please Aunt Morgan's temperament more than the others.

On the evening of the seventh day, with the sun low and red on our left, we came in sight at last of the Castle Haut-Desert. It stood on a high crag, rising out of the trees, and the evening sun caught and flooded it with amber light, picking out its intricate battlements and its gilded weather-vanes. A lovely picture it looked, and certainly the first human habitation we had seen in all our journey. We pressed on with good

courage and soon reached a wide path leading up to the
drawbridge, which had been let down for our reception. A
bodyguard of house-carles was drawn up to welcome us, and
at the outer gateway was my host himself.

And here a strange thing happened. We lost sight of the
welcoming party for an instant, rounding a belt of trees, and
then came full in sight of the castle's owner, quite close at
hand. I looked – quite plainly and calmly in full light – and
saw him as a young man in his early twenties or younger,
with dark glossy hair cut straight below his ears, with a clean-
cut and well-proportioned nose, brow and chin – with grey
eyes – but, well there! all I could say is that beside and
beyond, there was something that said to my whole heart and
soul and body: 'This is he.'

Not knowing what I was doing, regardless of all manners
and modesty, without a moment's hesitation I slipped from
my horse and ran across the intervening space with my hands
outstretched. I could not have done otherwise for my life.
And then, somehow, the man to whom I was stretching out
my hands was a thick-set, greying bullet-headed man of fifty
– sturdy and powerful and jovial, with a short chin-beard and
grizzled curls, eyes twinkling under bushy brows, thick lips
coarse but cheerful – nothing like the young man I had just
seen.

I almost fell forward into Sir Bertilak's arms – he put out
his big warm hands and caught me, exclaiming, 'Little Lady
Vivian! Welcome, child, and come in. Shall I call you niece, or
would I do better as your grandad?'

I knew, almost on the instant, that this must be just another
of Aunt Morgan's sleights; but why, why had she done this
to me? There I was, stirred and shaken to my heart's core by
the sudden glimpse of the man I would have died for – and
there was Sir Bertilak, bussing me heartily on both cheeks,
and rallying me for their paleness and coldness.

And so I went over the drawbridge into the Castle of Haut-
Desert, commending my soul to God and Our Lady – but not

daring to cross myself because of my aunt Morgan le Fay who followed close behind me.

Very soon my aunt Morgan began to educate me as a sorceress. This was unexpected and very interesting. Of course I was already lettered, for at the convent we learnt to read and write, and to understand Latin and French and a certain amount of ciphering; but now I had to go further and even learn a little Greek and Hebrew, as well as hard calculations about planets and stars and their positions in the sky. Astrology made up a large part of my studies, and I became quite good at casting the nativities of purely imaginary persons – my aunt would never let me try real ones, and strictly forbade me to cast my own, threatening me with such dire bad luck that I did not care to. I also learnt a formidable quantity of correspondences, attributions, Names of Power and such; with strange lore about the properties of herbs and stones, and the secrets of the four elements. When I had learnt enough, my aunt said, I should be able to command those odd people we had seen in the woods on our journey – but only if she told me the right words, which she might do in the course of time. For those things, the elementals, were real beings, she told me, not shapes conjured up by her power. That power, the art of raising illusions and deceits, she kept to herself – it was her own in a very special way.

There were also exercises, such as sitting very still and concentrating all the power of my thought on one object; and sometimes she would send me into a kind of dream, from which I would awake cold and shaking. She would fire questions at me then about what I had dreamt, but I never could remember anything very clearly, and that annoyed her.

She said to me one day, 'You know, Vivian, you are a witch by inheritance, and you certainly have some of the powers; but you will not have all the powers till you become a witch of your own will, and take the vows.'

I said, 'What vows, Aunt?'

'You will know when you come to them,' she replied.

'But whom do I make them to?' I persisted, and then, very daring, 'Must I make vows to Satan?'

She smiled. 'Well, in a way no, and in a way yes,' she said. 'It depends on how you look at it. In the long run, you see, you make the vows to yourself, for your allegiance is to yourself, and in the end it is yourself you will serve. Do you understand?'

'I understand,' I said, and in that moment I did understand indeed. I felt a cold sinking in my heart, and a shudder. 'Give me time to think about it,' I said. 'I can't make any vows suddenly.'

So time passed. The castle was a pleasant place, full of people, Sir Bertilak's retainers and men-at-arms mostly, with their wives and families. I came to know them, though Aunt Morgan was not on very intimate terms with any of them, and tended to keep me at a distance from them as far as she could. My lessons, and the work in the kitchen and still-room and garden, took up a good deal of the time; but there was hunting too, and that was where Sir Bertilak came into his own. Almost every fine day he would lead us all out on horseback; all the men, and a few of the women, with a straggling of children following on ponies or donkeys or on foot; and we would scour the countryside, hell-for-leather, after the fox or the hare or the deer – or in the winter, with care and organization, for this was difficult and could be serious, the dangerous wild boar. I came to love the vigorous exercise in the fresh air. Uncle Bertilak, as I came to call him, was the best of company, and I became very fond of him. He was cheerful and loudmouthed and downright, and called things by their plain names in such a way as made the seneschal's wife frown, and the huntsmen's wives blush and titter – but Aunt Morgan never turned a hair. I was puzzled as to the relationship between them. They were of course not husband and wife; she had her wing of the castle, where I lived with her, and he had another, and their manner when together was in no way like lovers; yet even I could tell that he was entirely dominated by her, and afraid of her too.

My room was a corner turret, up a winding staircase that opened below into the great hall; and above it was my aunt's room, at the top; there was a way out from her room on to the leads, and there she kept a pigeon-cote with carrier pigeons. About once a week a carrier pigeon would come in, with a letter rolled up in a small case strapped to its leg. These were from her spies in Camelot, but who they were, or how the pigeons were conveyed to Camelot in the first place, I never learnt. Sometimes she would caress and feed the pigeon after taking the letter from it; but now and then, when the news displeased her, she would grab the poor thing in her strong, thin hands and wring its neck. I would find the pigeon dropped casually on the winding stair, and I grieved for the poor birds, who journeyed so far and so faithfully only to meet their death because of unwelcome news for which they were not responsible.

After a long time of studying and trying, I at last found myself able to do one little piece of magic – I succeeded in making myself invisible. It was only a small degree of invisibility – it would last, so my aunt told me, about half an hour, and during that time I could escape the notice of anyone who wasn't expecting to see me or looking very hard. It was partly a matter of mental concentration – the rest, of course, I can't divulge.

It was a horrible, cold afternoon before Christmas – so black and cheerless and chilly, especially in our dark stony castle. The time of year when if you hadn't Christmas to look forward to, you'd give up altogether, and even with Christmas only a few days away, there was something so utterly depressing . . . I had shut myself in my room and was keeping myself warm as best I could with a brazier, and amusing myself by working hard at the invisibility experiment – when suddenly the image of myself in the big steel mirror on the wall flickered and went out. I thought, 'I've done it at last!' and almost at that moment one of the castle maids came in to put more charcoal on the brazier. I could tell at once that she couldn't see me, for she came in without a word of greeting or apology, looking all around as if there was no one there, and walked straight past me – she would have walked into me if I hadn't stepped smartly aside, for I didn't want to give her a shock and have her knock the brazier over. So I skipped out of the door she had left open and ran down the stairs in high glee to show my aunt that she couldn't see me, so to speak – at least, to let her know that the experiment had succeeded. I could hear her voice in the hall below.

But on the stairs I nearly stepped on yet another of those poor pigeons – not only with its neck wrung, but mangled almost as if by a cat. My high spirits sank, and I stole down to the hall and stood invisibly at the stair foot, holding the newel-post.

The hall was at the moment flooded by the afternoon sunlight, cold but coloured by the stained glass of the high windows; a fire burned in the wide hearth; and there was my aunt, pacing to and fro, with Sir Bertilak standing uneasily by the fireplace.

'But this must not be,' she exclaimed. 'I say it must not be.'

'No, indeed, my dear,' he said in his kind but rather dim way. 'I'm sure – but what?'

'This news – this news,' she said. 'Don't you understand? Guinevere is with child.'

'Why – well,' he said. 'I suppose that's excellent – oh yes, very. We all would wish—'

'What I wish and what you wish,' she snapped, 'are two very different things. You ought to know that by this time, fool. Arthur must not, must *not* be allowed to establish his line. I would – you've no idea what would happen. I *will not* have it. This child must not be born. Do you understand?'

'Yes, my lady,' he said, drooping; and I began to feel a chill steal over me, as the sunlight died out of the coloured windows and a flurry of snow burst against them.

'I can't do it myself,' she went on, pacing up and down in agitation. 'I am not welcomed at Camelot, and she wouldn't accept anything I sent her.'

'Anything you sent her?' he repeated in a horrified tone. 'You don't mean you'd—'

'I would, but I couldn't. She'd take nothing that came from me. And there's a reason why I can't get at her by magic. I can't tell you why, but it is so. And so—' she rounded on him – 'you will have to go.'

'What, me?' he said.

'Yes, you – and you'd better if I tell you to. You know that.'

'Yes, my lady,' he said helplessly. 'But what can I do?'

'Put fear on her. Fear. That's poison enough, to a woman or to the child within her.' She gave her low secret laugh, and the poor old knight hid his face in his hands.

'But you know,' he said, looking up after a minute. 'Guinevere's a stout-hearted lass. It will take more than a fright to do her any harm.'

'Fright? You talk of fright? Do you think I mean a nurse's bogey to scare a naughty child? – Real fear, my Bertilak – real terror. Have you forgotten? The terror that freezes the breath, paralyses the limbs – before the vampire bites, before the werewolf leaps – you should know, Bertilak, you should know.'

'No,' he said in a smothered voice. 'No. You don't mean – you don't mean to send me back into what I was?'

'That is just what I do mean,' she said.

To my horror, as I watched them unseen, I saw him fall on his knees in front of her, reaching up with his hands.

'Not – not the Beast!' he said in a more broken voice than I ever heard a man use. 'Oh God! Not the Beast!'

She gave an impatient exclamation.

'All right, then. The Beast will not be needful. The Green Man will suffice.'

He groaned, and then – before my eyes I saw him change.

He rose slowly and heavily from his knees, and went on growing taller – her hand was outstretched towards him, and seemed to be directing power at him – he grew not only taller but broader, rougher, darker – a shadow overspread him, as shadows seemed to rush inwards from the corners of the dark hall. Out of the shadow a dark glimmering green outline seemed to cover him and build up over his own shape, and then came clearer. The thing that stood there was half as high again as the tallest of men, vast and shaggy, and everywhere bright green. Its clothes were richly encrusted with gold and jewels, though strange and old-fashioned – the hair and beard were that same bright unnatural green, hanging down in a thick mane over the rich clothes whose ornateness somehow added horror to the savage face. Never could I have imagined a face of such brutal malignity – to say it was animal is not enough, for no animal's face could convey such repulsive, hideous evil. The skin and hair and all were a luminous diseased green – all save the fiery eyeballs, which were red, as were the gums that dripped red around the jagged yellow-ish teeth.

I don't know how I stood my ground, and did not cry out or faint. I knew I must not, or I should betray my presence to my aunt; so I clung on to the newel-post, shaking. I watched while my aunt gestured towards the terrible creature – who stood drooping stupidly before her – turned it round, saying, 'Go!' – and steered it out through the door as I had seen her steer those witless servants of hers. It – I could not call it Sir Bertilak – went out of the door, and I broke away from the stair-post and dragged myself up the stairs almost on hands and knees, knowing that I must surely be visible now, and Aunt Morgan must not know what I had witnessed. I locked my door and lay on my bed trembling for a long time, till I fell into an exhausted sleep.

That was a gloomy Christmas for me, you can be sure; it took me a long time to get over my fright, and everyone in the castle missed Sir Bertilak but none dared ask where he had gone. The castle people of course had their feastings and mummings, in which I took part but languidly; and there was the High Mass in the castle chapel at midnight, which my aunt dared not omit, no matter what she may have felt about it. She gave courteous hospitality to the priest who had journeyed over from a distant monastery, and attended the service with the same face of demure hypocrisy as I had seen her put on at the convent; but I noticed that she did not receive the Sacrament, nor touch the holy water. But oddly enough, where the house-carles' children had hung up the heathen mistletoe in other parts of the castle she seemed to avoid that also.

And then on Twelfth Day, when my aunt and I were sitting to noon-meat at a small table in a corner of the great hall, there was the sound of a horse in the courtyard, and Sir Bertilak strode in at the door, in his old leather jerkin and hose, as if he had been hunting. He flung across the room shouting for meat and drink, kissed us both on the cheeks as was his custom, and sat down in his big chair. I cannot say how glad I was to see him again. He was no different except – except that round his neck, if you could see between his beard and his collar, ran a thin green line.

He was surly and silent at first, and ate as if famished.

'Well?' my aunt thrust at him, caring nothing, it seemed, for my presence. 'Is it done?'

'I did what you told me,' he said, without looking up from his meat.

'But did she – is she—?'

'I don't know. How could I tell? – I ask you how would you expect me to know?'

She frowned, and tapped her fingers on the table.

'Oh very well, very well. But did Arthur take your challenge?'

He looked up for a moment.

'Arthur? No. A young fellow stepped in and took the challenge for him – so of course he must come here next year, and not Arthur.'

My aunt sprang up, knocking her wineglass over, spitting with rage like a cat.

'You fool, you fool! You've let everything slip through your fingers. We could have had Arthur here, alone – do you understand? – and bound to submit his neck to your axe. The Old Sacrifice would have been made by you, and I would have taken my rightful place by your side – oh, the chance that's lost!'

She paced up and down the hall, wringing her hands. He went on stolidly eating and drinking.

'Who is this young man that comes in his place?' she asked, halting and turning to him.

'I don't know. Some unknown youngster. Gawain, the name was.'

'Not Gawain of Orkney? He's no youngster. Morgause's boy – King Lot's heir ... at least he's royal, and next in descent—'

'No, no – it wasn't Gawain of Orkney. I'd know him. A younger one altogether. Oh, I don't know. Anyway, he'll be here in a year's time, according to the custom.'

'Well, well,' she said, biting her lips. 'Not even one of the distinguished knights. You've made a pretty mess of things, I must say. Anyhow, something might be done with that young fellow. Something will have to be done.'

'And now,' Sir Bertilak suddenly boomed out, having finished his blackjack of ale and evidently feeling better, 'now do you realize that's the first decent meal I've had for a fortnight? No Christmas dinner, by the Mass! Here—' he pushed his chair back noisily and stood up, 'Here – I've done what you told me to do – what you made me do, my lady – and by the Splendour of God, I'm going to have my Christmas now, in spite of you and the Devil and his Dam. Come on – house-carles, hullo! It's Twelfth Night, and we'll feast tonight for the blessed Christ's sake. Go get a feast ready.'

He put a warm protecting arm round me.

'Little Vivian – you look frightened. You look as if you'd seen something, or heard something. Now listen and I'll tell you, so you won't be afraid any more – listen now—'

He lowered his head to my ear, but my aunt broke in between us.

'What, whispering in a corner, old lecher?'

And from that moment she never left me alone with him, but watched us as if she had indeed been a wronged Juno.

Even in the revels that night (which at last I was able to enjoy) she would not risk his having a moment near me, not even in the figures of a dance when we could have put mouth to ear for the fraction of a second – so that whatever he might have had to tell me for my reassurance remained untold.

It was on Midsummer Eve that she next had news from Camelot. I heard the fluttering of pigeons at the window above mine, and an ominous pause – then the carrier pigeon came whirling away downwards, as if she had carelessly flung it aside – at least with its life and limbs, poor creature – and I heard hysterical laughter, and the tapping of Morgan's shoes as she raced down the spiral staircase, past my door and into the hall.

Her laughter was mingled with harsh dry sobs, and seemed more of rage and frustration than anything.

'Bertilak!' she screamed. 'Bertilak! Come here at once!'

'Yes, my lady,' he answered, obediently as ever, appearing from behind the leather curtain that screened the little cubbyhole where he liked to polish his armour. She ran across the great hall to him.

'Look here – did you ever hear anything so – so—' She went off into another hysterical, angry peal. 'All our trouble for nothing! After all that! – The woman Guinevere – she's – she's – she's delivered of a daughter.'

'A daughter?' The old knight stared rather stupidly at her, shaking his head. 'A daughter? Not a son after all?'

'That's what I said, idiot – can't you hear? A daughter!' and she seized his jerkin and did her best to shake him.

'And you – I – *we* had all that trouble, and wasted all that effort – and she goes and has a daughter. What do I care if she has forty daughters? And you – you – don't you care, that all my plans came to nothing?'

'Of course I care, my lady,' he mumbled uneasily, but I could see he didn't even understand what she was getting at.

'And you didn't even get Arthur,' she went on, 'the best chance I've had to get him since he began—'

'I did my best,' the old fellow growled. 'How could I help it if a younger man stepped in? After all, my lady, if you *must* work your devilment – and God help us all! You'll have that young man come here next Christmas, and won't he do for you instead of Arthur?' He spoke as one long tired out and resigned to evils he was helpless to prevent.

She stood still, releasing her hold of him, and then paced over to the window; there she stood looking out for many long minutes, while Sir Bertilak and I exchanged uneasy glances and waited in suspense.

Then she spoke, thoughtfully and quiet.

'Yet I mistrust this daughter of Arthur's. Gawain, Vivian, the daughter of Arthur – no, I can see something, and I mistrust it.'

She came rustling back from the window.

'I have it,' she said. 'You and Vivian must be married.'

Both of us said, '*What?*' as with one voice, and then held our breath.

'I said married,' she said, with her light shallow laugh.

'But, my dear aunt—' I cried.

'But, good God Almighty—' cried he.

'And when I say you must be married,' she said, 'of course you know you must.'

And that, we felt with sinking hearts, was true. What could one do or say when she said 'You must,' like that? If anyone doubts this, or finds it strange, I can only say that they never knew Morgan le Fay.

'And – when?' he managed to utter.

'At once,' said she. 'No time like the present. Midsummer Eve, a good day and a short night. Preparations? – pooh! what need? I'll see to that forthwith—'

And suddenly the hall, and all the castle, was full of people, servants, ladies-in-waiting, tradesfolk with baskets and bundles – all the house-carles and their families were there, somehow mingling with those shapes she had called up, I knew, out of thin air. In the instant, they had begun to prepare a wedding. The whole castle was being furbished up – I could see Hilda, the wife of a house-carle whom I knew well, stretching out a rich gold arras with the help of a tall pale woman in green whom she certainly couldn't have met before – for the woman was just a little taller than a woman possibly could be, stretching out her skinny white arms to fix the arras, and when her green skirt lifted a little, I could see she had feet like a cow's. The rest of the strange helpers were like that too. There was a short fat man rolling barrels up from the cellar, who seemed to have four legs as well as his two arms. But my aunt bustled me away up to my room, where thin spectral ladies in black were unrolling garments of such delicacy and magnificence that I could almost forget their grotesque faces and their fingers like dry scaly twigs.

My dress was a shimmering cloth of silver, with a tall pointed headdress from which dropped a transparent veil spangled with gold; and I could scarcely be blamed for enjoying its beauty, and the picture I made in the great mirror. I felt all the time that this could scarcely be real – but then, there were the real people whom I knew quite well – there was the falconer's little daughter, Maud, helping to spread my train out, and there was Ralph from the stables stealing sweetmeats off the sidetable, and it seemed he could taste them too. And yet it was all quite absurd – all in one moment like the snap of two fingers, I was being married to old Sir Bertilak. Oh yes, it was usual enough for a young maid to be given away ruthlessly without her consent – but he? He didn't want this any more than I did, but neither could he raise a finger nor a voice against this woman Morgan. Oh God, if only all this were a dream . . . yet I knew well that it was not. The things that Morgan le Fay caused to happen were all deceits and lies, but they were not dreams – they were nothing so harmless as dreams.

And here she was, proffering me a goblet of wine to drink.

'Here's courage for you, my dear niece,' she said sniggering. And I took the cup from her, and drank a sip of it – about half, maybe – and then I thought of what I was doing, and when her back was turned I poured the rest of it into the

rushes on the floor. So, when I began to see things even more
oddly, it was only in about half measure. The phantom people
faded a little, and I could tell them from the real ones; but the
most startling effect of all was that, when I slowly made my
way down the staircase, across the threshold of the hall,
towards the chapel door where Sir Bertilak waited to meet me
– I saw, mirrored across Sir Bertilak's shape, like a reflection
on a transparent glass window, the shape of that other man –
the young man I had seemed to see when I first entered the
castle – the man I was meant to love. And I knew that, had I
drunk all my aunt's potion instead of only half, I should have
been quite sure that *he* was there instead of Sir Bertilak, and
that it was *he* to whom I should be married.

So, in a world full of half-seen shapes, I went on into the
chapel for my wedding. My aunt's magic must have been
potent indeed, for it worked even in the holy building. All the
real people were there, for this had to be a real wedding,
before witnesses; and there was a priest there too, a stranger,
but certainly a real priest. But all the vacant spaces were filled
up with unknown people, richly dressed, smiling and amiable, and yet somehow not quite right as human beings, and
thinner, less certain of outline to my half-enchanted eyes, than
the people I knew to be flesh and blood.

And always there floated before me, sometimes clearer and
sometimes less clear, the image of the man who ought to have
been my bridegroom.

In a dazed, almost drunken state I was led through the
service, said some words – I hardly knew what – placed my
hand in Sir Bertilak's, which was hard, strong, dry, and yet
somehow cold and remotely trembling – and heard the priest
pronounce us man and wife; and then people on each side of
us led us, still hand in hand, to the feasting dais.

I had seen a few weddings in the castle during the time I
had been there, and they all struck me, at the time, as
terrifying affairs, at least for the bride. Always there had been
the long-drawn-out feast, and then the dancing, until anyone
who wasn't drunk must be tired to death – and then the bride

would be at last dragged upstairs by a shrieking crowd of bridesmaids, and the bridegroom dragged off in the opposite direction by an even noisier crowd of groomsmen. Then would begin the undressing of the bride, by all the brides-maids and all the dames of honour. This was both a ritual and a game, and everyone made the most of it – the bride's garments would be dragged off one by one, each with an appropriate song – and what songs. The respectable matrons, the house-carles' wives, seemed to see nothing wrong in them, but I – I was convent-bred . . . The whole thing always became a riot in the close, stuffy, curtained room, with the girls shrieking and almost pulling the poor bride to pieces – then at last they got her into bed, usually stark naked, and then began an interminable wait while the groomsmen, in another room, were doing the same with the bridegroom, or worse, and all getting roaring drunk. Then eventually, when the men thought they had got the bridegroom sufficiently encouraged, he would be led in, usually too drunk to stand, and tumbled into bed beside the bride. Everyone would contemplate them there in the great decorated bed, and sing some more songs, and pelt them with flowers and sticky comfits. At last the bride's mother would draw the curtains, and the party would retire, but no further than outside the door, where most of them would wait the rest of the night still singing and shouting jokes, and waiting avidly for evidence that the marriage had been consummated and the bride found a virgin. And at daybreak they would be back again to wake the happy couple up – assuming that they had slept at all. No wonder I dreaded what was before me.

I sat through the banquet, and whether the food was real or illusory I couldn't have told. And afterwards I led the dance, as best I could, with Sir Bertilak. Just for one moment he came close enough to me to whisper, and what he whispered was, 'Don't be afraid.' Bless him! My heart warmed a little to him even in my bewilderment and despair. But the festivities dragged on, and the hall was so hot and smoky and airless, and people crowded so upon me – at last I was almost relieved when my aunt, with the bridesmaids, came and led me firmly upstairs – although now came the time of which I hardly dared to think. I, who had lived so quiet and with-drawn among the nuns at Amesbury, to be suddenly exposed to all this public performance . . .

At least the undressing was over quickly – my aunt, smirking like a cat and trying to look maternal, set a limit to the number of songs, and cut short some of the feminine horseplay – I can remember her tossing my garters to the bridesmaids, and one was caught by little Maud, but the other by a slender strange girl who seemed to have a face like a vixen. To my relief they did not put me naked into bed, but arrayed me in a furred robe of white satin. And there I lay trembling against the great embroidered pillows. Fortunately the waiting was not too long. There were shouts and torches outside, and the groomsmen led in Sir Bertilak. I no longer saw him overshadowed by the shape of that other, or I think I could not have borne it. I knew by that that the half-measure of enchantment was passing off. He wasn't drunk but looked dazed and unhappy. He wore a red brocade bed-gown, and I remember thinking that he was a fine figure of a man, well-built, clean and tough, and his face was handsome in its way, and gentle. Indeed, an older woman might have found him attractive.

The groomsmen, who were all of the strange people, thrust him roughly into the room and into the bed. My aunt, with a revoltingly sly smile, drew the covers up over us, and then dragged the curtains together; the company raised a cheer, and trooped surging to the door. And then the door was shut.

I lay crouched up in my corner of the bed, shaking. Fortunately the bed was a large one. Presently, as the noise died away outside the door, Sir Bertilak said very quietly:

'Don't be afraid, my girl – I'm not going to touch you.'

I could feel his thick robe near me in the bed, but, indeed he didn't touch me.

'It's all a deceit of Madam Morgan,' he went on, speaking low. 'I can't say much, or she might hear us even now. I believe she hears what I think. I can't fight against her, neither can you – but I shan't let her hurt you. There are some things even she can't make me do.'

He put out his hand and rather clumsily patted my shoulder.

'You've nothing to fear now, little Vivian. There, roll yourself up in your robe and go to sleep.'

And so I did, and to my surprise I slept soundly.

2 · *Gawain*

I am Gawain – but I have to keep on explaining, till I am embarrassed, that I am not the 'great' Gawain – I am only the 'little' Gawain. I am only his nephew: great, rough, irascible, terrifying, sometimes lovable Gawain is my awesome uncle – Gawain, the most famous man after Lancelot at King Arthur's court – Gawain of Orkney, son of grim old King Lot and the witch-queen Morgause, brought up in the fierce bleakness of Orkney with Gaheris, Agravaine, Gareth and the sinister Mordred. I am older than Mordred, but I am Gareth's son, and as long as I can remember we have lived apart from the Orkney family, in the south, in Lyonesse. My mother is the Lady of Lyonesse, Madam Leonie, whom Gareth, the gentlest of the Orkney knights, rescued from the Knight of the Red Laundes (now a very harmless old gentleman, and about to retire into a monastery, they tell me). Her sister Lynett, who accompanied my father on his quest and treated him so badly, is my aunt, of course, and lives with us – she was married to Gaheris when my parents were married, but it didn't last – Gaheris hadn't my father's patient temperament by any means, and after the marriage night, she left him and became the King's messenger. Later she came back to her sister – and to my father, who I fear is the only man she really loves. She's a queer creature, is my aunt Lynett. I often think that if Arthur had given her to my uncle Gawain instead of to my uncle Gaheris, he would undoubtedly have swapped off her head in one of his bloody rages. As it is, she ranges about the forest roads on horseback, and is never happier than when carrying letters from Arthur to his knights. We wonder every time she sets out whether she will return alive – it isn't really safe, and she takes nobody with her but my father's old dwarf – but the ruffians of the forest seem to have some respect for her, perhaps because she is a remarkably good physician. That always brings a woman under suspicion of being a witch, though there isn't much of a witch about my aunt Lynett. Or perhaps it's her sharp tongue they are all afraid of.

We have lived as far back as I can remember in the land of Lyonesse, a sunny country stretching south from Cornwall. The sea surrounds us on three sides, a narrow neck of land joining the peninsula to St Michael's Bay, where we can see the great Mount whence they flash signals on a polished shield all the way to Scillonia, which lies in sight of us. Ours is a rocky land, like Scillonia, but not high. The sun beats off the sea and warms it, and the spring flowers come early; for nine long months of the year there are soft breezes and the scent of honey; but for the other three months the sudden storms pounce on us like beasts of prey, and it is recorded that Merlin said that in a hundred years' time there will come a day when the sea will sweep right over the land and nothing will be left of it. And the thought of it is a grief to me.

Before I went to Arthur's court to be made a knight, I served my time as squire with my father, and learnt all that is required for a knight to know. I did not have to serve as a page, since I came of a noble house and had been bred up to courtly usages by my mother, who taught me every kind of noble manners. With my father I would gallop about the countryside after hares and foxes and deer and wild boars and sometimes wolves – dressed in rough leather and plastered with mud, stopping to snatch our noon-meat at some dirty, smoke-blackened alehouse, or swigging our leather bottles of ale and munching our lumps of cheese under a tree. Then when I came home I would wash, and comb my hair, and put on silk and satin, and wait upon my beautiful mother, handing her the dishes and cups on my bended knee. Then presently she would laugh and tease me, and we would sit in her cosy bower, with the bright curtains to keep the warmth in, and tell long stories of the heroes of old and of the world of Faery.

There were no others of my age and rank in the castle – the house-carles' boys and I came together but little, and otherwise there were only my father and mother, my aunt Lynett, and such guests as sometimes came our way; and I grew up rather solitary, and very much of a dreamer. And what did I dream of? Why, of knighthood, and King Arthur, and his great Round Table, and how one day I should be numbered among them, and be the best – oh yes, the bravest, the truest, the noblest knight of them all. And of course, of women. That is, of fair ladies. For in my mind I saw them all as goddesses. How wonderful they were, I thought – starting with Our Blessed Lady, to whom I prayed day and night – then my adored mother – then my aunt Lynett in spite of her sharp tongue – and my comfortable old nurse, why, she was a woman too, and so I must think of her with respect – and then all the wonderful ladies of whom I had heard tell – Queen Guinevere and Queen Yseult (no one had yet whispered a word of scandal to me, nor would I have suffered it) – Queen Morgause my grandmother (I had never seen her, and no one called her a witch in my hearing) – Ygraine, that far-off great-grandmother, and all those others: damosels and ladies in story and song, beyond number, all beautiful, all saintly, all to be served and protected. True, there were old crones who came to the back door for alms, and loud-voiced greasy kitchenmaids with red noses and bad teeth, and silly yellow-haired dolls who fooled about with the men-at-arms – but what of that? I was taught to look beyond the outward appearance, and remember all the tales of goddesses who had walked the earth disguised as peasant lasses or old women in rags. As I grew older the idea haunted me, obsessed me, that I must respect all women, protect them, shield them from danger. Men did dreadful things to them, I learnt with a shudder. The priest who came to teach me my catechism talked to me about Temptation. I, even I, he said, might be tempted to do dreadful things to those sacrosanct creatures. Dear God, I . . . ? – How I prayed, how I resolved. I would be a pure knight to my life's end. I would love the most beautiful lady in the world, and lay my chaste adoration at her feet. Perhaps she would take my hand in hers and accept me for her true-love, and I would love her, but never, never touch her beautiful body. I would vow myself to virginity for her sake, all my life long. It never occurred to me that the lady might not care for the arrangement.

By which it can be seen plainly that I wasn't a very wise young man – in fact it might be said, with some justice, that I was a good bit of a young prig as well. I don't deny it, neither do I deny that I was as green as little apples, long after I should have known better.

The time drew near for me to be made a knight – as a knight's son, I could be knighted at eighteen years, my father standing sponsor for me, and vouching for me as having served my time as his squire. My birthday fell in November, so at Christmas, as ever was, I should be taken to Camelot, and presented to King Arthur, and there fulfil the solemn rites of knighthood.

You can imagine how the castle was in a flutter, and how my parents busied themselves in providing me the best outfit that a knight could have. My father journeyed to Winchester, to procure me a magnificent suit of armour – part chain-mail, part plate, ingeniously jointed, decorated with damascene-work, and padded with soft leather inside to make it easy in wear. But the sword he bought at Marazion, from the Jewish merchants who came there from the Holy Land as they had done since time began – and this was a real blade of Damascus, than which there are none better unless they are of elvish work. My mother and Aunt Lynett made the rich crest and hanging silk draperies that should crown the great jousting helmet; the crest represented the hawk of the Orkney family, but white to distinguish it from the others; and my shield had no device at all, but was maiden white until such time as I should win myself an honourable blazon. Besides all these, of course, there were jerkins and hose of leather and of wool, and of stout linen, and shirts of fine linen; and courtly suits of silk and velvet, with a short mantle trimmed with squirrel's fur, in which to wait upon the King and Queen. To say nothing of boots and shoes and gloves and nightcaps and God-wot-what. It took three sumpter-mules to carry them all, in the end.

My father had often told me how he, in his time, came to Arthur's court in an old leather jerkin without a penny in his purse, plodding on foot till he was so footsore that he arrived at Camelot unable to walk at all, and had to lean on two old men to hobble up to the dais; and how he hid his identity, and became a scullion in Arthur's kitchen, because he was afraid of the scorn of his big brothers who had always bullied him, and also because he was too proud to bear their patronage and pity. He bided his time, watching and learning, and won his prize in the end. His mother Morgause, indeed, would have overwhelmed him with knightly equipment, and helped him with magic too – not for affection, but for family pride – but he would have none of it. He set out on foot without even a sword. But he was determined that my start in life should be different, and so was my mother; and as for Lynett, she looked me up and down, but there was no knowing what she thought.

For my horse, I had my father's own, a good reliable fellow called Trojan, not too large for me, not too fierce; perfect in manners and manage, and an old friend of mine. I had been secretly afraid that knightly honour would oblige me to ask for a taller and more fiery horse, so I was relieved when my father insisted, on my obedience as a son, that I should have Trojan and no other. Trojan could be trusted in every emergency. I had practised jousting on his back, with my father and various of his friends, and we knew what to expect of each other. Jousting is a game like any other, and I was pronounced to be reasonably good at it. I would, of course, have to take part in the tourney after I was knighted.

The journey was a long, cold, tedious one, and I wasn't at all surprised that my mother and aunt Lynett had excused themselves from it. There was only my father and myself, besides the men-at-arms. I was glad – the nervous tension was quite enough without the ladies being there to make me more anxious. I don't think I could have borne it.

After rain and cold, mud and fog, we came in sight at last of the towers of Camelot, a little after noon of the short, dim day. A thrilling sight – how all its towers and pinnacles glistened, and its banners waved, above the massive stone ramparts and the little bright-coloured town that clustered at its foot. The great gate stood wide open, with the drawbridge down, and folk of all sorts went in and out with noise and cheerfulness; music played, trumpets sounded from the turrets, bells rang, and already lights gleamed in the windows. My father said he could smell the dinners cooking a mile away. We clattered through the great gates, where men-at-arms in Arthur's livery stood more as if to welcome guests than to guard; a trumpeter above the gate blew notice of our arrival. Through bailey and keep and across the courtyard we went, to the royal hall, and there all was warmth and light and the colour of rich robes. I expected that we would be presented to the King and Queen with ceremony, after we had washed and changed; but the King made no formality with us. From the high dais he had seen us come in, and he came striding down the hall, hand outstretched. He was dressed only in a huntsman's suit of leather, for it was not yet the hour of state; but his look marked him out as the King. A tall man, taller even than my father; fair-haired and with a close beard, and I should judge between forty and fifty years old, with a head like one of those marble statues the Romans left behind, and large, bright grey eyes. If he had been in rags you would have looked at him twice and three times. He seized my father warmly by the hand and greeted him as an old friend; looked me up and down and laid a firm, rather heavy hand on my shoulder, and led us both up to the dais, where the Queen was sitting.

They say her name means 'The White Apparition'. Truly I have never seen a lady so white – her hair like pale gold thread, but her face and neck and arms all like gleaming pale ivory, or like a sea-cliff in the summer with the sun beating on it, as you look from the sea. Her eyes were luminous too, light and clear, like the sea on a calm day. A beautiful white ghost of a lady, the moon to Arthur, who was the sun. She was robed in white and silver, loose and flowing. I knew that she was said to be with child, and as such she seemed to me very sacred indeed, hardly less than our Lady herself; and I thought my heart would stop beating at the wonder of her. Falling on one knee to kiss her hand, as I had been taught to do, I could hardly get up again, and my father had to jerk me, but not unkindly, to my feet.

Guinevere dismissed me with a rather remote smile, and my father took me to meet some of the other knights. Mostly he greeted the older ones, who had been with Arthur from the beginning, some twenty years back – Sir Kay the Seneschal, and Sir Lucan the Butler – their jobs must have been honorary by that time, or at least supervisory, for Sir Lucan never drew a cork or tapped a barrel in those days, and Sir Kay's concern was more with the ciphers and lists of supplies in the chancellerie than with the kitchen; though my father still looked at him rather askance, as if he remembered being set to wash the dishes and nicknamed 'Pretty-Hands'. There was Sir Griflet, who was the first knight that Arthur had made, now, like Arthur, a strong man of forty or upwards; and Ulphius, who had been in his first great battle; and old Ector, who was Arthur's foster-father, now very grey and long-bearded. Some of the younger knights were there too, for a second generation of the Round Table was growing up; Lamorak and Percivale, the sons of King Pellenore – Percivale, a noticeable young man, rather over-tall and drooping, but with luminous dreaming eyes. There was Tristram, pale-skinned and dark-browed, but formidable; there was Dinadan, the cheerful, lovable joker, light-footed and light-tongued, leaning over the left side of Guinevere's chair, and trying to make her laugh; and there on her right side was Lancelot—

But now my father was greeting his brothers, the three Orkney-men, my uncles – Gawain, my namesake, Gaheris and Agravaine. They were big, overwhelming, loud-voiced men, with Northern accents I could hardly understand. The four of them were caught up in a clamorous family clack, full of loud laughter and obscure allusions. I heard Gaheris asking after his wife with a sour smile, and not waiting to hear the reply. My father drew me into the middle of the group. 'Here's the boy,' he said. They all bore down upon me and made me feel very small.

'He's thin,' said Gawain, pinching my shoulder. 'No muscle there. By God, Gareth, why couldn't you have married a good Orkney lass?'

'Why couldn't I, you mean,' interjected Gaheris. 'There's a dozen I could have if some obliging robber would—'

'Enough said,' interrupted my father. 'We know all about that. Well, here's my son, and I daresay he'll do as well as any of them here. Will you give him the buffet tomorrow, Gawain?'

'That I will,' said Gawain, and I knew I was in for something.

Then he took hold of my father's elbow, and drew him a little aside; and I heard him mutter out of the side of his mouth, 'Mordred's here.'

'Mordred?' My father's eyebrows went up. Of what followed I could only hear the word 'Sixteen', but there was a great deal of secretive grimacing and jerking of heads and thumbs, that made me faintly uneasy.

Then my father led me out of the great hall into the long

cloister, and approached a door from which an uproar was coming that made the big hall seem quiet by comparison.

'That's where you must go,' he said. 'The squires' hall, till you've been through the ceremony tomorrow and the next day. I can't be with you now – you must manage on your own.'

My heart sank.

He gave me a bundle of clothes.

'Here's your things for this evening. Not your best. I'll keep them for you, and send them to you by a page when you need them. No good having more with you now – you'll soon know why . . . Now go on, and God be with you.'

He pushed me towards that door.

'Go *on*,' he insisted, and feigned a playful kick towards me. I braced myself, and opened the door.

In the middle of the bear-garden roar that came from the crowd inside, a rather high, drawling voice was saying, 'And now this lady, as I said – well, she took off her clothes—'

'*All* her clothes?' chorused several voices.

'All her clothes, and was about to . . .'

The voice stopped suddenly, and the whole crowd turned and looked at me.

I suppose they weren't bad lads really, but I saw them as a hostile pack of wild animals; and they looked back at me as such. The boy who had been telling the story, who seemed rather younger than myself, put himself at their head. He was fair-haired and complexioned, and vaguely reminded me of someone; but his whole texture was coarse – heavy eyelids, thick lips, swollen nostrils, spotty skin, and small reddish hairs shining all down his cheeks. His hair lay on his neck in thick blond curls, and his eyes were like blue marbles. He addressed me.

'Oh . . . a newcomer. Well, how delightful. And what might you choose to call yourself?'

I stood up to him with what courage I could muster.

'Gawain,' I said.

'Gawain!' – The name was greeted with a shout of incredulous laughter.

'That's lie number one,' said the ringleader.

I felt my face getting hot.

'I'll have you know that it's my name,' I said. 'I'm Gawain the son of Gareth of Orkney.'

'Oho!' said he, stretching his marble eyes a little more. 'Are you so? Why, then you're my nephew. Meet your uncle Mordred.' And he held out his hand to me.

I didn't like the look of that hand, but I felt I could hardly refuse to take it; so I took it, and he swung up his left hand and caught me a stinging blow on the side of my face, that sent me skidding across the room to crash into the row of washbasins. A pewter basin went over, drenching me and the clean clothes I was carrying. I picked myself up off the floor, dazed and hurt and wet.

'There's your knightly buffet,' he said. 'You'll be glad to know,' he addressed the room, 'that this person here – my nephew – is to be made a knight tomorrow – at eighteen! Because he's his father's son. Some people have all the luck. Come here, nephew, and kiss the toe of my boot. Come on.'

'I'll see you in hell first,' I said.

The others laughed. I couldn't tell if they were for me or against me, but I rather thought the latter. Then a chap whose face I didn't at all dislike came up. 'Give over, Mordred,' he said. 'That's enough.' This new fellow had a wide, good-natured mouth, a short nose, smudgy brows. 'My name's Bedivere,' he said. 'Let's see what's happened to your clothes.'

Mordred drew off with the crowd, but they went on chattering and guffawing, polishing bits of equipment as they did so, and tidying themselves for the dinner. Bedivere did what he could to sort out my general dampness.

'His Majesty's looking pleased tonight,' someone remarked casually.

'And well he might,' another voice put in. 'Everyone knows about the Queen. Next Midsummer, they say.'

'So the old chap will have an heir at last?'

'As if he hadn't one already,' came Mordred's voice. 'And as to lawful heirs, well – it's a wise child that knows its own father, they say. No doubt our good King will be very pleased about the *Queen's* child.'

Rather incautiously I emerged from my corner.

'What do you mean by that?' I said across the intervening heads. Mordred fixed me with those blue pebble eyes.

'What I say, my good greenhorn. We all know about Lancelot – don't we? About Lancelot and my lady Guinevere? Don't we? – All, that is, except our good King himself – who *thinks* he's going to have a lawful heir to the throne—'

This was too much for me. I pushed forward through the crowd.

'Draw your sword,' I said in a voice I hardly recognized as my own.

'Eh? Oh, it's me nephew. Now then, boy, none of that—'

'Draw your sword,' I repeated.

'Oh, God! What's the child think he's doing?'

'You shall *not*,' I said, 'you shall *not* say what you have said – about our Lady the Queen. Draw your sword, I say!'

'Oh, don't be a fool!' he laughed. 'I'll say it again if I please, I'll say she's a—'

With one bound I was across those who stood in my way, and had my hands on his throat – a bench went over with a crash, and we rolled on the floor together. My heart was pounding and my head buzzing so that I hardly heard, but rather felt, the sudden silence as the door opened and an older voice said:

'What's this brawl? Get up there.'

Mordred and I both scrambled to our feet. Old Sir Griflet, who I later learnt was in charge of the squires, stood frowning.

'Well? Fighting like drunken churls in an alehouse?'

'Sir,' I said, with my eyes on his feet, 'he spoke shamefully of – of a lady . . .'

'So. The ladies here, as well as their Majesties, would be better pleased if you kept the peace. You – you're Sir Gareth's boy, I believe?'

'I am, sir, so please you.'

'To be knighted on Christmas Day. A bad beginning. No, I'll not report the matter, for that cause only. Be quiet now, all you cubs, and get yourselves ready for the hall. The meat's about to be served. Now get to your stations.'

He swung the door to, and we went sullenly to our washbasins and combs. Bedivere stood by me.

'Don't heed Mordred,' he said quietly. 'We all know what he's like. Let him alone. We none of us like him, but the weaker ones follow him, and we have to put up with him because of his—' here he checked something he was about to say, and amended it with: '—because of his mother.'

Bedivere kept by me for the rest of the evening, and made up his straw pallet next to mine for the night, so keeping Mordred and his followers away, or I don't think I could have endured it. Bedivere was a good chap, very dependable, but with strange dreamy ideas too. In the course of a long, whispered conversation that night, he told me that he had once had a dream about being the very last of King Arthur's knights to be left alive after a great and terrible battle – the very last, and Arthur dying in his arms. He had awakened in a shaking fright, as cold as stone, and had never told anyone about it till then. He was to be knighted at Easter.

We were all up long before light, on the chilly morning of Christmas Eve; and came to a good breakfast in the big hall, the squires alone, the knights breaking their fast in another chamber. We had broth and bread, salted butter and small ale: and I was counselled to make a good meal, for I had to fast until breakfast next day. All very well, but I was feeling sick with excitement and apprehension and the sense of the occasion. I swallowed some broth, but no one could say I made a good breakfast.

I was very glad when presently a monk in a brown habit appeared, and beckoned me. Bedivere said, 'Now for it – good luck!' and gave me a handshake; but Mordred looked up from the end of the table, pushed out his thick lips, lifted his coarse nostrils in a sneer, twitched an eyebrow – as it were casting a smear over the whole thing. Just when I wanted my thoughts to be serene and undisturbed.

The monk led me into the great church, where I made my shrift – and how I tried! I was determined that my soul should be as clean as I knew how. Painfully I scrutinized every corner of my mind, and accused myself of sinful intentions that I probably never had, just in case ... After the effort, and the priest's quiet words, I felt very clean in soul, and all the discord and unpleasantness of Mordred and his friends slipped away. I was then led into a big echoing room next to the kitchen, where I had the ceremonial bath. There was a large round tub of hot water, filled up by scullions from the great cauldrons in the kitchen next door – the last of these had just tipped his canful in as I entered the room. There were perfumed herbs in the bath, and rose petals floating on the surface. My father and my uncle Gawain, being my sponsors, were there, and undressed me, saw me step into the bath, and then laid embroidered cloths over the bath so that only my head could be seen; they then recited to me, by turns, a long exhortation about the duties of knighthood. For myself I sat at ease on the wooden stool in the tub, with my back resting against its side, relaxed in the warm, sweet-smelling water – after all the excitement rather drowsy and dreamy, with the sonorous, monotonous words going on and on – and nearly fell asleep. It was pleasant and peaceful, and I wished I could stay there for ever. The words of the exhortation just ran together in my mind as a kind of vague magnificent music – I couldn't have told you what they meant. I was miles away – till suddenly the words stopped, the covers were ripped off, and my father was hauling me out. The air was wretchedly cold as I struggled out of the warm water. My father and my uncle wrapped warm towels round me and led me off, padding barefooted, into a little room close at hand, and laid me in a fine white-draped bed. And now, I thought, I'll be allowed to have my sleep out. Not a bit of it. The rest in the bed, it seemed, was only symbolic. I had hardly lain there a minute when, after a prayer, they hauled me out again, thrust a new shirt, tunic and breeches at me, and bade me be dressed – for, they said, I was now a new creature, just born, and must rise and take up a new life.

It must have been late by this time – I don't know how the time had passed, but it was already dark, and the torches were lit. In the great church the knights were assembled, glimmering in the candle-light. Here there was long chanting and praying, and reading from the holy words; and here they showed me my breastplate and my helmet, my shield, my sword, my spurs and my belt, and explained what each should mean to a knight; and laid them, one by one, hallowed with both holy water and holy incense, on the altar of the little dark chapel behind the high altar.

The officiating priest, a distant impersonal figure, led me by the hand, bareheaded and clothed only in tunic and hose, to a faldstool before this, the eastern altar, and directed me to kneel.

'Remain here,' he instructed me in a whisper, 'and watch your arms upon the altar till the hour of prime. Do not move from where you are, and do not look behind you even once. The Lord be with you,' – and he rustled away from me. Behind me I could hear the choir and the knights going out – from the dimming of the light that shone on the eastward wall behind the altar, I could tell how the candles were being extinguished one by one; in the end one candle, as I could guess, still burned. The footsteps died away down the long length of the church. I was left alone.

Now, knowing the long vigil before me, I tried to fill my mind with the thoughts that should be there. At first this was easy, for I had much to think about – how I was at last and indeed being made a knight, and that power would descend upon me, as it had done at my First Communion, and how I should never be the same again. I would be a perfect gentle knight, always courageous, always gentle, always strong, always trustworthy. Now both my soul and my body were clean, so clean that I was afraid to brush the bloom off them. If only I could die now, I felt, surely I should be safe for ever and go straight to Paradise? But no, I was to be a knight, and have duties to do. Oh, I would, I would ... And then the spate of fine inspiring thoughts began to spend itself and die down, and I began to be more aware that I was alone, that this place was dark and vast and silent, and that there was no escape for long hours yet; that I must not move from where I knelt, nor turn round ... not turn round, when who knows what might be behind me? I listened behind me, with my heart sinking. Silence – silence broken by all those little uncanny creakings and rustlings and tickings that belong to a large dark empty building at night ... How cold the back of my neck felt ... Rustlings and sighings, the creaking of old wood. No, I mustn't look round. Before me lay the altar, an old plain stone one, with a purple cloth whereon lay my armour, high above was an arched window, and on the plain brick wall between altar and window a black wooden cross, on which I tried to keep my eyes fixed; but to right and left of the cross was pale blank wall, on which the single taper behind me cast its light; and as I watched, in the space to the left of the cross a shadow rose up, and took shape – the shape of a head, with horns and wagging ears—

I stifled a scream – but I must not, must not look round. I was a knight – or was I? I had to *be* a knight, God help me – and with that horror looking over my shoulder—

And then I heard a footstep, and a rustle, and a malicious chuckle behind me. Mordred! My relief was more than half anger that he should have tried to frighten me with this childish trick. Why, I knew how to make better shadow-pictures than that ... But that he and his hangers-on – I couldn't tell how many – should come and bait me now – intruding on my solemn trial with their silly horseplay – I was all alone too, and at their mercy. What should I do if they attacked me? Should I snatch my sword from the altar and round on them? I had been told not to move or turn my head. Oh God, it was hard.

They remained there behind me for quite some minutes, making their devil-shadows, sniggering, waiting to see how

I'd take it. They made noises too – hissing, whispering, tapping, groaning. But now that I knew what the noises were, I took no notice – only praying that they would do no worse than make noises. And after a while, as they became sure that they would get no response from me, they gave it up and went away, and I heard their footsteps clank away down the far end of the church. Once more I was alone.

And now it was harder to collect my scattered thoughts. Supposing – my mind said to me – supposing that thing on the wall had *not* been just a shadow? But no – I must think of the ideals of the knightly life. To be good and true, to respect and protect damosels and virgins – oh, yes, yes indeed, certainly I would ... in spite of the ... what? In spite of that old man I could see out of the corner of my eye, who kept on saying '*You* – *You* protect damosels and virgins? – You know what you'll do – you'll deflower a virgin some day. Yes, you will. *You!* You will ruin a helpless girl, and take from her what she can never have again – and she'll be disgraced, and perhaps she'll kill herself. And you! The finger of scorn will be pointed at you – you'll have your spurs hacked off by the cook – they'll cast you out, and what will you do then?'

I tried to swivel my eyes round to see him – he was grey and long-bearded, with yellow teeth that hung over his lips. He seemed to be palely luminous. As fast as I moved my eyeballs to try and see him, he went further back behind my head. And he went on saying:

'And perhaps nobody will ever know it was you, and that will be worse. You will be torn with remorse, everyone thinking you are a faithful knight, and all the time that poor girl— perhaps several poor girls. You will know yourself vile. You'd be better dead. You know you'll do it. You know you will. You a knight! Better jump up from your knees now, and run into the hall, and tell them all you're no good. You daren't? You haven't even the courage? You'll go on then, and fall and be damned.'

I could hear him cackling and chuckling, and this time I knew it wasn't the squires. It was something quite different.

Was it the rattle of charnel bones I could hear, as he rubbed his hands together? and couldn't I smell the awful reek of the grave?

And then at the other side of me a round, floating thing, like a ball of light, came oscillating across in the tail of my sight – came a little nearer in, and I saw it was a shining globe, and in it the face of the loveliest woman I had ever seen. The beautiful face brought tears into my eyes, and I felt like stretching my arms out to her in entreaty. The vision, a face and nothing more, hovered so close that I almost thought she would have kissed my cheek; she was so close behind my elbow that I could only with the very greatest effort forbear to turn round. She seemed to be calling me, too. Then she rustled forward again – surely it was the rustle of silk and satin that I could hear on the floor at my side? From the shining head a form seemed to extend – and then as I dropped my eyes as far towards her as I dared, the light from that gleaming globe hit the form below it – and it wasn't human at all, it was a huge, dark, glittering snake – a snake with a body thicker than my arm, dark indigo blue and iridescent, coiling away into the dark behind me, and its head, its head that heartbreakingly beautiful face—

I could hear myself sobbing aloud, and the sweat poured off me. Pray? I prayed frantically – and all the time the grey old man at my other elbow was saying, 'It's no use, you see, it's no use . . .' But I held on – literally held on, for I gripped the faldstool with both hands, fixing my eyes on the cross in front of me and trying to imagine Our Blessed Lady and the holy angels – and then at last I heard the great bell begin to ring, and the footsteps of the priests coming to release me – and at that the phantoms were suddenly gone. But I was shaking all over, and as the priest raised me up he looked at me strangely and said, 'All right now – poor lad, you've had a hard vigil. See, your limbs are stiff – that's from the long kneeling. There, easy does it, my son.' Indeed, I had to lean heavily on his arm as I got up, for I could hardly stand.

They helped me into a vestry, and let me sit down for a few

minutes, slumped against the back of a chair, and one of the
monks sponged my face with cold water – they couldn't let
me break my fast yet. And then beyond the vestry door there
were lights and chanting and the smell of incense – the
rumour and rustle of a great and brilliant crowd collecting,
and the holy voices of priests. One of the monks said, 'Come,'
and drew me to my feet, and with a monk each side of me I
stepped out again into the church. It was ablaze with lights
now, lamps and tapers in shining groves, and the high altar
draped with white and gold; and the whole building was
packed with knights and ladies, bright with polished metal
and coloured silks, with faces of solemn exultation turned
towards the altar. So the first Mass of Christmas Eve began
(not of course the great Mass of Christmas, which would be
at the coming midnight). There was built up a white and
glowing glory around us all; and when the Holy Office was
over, the King himself stepped from his place and stood on
the altar steps; and the monks led me before him. Two squires
closed in on me, and as the priest brought from the altar my
helmet, my breastplate, my sword and belt and the rest, King
Arthur himself gave them to me, and the squires buckled
them upon me. Then, full armed all but my helmet, I knelt on
the steps before King Arthur, and received the accolade.

One cannot speak much of moments like this. It was all I
had expected and more. From that moment I was King
Arthur's man for life or death, and I was something more
than myself. Something of Arthur's spirit, his personality, his
special interest, entered into me – a feeling that he could trust
me, use me as a limb, a sword in his hand. That was what I
felt when, having bent before him for the accolade, I looked
up when he bade me rise and saw his face.

Then bells were ringing overhead, and people were throng-
ing and jostling round me to shake my hand and call me Sir
Gawain. My father was first, of course, unashamedly kissing
my cheek; and then the Queen, who had let him go before
her, held out her white hand for me to kiss; then Lancelot's
handclasp, and Sir Griflet, and Sir Ector . . . Sir this, and Sir

that, and all the while the bells went on ringing, and suddenly I was tired to death and very hungry. We slowly passed out of the church door, and there was my uncle Gawain, coming up smiling, and the people cleared a space before him. He held out his hand – and then I felt a smashing blow at the side of my head, and went down into the dust like a ninepin, and all the people cheered. I heard him say, 'And be thou a good knight,' and he hauled me to my feet. This was too much for me, overwrought as I was, and I felt the tears spring into my eyes, and my chest tightening to explode into a catastrophe of weeping; but I held so tight to what was left of my control – I held so tight that everything went dark and I lost consciousness.

I opened my eyes again, and I was in a small, warm, light room, with my father propping me up and putting a cup of wine to my lips, and my uncle Gawain saying awkwardly, 'Och, maybe I hit you a bit too hard, but it's the custom, ye ken – I'm sorry, laddie, but ye see, my hand's a bit heavy – ye're no hurt?' My father was a bit short with Uncle Gawain, and very gentle and understanding with me. I think he knew what my last effort had meant.

Then, when they had recovered me somewhat, we went in to a great breakfast at the Round Table itself. The Hall of the Round Table was a different place from the great hall of the castle, where all would assemble and where the King and Queen and their peers sat on the dais, and the lords and ladies, the knights and gentlewomen, squires and pages, men-at-arms and all, sat before them in their degrees at the long tables. The Hall of the Round Table was a place reserved for the knights alone. It was four-square, with the Table in the midst; the Table was divided into three times nine sieges; for twenty-four knights, the King, the Queen (the only woman who might be present) and Merlin. Of course there were more than twenty-four knights in the Order now, but when there were more present, the rest sat along the square sides of the hall. One seat was left vacant at the Table, and that was the Siege Perilous. Each knight had his name painted on his place at the Table, and those that were present would sit in their own sieges if possible; but of course not all of them were present at any one time, and many of the original twenty-four were dead and gone, but their names remained there, with the names of the new owners added above them. My uncle Gawain arranged that I should sit in his siege over his own name, Sir Gawain, which was now mine also; and he himself sat elsewhere. I had hoped to see Merlin there, of whom I had heard so much; but he was not at court any more – people said he was growing too old – a younger magician took his place, much to my disappointment.

Meals at the Round Table were always very special – like this one, they were solemn, and yet they were merry, as if we were all a little light-headed with wonder, after the high and holy daybreak. That was the Table where, once or twice before, and as I was to learn later, once or twice after, the Sangreal itself appeared.

I ate and drank heartily, for I certainly needed it, and it was a good breakfast too; and everyone made much of me and was amiable to me, as the new knight. I felt better, and after breakfast my father took me away to one of the small rooms in the knights' quarters – no more keeping with the squires, thank God! and let me sleep in a soft bed for the rest of the day and part of the night.

Before midnight I was roused again, to take part in the Midnight Mass of Christmas. By this time I had become quite bewildered as to day and night, and fairly lost between today and tomorrow and yesterday. But having slept since long before noon, I was rested and fresh, and enjoyed the late collation after Mass more than those who had stayed up singing carols and waiting for midnight; and when they all went to bed I was still wakeful, and roved about the hall, warming myself by the fire, polishing my armour for the tourney the next day, and killing time as best I could.

At last, at early light, the company bestirred themselves, and all prepared for the great event of the day, the jousting. This I knew was going to be my great test. I had practised and practised, and gone through every possible exercise and training at home, and I knew all the techniques, and had ridden in small jousts with neighbours and visiting friends; and my father assured me I ought to do reasonably well if I kept my head. As for old Trojan, he knew it all backwards.

Everybody knows how a tournament is set out, how the lists and the barriers are arranged, how it all looks – the pavilions, the royal gallery, the banners and pennons, the colour and glitter, the noise and the excitement. And there was I, in my brand-new jousting helmet, out of which I could only see through a narrow slit. Nonetheless, I had learnt to calculate my distances, from what I could see through that narrow slit, to a considerable degree of accuracy.

We drew for opponents; if you beat your first opponent you went on to the next in line, and so on as far as your success lasted. I waited in line, watching, through that slit, the knights on the opposite side as they came up one by one, but having no means of knowing one from another, hidden as they were by their armour, save by their crests and the devices on their shields, and those didn't as yet convey much to me – they were all strange. The herald cried their names as they rode up. Each rode against the barrier, sideways on to his opponent, meeting him with a slash and trying to sweep or thrust him off his horse. One or other always went down with a huge clatter of armour, but the armour was so padded that, though their spears were usually splintered, hardly anyone was hurt more than a few bruises. Of course, accidents did sometimes happen . . .

Now my turn came. I heard the herald shout, 'Sir Segwa rides against Sir Gawain le Jeune . . .' and I gave a shake to Trojan's reins and was off.

I saw my opponent riding up the other side of the barrier, a big man in blue armour. Carefully I remembered everything I had been taught, and followed the formula exactly. It worked like a spell. Aim, point, slope, sweep – so! He was off his horse with a rattle like a ton of old iron, and I swept on along the barrier, round and back, and the crowd roared applause. I lifted my beaver and saluted the King and Queen, and saw my father's delighted face beside them. Then I wheeled about ready for the next course.

'Sir Gawain le Jeune against Sir Leontine . . .' shouted the herald, and I was off again – but as I swung my lance I felt something was wrong. My balance was gone – my girth slipped, the saddle turned under me, and I crashed to the ground. I heard the crowd groan as I felt the pain of the fall in all my joints, and with an effort rolled clear of Trojan's hoofs. Some of the crowd applauded my opponent, but most were disappointed because of me. I struggled to my feet, and stood dazed, while one of the squires caught Trojan – it isn't easy to run in jousting armour – and brought him back to me, carrying the saddle. I plodded from the lists on foot, heavy-hearted and mortified. But what had happened? I was sure I had tightened that girth properly. How had it worked loose? Hadn't I secured the buckle?

My father came up behind me as I took my helmet off. 'Hard luck, boy,' he said. 'But how did it happen? Didn't you tighten the girth?'

'Of course I did, Father,' I replied, and then suddenly it flashed into my mind that someone could have undone that buckle – leaving it so that it didn't slip at once, but only after I had ridden one course – and even while I thought of it I saw, over the heads of the crowd of stable-boys, the sneering face of Mordred. It was on the tip of my tongue to cry his name aloud – and then I thought that an honourable knight could hardly do so without any proof at all; neither would it be knightly to start making excuses and saying it wasn't my fault. So I held my tongue. My father went off shaking his head, and soon I learnt that he persuaded the marshals to let me ride another course. I led Trojan back to the horse-lines and put his saddle on again, very carefully you may be sure. I took a good look at the buckle of the girth, but it told me nothing. (It was a very good thing that we were not using the full caparison, with the great flouncing skirts draping the

horse's legs, or the whole thing would have tangled up, and
Trojan's legs might have been broken.)

And, of course, after that I should not have left Trojan alone
for one single minute – nor would I have done, but that my
uncle Gawain called me out from the horse-lines and I
couldn't say no to him; so I gave the reins to one of the horse-
boys and went to his pavilion. It was just to tell me that I was
to ride once more, against Sir Dinadan – a kind and jolly man
who was anxious to give me another chance. My uncle also
advised me, rather gratuitously, to look well to my girths this
time. So I took my leave of him as soon as I could, and
hastened back to Trojan.

The herald announced, 'Sir Dinadan against Sir Gawain le
Jeune,' and I mounted and moved in. The moment I was in
the saddle I knew there was something very wrong – Trojan
winced and started and sidestepped – then as I put him to the
gallop and lowered my full weight with the lance into the
saddle, he seemed to go mad. He plunged and reared, threw
up his forelegs and then his hind legs; struggled, raged – he
bore me out into the clear space of the field, away from the
barrier where Sir Dinadan had already hurled past – I clinging
on desperately, being tossed about, hardly knowing what was
happening to me – at last, with a scream such as horses give
in battle, Trojan reared right up, pawing the air with his
hoofs, and as he came down again, threw me. I crashed across
the width of the lists and fell heavily against the railings. I
could see nothing in my helmet, but I could hear Trojan
scream again, and the thunder of his hoofs. Then someone
dragged me clear and pulled my helmet off.

My father and uncle supported me away from the field –
three or four grooms were struggling with Trojan, who was
lashing out and foaming at the mouth.

'I think you'd better quit now, son,' my father said, very
kindly and quietly.

'That's a vicious horse,' said my uncle. 'Why d'ye let the
boy ride him, Gareth? Ought to send him to the knacker's
before he slays someone.'

'What, Trojan?' said my father. 'Trojan's not vicious. I don't know what's come over him. I trust him like – like my son.'

I was too miserable and humiliated to speak. I just went with them, back to the horse-lines, with Trojan being led clattering and stumbling behind us. Knights came up and spoke to me, saying how well I'd tried and how sorry they were. They were all so dreadfully kind to me.

And then Mordred came up, with his rancid smile, and said, 'I hope everybody is being kind to you, nephew?'

I couldn't go for him then and there. There was absolutely nothing I could do. I felt I wanted to scream aloud, or to lie down and kick, or be sick, or throw myself out of a window—

Only one thing I could do. I got two men to hold Trojan's head firmly, and I carefully removed his saddle. There was a beech-nut under it . . .

And so it was that I came to the great Christmas banquet, miserable and humiliated, my pride in the dust, hurt and angry, and altogether at the bottom of the world. As the new-made knight and my father's son I was given a seat on the dais with the King's special friends, and placed next to Lancelot – just when I was longing to crawl away and hide myself in a dark closet. Nobody spoke of the jousting, and in my hurt pride I imagined that they were all carefully, kindly refraining from speaking of my humiliation.

We went early to the feast; such sun as there was, low and cold on the snowfields, was still in the sky, and glowed in redly through the leaded and coloured windows of the great hall. Where we sat, on the dais, the big outer doors faced us where important strangers, embassages and heralds were wont to enter; but now they were closed against the cold. Yet we sat waiting, and everyone looked at those doors.

'It's as well we are assembled early,' Sir Dinadan said to me in low tones – he was on my right, and on my left was Lancelot, who was on the right of the Queen. 'I hope you're not too hungry, for dinner won't be for another hour. I took a nuncheon of bread and ale before coming in. You see,' he

went on in reply to my enquiring look, 'it's our King's custom
at the big feasts. Dinner can't begin till he's seen a marvel . . .
as if it wasn't marvel enough that we all wait patiently for
our meat. So they all know about it, and Sir Kay brings us all
to table a full hour before the meat's ready. There's always
something turns up. When Merlin was here he used to
manage one of his sleights or phantoms or whatever they are
– that is, if no real adventure presented itself. Now poor old
Merlin's decided to leave us, we have to make do with what
we can – I think they've got some mummers with a masque –
unless, of course, anything *does* happen—'

'I'm sorry to miss Merlin,' I said. 'Why has he left?'

'Oh – poor old chap, he's growing very old. Very old and
feeble. We're all sorry he's gone. It's – somehow not so safe
as when he was here.'

A silence fell – everyone sat quiet, looking towards the
King, who gazed towards the door. Some of the pages giggled
nervously – they were silenced.

'Why is it getting so dark?' I whispered to Dinadan.

'It's the snow – yes, here it comes,' he replied as a gust of
wind hurled itself against the windows. And then far off we
all heard something. It wasn't the wind – it was a drumming
– a horse approaching, yes, no – larger and heavier – der-um,
der-um, der-um – nearer, nearer, louder, louder—

A shudder, without reason, swept through the hall. Men
held their breath, as the thundering drew ever nearer, and
every face was white; for the drumming, drumming, carried
a menace beyond words – Dogs below in the hall slunk under
their masters' feet. The Queen's two little trainbearers, little
damosels of twelve or so, were clinging together and quietly
weeping for fear. Arthur and Lancelot closed up each side of
the Queen, and I saw her reach out a thin pallid hand to each
of them . . .

Then the drumming ceased, and was followed by a heavy,
dull plodding, as if some heavy beast approached, step by
ponderous step, shaking the earth. Then on the door, three
shattering knocks – and the door flew open with a rush of

cold wind that swept the torches sidelong; and in the doorway stood That which had come.

The thing was a monster.

No other word would describe it – it was human in shape, but too big – terrifyingly too big. It stood all of eight feet high, and with its shaggy head and great hulking shoulders filling the width of the door – its head drooped like a bull's about to charge, and its arms swung forwards – the fingers of one hand dropped down, well below its shambling knees, and the other hand clutched a weapon. At first, against the wan gleam of the snow, the figure stood as a shape in black – then, as the light of fires and torches shone upon it, I could see that it was green, a strange gleaming green all over – its tangled hair and bristling brows, like a tussock of rank grass; the flesh of the face, the neck, the bare arms and great coarse hands, all an unnatural, reptilian green – as well as the figure's clothes and armour, rough and ancient, yet encrusted with gold and gems as if arisen from some older world. Only the eyes were red, and the teeth were an unclean yellow with red and drooling gums; and on the face was the most bestial ferocity that I had ever seen on man or brute. And the weapon it leant on was an axe.

I had heard that there were still such creatures in the world – offspring of an older time, hardly human, dwelling upon the fringes and in the outer wild. But here was one, in the midst of us, in the light of the torches and between the dressed tables, within arm's reach of the gaily dressed women and the little pages . . . as if it were a dangerous wild beast, a deadly snake raised to strike. We were forty knights and sixty men-at-arms, but most of us were unarmed, and if that Thing had but swung its long axe it would have mown down ten before the rest could stir – and worse, the front ranks were the women and children . . .

None moved.

With deliberate heavy step the monster advanced into the hall, and then we heard its voice – harsh, deep, croaking, as from long disuse.

'King Arthur.'

'I am King Arthur,' he said, in a voice that did not shake.

'I come in peace.'

A sigh of relief went round the hall, but we still held ourselves tense and apprehensive. What might this Thing mean by peace?

'I ask a boon.'

'Say on, and I will – grant it.' Arthur's voice in the known formula, only hesitated a fraction.

'A Christmas game!' and the monster gave a slow, cackling laugh. 'No more than a game! – Give me a man here to exchange blows with me. One blow for one blow. No more. Have you one brave enough?'

I could hear the hissing sound of a deep indrawn breath from all in that assembly. None answered.

'One blow for one blow,' the monster persisted in its creaking voice. 'With this axe of mine. Let your champion strike me first – one blow on the neck – and then let me strike him. Come now, is there none of you—?'

Heads were turned, and now the hall rustled with men looking this way and that – but none came forward.

The creature grinned, convulsing its horrible features, rolling its red eyes. One hand smote the heft of the axe on the floor before it, the other thumped its breast like a drum.

'What – not one? Not to save the name of the Round Table? Cowards and cravens – ha, ha! Not a man to stand up to me! Not one! All, all afraid of me. Oh yes, I could lay my hands on your pretty ladies, pick up your little pages and swing them against the wall, and snatch at your lovely Queen there – but I won't, though I could. I only ask you for one man, one man to stand up to me, for one blow – and you can't give me one!'

I saw Lancelot, who was on my left, start from his place – but in the same instant I saw the Queen, whose hand still rested in his, tighten her hold, while her lips framed the word 'No.' Then Arthur himself rose, loosing her other hand from his.

'I answer the challenge,' he thundered across the hall, 'I, myself, will defend the honour of the Round Table.'

I saw Guinevere's face then: and whatever men may now say of her, I know and will always maintain that though she loved Lancelot, she also loved Arthur, and she loved him with compunction and sorrow. In her eyes I could see the torment of her soul. And that was the moment that decided me—

I stood up, thrusting back my stool clumsily with noise, and stepped to the edge of the dais. Then I raised my voice.

'My lord King – I pray you let this aventure be mine.'

All were silent as I spoke. So far the words of the formula, but I must needs go on and add more.

'My lord King, I'm the youngest knight here, the least of you all – quite useless, quite valueless. Nobody here will miss me – the Round Table won't be the poorer for just me – while you, my lord—'

I stopped, embarrassed at the sound of my own voice. Arthur, who was already on the floor and had received the axe from the hand of the giant, turned to me, and I saw his eyes light up. He held the axe out to me horizontally in both his hands.

'My good knight,' he said loudly, 'yours be the aventure, and may God give you joy of the due performance thereof.'

That, again, was the formula, but there was more in it than a ritual utterance. I came down from the dais – I could feel the tenseness all round me as the company watched me. Arthur placed the heavy axe in my hands, while the giant shambled to and fro at the far end of the hall, snuffling like a bull in a field.

'My lord,' I whispered to Arthur, 'shall I strike to kill?'

'Surely,' he replied. 'Strike once and make an end, and you'll not have to fear his blow.'

'I will, my lord,' I replied, with a confident smile that was a long way from my heart.

I approached the monster, who looked me up and down, as if it only dimly appreciated that a change had been made.

Then to my surprise it sank on one knee, placed its clasped hands on the knee that was upraised, and bowed its head. The rank green hair fell forward, baring its neck – I could see the coarse yellowish-green skin, with larger pores like a pig's, and the short hairs springing up blackish-green and bristly.

The axe was not a weapon I had ever used much, being no part of knightly warfare, but belonging to an earlier age; but I had chopped wood, and sometimes jointed the carcase of a beast. The edge, I saw, was sharp enough for any work. But this must all be done with one blow – there could not be a second. I swung the axe for a minute to get the feel of it, then made a prayer and heaved it high, and with a good bold swing brought it down. It fell true and with all my weight behind it – I felt it bite bone and gristle ... it went through, and the head leapt forward and rolled on the ground. Rolled and rolled and went on rolling – it spun horribly right across the hall, and thudded against the booted feet of a man-at-arms, who, with an instinctive movement that was half a shudder, kicked it back into the middle of the hall again. I saw with sickened fascination that the blood that dribbled from it as it rolled was not red but green – a sticky dark green like green paint. Then I heard gasps of amazement all round me, and I looked back at the body of my adversary.

The headless trunk, that should by rights have fallen prone on the floor, still knelt, with green blood pumping from the severed neck – and then, incredibly, it heaved itself to its feet, headless as it was, dead as it ought to have been – and stood, tottering and bleeding. Then, step by step, groping before it as a blind man walks, it stumped across to where its head lay, and scooped up the head in one huge hand. The creature held its head thus, and waved it before us all – the eyes open and rolling horribly, somehow still alive, the mouth twitching, the neck still dripping green blood. Right before Guinevere it held the head – she closed her eyes and sank back, and her women gathered quickly round her and carried her out of the hall.

A voice came from the head – or was it from the headless body, where the head should have been – how could we tell?

'Haaaa—' it said, a long mirthless laugh. 'Your champion has struck his blow. Let him abide mine—'

And at that, I felt that there was no more blood in my heart. And I do not think the bravest of knights could have felt otherwise.

'But not now,' went on that hollow unearthly voice, as if indeed something else, that was not visible, spoke through those dead lips. 'Let him come in a year and a day. Let him come to the Green Chapel that is by the Castle Haut-Desert, north-west from here – and let him call on the Green Knight. Write it down, you scribes of the King. And let him not fail, or your Round Table is shamed for ever.'

The axe lay on the floor where it had fallen from my hand. The giant touched it with its foot.

'Let him – bring – this – axe,' it said, slower and slower, like a clock that is running down, 'for – his – token.'

And then – good God, it would have been a thing to laugh at if it had not been so horrible – it thrust its head back on its shoulders, and strode out as it had come, all men drawing back to make way for it. None followed to see where it went. The great doors swung together behind it, and it was gone.

And all at once the hall was full of noise – made up of laughter and shudders and excited talking – we had to laugh, it seemed, to shake off the fear – though some were crying, and not only the women either. And Arthur descended from his dais again, and laid his hand on my shoulder, and everyone looked at me. I saw my father's face, and he was as pale as death. Guinevere had taken her seat again, whiter than her usual white, but composed, and Arthur led me up to her. I knelt and kissed her hand, but she bent forward and pressed her lips on my brow. And I heard my father say, 'Oh, my boy, my boy – God knows I'm proud of you – but did it have to be – like this? What shall I tell your mother?'

And I knew that they all regarded me as under sentence of death.

3 · Vivian

*T*ime went on, after that fateful Midsummer, and the year turned towards Christmas.

Bertilak, now my husband, never came to my chamber after our wedding night. He was gentleness and consideration itself, and gave me full honours of my position as lady of the castle, seating me on his right hand at the table, and setting my aunt Morgan on his left – she didn't like that, I could see! – and insisting that the castle people should call me 'Dame' instead of 'Demoiselle'. He gave me presents too, and spoke to me always with a wistful gentleness; hardly ever did he lay a hand on me, save in the formal gestures of courtesy; but sometimes he would take my face between his hands, and very gravely kiss my forehead, and then there seemed to be unshed tears in his eyes.

But I could still see the little green line that ran round his neck, and it made me shudder in spite of myself.

He was still afraid of Aunt Morgan, and under her power. Once I overheard him saying to her, 'For God's sake, madam, let me alone now – I'm a married man – 'and she replied by laughing in that horrible way I knew only too well.

I occupied myself now with learning as much as I could of magic, without committing myself to Aunt Morgan and the powers she served. She was always saying that there were things she could not tell me till I had taken the vows and undergone the rites – but I put her off from day to day, and meantime set myself to learn how to protect myself against her powers. For there is a white magic as there is a black magic. Never would I perform the sacrificial rites with her, or invoke the names she invoked; but from her books I learnt the angelic names, and the prayers to the high powers; I learnt the stars, and the times, and the correspondences; and all that could be done by increasing the power of the will and the mind, without calling upon the demons. And after a while I mastered a few small arts. As I have related, I stumbled upon invisibility, and learnt to use it a little; and I became fairly proficient in the outward art of shape-changing, when given time and the help of such things as clothes. I could not instantly become a cat or an owl, as Morgan could; but I could make my face and body pass for that of an old woman, or an old man, or a country yokel, a nimble small boy, or a grave priest, when I had dressed myself in the right garb and had time to think about it. Now and then I would amuse myself, and gain practice, by walking about the castle precincts in a disguise, and mingling with the folk. But Morgan would always know me. Most of the disguises I enjoyed – I liked being a swaggering man-at-arms, or a page-boy, or a mincing clerk; but one I disliked, although it was a useful and effective disguise, and that was an old woman. I hated to have to impair my fine healthy body, and make it withered and feeble – to see my face so wrinkled and colourless, and my teeth seem to disappear; to feel my limbs heavy and stiff, and my eyesight dim. It seemed a horrible anticipation of what old age must some time make me.

Christmas was coming, and something important was to happen at Christmas. Preparations were being made as they had never been made before. As November drew on and December approached, I was surprised to see room after room hung with rich arras, new tables spread with Eastern carpets, carved chairs with cushions, sideboards with silver vessels, screens of Saracen work – I had never seen such a display. Of course I suspected it of being illusion, and went about fingering cushions and hangings, and carefully sitting down in chairs, to see if they were real. Usually they were – except when Morgan was in the mood to play me a mischievous prank, and the chair disappeared the moment after I had sat down in it . . . But mostly it looked as if this display were to last, and be used. The castle people were surprised, of course – but they all knew better, by this time, than to ask questions. And the odd people who had appeared on my wedding night kept on cropping up, too, and mingling with the house-carles and bower-maids and pages. Sometimes they were there, and sometimes not.

December set in, wild, cold and rough; and just before Christmas it snowed for a week, and the wind howled. All the rich new furnishings couldn't make the castle anything but cold, especially at night. In the long, long evenings we sat by the fire in the solar chamber, our fur mantles heaped over our backs to keep out the chilly draught behind us, with little to do but talk and listen to the same old storyteller. But Morgan would stare into the heart of the fire as if communing with the spirits there, and waiting for someone to arrive. Often I tried to see what she saw, but no picture would come.

And then one night, just before Christmas, as we sat thus, I saw Morgan lift her head, as if she listened; and far off a hound bayed, and another hound in the yard took it up. Then, over the sound of the cold wind, very, very far off, came the faint blowing of a horn. And at that sound my heart turned over in my body.

Morgan rose from the fire, and spoke at the portal curtain to the servants, quiet and purposeful; and I listened where I sat in my corner. Half an hour, maybe, passed, and then we could hear a horse, and the heavy clanking of the armour of him that rode it, coming nearer across the wild. Heavy and slow it came, as if lame; then once again the horn rang out, and this time an answering trumpet from the battlement startled me, blaring out over my head. And then the castle's bell pealed.

'He has come,' Morgan said.

'Who has come?' I said faintly.

'Go and see.'

I ran down the winding stair from the solar, and rustled in my long stiff gown across the hall. The men-at-arms were grouped by the door – the stranger, I could tell, had crossed the moat and passed the guard-house and through the court-yard, on Morgan's orders to let him through, and now he stood outside the hall. The seneschal stood directing a man to unbar the door. As the door swung open, all the torches swept one way in the wind, and a man in armour toppled off his horse as if unable to stand. The icy blast seemed to sweep him into the hall. For a second he clung to the doorpost, swaying on his feet, while the snow blew in behind him – then he recovered himself a little, took a step into the hall, and as I put out my hand to welcome him, stumbled and fell forward at my feet. The seneschal lifted the helmet off his head, and there, looking up at me, was the face I had seen at my wedding – the face I had seen when I first entered the castle. The face of the man I was to love.

I hardly heard his indistinct words of greeting and apology. Bertilak was close behind me, exclaiming.

'Good God, the man's half dead with cold! Bring him in, Walbert – look after him there, can't you? Wine – no, the fire – no, best take him off to bed – come on, you carles—' and all was bustle and solicitude round the new arrival. The men carried him off to restore him, and I looked round to see Morgan at the far end of the hall, very composed and smiling, saying, 'In an hour we dine.'

Now all the strange glamour that had been laid upon the bare bones of the castle took gloss and lustre. There were already curtains and carpets all over the stony walls and floors, but cressets of soft white flames were now lighted, and braziers steamed with delicate perfumes. And those peculiar attendants, always unobtrusive, filled up corners and alcoves. It was like a king's court – but a king's court in some far outlandish region.

The stranger-guest, rested, warmed, restored and clothed in a handsome fur-edged mantle, took his place in the hall, and I, in a new plum-coloured satin gown, came forward to meet him. But when I looked back at Morgan following me, I caught my breath in astonishment. Her bold dark beauty was altogether hidden. Not only was she clothed in the severe black-and-white that becomes an aged dowager, but her face was a mass of wrinkles – her eyelids like paper in the discoloured sockets, under straggling grey brows – her neck sagging, save where the severe white wimple braced it up.

One heavy gold ornament clanked on her breast, and her wrists and hands were a mass of bangles and rings. She was the perfect respectable duenna to complete the picture I made, as I sank down in my curtsey before that dark-haired, pale-browed knight, and felt his eyes searching mine.

The meal was magnificent, there was no denying it; and Sir Bertilak, sitting next to the stranger, plied him and cheered him in his hearty, noisy way. There was no need for me to say anything. Sitting sideways to him I could not look directly into the stranger's face, and it did not seem to me that he had looked at me with any notice at all, except for that one strange intense look he had given me when he had fallen at my feet at the door. That might have been in a dream, and now he was awake and had forgotten all about it.

It was the convention that no stranger was asked his name or his business until he had eaten and drunk. Presently, when the meal drew to an end, Bertilak, with much clearing of his throat as if squaring up to the occasion, filled his glass, and said in the usual set form of words: 'Now, sir stranger knight, if it so please you, declare unto us your name and your errand.'

And the stranger got to his feet, and still following the formula, answered, 'Gramercy, good mine host, for your kind welcome. My name is Gawain the Younger, of the Court of King Arthur, Knight, and I come in search of the Green Knight whom I must meet at the Green Chapel, near to the Castle Haut-Desert, on the day following Christmas.'

A silence fell, and many in the hall drew in their breath. The lights flickered just for one moment – and shuddering, I glanced at Sir Bertilak.

But he was his hearty, mortal self, red-faced and jovial, and I could not see the green ring on his neck at all. Rather, he glowed with warmth and wine, and broke the formality with his next words.

'Castle Haut-Desert? This is it, my dear fellow, this is it. And as for the Green Chapel – know it well. Not a couple of miles away. You're at your journey's end here, what? Nothing more to do. Just stay here a couple of days – it's – what is it now? – three days – and then you'll be right at the day. Tomorrow, then Christmas Eve, and then Christmas itself, and then St Stephen's, that's the day. St Stephen the Martyr's.'

Morgan turned to the stranger, graciousness itself, and said, 'Good Sir Gawain, since that is your name, come you within to the bower, and there tell us more of your strange adventures.' She wheeled about with a rustle of skirts, and led the way up the winding staircase to the solar above. As I followed her, Sir Gawain stood back to let me pass, and extended his hand in a courteous gesture – his eyes met mine, and our hands touched just for an instant – and in that instant something passed between us – the sympathy of two lonely people? – Much more than that; but I have no words for it now. And in an instant it was gone, and he had become once more a man guarded, aloof and dedicated; and I was tense and apprehensive of horror and cruelty to come.

The solar was warm with the big fire in the chimney, and the many-coloured hangings closing us in around a gilded table, where flagons and cups had been set, and chairs for the four of us.

Bertilak, still laughing boisterously, turned to the knight. He had altogether dropped the archaic, ritual form of speech.

'Now, my dear chap, we'll have a jolly evening together, and make you as welcome as we can. You needn't worry about the Green Knight. In a matter of single combat I've no doubt you'll come off the best.' He stretched himself in his big chair before the fire. But Gawain, seated upright and unrelaxed in a straight-backed chair, replied frowning.

'It's not quite like that, sir. Not exactly single combat. I have to go – to – give myself up.'

This, I felt, was the thing I feared.

'To give yourself up?' came Morgan's voice, soft and purring. 'But pray, how can that be?'

'This Green Knight,' said Gawain, pale and serious, 'is no earthly man but a monster. He came to Arthur's court last Christmastide, and defied us all to exchange one blow for one blow. For – for the honour of the Round Table I took the aventure. There and then with one blow I struck his head from his shoulders, and – and – he did not die.'

His voice faltered into silence; the others watched him, saying nothing, and I watched them.

'He – still living – bade me meet him in a year and a day, and bide one blow from him, without defence. So of course – I have come. And when I meet him – there will be nothing I can do but – keep my bargain.'

Again silence fell – and then Bertilak shattered the silence, slapping his hand on his thigh.

'Why, it's like a tale of old times!' he roared. 'Come now, it does my heart good to find one so young and valiant. So you'll keep your tryst with this hobgoblin on St Stephen's Day? Fine, fine. Ah, never look downhearted, man. What must be, must, and yet there's much can happen between now and then. Have another cup of wine.'

'You'll keep Christmas with us, and then we'll see you on your way with goodwill,' said Morgan smiling.

I was aghast. They knew *what* they knew, and yet they could laugh and cheer him? Up to that moment, indeed, I had known that he must meet the Green Knight that was Bertilak's other self – but I had not suspected the manner of their meeting: that he, mortal, must bow his defenceless neck to some unimagined shape of evil from the other world, and lift no hand to save himself . . .

'You must have a good rest first,' went on Bertilak. 'I shall be off early tomorrow, to hunt for this feast, but don't you stir. You lie in bed as long as you like – you'll need it after your journey. One of the serving-men will bring you your breakfast. Promise me you'll have a good long rest? You can do the same for the next three days, and after that you'll be fit for anything—'

The chattering and vociferating went on, and presently they called in a couple of jongleurs to play an interlude; but I was sick at heart, and hardly knew a thing till we had parted for the night, two handsome serving boys (but not quite earthly) leading the knight to his chamber.

As I went into my turret room, and Morgan passed up the stairs to hers, I caught her sleeve and drew her back.

'Aunt,' I cried, 'in God's name what are you doing? What are you making Bertilak do? Do you mean to murder this man?'

She held me off at arm's length, and under her disguise of wrinkles her face was mocking.

'Oh, so we're interested, are we? I thought so. My poor silly niece, it's little you know of magic and its workings. True, your fine cavalier is in great danger – you've found out something, but not enough, you see! But he can be saved, and it is for you to save him.'

'Me? It is for me to save him? Oh, God knows, I'd do anything – anything to save him – only tell me how.'

'Come and see me at daybreak tomorrow,' said Morgan, coolly drawing her sleeve from my clutch. 'I will tell you then. Meantime, go to bed, and sleep soundly.'

She kissed me on the forehead, and I shuddered from head to foot; and then she passed on up the stairs and left me – but not to sleep soundly.

The winter daybreak was late and dark – I had slept very little, all those long dark hours. At last, when the faint light came, I dressed, and stole upstairs to Morgan's room.

She was up and walking about in her furred night-robe, her disguise all gone and her face boldly handsome as ever, even at that hour. She handed me a silver tray, with a stoup of ale and a manchet of white bread.

'There,' she said. 'You will take him his breakfast in his chamber. And then you must tempt him.'

I felt as if I had been struck a blow over the heart.

'I don't understand you,' I gasped. She turned on me, suddenly furious.

'Oh, in hell's name! – I knew they bred fools in convents, but *such* fools! "I don't understand you!" – Then have it in plain words – you must offer him your body, make him take you to his bed. Or must I say it plainer than that?'

I set down the tray, or I should have dropped it.

'But why – why must I do this?' – I know my voice was stupid, but I was stupefied.

'My good foolish niece,' she said, suddenly calm again, 'didn't you tell me last night that you wanted to save this man from the danger he is in? Come, I know you love him – you've made it plain enough. Well, do you want to save him or don't you?'

'Oh,' I said, fighting to get my breath back – 'I do – I do – I'll do anything to save him – anything you say – but why that?'

She turned away from me and stared into the fire that burnt under the chimney-cowl. 'This, my girl, is a magical matter, and you know nothing, nothing at all about magic and its operations. All you know is that he is in danger from an enemy from the Older World, and you're right in that. Now understand this: this man Gawain stands in danger now from the operation of the planet Mars, under whose dominion he is. You must bring him from the dominion of Mars to that of Venus. If you can place him under the power of Venus, then Venus will protect him and he will be saved. Otherwise, Mars must have his life.'

As she told me this, it sounded very convincing. How was I to know how altogether false it was? I was not to find that out until much later, when indeed it was too late. I should have known that all Morgan's words were lies; but who else had I to guide me in the dark region where I was wandering?

She turned and handed me the tray again; but I did not put my hands out.

'No – I can't do it,' I said. 'I can't bring myself to do it.'

'Ha!' She gave her bitter, nasty laugh. 'Well, you're a fine ardent lover! Maiden modesty, is it! Convent-bred, I know. Oh yes, you think you love him, you say you do, but you won't do that much to save him from death. Not to save his neck from the axe – come, you'd rather see his blood flowing,

his brains battered out – rather than venture your pure body
– or is it perhaps your soul?'

I could not answer, but the tears ran down my cheeks.

'And much good your virginity will be to you, when he lies
a bleeding corpse—'

'Oh, God help me!' I cried. 'Is it true then – is it true that if
I make him yield to me it will save his life? Will you swear
it? What will you swear it by?'

She relaxed a little, and smoothed her brow.

'My dear niece, your hallows and mine are not the same. If
I swore by anything that you worship, I would swear without
faith, and you would not believe me; and if I swore by my
own hallows, they mean nothing to you. So let's have no
swearing. Only I do assure you that what I have told you is
true. Come now' – for seeing me weakening, she suddenly
changed her mood – 'poor child, you are shivering with cold.
You've not broken your fast. Come, sit down and share my
morning posset.'

She had a milk posset, with honey and spices, keeping
warm in a chafing-dish; and it is true I was cold and wretched
and very thirsty, after a long sleepless night. I took the posset
and drank it eagerly – never remembering about her subtle
potions. But as soon as I had drunk it, my mind changed, and
I had no more scruples nor doubts. I saw everything differently, as it were drawn to one point with nothing before it or
after it.

I stood up and took the tray.

'I'll do it,' I said.

'That's my girl!' and she held the curtain aside for me to
walk out.

And then she threw me a last word.

'Remember, he can't scorn you altogether, or he fails in his
knightly courtesy.'

I went down the stone staircase, across the empty hall, still
dark, and up into the opposite turret where our guest lay. The
illusory power of Morgan's potion was strongly upon me, and
I had forgotten fears and scruples, as if I were not myself at

all. The heavy oaken door of the chamber was not barred; I opened it by the latch, quietly, and went in, closing it behind me. The room was small, as most of such rooms were; the thickly curtained bed took up most of the space, and all the curtains were drawn; but light came from a little window by the side near the door, glazed with coloured glass, and below it stood a small chest. I set my tray down on the chest, and stealthily drew back the curtain.

He lay in his bed, relaxed in sleep, his head thrown back so that the red and purple light from the window played on his face and throat. He slept like a child, and my heart turned over in me as I looked at him. So beautiful, so unconscious, so strong, and so helpless. I was emboldened by the potion, it is true – but it was something quite other than any magic of Morgan's that came over me at that moment, and made me stoop over the bed, fling my arms round his neck, and press my lips to his.

He woke, his eyes looking right into mine with a look of unutterable bliss and sweetness; the lovely moment hardly lasted the time of a heartbeat before recollection came, and a look of horror wiped out the smile, and he thrust me away from him, and clutched the sheet up to his neck, crying, 'Who are you? – What do you want? – Go away!'

Then, as I reeled back, he recollected himself still further, and a look of confusion swept over his face with a deep blush, and he stammered, 'Oh, I'm sorry – oh, my lady, I'm very sorry – forgive my words – I – I was taken by surprise – I was discourteous—'

I myself was taken aback now; I remembered what my aunt had said, that he must not repulse me altogether, because his knightly code forbade him to offer me any discourtesy.

'Oh, no, no,' I cried. 'Don't, don't distress yourself. I came upon you too suddenly. You see, I've brought you your breakfast—'

'That was kinder than I deserve, lady. You should have sent a serving-man.'

'And – I have brought you something more—'

'Yes?'

I didn't know how to go on; and like a fool I just blurted out, 'I love you!'

I saw him start, and draw his breath in sharply. I had said it now, and I went on desperately, 'And I've come to give you – all of myself—'

Again he breathed deeply and frowned, and his hands tensed on the coverlet. But he said nothing. I had to go on.

'Then will you not – eat the breakfast I have brought you?' I had heard of that kind of double-talk, but I wasn't very good at it; and he didn't help me by taking it literally.

'Lady, I shall be very glad of your bread and ale – it was good of you to wait on me. But – do not ask me anything more.' He looked straight before him, and it was hard to read his expression.

'No?'

'No. You – you honour me greatly, sweet lady, but I'm no paramour for you. Forgive me, but you deserve better. If it pleases you, I will be your true servitor, and hold you for my worshipped lady – will that content you? – I see it will not.'

'At least don't send me away,' I almost whispered.

'How could I do that? It would be unforgivable. I am under your roof. But, lady, you should not be here. Your husband—'

'He has gone to the chase, you know that.'

'Your aunt—'

I stifled the bitter laugh on my lips.

'The servants—'

'They will not stir yet.'

'Oh, I see you have arranged it all—' —and he frowned.

'No, no!' I cried wildly. 'Say that I just took the opportunity because – because I love you—'

He shook his head, and put on the air of a grave elder admonishing a child.

'My dear lady, it cannot be. You know I am a man under sentence. I cannot, in any case, be any lady's lover. Don't set your heart on one who has only three days more in this world. All you can do is pray for me.'

And at that, the recollection that all this desperate strata-
gem was for the purpose of saving him from his fate so
overcame me that I burst into sobs, my face in my hands.

He was all concern at once.

'Oh, lady, dear lady, you mustn't cry. What a brute I am –
how could I hurt you? Oh, forgive me—'

I raised my face from my hands.

'At least you don't hate me?'

'Hate you? Heavens, no. But, my dear, I cannot do what
you ask. Please understand this, and leave me.'

And I could do nothing else.

At the foot of the stairs to my own room, Morgan met me.
She took one look at me.

'I see you've failed.'

'Yes, I've – failed.'

'Well!' she burst out, 'of all the weak ninnies – of all the
feeble niminy-piminy, milk-and-water minikins – you demi-
nun, you! Failed, and there's a man's life at stake! I love him,
says she – I'll do anything to save him, says she – and then at
the pinch she can't take her lover to her, to save his precious
life!' She stopped for breath, and I put in, 'He wouldn't. He
refused me. What could I do?'

'What could you do? Oh, of course, you could take no for
an answer, couldn't you? Call yourself a daughter of Eve?
Come now, this won't do. You've got two days more, and
you must try again tomorrow.'

'Then,' I said, 'be sure you give me your potion again, or
I'll never have the boldness—'

'What's that? Oh, ay, that I will!' and she went away
laughing.

But I crept up to my room, and stayed there all day. I did
not come down to dine, though I listened down the stair, and
heard Bertilak come back from hunting, noisy and cheerful as
ever. He flung down a load of heavy carcases – I could hear
the horns click on the stone floor.

'Deer – a good bag. Need them for food. Oh yes, we'd good

sport. You have to take them by surprise, you see, for your deer's a timid beast – if you don't creep up on him and take him suddenly, he's off and away and you'll never catch him, this time of year. Now tomorrow we hunt the boar. The boar, now, you must take by bold assault, and fight him hand to hand—'

'I'd like to come with you,' I heard Gawain say, and I hoped fervently that perhaps he might, and I be excused from the task I dreaded.

'No, no – you must gather your strength. You stay and rest tomorrow and the next day. You've enough before you. No, you stay and rest while you can.'

And so the next morning found me again at his door, with my platter of bread and stoup of ale. As before, I stole in quietly, but he was awake, and I think he had been expecting me, for he looked up from his pillow.

'May I come in?' I said diffidently. 'I've brought your breakfast again.'

'Certainly, come in. It's very good of you.' He sat up and took the tray from me.

'Are we friends then?' I ventured.

'Why, of course we are friends—' and he smiled, so that I was encouraged to seat myself on the side of the bed.

'Then let us talk as friends,' I said. 'Talk to me while you eat.'

'Will you not share my breakfast?'

With a little ceremonious gesture he handed me half of the manchet, and then the stoup of ale to sip from.

'Tell me,' I said, 'all about yourself – your home, your family.'

So he told me, warming to the subject as he went; how his father was Gareth Beaumains, and his mother the proud and beautiful Lady Leonie of Lyonesse; and about his aunt Lynett, the bold lady that rushed about the country running errands for King Arthur; and of his three uncles, the brothers of Orkney, the greatest of whom was the other Gawain, whom he called Gawain the Great, saying that he himself was only Gawain the Little. But I wouldn't have that, for I said he was as good a knight as any of them. Then he told me of how he was knighted by King Arthur, and all his trials and humiliations, and how in sheer despair and lowness of spirit he had taken the challenge of the Green Knight; and how he had spent the past year in discipline and exercise to prepare himself for his ordeal. But I tried to lead his thoughts away from this, and asked him what he thought of ladies, and damosels, and women in general. He told me he had been taught to give worship to all ladies, and discourtesy to none, and to serve them all, and in particular lovely Guinevere, the Queen.

And all this while, I sat on the silken coverlet, with the silver tray between us.

'But did you,' I said, 'never love a lady of your own?'

'No, never,' he said.

'Then,' I said, leaning towards him, 'then—?'

'No!' he cried vehemently, and swept the tray and all that was on it to the floor, so that it crashed down noisily. 'No, don't speak of *that* again. I tell you, I won't listen—' and he glared at me with such a look of terrifying hatred that I gasped in fright, and burst into sobs like a child. It was all too much for me, and I cried and cried without control.

Suddenly, to my astonishment, I felt his hands on my shoulders.

'Oh, lady, lady, I'm sorry- that's twice I've made you cry – oh, I'm a clumsy brute—'

'And don't call me lady,' I sobbed, slapping down his hands from my shoulders. 'Call me by my name, which if you remember is Vivian.'

'Oh, Lady Vivian – I mean, Vivian – dear, dear Vivian, don't cry—' and in spite of my feeble slapping hands, he gathered me into his arms, and I lay there with his hands caressing my head and shoulders – and oh, heavens! in that moment I knew, and he knew, that thus it was meant to be,

and that this was love. I had forgotten all about the part I had
to play; I only knew that we were meant for each other.

But after just an instant he put me gently from him. 'We
forget ourselves,' he said.

'Oh no,' I said bitterly, gathering myself up from this
repulse. '*You* don't forget yourself. You remember yourself.
You don't forget. You'll go no further.'

'How could I?' he said, and it maddened me that he should,
as it were, preach at me.

'You'll venture nothing,' I said. 'You'll not venture your
body – or is it perhaps your soul?' The moment I had said it I
remembered where I had heard those words before. These
were Morgan's words – how had she put them into my
mouth? I hadn't *wanted* to say them.

'That was cruel, Vivian,' he said.

'Oh I know, I know,' I cried wildly. 'I didn't mean to say
that. Forgive me,' and I seized both his hands and held them.

'You know I cannot give love to any woman,' he said. 'I am
a man under sentence—'

'Not even for the first and last time?' I pleaded.

'Not even for the first and last time. You are my host's
wife—'

'His wife only in name.'

'Even then, I am trusted. So you see—'

His hands were very warm in mine.

'But if,' I said, 'if it were not so? Just supposing it were not
so? What then?'

Our faces were close together, and his eyes burned into
mine.

'If it were not so—' he whispered. But then he lowered his
eyelids over those burning eyes.

'Let us remain friends,' he said. 'Go – and go quickly before
I weaken.'

'Let me stay here till you weaken.'

'No – no. I wish that we may remain friends. Go, before we
become enemies.'

And so sternly he looked at me, that I could do nothing else but gather up the tray from the floor and go, without looking back.

I know I was shaken and flushed when Morgan met me, and my cheeks were still stained with tears. She looked me up and down.

'So? Not unmoved. Well, try again tomorrow. You might save the man's life yet.'

Once again I did not show myself all day, though it was Christmas Eve. At dusk Bertilak returned, blood-smeared, and flung down the carcase of a boar.

'He fought well, and it was a near thing,' he said. 'Tomorrow it's the fox – he's more cunning, and we have to use indirect ways.'

Now I could no longer keep to my room, because the customs of the feast demanded me; but I sat through it with a heavy heart, in spite of the glow of tapers and glamour of holly and mistletoe. Never once did I raise my eyes to Gawain's face, though he sat beside me at the table; nor did he address any but formal words to me.

But as soon as the dinner was over, I slipped away, though by rights I should have kept the Christmas Eve vigil and gone to the midnight Mass. Instead, I went up to my room, made fast the door, and took down from the shelves certain books I had been carefully studying all the day. These were books of my own, into which in days past I had laboriously copied all that I could learn of Morgan's magic, as far as it was not tainted with the names of devils.

Now I took from my coffer a knot of green ribbons, and having drawn a circle upon the floor, and traced out the signs, I sat down within the circle and plaited those green ribbons into a belt. I plaited them intricately with many twists and turns, for that way the evil influences are twisted and turned aside and made to lose their way as in a maze. I fitted it with a copper buckle – for copper is the metal of the Lady Venus;

and a beautiful thing it looked when it was finished. Then I laid it in the centre of the circle, and having sprinkled it with water and blessed it with the smoke of incense, I put upon it the strongest magic that I knew, to fill it with the protecting power of Venus, that he who wore it should be safe from all the strokes of Mars, from iron and bronze and brass and stone and wood and fire; and that no power of the leaden Saturn should touch his life, but that the power of Mars in him should turn to valour and victory, and that of Saturn to peace and length of days, all under the dominance of sweet Venus, the bringer of peace, the mother of us all.

Then, when I had completed my work upon the girdle, I buckled it round my own waist and hid it under my robe.

... And so, I thought, I might even then save his life, without doing what Morgan wished me to do. God knows how I longed for him in body and soul – but why, oh why had Morgan brought him here – as I was sure she had contrived it – I so unnecessarily tied to Bertilak, and Gawain a man devoted to his fate, from which only dishonour could save him? But perhaps my magic would prevail over Morgan's, and save him without dishonour either way. I would try.

Down below in the hall I could hear those who had been present at the midnight Mass, still carolling for Christmas, and I felt very remote from them. But when I set the tray for Gawain's breakfast, I laid on it a sprig of holly, and a rosy apple, and a comfit of dates and spices, and filled the cup with wine instead of ale. I was in my best robe, too, a beautiful crimson damask, sweeping the floor and cut well away at the neck, where a soft edge of fur warmed my bare shoulders.

So I lifted the latch and opened the door.

Once again he was awake, and I think he had been expecting me, but his first words were, 'You should not have come.'

'Why not?' I said, stepping up to the bedside and placing

the tray across his knees. 'You had to have your breakfast –
could I let you starve on Christmas morning?'

He smiled and fingered the rosy apple.

'Then lady – no, I should say – Vivian! – I'll wish you a
merry Christmas – and thank you – and now you must go.'

I frowned at him.

'Not much of a Christmas greeting? – Oh yes, I'll go – but
first I've a present for you. At least you'll let me do that.'

'A present? Why, that's good of you, but I don't think I can
take it, for you see, I've nothing to give in return.'

'You must take it, you must!' I burst out wildly, and
unbuckled the green girdle from round my waist, and held it
up before him. 'Gawain—' (and this was the first time I had
called him by his name) – 'this time I ask nothing more of
you, but just that you accept this, and wear it.'

He fingered it doubtfully, as it lay all across the bed, the
green boldly contrasting with the red and purple lights from
the window.

'And wear it? But what *is* it – what is in it?'

'Do you mean – '

'Yes. A thing like this can only be magic.'

'Then I will tell you. Oh, my dearest, my beloved—' (and
now once more the tears were streaming down my face) – 'It
is a charm to preserve you from danger, the strongest charm
I could make. Tomorrow I know you must go and meet your
challenge, and I shall never see you again. Go then, but take
this and go in safety. Your life will be safe, though I shall
never – never—'

I could say no more. To hide my face I bent and took up
the tray and laid it on the chest under the window, and stood
with my back to him. I heard his voice.

'Sweet friend – what else can I call you – you are so kind.
You know that I ought not to try to shield my life with any
magic, for I have to offer myself willingly.'

'Was *he* protected by no magic?' I cried. 'That monstrous
Green Knight who – who was not what he seemed?'

'No matter. That was his way, mine is another. I made a

bargain and must keep it. And I do not – admit to fear.'
(Perhaps not, but his voice shook ever such a little.) 'So I do
not accept your gift as a protection to my life. But I accept it
for your love.'

I turned back to him with a sudden leaping of the heart. He
drew me to him and kissed me gravely on the forehead.

'And so goodbye, my lady and my only love. As we met so
let us part, in honour and worship. My heart is yours if I live
or die, and so God be with you.'

And so we made our farewell.

Saint Stephen's Day – Saint Stephen the Martyr. And how
cold, cold, cold a morning!

Christmas Day had been a bitter one for me. As in duty
bound, there I had had to sit on the dais throughout the
revels, with Morgan, in her dowager disguise, one side of me,
and Bertilak the other, while below in the hall a gay party of
pretty girls, and a few smooth young men, led Gawain
through his paces in all the traditional Yuletide games, as if
he had been a pet animal or a child they were determined to
spoil. I don't know where they came from, but strongly
suspected that they were only some more of Morgan's phantoms. They fussed over him and flirted with him, and ever
and anon broke into sentimental lamentations, that such a
fine young man should have to go and meet his fate ... I
don't think any real human beings could have acted so.

And Bertilak – there he was, the hearty, courteous host,
urging him to drink and enjoy himself, whipping up the fun.
A wave of disgust swept over me – how could he, knowing
what he knew? – He had come home from hunting soon after
noon, and flung down a bedraggled fox. 'That's all we got,' I
heard him say. 'He's clever, the fox, but he breaks all the
rules. Does things you wouldn't think of. Not a chivalrous
beast—' and with that he turned and looked straight at me.
But I looked back at him. If I was a deceiver, so was he. So I
reflected while I sat beside him on the dais. But how could I

condemn him if, like myself, he was only a tool in the hands of subtle, smiling Morgan?

And now the morning of St Stephen's Day was breaking, and it was the day appointed for Gawain to go. A bitter cold morning – no wind, no rain, but a grey pall of cloud, through which the sun showed as a red globe for a few minutes after sunrise, and then vanished again into the greyness. Snow everywhere, and a bitter frost hardening it as it lay. Glimmering white fields extending out to a comfortless horizon, and long icicles hanging from battlement and balcony. The far-off trees made caves of shadow below their laden branches, and the black specks that moved in the distance here and there might well have been wolves.

From my turret window I could see the courtyard, where the great hall door opened out, and here were Morgan and Bertilak – Bertilak – saying goodbye to Gawain, and seeing him mount his horse. A serving-man went with him on a mule, to guide him to that place, the Green Chapel, wherever that might be. I disliked the look of that serving-man. He wasn't one of our honest house-carles, but only too plainly one of Morgan's creatures. I had the impression that under his cap his ears stood up straight like an animal's.

The murmur of words came up to me – endless, ceremonial goodbyes in the old formal speech, handshakings, bowings. There – he was mounted at last, and that sinister serving-man took the lead, and they went out through the great portal and over the moat. For a moment I lost sight of them behind the curtain-wall; and they were on the road and going up the hill.

And at that moment I took a resolve. I hurried into my warmest clothes, such as I would wear for hunting; and summoning up all I knew of magic, I made myself invisible. Then I slipped downstairs – carefully avoiding Morgan, for I was not sure how far my invisibility was proof against her – and hastened out to the stables. My favourite horse, Deerfoot, knew me by touch and voice – I do not think he minded not being able to see me. I saddled him, mounted, and was off by the postern gate. Quickly I slipped round the circumference of the castle walls, and picked up the line of the road that went up from the main gate; as I did so working hard in my mind to extend my invisibility to Deerfoot, and as far as I know I succeeded. I knew the path that Gawain must take for the first three miles, for there was no other; but after that the road forked, but his tracks and that of the serving-man's were plain enough, and I followed them, through that dead, cold, miserable landscape, and presently I sighted them, going away towards the desolate north. So I followed, just keeping them in sight. Why? Just because I had to know what became of him.

The road grew wilder and more desolate still. Woods closed round it, their snow-weighted branches roofing sinister caverns. What might be lurking there, I dared not think. I remembered the strange creatures I had seen in the woods when Morgan and I had ridden up from the south – some of those were terrifying enough, and that had been in the summer – but what kind of beings might hide in these darker, grimmer places? – And wolves, undoubtedly there would be wolves. It was little comfort to me to know they could not see me – they could hear me and smell me. I wondered if, in a crisis, I should become visible quickly enough for Gawain to see me if he turned at a cry for help – or would he just see a struggling mass of wolves devouring something, and leave them to their feast?

I kept Gawain, with the serving-man, just within sight, and if he heard me he would no doubt think it all part of the spectral torments of his road. They pressed on until the day was far advanced. We went up into hills, zigzagging up the sides of sheer cliffs. At the top of one such climb, where a dark coombe opened between the shoulder of that hill and the next, I found they had halted, and an argument was going on between Gawain and the servant. They sat on their mounts, facing each other, and a steam went up from the horse and the mule into the frosty air. Their words came down to me clearly.

'Good sir, this is where I leave you – and – and—'

'And what, my good man? You seem afraid to speak.'

'And – if you wouldn't take it amiss – you won't go on either. I know the place, and I know about it – that man you're going to meet. I tell you, sir, I wouldn't go on for a fortune.'

'No one is asking you to.'

'No, sir. But you yourself—'

'Never mind myself. You were sent to guide me to the Green Chapel, and that's all that concerns you. Now, are we near it?'

'Just up that valley, sir, straight before you. But – if you please, sir – I *don't* like to think of you going up there. To put it plainly, it's certain death.'

'Supposing I know all that?'

'Yes, sir. But I beg you – now supposing, sir, you were to go off down *this* way, which will lead you towards Wales and the sea. I'd go back, and never say a word to anyone, except that I left you just here, and no one would ever know—'

I could hear the harshness in Gawain's voice, as he replied, 'Go away. Go away and leave me. You may not understand, but I have to go on. I tell you, you miserable coward, that if you go back and spread any lie about my backing out and running away, when my bones are lying dead in that valley up there, my skull will fly after you screaming – Now, go your way and let me go mine.'

He gathered up his horse's reins and turned him with the spur; the stones his horse kicked up in turning went rattling down the face of the precipice. I saw the servant turn the other way and begin to pace down the hill path. From where I was placed I could see them both when they were out of sight of each other – and as soon as the servant was hidden from Gawain by a spur of rock, both the man and his mule just vanished. I knew then for certain that he was one of Morgan's phantoms. If he had been an earthly man under enchantment, I should have been able to see him, being myself at that moment partly in the Otherworld; but this creature had no underlying substance at all, and had now disappeared completely. As I passed the spot where he had last stood, I was conscious for a moment of a colder breath, and that was all. So I hurried on up the slope after Gawain, and shortened my distance. His moment of peril was approaching.

The ravine was like a narrow dark passage, where the light hardly penetrated from the weak, clouded sun above, and the winter air rushed through it in a deadly draught. Then it widened a little, into a dell, with a torrent breaking through under icicles; and in the middle rose an ominous shape – a high, rounded mound, shadowy and grass-grown, the grave of a giant. A dark doorway opened in its side. I had heard of places like that – ancient burial hills of the men of old, hollow inside, and with winding entrances at the quarter-points of the sun, leading away into darkness within, where, they said, the Old Dead sat in a circle, crowned with gold. If this was the Green Chapel, what unholy prayers were offered here?

Then as I approached, I heard a strange and frightening noise, coming up as it were from under the ground. First a thudding, a vibration that shook the road below so that I felt it all up through my horse's body – then a sort of grinding roar, with a shrill edge to it – what on earth, or under it, could make that noise? Deerfoot threw up his head, checked, trembled – I could see Gawain's horse, that was much nearer the source of the noise, wince and shy and dance. Gawain held the reins firmly and coaxed the terrified animal on. But after a few yards forward, he dismounted, tied his horse to a thorn tree, and proceeded on foot. He held in his hand the great axe he had brought with him, but he put himself in no posture of defence with it. He had cast aside his cloak, and with a little comfort I saw that he was wearing my green belt.

The horrible noise ceased – then broke out again, juddering back from the stony walls. And now I knew what it was – a grindstone. Somebody within there was sharpening an axe.

I dismounted, tied Deerfoot, and moved quietly forward till there were perhaps three hundred yards between us. Then the noise ceased once more, and this time there was quietness, deadly expectant quietness in which I could hear the stream, and the melted ice dripping from the trees, and the piping of a forlorn small bird. Nothing else moved – until, when I thought I could bear it no longer, Gawain shouted.

'Hola—'

and the echoes mocked,

'Hola – a – a—'

Then out of the dark twisted entry of the barrow, shouldering its way through the overhanging growth, came that green horror I had seen before. Shambling and huge, it walked like a bear, but it was larger than a bear. It – I could not think of it as Bertilak, though I knew – it was larger than I had seen it before. Its eyes and nostrils glowed red against the horrible green flesh. It strode forward, leaning on an axe, a much larger axe than that which Gawain carried, an axe freshly sharpened; and it loomed over him.

He looked up at the frightful thing, but I could not see his face.

'I have come,' he said, and his voice was small but steady.

The monster spoke, slowly and creakingly.

'You keep faith. That is well. You have struck your blow. Now I strike mine.'

Gawain laid on the ground the axe he carried, and very deliberately removed his helmet. He wore no plate-armour, only a leather jerkin. And so he stood, quite still, and bent his head forward. The monster wheeled up his huge axe – and I could watch no more. I shut my eyes – I heard the whipping sound as the axe descended, and then a kind of muffled shout.

'You flinched,' the monster said.

I opened my eyes – Gawain still stood there, unhurt, and the axe swung in the monster's hand, to the right of his victim.

Still I could not see Gawain's face, but I heard his voice.

'I am sorry. Strike again, and this time I will not move.'

Once more the axe swung upwards, and this time I watched as if spellbound. Incredulously, I saw it fall past his ear, to the left this time, and not touch him. Gawain did not move as it fell, then he tossed his head up, puzzled and angry. The monster let out a roar of ugly laughter.

'I did not move that time,' Gawain said. 'You, whatever you are – for God's sake don't make a mockery of me. Strike and make an end of it.'

'I will so,' grunted the giant, and once more swung the axe.

Down it came, and – I think I must have cried out, for I saw it gash his shoulder, and suddenly there was blood running all down him. But he was still standing, while the giant stepped back and made no move towards him.

A breathless moment they stood so, and I waited to see Gawain stretch his length on the ground. Instead, he snatched up the smaller axe that lay at his feet, and with a laugh, whirled it in the air and leapt towards the giant.

'You've had your blow,' I heard him shout, 'And I'm still alive and now I can fight you. Come on, you hobgoblin – '

With an answering laugh the monster parried his stroke with one arm, wrenching the axe from his grasp – and there was Bertilak, and no monster, holding Gawain off at arm's length as I have seen him hold a puppy.

Bertilak's huge laugh rang against the rocks.

'No need to do that, lad – that's enough. Steady now – you've done very well. It's all over now.' And then, taking up the formal language of knighthood, 'Hold, Sir Knight, for thy quest is accomplished. Right well hast thou endured, and here I yield thee the mastery.'

He released Gawain, who staggered back against the rocky wall with his hands spread out behind him to hold him from falling – more shaken than I had seen him in all the time before. Bertilak leant on the axe, which still remained in his hand, and addressed him confidentially.

'You did very well, my boy. I'm sorry about that gash, but it isn't very much, only a flesh-wound, and I had to do it. You see – the once that I didn't touch you was for the first time you resisted my wife. It would have gone hard with you if you hadn't. Twice was for the second time. But the third time

I had to wound you just a touch, because, you know, you did fail at the third test just a little.'

Gawain's face, that had been so white, reddened slowly.

'But I swear to you – I swear to you – I never – oh, believe me, never, never—'

'I know you didn't, my boy. Mind you, I'd have smashed your skull in if you had – I'd have had to, d'you see? No, it wasn't that at all, so don't worry about it. It was that green baldric you're wearing.'

'This? – oh, heavens, take the horrible thing away,' and he tore it from him and flung it on the ground.

'Yes – you accepted it from my wife, you know, not just for a love-token, but as a charm to save your life. That was against the rules, now wasn't it? Am I right?'

'Oh yes, you're right,' said Gawain, miserably, with hanging head like a chidden schoolboy. 'That's absolutely true. I did fail, and I was afraid, just a little. Oh Lord, that's all the good I am.'

'No, my boy,' said Bertilak very kindly. 'It was a hard trial – you had to be tested in all sorts of ways, you see, and you've come out of it very well. Look, you must wear this,' and he picked up the green baldric and handed it back to him, 'when you go back to King Arthur's court, as a sign of your victory.'

'As a sign of my defeat,' he insisted. 'A sign of my failure and humiliation. I'll not wear it.'

'You must. You must wear it to let them know you have accomplished your geste. Look, lad, you mustn't blame yourself – the forces against you were very strong. It was all devised by Morgan le Fay – the old lady in black in the castle was herself in one of her disguises. Part of her schemes and deceptions, directed against Arthur and Guinevere, but you've beaten her after all. And you mustn't blame my pretty wife either.'

'What?' Gawain looked up sharply.

'No – she was put up to it by Morgan as well. It was all part of the scheme to try you. I had to agree to it, of course.

She didn't really want to do it at all – you've no idea the difficulty Morgan had in persuading her.'

If Gawain's face had been pale before, it was paler now. He put his hands to his forehead, and leant back against the rock.

'Oh, my God!' I heard him say. 'Oh, my God – I thought it was because she loved me.'

Silence hung between them for a long minute.

Then Bertilak, with his broad, heavy, kindly, stupid face all concern, stepped to Gawain's side with a pad of linen for his wounded shoulder, exclaiming, 'Now, now, my lad – don't take it to heart. Come on, no harm's intended. Here, you come on back with me now, and get that cut seen to, and have a good meal and a rest – there's ten days of Christmas still left. And you must meet the lady wife and make your peace with her.'

'No, no!' cried Gawain wildly. 'No more women! No more women ever at all! I'll never look at one again. They – they deserve all that has been said about them. Ha—' (and he shuddered) – 'I had a vision once of a serpent with a woman's head. No, I beg your pardon, my lord. I forget my courtesy – it was kind of you. But I'd rather not come back with you. I'm no fit company for anyone in my present mood. Let me go my way.'

'Well, if you must, lad – back to King Arthur's court by the shortest way, I hope?'

'Perhaps. I don't know. I can't think. I must just be alone for a while.'

'At least get that cut seen to. Look, follow this track out of here the way you came, and the first path that branches to the west – see the sun? – will take you to an abbey. Don't wander about in the cold, in the state you're in—'

'Thank you,' he said shortly, and moved towards his horse. He walked right past me, and never even felt that I was there, and I saw his stricken face.

'Goodbye, lad, and take care of yourself,' said Bertilak, 'and don't think too hardly of us all. You've shown yourself a brave knight, and never let anyone say the contrary.'

I mounted my horse as quietly as I could, and followed
Gawain as he rode away out of the dell, as shattered and
dejected as he was; Bertilak remained behind, leaning on his
axe, frowning and screwing up his eyes in puzzlement. All I
understood now was that Gawain hated me; but that lief or
loth, I must go with him to see what befell him, though it
were to the world's end.

4 · Gawain

When I turned away from the Green Chapel and rode
alone down the mountain path, I was too sunk in
misery to know or care what became of me or which way I
went. I had no feeling of having passed successfully through
an ordeal, or of having fulfilled the purpose for which I was
sent – on the contrary, my pride, my love and my faith were
shattered, and I had nothing left to live for. Add to this that I
was weak with shock, that my wounded shoulder ached and
burned, that I was tired and empty, and that the cold wind
blew right through to my shivering skin. It was more thanks
to my horse than to myself that I took the turn Sir Bertilak
had suggested, and came in time to the abbey, where the
good monks were very kind to me, and put me up comfortably for the night, and did what they could for my wound.
They pressed me to stay for a few days till I was properly
recovered, but I was restless, and with the sheer perversity of
a sick man I insisted on going on the next day, though I felt
far from well, and the old infirmarian was most reluctant to
let me go.

Without much definite purpose, I set my face to the south,
perhaps having a notion that the south country might be a
little kinder than that rough north, where the snow still lay
and the wind blew chill. I kept on feeling suddenly hot and
sweating in my heavy accoutrements, and then shivering

again – the wound in my shoulder throbbed, and my head ached so that I hardly knew what I was doing. I rode along in a miserable half-dream, in which the shapes of my unhappiness rose before me and tormented me.

Presently I began to take notice of small sounds behind me, as of a rider approaching. In that haunted country I had experienced a number of times the sound of phantom steps seeming to follow my way, and anyhow everything seemed phantasmal to me now – I hardly cared what spectre rode behind me; but now I felt that it was something real. Round the corner behind me came a small brown donkey, with a small black bundle on its back. I drew rein and waited while the donkey picked its way delicately up the road; and then the rider was revealed as a little old woman.

She dismounted and came up close to me. She seemed very old indeed – the skin of her face was like parchment, such wisps of hair as escaped from her white wimple under the black coif were like faded winter grass, her mouth was fallen in so as to show no lips at all; yet she seemed spotlessly clean, and her eyes, though deep in the bony sockets and without a trace of eyebrow or eyelash, were bright and, I thought, kindly. She was so little that her face hardly reached to my stirrup.

'Please you, sir knight,' she began – and her voice, though high and thin, was clear, without the annoying tremolo of so many old women.

'Sir knight,' she said, 'this is a lonely road, and I am unprotected. Would you be so kind as to let me ride with you till we come to a better place?'

And now I was seized with doubt and misgivings. A woman! No more women for me. The very sight of a wimple and gown made me wince with pain. Oh, to be able to forget that such creatures existed!

'I am sorry, dame,' I said, 'but I am resolved to have nothing to do with any woman—'

'Resolved?' said she, with a wrinkling smile. 'Not under vow, but only resolved? – But then, good sir, look and behold you'd hardly count me as a woman. St Anthony himself would hardly trouble about me. No woman, sir, but only a poor old nurse out of employment.'

I looked her up and down, and certainly, there seemed little enough of Eve's allurements about her.

'I was a nurse, good sir,' she went on, 'to the family of my Lord Egerton, but the children are all grown up now and need me no longer, so I'm on my way to my sister's daughter at Sarum, who I trust will take me in. But it's a long road, and I'm afraid of robbers.'

I took another look at her, for another thought had struck me – what if she were a witch? That was always possible with an old woman.

'Nay, I know what you're thinking!' she exclaimed. 'No, I am not a witch. Look, I wear a silver cross round my neck. My feet are not cloven – see here,' and she lifted her long skirt to show me her little feet in thick worn shoes. 'And you may prove me with holy water at the first church we come to.'

'No, no, good dame,' I said. 'I'm sure you're not a witch.' I was indeed in great perplexity, for all my life's training had been to respect and help all women, old or young, high or low; and hurt and suspicious though I was, I could not quite go against it now. 'Fair enough, good dame,' I said, 'you can ride with me and welcome. I'll see no harm comes to you. But forgive me if I'm but poor company.'

'I'll not give you any trouble,' she said. 'I'll ride behind you on my little donkey, and I'll promise not to speak unless I'm spoken to.'

So we rode on in silence, I feeling more and more miserably ill with each hour that passed. At length she called to me from behind as she rode.

'Sir knight – I think from the sun it's time for noon-meat. There's a cave over yonder would give us some shelter from this cold wind.'

I was glad enough to agree; and I was so weak that as I dismounted I lurched and almost fell to the ground. She steadied me on my feet.

'Why, the man's sick!' she exclaimed.

'It's nothing, dame,' I said. 'Just a touch of fever brought on by a slight wound – a trifle—' As I spoke everything seemed to spin round me, and a horrible wave of cold shivers swept over me.

She kept her hold of my arm. 'Men!' I heard her say. 'Call a high fever a trifle . . .'

And then I must have fallen forward, and been for a long time wandering out of my mind; for there was nothing for me but uneasy dreams, and struggling in the darkness, and burning heat, so that sometimes I thought I must be dead and in hell. Meaningless words echoed in my ears – horrible faces swam up before me, some of them with horns and double noses and gnashing teeth. I seemed to run and run, round and round in circles. Then at one time I thought my mother was there, I clung to her, and laid my head on her breast, and cried bitterly for a long, long while. And then, I think, the faces ceased to trouble me.

At last I awoke, easy and relaxed and cool, but very weak. I had no idea where I was, but before I opened my eyes I could feel that I lay on a comfortable bed of sheepskins, with a clean linen shirt next to my skin. I opened my eyes, and saw firelight flickering above me on the rough roof of a cave. At first I thought I was still at the abbey, and wondered why they had moved me from a cell to a cave. For a cave it certainly was, with a fire that burned in the crevice at the back, where I lay warm and cosy on sheepskins; and then a shadow came over the mouth of the cave, and the little old woman entered bearing a bowl of broth.

'Awake at last, son,' she said. 'That's right. Now sit you up, and sup this good broth.'

With a shock of shame I realized that this woman must have stripped me naked and put me to bed. I was horrified. But what could I do? To jump up out of bed then and there in my shirt would be more and worse shame – moreover I felt extremely weak, and extremely comfortable where I was, and the smell of the broth was very appetizing. I gave up resisting.

'How long have I lain thus?' I asked.

'Three days.'

'Was I sick?'

'That you were, and not too well yet. You can thank God for sending you a nurse, for by the Rood! you needed one.'

'You nursed me?'

'You'd have died else.'

'Then,' I cried, 'I owe you my life?'

'No doubt you do,' she replied drily. 'Now be a good lad and drink your broth, and then rest again.' But she turned her face away from me, and her voice shook in a way I hardly understood.

Later, as she sat by my bed, I asked her, 'What are you called, dame?'

'My name is Dowsabel,' she replied.

'Dowsabel,' I mused. '*Douce et belle* – gentle and beautiful.'

'Beautiful I was once,' she said, with her eyes cast down to her clasped hands. 'And gentle I can still be to you, if you will let me.'

'Gentle you are indeed,' I cried warmly, 'and beautiful you will still seem to me for your kindness.'

She did not answer, and I almost thought she was weeping.

That night the fever came on me again, and once more the ugly faces rose, and I wandered through hot deserts and up unending flights of stairs and through crowds of cruel people, perplexed and hot and frightened – then, as before, it seemed that my mother came, and I clung to her and cried. Then for a moment I awoke, and as I opened my eyes I realized that it was dark, and I could not see the face of her that held me.

'Mother?' I said.

'Lie still, lad,' said the gentle voice. 'It's only Dowsabel, old nurse Dowsabel. Lie still and rest.'

And so weak was I, that I lay back in her arms, and let her put a cooling drink to my lips, and presently slept again.

*

We remained there a full ten days more, as I grew stronger. Each day Dowsabel would ride away on her little donkey and get provisions from some lonely moorland village – whether she bought them or begged I never knew, but we always had enough. In the early afternoon she would be back – I would be glad to hear the donkey's little hooves on the stony path – and she would make up the fire and cook supper, and we would sit together by the glowing hearth, warm and snug enough in spite of the cold and rain outside. We would talk, and gradually I would forget that she came of the treacherous and accursed race of women – or perhaps it was that as my health returned I tended to forget my griefs and grievances. I told her all my story, though she would never tell me hers. When I told her of my betrayal by the Lady Vivian, I was surprised to see, in the firelight, tears running down the old woman's cheeks.

'Why do you weep?' I asked her.

'I weep for that poor lady,' she said.

'But, Dowsabel, she was a traitress as well as a temptress—'

'Listen, lad – suppose she too suffered? You were told that she was forced to do what she did, by the power of that wicked Morgan – supposing she did indeed love you?'

I shook my head. 'Not possible, not possible.'

'Remember she gave you the green baldric for your protection.'

'For my protection! It was for my downfall. Had I not taken it, I'd never have had this wound, to remind me of my failure.'

'Yes, but suppose she had indeed meant it to save your life?'

Her look and her voice were strangely urgent, but I could only murmur. 'No, no – let's speak no more of her,' and turn away.

Dowsabel would not let us move from our encampment until she considered I was well enough, and indeed as long as I remained there she was the mistress. I well remembered how when on the sixth day I put on my riding armour and tried to get on my horse, she scolded me as stoutly as if she had been my good aunt Lynett herself. I had to give in and wait her time.

I never knew where she slept – I think she had another cave near at hand, for there were many along the hillside. There was one where my horse and her donkey were stabled, and it may be that she slept there. But for the first week or more I doubt she slept much at night – whenever I woke I would find her watching by my bedside.

The weather grew milder as we advanced into January, and by the tenth day after I had recovered consciousness, she let me mount my horse and ride about a little, to get my strength back. It was strange how I obeyed her as if she were truly my aunt Lynett – or my mother.

One early afternoon, as I had ridden out in the watery noon sunlight and was returning, I came upon a strange sight. I had stabled my horse, and was walking round the foot of the cliff where our dwelling was. Beside the mouth of our cave there was a kind of niche in the cliff, facing south, sheltered from the wind and open to such sunshine as there was; the first aconites and snowdrops had broken through here, in the short pale grass, and overhead the brambles and ivy hung like a canopy and dropped down like icicles. Inside this little bower, Dowsabel was sitting; and as I live! – stretched out at her feet was a great white unicorn, with his head in her lap. The great beast was as huge as a warhorse, but as gracefully built as a deer; his limbs were drawn up under him, at rest, and showing the silver hoofs; his eyes shut, save that between the long black lashes came now and then a gleam to show he was not quite asleep, as she caressed his pearly horn. She sat there, calm and composed, like an image of Our Lady amongst the frosted boughs and the early flowers; save that her poor old ravaged face was more fitted to a St Anne. Yet the hands that played over the unicorn's noble head were, I noticed, smooth and white and shapely like the hands of a young girl.

When she heard my step she looked up, smiled gravely, and laid her finger on her lips; so I went softly away. When I returned, in about an hour as far as I could tell, the unicorn was gone, and Dowsabel was inside the cave and busy about the fire.

'Where is our beautiful guest gone?' I said.

'Oh – just gone,' she answered.

'Gone – but where?'

'Why, I don't know. Just gone.'

'Were you not cold, sitting out there in the snow?'

'No, he warmed me with his breath.'

'So, little Dowsabel,' I said (for I knew the meaning of the unicorn), 'it seems you have never known love?'

She stopped what she was doing and turned to face me.

'It is true,' she said, 'I have never known the happiness of love. That is not to say that I have never loved.' And there seemed to be all the sorrow of the world in her eyes.

Impulsively I took her hand and held it. (Had I thought her hand was white and smooth? But now it was veined, twisted and blotched with brown, as an old woman's hands are.)

'My Dowsabel,' I said, 'when I first met you, I could no longer trust any woman. But I trust you now and always will.'

She drew in her breath sharply, as between delight and pain, and stood for a moment searching my eyes. Then she said,

'But if I were young and lovely, would you trust me then?'

'I don't know,' I answered slowly, for I was trying hard to be honest. 'That would be different. I don't know.'

At that she drew her hand roughly away from me, and turned abruptly, and went into the inner part of the cave. There I heard her weeping bitterly, but I did not dare to go to her.

On the twelfth day after I had fallen sick, being the middle day of January or thereabouts, she said we might take the road again on the day following; I was stronger, but she wanted to push on to some convent or abbey where I could rest in better comfort for a time, till the weather was more reliable and I had gathered strength; after which we would make for King Arthur's court at Chester. As to her sister's daughter in Sarum, Dowsabel said she might wait. Dowsabel was resolved to stay with me and do all the offices of a squire as well as a nurse, and for my part I felt I could not do without her.

So the day before we were to set out, she went to the village as before, to get provisions, and while she was gone, the messenger came.

It was a young monk, and I saw him from far off as I looked down from the mouth of the cave, over the snowy slopes. That was the first time I had seen anyone on that path except Dowsabel. He wore a brown habit with the hood drawn up over his head; as he came up to where I stood he put the hood back halfway, and I saw a pale young man, not ill-looking, with dark brows, a shaven chin and a tonsure; he kept his eyes lowered as he spoke to me.

'You are Sir Gawain?'

'I am he, good brother.'

'I bring a message from King Arthur.'

You can imagine how my heart leapt at that. So Arthur knew where I was, and how I had sped! He must know I had fulfilled my trust with the Green Knight, and done what I was sent to do; but – and here my heart sank again – he must also know of my failure. But I must not shrink from whatever my payment was to be, good or ill.

'Give me the King's message.'

'King Arthur says: To my trusty and well-beloved Gawain. If thou hast fulfilled thy geste, I bid thee come to me at Candlemass, no later, in the City of Sarum. And thereof fail not as you love me.'

He recited all this as a lesson learnt by heart.

'At Candlemass!' I said. 'That is fourteen days from now, is it not?' The monk nodded, his eyes still on the ground.

'Do you bring any token from Arthur?' I asked. For answer

he withdrew his left hand from his sleeve, and I saw on his finger a ring of rubies and emeralds, wrought like a winged dragon. Such a ring I was sure I had seen on Arthur's hand. So I knelt and kissed the ring.

'Say to King Arthur,' I said, 'that I his knight will obey his command, and will be in the City of Sarum on the day of Candlemass.' Then I rose to my feet, and dropping the courtly speech, said, 'And now, brother, won't you come in and rest? This is a poor place, but the best I can do.'

'I thank thee, no,' he replied, for his part never leaving the courtly speech. 'Gramercy for thy courtesy, but I must needs haste on my way, Benedicite—' and he raised his hand in blessing, and paced rapidly away round the corner of the hill and out of sight.

When I told Dowsabel, I thought she would be pleased that we should go to her niece's place; I was quite unprepared for the harsh look of suspicion that came into her face.

'A monk – what kind of monk?'

'Oh, young – brown-habited, tonsured, what else would he be?'

'What cloister was he from?'

'I never asked him. He came from Arthur, that was all.'

'How do you know he came from Arthur?'

'He showed me Arthur's ring.'

'You mean, he showed you a ring you thought was Arthur's.'

'Heavens, Dowsabel! Must I doubt the evidence of my own eyes? He was a messenger from Arthur – Arthur himself – should I have put him through his catechism?'

She persisted: 'Did he wear a cross about his neck?'

'I couldn't see.'

'Did he give you his blessing?'

'Of course.'

'In what words – what sign?'

'Why, I suppose the usual ones. I remember he said "Benedicite", and held up his hand—'

'But did he invoke the Father, Son and Holy Ghost? Did he speak the name of God? Did he make the sign of the Cross?'

'Really, good dame,' I said, 'when a man brings a message from the King, and a knight receives it, do they stand upon ceremony – even if I could remember exactly the words of his blessing—'

'I wouldn't trust him,' she said.

'Maybe you wouldn't,' I said, rather acidly I admit. (I was peevish in my convalescence, I think, and her questions had put me out of patience.) 'This was a man, and it is a matter between men, and between me and the King. I have received orders from the King to go to Sarum, and to Sarum I will go; and I will thank you, my dear dame, not to hinder me.'

I knew that I had hurt her, but fool that I was, I didn't care.

So next day we packed our belongings and started away south and east.

I had very little strength for the first day's travelling, although my wound was well healed; but by evening we reached a nunnery, and there Dowsabel arranged for us to stay three days. I'll admit that I was glad of a decent bed in a decent dry room, and it did me a great deal of good. I was, of course, lodged in the infirmary, while Dowsabel was with the sisters inside the cloister, so I hardly saw her at all till we came to take our departure; which was perhaps as well, for we were not friends. We had, I think, worn off the edge of our mutual anger when we set out again, and of course I was feeling better and therefore more cheerful; so we talked civilly enough, as we rode along, on indifferent subjects; but there was a constraint between us.

We took the road south and east, towards Sarum – at that time it was not hard to find one's way, for the great roads the Romans made were still there, and directions marked upon them at the crossways; and although the ways might be open and lonely, they were not quite so lonely as those in the wild north which we were leaving behind. Each night one could be reasonably sure of a monastery or a nunnery, or an inn, or at least a farm or a cottage to give lodgings to a knight and a pilgrim. So we journeyed on, and became more at ease with each other, and almost forgot our discord. Then within two days of Candlemass, we came out of Savernake Forest, and reached the edge of the great plain.

We had spent the night at a lonely farmhouse, and were preparing to set off in the morning – a damp, windy, black morning, with the gleam of bleak light in the east like a glimmer under a black roof. I was standing outside the brick archway of the farmhouse wall, tightening my saddle-girths, while Dowsabel was still in the house settling our reckoning with the housewife; when I looked up, and there, suddenly, was the monk.

I started at the sight of him, and my first thought was to call Dowsabel that she might speak with him for herself; but he said, quickly and quietly, 'Do not call your nurse. This is between men. King Arthur bids you go to the great circle of Stonehenge, and there on Candlemass Day to meet with Merlin. Hereof fail not on your love and obedience.' He held out Arthur's ring – it gleamed in the dim light by the wall, and I knelt and kissed it.

'I will be there,' I said. 'Will you not come in?'

'No, I must go. Farewell,' and abruptly he was gone, round the turn of the dim road.

In a few minutes Dowsabel came out.

'Dowsabel,' I said as she mounted her donkey, 'the monk has been here again. He says I am to go to Stonehenge, to meet with Merlin.'

'What?' she cried. 'That monk? Why didn't you call me? Where did he go?'

'I don't know where he went,' I said frowning, 'and he spoke to me alone. You understand – he is Arthur's messenger, and I must obey.'

'I don't trust him,' she said, her old face paler than before, and her papery eyelids fluttering. 'I don't like it. Why must he call you to Stonehenge? First was to Sarum, and now it's changed. He brings no token—'

'He brings Arthur's ring.'

'I say he brings no token I can trust. There's nothing to show what he is. He might be a demon, or a shape of magic—'

'Dowsabel,' I said, 'no one asks *you* to trust this monk. It was to me the message was sent.' And then, for I was mad with irritation and impatience, 'No one asks you to go to Stonehenge. Go on to your niece at Sarum, and God be wi'ye. It is I who must go to Stonehenge.'

She reeled in her saddle, and pulled her donkey to a standstill. The reins dropped from her hands.

'Is that what you wish?' she said in a small faint voice.

'Yes,' I said. 'I am under a man's orders now, not a woman's, and I think it best we should part here.' She gave a sudden dry sob, and said, 'Very well,' and immediately turned her donkey, and rode away quickly down the other fork of the road. I stared after her – I knew that I had been boorish, and that at least I should have thanked her for all she had done – but I was still angry and proud, and she had gone very quickly. While I was still doubting as to what I should have said, she was out of sight.

The loneliness of the great plain beyond Sarum is something no man can imagine who has not been there. The wild country of the north is savage enough, with its crags and forests; but here there are no crags, no mountains, no trees – nothing but wide barren land going on and on, over distant slopes and long undulations, as if for ever; blackened ling and shrivelled juniper bushes, and yellow grass faded to beaten straw from last year's growth, are all that clothes the earth. Not even the white thorn grows here – only in some places the gorse shows a faint gleam of yellow, and the scars in the ground, far off, show the white flints gleaming in unlikely shapes; and away on the skyline loom the burial mounds of forgotten kings. Through this country my road lay, and I was alone, alone and beyond all loneliness.

I tried to talk to my horse – good old Trojan, whom I still had – but my voice mocked me, and made me afraid. Over and over I told myself that I should not regret Dowsabel –

God's pity, hadn't I ridden alone before? Was I a child, to
need a nurse? While she was with me, what was she but an
encumbrance – a frail old woman, who would have to be
protected if we ran into any danger? Wasn't I better off
without her?

The day was short, and the rain fell pitilessly. No trace of a
farm, or an inn, or a convent, not even a shepherd's hut; and
I knew there could be no riding by night in such a time and
place. Darkness came upon me rapidly – so (by God's mercy,
or how would I have fared?) I found, by the roadside, the
only clump of trees within miles, and decided to make camp
there.

It was a dark, ill-omened spot, but better than the open
plain. The trees were black twisted pines, and below them
were hollies. I was in luck, for the largest of the hollies made
a green bower within, under its leaves, and the rain had not
penetrated there, so there was a dry sheltered place for me
like a little tent. So I tethered my horse outside, and before
the light had quite failed, gathered sticks and made a small
fire in the heart of my leafy shelter. But by the time I had
really got the fire going, it was pitch dark; and far off I heard
a sound that made me shiver – the howl of a wolf. Trojan
heard it too, and started whinnying and plunging. I couldn't
leave him outside the holly-bush to be eaten by the wolves;
so I untied him, and throwing my cloak over his head to
shield his eyes and muzzle from the prickly leaves, somehow
coaxed him in under the holly boughs, to my cramped little
circle of firelight, and made him lie down. Then I laid myself
down against his warm belly. It was not the first time Trojan
and I had slept so – I had taught him the trick of lying down
and letting me rest against him during my year's wanderings,
for it was useful to have that resource, and we had slept so
under haystacks and in woods, but never before in such
cramped quarters. For I could not make my fire too close to
the stem of the holly for fear of setting it alight; neither could
I bring Trojan too close to the fire; but the circle of the green
holly leaves confined us closely, and outside was rain, dis-

comfort and danger. I had to talk to Trojan all the time I was arranging him, and maybe it saved my sanity that night, for here was at least a living creature, though dumb, able to understand some of what I said to him. His big eyes, when I uncovered them, met mine and we exchanged our fear and loneliness and unhappiness.

So we lay and waited for the long night to pass; a very long night, for at that time the night is far longer than the day. And my thoughts turned to Dowsabel – I hoped that by now she was comfortably bestowed in some safe lodging, or perhaps already with her niece in Sarum; and certainly this was no place for her – it wasn't like the cave. I could not wish her with me – but I did realize how desperately I missed her.

The rain continued to fall, black and dismal; far off I could hear that howling, and nearer at hand there were noises that were harder to define – rustlings and cracking of twigs, a soft footfall round and round outside the holly, and sometimes a sound of breathing. I could feel the hair rise on Trojan's neck; he twitched and snorted, but I spoke to him quietly and bade him lie still, though I myself was tense in every limb. Then I began to know a worse thing. Nothing that I could see or hear, but I could feel it with my inward sense and see it against my eyelids whenever weariness made me shut my eyes. It was a thing like a net or veil of mist, drawing up from the earth, one and unbroken for miles around, for it *was* the earth of that land – but strong and stinging like a spider's web, and pulling itself up in a thousand places at once into a thousand heads, a thousand mouths, open, hungry and eyeless. It gaped and sucked with all its mouths – immensely old, and cruel, and greedy. It was thin and barren and craving. Mile upon mile it stretched away, heaving up, wave upon wave into the darkness, blindly searching with those starved mouths. And somewhere out there a small helpless living creature, a little animal, or worse, a child, was being chased to and fro, running from one horrible mouth to another, whimpering in terror – and that helpless creature, I began to feel, was I. It was a nightmare without sleep I was drifting into. Trojan recalled me, by plunging and struggling and trying to rise; I held him down and quietened him, and made myself think of him instead of that thing outside; and I sat and fed the fire with twigs, and tried to pray to God and Our Lady till the light came.

At last it came, a sad and watery daybreak, parting the heavy clouds, but as welcome to me as good news. I struggled out of my cramped den, and seeing the desolate country at least free from wolves and nightmares, I helped Trojan out, once more covering his eyes against the prickles; he shook himself vigorously and snorted and stamped and then searched the ground for such small thin grass as there was. I had some corn in a bag, which I fed to him. For myself I found some bread and cheese in my pouch, and a flask of wine, which put a little courage in me, and so we went on. The rain had ceased at last, and the grey light of the second day of February grew clearer, and showed a wan streak of blue. Candlemass Day had come.

I could tell I was approaching Stonehenge, for soon I came upon a long, wide road, bordered with solemn great stones, standing like grim men in grey, ranged in two lines to watch me go past. The sound of Trojan's hoofs echoed against them, and intensified the silence in which we rode.

This awesome avenue led straight before me, over a hill and down into a valley, and then as I breasted the next slope upwards I saw it – Stonehenge. Tall, stark and beyond all words solemn it stood, dark against the pale gleam of the sky. The huge stones stood round in a perfect circle, the lintels above them joining stone to stone, regular and straight; over the heads of the lintels five taller trilithons loomed; but the oldest circle of all, the foreign blue stones, lay within, hidden like the secrets of that place. Yet on the outside of the great round temple stood, right in my path, a still older thing – one tall stone, like a pillar, standing alone, and behind it, another stone flat on the ground, like an altar. And in front of the standing stone, waiting for me, was a man.

He was so wrapped in thick black robes that at first sight I took him for a woman; but as I came nearer I saw that it was a man, old but vigorous, with a pointed grey beard that retained a tinge of red, and raking reddish eyebrows; his eyes, beneath fair well-shaped brows, I should have expected to be blue and benign, but they were black and keen, and glittered like a snake's. But his lips smiled, and his voice when he spoke was musical, and slow as if clogged with honey.

'All hail,' he said, 'Chosen of the Stars.'

I drew rein, and stared at him, for at his words a cold hand was laid on my heart.

'Hail to you, good father,' I said, and I hoped my voice did not shake. 'And who are you that hail me, and for what end?'

'For your own end,' he said, with his sweet smile. 'I am Merlin, and I hail you who must give your life for Arthur the King.'

A fight at last! I thought, and my hand sought the sword-hilt.

'Willingly – and whom must I fight?'

He shook his head, still with that smile.

'Put up your sword, brave knight. You are required not to fight, but to lay down your life willingly, here upon the Stone of Sacrifice.'

'No!' I cried. 'Not that way! Let me fight, but not—'

'No?' he said. 'You do not understand.'

He moved his feet, and took up an easy stance, leaning on his tall staff, and began as if instructing a pupil.

'Listen now and learn. It is the law of ancient custom, time out of mind, in this our land of Britain, that once in every seventh year of the King's reign, one must be offered in sacrifice for the King's life, or else the King must die. This we know from our fathers before us. You should have known, when you undertook the aventure of the Green Knight, that you were the one chosen to die in place of the King. You know when and where the sacrifice should have been made – and you know that it was not made, and you know *why* it was not made.'

He looked strongly at me, and I was desolate with shame,

feeling that green baldric burning into my shoulders. He continued.

'And now it is the fourteenth year of the King's reign, and he lies grievously sick. The holy time of the sacrifice is from Yule to Candlemass. This is the time and the place. But it must be with the victim's consent. Do you therefore consent to give your life, here and now, in exchange for your King's?'

To say that my mind was in a turmoil is to say little of what I felt. I cried.

'I would do all I could to save or serve my liege lord, as I am sworn – but must it be this way?'

'This way, and no other.'

'But this is a heathen thing! What have I to do with it, since I am a Christian knight and serve God and His Mother?'

The old man smiled, as from deep wisdom.

'Oh, my son, here we are among the older things. What do you know of gods and their mothers? What you profess to serve will avail you little here.'

I drew my sword and held it crosswise before my face.

'Avaunt, then, Satan and all heathennesse!'

He put my sword easily aside with his hand.

'Put that away. This is not the time nor the place for such. Here are things far older. I tell you, my son – pray what prayers you like, to whom you like, but unless you give your life, willingly consenting, here and now, Arthur will die.'

'Is that true? 'I sighed.

'True it is. He will die this night, and you, Gawain, will be to blame. It will be because you willed it so. Oh, I cannot compel you. Have no fear of violence from me,' and he smoothed his bristling brows – 'I will lay no hand on you against your will. You can ride away from here free – and go to Camelot for Arthur's funeral, with Arthur's death upon your soul.'

I could not stand against his words.

'Well and good, then,' I cried. 'I am Arthur's knight, and for his sake I will give my life. But be quick, and despatch me before my heart cools,'

'Not so fast,' said he. 'Here comes one who has a part to play.' And he drew aside so that I could see the curve of the stone circle.

Round the circle came riding Dowsabel on her donkey – she halted and dismounted, and ran towards us over the short grass, but as she ran she was changed – I saw, as I should have known long before, that it was the lovely lady Vivian herself.

And in that instant I understood how great a humiliation she had undergone for my sake, laying aside her youth and beauty and all her pride, that I might learn to trust her. Without a word I held out both hands to her, and without a word she came to my arms.

The old man stood looking at us, his black eyes twinkling.

'So,' he said 'do you love this lady?'

'With my life,' I said.

'With my life, says he about to die,' he mocked me. 'And you, lady, do you love him?'

'Utterly and for ever.'

'That is good,' said the old man.

'Oh sir,' I cried, 'if you are a priest as well as a magician, do us this last charity – let us be wedded before I die!'

'I will do better than that,' said he. 'She is to be your executioner.'

'What!' we exclaimed together, and turned to face him, yet she never left my embrace.

'It is for you, lady, to drive the sword through his heart. Only so can the sacrifice be made perfect.'

'I cannot do it,' she cried.

'You must, or Arthur dies.'

'Rather will I die with him. I beg you to let me die with him.'

The old man seemed to consider for a moment, then he lifted from beside the recumbent stone a long, thin sword of steel, exceedingly bright and sharp.

'So be it, then,' he said, and his voice was caressing. 'Thus it shall be done. You, Sir Gawain, will lie upon the stone of sacrifice, and your lady shall lie upon your breast, with her face to the sky. Then with my hand to give the thrust, her hand shall guide the sword to pierce first through her breast and then through yours. So you shall die united.'

I felt my dear Vivian tremble in my arms, but her face was resolute.

'Death is an ecstasy,' the old man was saying. 'No more than the consummation of love. It will be very beautiful.' And his voice was like soft music as he talked calmly of our death.

Desperately I tried to recall the comforts of my faith, but they seemed far away from this dark ancient place. I could only make an inward act of devotion and commend my soul to God as I might on a battlefield. I looked deep into the eyes of my dear lady.

'My love, I have only just found you,' I said, 'and must I lose you so soon? There was so much to say—'

'There will be time in Paradise,' she answered. 'Lead on, magician.'

So, in the dimness and coldness, with the lapwings crying overhead, and the clouds racing, he divested me of my armour and my leather doublet, and laid me down on the great flat stone. And then he laid my dear love on my breast, and I closed my arms round her to give her what comfort I might. Her red hair flowed over my face and partly covered my eyes. The old man towered over us, throwing back his hood – I heard him chant some strange form of words, that echoed far away over that still plain. He stooped and placed the sword to Vivian's breast, clasping her hands on it—

Then suddenly she gave a great cry, and struggled to be free—

'Stop, stop – *this is not Merlin!*'

But it was too late.

5 · Melior

I am called Melior, the disciple of Merlin. The name Melior means 'honey-mouth', and has been given me because I have a sweet voice by the grace of God, both for singing and speaking; and also some small skill in words. So it falls to me, according to this same gift of words, to set down the last record of these things, as I saw them; as I sit here in my cell in Amesbury, with a blind man by my side who was once a knight.

I was Merlin's close companion for more than five years, and lived with him in his little cottage outside Marlborough. I am setting out now in writing the tale of the last days of his life, but if I should try to tell his whole life-story, I could never worthily portray his greatness, his wisdom and his kindness. For he was the Mage of Britain, and there was never any like him, nor shall there be again.

In looks he was a short, broad man, powerfully built – he must have been a formidable man in his youth, and handsome too, for he was still comely even in his oldest age, and no one knew how old that was, His skin was fresh and without blemish, his snow-white hair parted smoothly over his brows, and hung in curls on the nape of his neck, and his great wide beard, equally white, swept down over his broad chest like a cataract on a mountain. His eyes were large and blue and clear, and looking into them was like opening a window on a bright and frosty morning, Such was Merlin, my friend and teacher. I was his clerk and pupil of his hermitage, but neither he nor I were ordained priests of the Church. Yet I always thought of him as a great priest of an older fashion. Nonetheless we were not heathens. We were true servants of our Blessed Lord, who once walked in Glastonbury, and of His dear Mother, who ended her days there. And may I, when my time comes, be laid in Glastonbury's holy earth, as I know Arthur will be, and our poor Guinevere by his side.

Since the time I came to him (being then a young lad of fifteen) Merlin had gone very seldom to Arthur's court, and for the last three years not at all. He would make excuses, saying he was growing old, and that Arthur must rule for himself now and not lean on another. But each Christmas he used to set out, two days before the feast, and journey slowly along the wintry roads to Avebury. There, where the great solemn stones stand, he would go before daybreak in his white robes, bearing the mistletoe bough, and take his place in front of the Ring Stone, bidding me place a vessel of water on the flat stone below it, on one certain spot. When the sun of Christmas Day rose, small and red and low in the southeast, its rays would shine through the Ring Stone and strike upon the vessel of water; and gazing on its reflection, he would prophesy.

And now Christmas was drawing near again, and it was time for him to think of our journey. I came in to him on the morning of St Thomas's Day, in his little bedroom at the back of our cottage, where he lay in his curtained bed. It was snowing outside.

'No, Melior,' he said, 'I don't want to go to Avebury this year. Why should I? I'm too old.' And he coughed – but I, who had known him a long time now, knew that it was no true cough. Sometimes, wonderful man though he was, he could be as trying and awkward as any other old man.

'You have always gone, up to now, Master,' I said.

'I know, I know – but times change, times change, Melior, and perhaps the world doesn't need me any more.'

'Never say that, Master,' I said.

'Oh, ay, but I do say it. Arthur doesn't need me, his court doesn't need me. They want a younger magician.' And he humped himself up in his bedclothes.

'Are you sick, Master?' I inquired.

'Yes – no – well, yes. Sick enough, and old, old, old. It's snowing – what's an old chap like me to do with trudging about the country in the snow? It's cold, and I'm comfortable here. Bring me a bowl of broth and my Plato, and leave me alone.'

'Is the rite at the Ring of Stone no longer important, then?' I ventured to ask.

'Not important? Yes, yes, of course it's important – but I can't go this year, I tell you, and I won't go. Certainly it's important, but this age doesn't value magic any more. Let them do without it.'

'Will you not send someone in your place, then, Master?'

'Who is there to send, in God's name? Don't be a fool, Melior,' and he picked up the three-legged stool from beside the bed and threatened to throw it at me. He hardly looked either sick or old, I thought. But I also thought it advisable to let him have his own way. So I brought his broth and his Plato, and left him alone.

The snow fell thickly all the day, and when I went in to settle him to sleep for the night – for he still played the invalid – he frowned and muttered and cursed, and insisted that he wouldn't go, though I no longer argued with him. He seemed to be arguing with himself. Every small cause of offence, every grievance that he might have had against Arthur and his knights, every fancied slight, he dragged up and commented on. This was unlike him, for never before had I known him to harbour grudges or bear malice. But he seemed anxious to prove to himself that he was no longer wanted at Arthur's court.

'I'm an old man, old, old, old,' he insisted. 'Time I was dead. I've lived too long. Let me go away and join my Nimue – how long before she comes to fetch me?'

I had never heard him speak of Nimue before, and I wondered who she was.

'So – blow out the light and leave me,' he concluded. 'I will – not – go.' And on the last word he pulled his curtains to.

But before the light had glimmered into the sky the next morning, in the dark and the cold, I was wakened with a start, and there was Merlin standing over me with a lantern.

'Get up, Melior – get up, boy, and don't delay. We must be off.'

'Eh – where, Master?' I stammered, bewildered with sleep and astonishment.

'To Avebury, of course. We haven't a moment to lose.'

I struggled from my bed and dressed myself in a clumsy huddle, my hands shaking with the cold. But he was not shaking – rather his eyes were blazing with excitement.

'Don't be so surprised, my dear Melior,' he said. 'Oh yes, I know I said I wasn't going, but there is something – it came to me in the night. Perhaps from this,' and he touched the mystical snake-stone that hung round his neck. 'I don't know what it is, but I know I must go. Come, let's start as soon as we can.'

The journey on foot to Avebury usually took us the best part of two days, but this time we had started late and had to press on hard. The snow fell thickly, and a cold wind drifted it against us, as if it were trying to push us back; and although Merlin had started out full of purpose and new energy, I did indeed wonder if he were not sick after all, for he struggled and staggered, and leant hard on me. Part of the time he rode on our pack-donkey, and I carried its load; and I began to wonder if he ought not to have stayed behind after all. We spent the night in a shepherd's cottage, and next day the cold wind had dropped and the snow fell no longer, but lay thick and gleaming under the cold sky; it was Christmas Eve, and Merlin hastened on, begrudging every moment's pause, hardly speaking, his eyes fixed far ahead. That evening we reached Avebury and were received by the two old Culdees who lived there – hermits, the people called them, but like Merlin, they were priests of an older order. They welcomed us kindly, and lodged us for the night, and in the morning they accompanied us to the place of the Great Stones.

We set out before dawn, one of the Culdees holding a lantern before us, but the glare of the snow lighted us in the dark and in the east a faint glimmer broke the clouds. Merlin was dressed in his white robe, as we all were, with the white hood over each one's head; but on Merlin's hood, over his forehead, was placed the symbol of the Three Bars of Light, and on his breast, below his beard, gleamed the snake-stone. In his hand he held the shepherd's crook, and on it he carried the bunch of sacred mistletoe.

In silence we threaded our way along the great stone avenue – very black the gigantic stones looked against the snow. We came at last to the place within the Circle of the Sun and Moon, where the Ring Stone stands, pierced with a circular hole through which the sun's rays shine. I carried a pitcher of water and a bowl, and the other Culdee carried incense; so when we had made purification by water and fire, and offered the mistletoe as by the old custom, I filled the bowl with water and laid it on the low stone, and we all waited.

At last the sun's face came up, like a burning ember, and a long red ray shone through the hole of the Ring Stone upon the mirror of water in the bowl; and Merlin gazed there earnestly. Then the clouds obscured the sun, the faint gleam had gone, and Merlin sprang back as if suddenly released from looking. His face was pale.

'Finish the rite,' he said in a low voice, and so we went on and completed the rite according to ancient custom, leaving nothing out. Only then, when we had left the circle in proper processional order and were outside the holy ground, he seized my arm and turned to our kind hosts.

'I knew it – there's trouble, and I must go at once. Brothers, I'm sorry – I would have shared your feast, but we must go at once. There is danger – I saw danger in the light on the water. Danger to Arthur and all the Round Table, and to all of Britain now and to come. I must go at once to be there in time.'

'Where will you go, reverend father?' one of the Culdees asked. Merlin looked to and fro in some bewilderment.

'Why – why- I can't tell where the danger lies at this moment, for one stands in the way of my sight, and hides the place from me. But if we don't know, there is only one place to go from which we can act as in every place.'

'To Camelot, Master?' I said.

'No, no – to the centre of magic – to Stonehenge.'

So that very morning, waiting only for a hasty breakfast, we set out for Stonehenge, and should have reached it easily in three days.

That night we stayed at a little rustic inn, comfortable enough. And as we got ready in the morning to take the road again, up the track towards us came a tall, swarthy man in the black robes of a scholar.

'Greetings, good sirs,' he said, bowing sweepingly to the ground. 'Am I in the presence of Merlin the great Seer of Britain, called Ambrosius? For if so I am greatly honoured.'

My master had his staff in his hand, and had taken the first step on the road, and I was behind him with the pack donkey; but he halted at this salutation, and returned it, though hardly so sweepingly.

'I am Merlin Ambrosius of Britain, courteous sir. May I know your name?'

'Names,' said the stranger, 'are a deep matter of philosophy. I might tell you many names, but if they were not the truth, would they profit you? Yet if I were to tell you that I were Pythagoras of Massila, or Empedocles of Sicily, or Plato of Athens, or even that Abares of Gaul who journeyed from Britain even to Constantinople – what would you say?'

'I would say, are you real?' said my master.

'You would say, are you real?' the other exclaimed, with his eyes lighting up. 'But who is real? What is real? What, indeed, is reality? Nothing that we can apprehend with our five dull senses.'

'True,' said Merlin, resting on his staff, 'and yet reality, being beyond apprehension, needs the mediation of the senses before human intellect can conceive it—'

'Master,' I interrupted, 'we have to be on our way.'

'In a minute, good Melior— but, sir, if our senses be not the channels of apprehension of reality—'

'Not so,' the other said, smiling, 'for how can the fallible be the channels of the perfect and eternal? For reality, you will grant, is that which is perfect and eternal; therefore if you ask me, am I real, I can but answer no, clothed in flesh as I am; neither are you, clothed in flesh as you are.'

'Master—' I ventured, but he shook me off.

'My good sir, come back here into the inn for a moment. Melior, wait a little – Come now, sir—'

And before I could stop him, he was swept away into deep argument with this stranger, whose eloquence and subtlety held him spellbound. At noon the innkeeper brought them meat and drink, which they ate without looking at it – at least Merlin ate, but the strange man ate nothing. The short afternoon went, and I unpacked the ass's load and sat back in the chimney corner. All night they talked – and all the next day too – and all the next day. Three days had passed since Christmas, and on the morning of the fourth day I thrust myself, rudely I fear, in front of my master. I had the saddlebags packed and loaded, the reckoning paid, and my staff in my hand.

'Master,' I pleaded, 'we must be going.'

He looked up, bleary-eyed, from the chimney corner, where he and the stranger had been huddled together, pointing fingers and hammering fists at each other.

'Eh? What's this?' he said, like a sleepwalker, as I led him by the arm out to the door. The stranger followed us.

'Master – is your errand of no more importance, then?'

'My errand? What errand?'

'Why,' I burst out, 'you said it was something of such importance that you must not delay for a minute – something you saw at Avebury—'

He blinked in the sunlight at the door. 'I don't remember.' Then passing his hand over his forehead, 'What is the time?'

'What is the time?' cried the stranger, coming up behind us. 'Say rather, What *is* Time? Do *you* know, Master Merlin? No. Do I? Perhaps.'

Merlin turned back to him, and the stranger laid hold on his sleeve.

'For Time is not what you think. Oh, do not go. Listen –
give me ten minutes more – bah! why do we talk of minutes?
What are they? – only wait, and I will tell you what Time is—'

I knew that I would never get him away now unless I did
something drastic; so (may I be forgiven for the cruelty, for I
never do such things willingly) I picked up a sharp nail that
had fallen in the road, and drove it hard into our poor beast's
backside.

The ass gave a screaming bray, and was off down the road,
and off the road, and into the heather, and out of sight. I
dragged at Merlin's other sleeve and pointed.

'The ass, Master, the ass!' I shouted.

'Let it go,' he replied. 'We can buy another.'

'But it's got your Plato in the saddlebags!' I yelled at him.
That worked.

'My Plato! Oh, my precious Plato!' And he plucked his robe
from the stranger's clutch, and pelted away down the road
after the ass, and I after him. About ten minutes' hard running
across the heather tussocks brought us up with the ass, poor
beast, now forgetful of its fright and quietly cropping the
strawy grass. Merlin hastened to make sure the Plato was safe
in the saddlebag, patted the poor ass, and sat down in the
heather to get his breath. The inn, and the stranger, were far
out of sight, and the spell was broken. I let him breathe, and
then I said, 'And now, Master, it really is time to hasten on
our journey.'

'Eh? What journey? . . . Oh yes, I begin to remember. Why,
were we talking very long?'

'Three whole days,' I said. His eyes grew round.

'No? I honestly thought it was half an hour. And all that
time without meat or drink?'

'Not quite. I and the innkeeper fed you, but you never
seemed to notice.'

'No more I did – and the stranger?'

'He neither ate nor drank.'

'Didn't he? Now that's very strange.' He grew thoughtful.
'Do you suppose he was real?'

'Oh, for heaven's sake,' I cried, 'don't start talking about reality again. But Master – you have an errand. Or at least you said you had. One of such importance that not one minute could be lost – and now you've lost three days.'

'Oh, heavens!' he said. 'That man made me forget everything – Melior, Melior, think of it – he made me forget everything, three days passed in his company in half an hour, and he neither ate nor drank – What if he were a deceit of the Enemy?'

'What, indeed?' I said. 'Oh Master, let us hasten on our journey.'

'But I don't know where we were to go,' he said helplessly.

'To Stonehenge,' I reminded him.

'To Stonehenge? But what to do there?'

'I don't know,' I replied. 'You did not tell me.'

He gave a cry of pain, and bowed his head, beating his forehead with his palms.

'Miserable old man that I am! I have forgotten it all, all – but I know it was a thing of deepest peril, and that the whole future of Britain hung upon it – and now, now, now it's all gone from me. Gone, like a dream one can't remember. Gone, stolen from me by the deceit of the Deceiver.' He laid his head on his knees, and for a moment he wept. Then he looked up bleakly at me.

'Melior, my son – what are we to do now?'

'Why not look in the snake-stone, Master?' I said. His face cleared a little.

'Ah, of course, the snake-stone. How could I forget? This man has upset me badly – I doubt I could repeat the Greek alphabet, let alone the Hebrew.' He laughed shakily.

'Don't try, Master,' I said, helping him up. 'Let us find a sheltered dell somewhere and make a fire, and then you shall consult the snake-stone.'

'I will indeed,' he said, 'and this time I will tell you everything, so that you can remember for me.'

After some casting around we found a dell, with a few birch-trees, which gave us a little shelter; I found enough wood and gorse to light a fire, and we took our noon-meat of bread and cheese and ale; then, when I had made Merlin as comfortable as I could by the fire, I sat down by him in silence. He drew the snake-stone from his bosom, released the cord that held it round his neck and laid it in his palm. I looked sideways down upon it. It was a large glass bead, between the size of a pigeon's egg and a pullet's, and quite round, of a cloudy green colour, with whirling threads of white and blue inside the glass. He stared at it a long, long time. Then he began the low, monotonous chant of the Wise Men, repeating one word over and over. Then the chanting ceased, as if he had fallen asleep, but his eyes were open.

'I can see now,' he said slowly. 'A man and a woman – a knight and a lady. He rides before and she follows after – why does he never look at her? She is veiled, and I cannot see her face. Why is she veiled? She is not a widow, nor a nun. She is a young maiden, fair and lovely, but I cannot see her face. I know *him*, but who is she? – They are riding into danger. They are riding to their death. I see a sword in the way they are going, a long sharp sword to pierce both hearts at once – and worse than that, worse than that—' His voice, that had been spellbound and monotonous, now quickened with excitement – 'Oh, much worse – the sword is to pierce far, far down into our land – not for this time only, but far ahead . . . Ah, the lady turns, she lifts her veil. I shall see who she is – Oh God!' His sudden sharp cry rang out, and then he moaned as if he had been wounded.

'Oh Vivian, Blaisine, Nimue – Oh my lost darlings!'

He let the stone drop from his hand, and leaned back; I supported him, or he would have fallen. His eyes were red-rimmed, and he trembled. After a while he recovered himself, picked up the stone, replaced it round his neck, and sat nearer the fire, which I was mending with twigs. Then at last he began to talk to me.

'I said I must tell you what I saw, Melior, so that if I forget again you may remind me. As you said, we are to go to Stonehenge and there meet this man and this woman I saw in the stone, who are going there into danger. The man is one of the best of King Arthur's knights of the second generation, his champion for those days; but the lady—

'Consider this, Melior. We men give our names to our line, and reckon it from father to son. We take a woman's name from her, and give her ours instead, and her name, and her lineage, are forgotten in history. And if a man has no son – and I have no son, Melior – the name dies out, and the line fails. But the mother-line, ah! the mother-line! *That* runs on, underground, hidden and forgotten – having three threads to the father's one, thus: mother to daughter, father to daughter, mother to son. So it spreads and spreads unnoticed, carrying with it all the treasures of the mother's blood, when the father's line that bears the name has dropped away and failed.

'It is a matter, now, of genealogy; and it is given to me to see the genealogies that may yet be, and also those that may not be, and the point at which a knife-edge divides "shall" from "shall not". Arthur has no lawful son, and I know that he will not have any – and God forbid that his inheritance should pass to Mordred. But he has a daughter, and no one will remember her name in years to come, or know that he had a daughter – yet the son that should be born to those two I saw in my vision should wed her, and from them should come no kings, but queens a few, and commoners without number, down through the ages passing through the mother-line, to be the nerves and sinews of this our land of Britain in long ages to be. All of them – I see them running like a silver network through the body of our land – all of them with some gift, some light within them, some high calling, that shall make this Britain what she is meant to be. But only if these two are allowed to live and love.

'For Melior, I have not told you who the lady is. I will tell you, and – and if I fail in any way, and you survive, you must go to her and aid her with your life. She is Vivian, the child of Blaisine my daughter, the child of Nimue whom I loved. She is my grandchild, Melior.

'So you see,' he said, with a brisk change of tone, getting

up off the ground, 'I must go to her at once. Pack up the things and let us go, and let nobody stop us this time.'

I began to put the things together as quickly as I could.

'But tell me, Master,' I said, while my hands worked, 'who is the adversary who threatens the lady and the knight?'

He looked at me as if I ought to have known.

'Why, the Deceiver herself – Morgan le Fay, the queen of all deceivers. She would be throned in Britain herself, and would root out now, in the acorn, the oak of Arthur that ages will not destroy, if only – if only – oh, let us hasten on.'

So, under the darkening January sky, we took up our staves, and I held the donkey's bridle, and we pressed on. But our flight from the inn door had led us far out of our way, and there seemed to be no tracks across the moor at all. Merlin guessed our position by the faint gleam of the setting sun, and bore southwards; but though we found some devious tracks of sheep and goats, we found no path of men, and the tracks we followed led us into terrifying quagmires, where our staves, as we thrust them in before us, sank and were sucked at by the hungry slough beneath, and we could hardly pull them out. We had to go round and about, further and further off our course, till at last when it was dark we saw lights, and stumbled into a lonely farmhouse which proved to be further off than where we started. There was nothing for it but to stay the night in the farmer's chimney corner. He told us we were lucky not to have been swallowed up in the quaking quagmire.

The next morning we pressed on, and the farmer set us on a firm track once more; and we ought to have reached Stonehenge by nightfall. But before noon we came to a village, and as we drew near a stench came out to meet us – not only loathsome but terrifying, for it spoke to the nostrils of danger – the smell of pestilence.

I said to Merlin, 'I think, Master, we would do well to go round this place and keep clear of it,' but at that moment a half-dozen people came running out from the wall that

encircled the village – chiefly women, with ragged clothes
huddled thickly around them, their hair hanging dank and
loose, some with children clasped in their arms and moaning.
One of the women, with a year-old child in her arms, fell at
Merlin's feet.

'Oh, sir, sir,' she cried, 'I think you are a healer by your
dress. Help us, for God's sake! It's the plague – three children
are dead already, and five men, and we don't know what we
shall do – my baby here is sick, and oh! dear healer, for the
love of Our Lady—' The tears ran down her pale tragic face,
and the baby in her arms coughed.

Merlin drew back the clothes and looked at the baby.

'What kind of sickness is it?'

'Oh, Master,' I said, 'we mustn't stop. You said so yourself.'
He shook off my hand. 'It seems I am needed here.'

'But if this should be another device to delay us?'

He turned and faced me sternly.

'There are children dying,' he said, and would say no more.
He went into the village with the woman, and I could do
nothing but follow him.

The plague was not the very worst kind – not the black
swellings, but only the sweating sickness – but any sickness
is bad enough if it means the death of a man, and the death
of children is the worst of all. There were perhaps two
hundred souls in the village, and over half of those were sick,
and the rest like to be; not only those the woman had spoken
of, but ten more died that very night, and the whole village
was in panic fear. Merlin took charge at once and did what
was needed. Really it was no hard sickness to cure, if the folk
would nurse each other with care and good sense; but if they
went running to and fro with the fever on them, eating no
meals because there was none to feed them, and becoming
weary and chilled and overwatched – why then they died
easily, sometimes dropping down dead by the bedside of
those they were trying to tend. The place was filthy, and no
wonder, and the filth spread the pestilence. Merlin's first
action was to muster all those who were still well, and give

them their orders to care for the sick, marshalling them like a small army, and bidding them clean and wash and cook and nurse. For though at times he was an arrant old dreamer, yet at a pinch like this he would bestir himself and plan and command like a chieftain; and always men would obey him. He did not use much magic, for there was no need to. All the people needed, really, was someone to tell them what to do. He sent some of them to collect herbs on the moor, and made herbal medicines; and perhaps he put a little of his magic into them. But sometimes he would stand by a sick one's bedside, especially if it were a child, and let the power run out of his fingers into his patient's body; this was a strong healing, but it made Merlin himself very tired, and in time it took disastrous effect on him.

Ten whole days went by; after that first night no more children died, and only one more old woman; everyone in the village had the sickness in their turn, but they recovered from it, taking heart when they saw that others had recovered before them. But when it seemed that the plague was abating, on the eleventh day after our arrival, I went into the little hut the people had allotted to us, and found Merlin crouched on his bed, shivering and clenching his teeth.

'I have taken it,' he said. 'No use. I'm a wreck now, Melior, but never mind about me. You must go on to Stonehenge.' He paused while a paroxysm of shivering ran over him. 'Don't you realize it's the fifteenth day of the month, and we should be there by Candlemass? Pack your things and go at once.'

'And leave you like this?' I said. 'Never!'

'Ah, don't be a fool. The village wives will nurse me – Gwennath, or Huw's wife.'

'I don't trust Gwennath or Huw's wife or any of them,' I said. 'Much good they did before you came. I'm sorry, and I know I'm disobeying you, my dear Master, but I'm staying here.'

He was really too ill to argue with me, and he said nothing more, but seemed to doze for the time. I sent for the village wives, and gave them orders as he might have done, to get me what I needed for him, but I tended him myself, and watched him through the fever day and night for five days. Then on the fifth morning, when he had woken cheerful and hungry but still very weak, what must I do, as I stood by his bedside, but drop the bowl I was holding, as I felt the hut spin round me and I sank down on the floor. Presently I found myself in bed, with Merlin's face above me.

'Go on now, Master,' I whispered hoarsely, for I could hardly breathe. 'Don't wait for me. Time is running out – you must get to Stonehenge. Leave me here.'

'And what kind of master would I be to do that?' he said.

So there I lay, and dimly knew that he nursed me as I had nursed him. In the first horrible night of the fever when I did not seem to be able to sleep but was assuredly not awake, I thought I saw a tall dark woman, proud and of devilish beauty, looking at us both, and laughing and laughing. In her hand, I remembered, she held a mask as of an old man.

Then at last I came up out of the cloud. I found Merlin beside me, in the grey light of the morning, and his hand held mine and poured strength into me.

'Master!' I cried. 'The time passes – we must go. What day is it?'

'The twentieth of the month,' he said, pressing me back as I tried to rise. 'No, stay there, my boy. You are too weak yet, and I'm really none too brisk myself. Five days more will give us time enough.'

'Five days?' I answered wildly. 'I thought there was no time to spare—'

'Hurrying won't help us if we both drop down by the way,' he said. 'Lie there and get your strength back, and try not to be anxious.'

There was nothing for it but to do as he said.

The villagers overwhelmed us with gratitude and kindness; but I was horrified to think that our enemy might have sent this plague upon them just to delay us, and I could not bear to pass by the graves of those that had died. But the rest of the village came slowly back to health; and on the twenty-eighth day of January Merlin and I set out again.

We had wandered far from our road, and since we went into the plague-village there had been heavy rains, and places where we could have passed before were flooded, so we were told, and we would have to go a long way round yet. Nonetheless, we should not need to take more than two days to cross the plain.

'We shall be there by tomorrow night if nothing stops us,' said Merlin.

'If nothing stops us!' I echoed.

For almost as I spoke, down from the north came the blackest and most towering of clouds, piled up in the sky like a castle and trailing below over the hills – slate-coloured, and blotting out all behind it; it swept over us like black wings, and out of it came snow, large and driving, pressing into our faces until we could hardly breathe. We clutched our garments round us, and made them as secure as we could, for the wind pierced into every loophole, and the snow found its way into every fold. The poor donkey stood with its head lowered and its feet braced, and it was all that we could do to urge it on, or our own bodies either for that matter. We could not talk, could not see where we were going. We pressed on into the snow and wind as if boring our way into something solid.

'Master!' I yelled into Merlin's ear at last, 'couldn't you use a little magic to help us?'

'What?' he shouted back.

'Magic – help us – possible?'

'Possible but not permissible,' he yelled.

'Oh, but why?'

He shook his head, and it was useless to try and carry on an argument. We pressed on as best we could, and presently to my dismay I found that the light was fading – the short day was over already. Then suddenly the wind dropped, the snow stopped falling and there we were in the dark on the bare downs, with drifts of pathless snow all round us, and no means of knowing which way to go. Just two lost human particles in the vast snowy night, out of touch of all life and help.

But Merlin seized my arm with his firm comforting grip and pointed. There below us were moving lights, and a sound came up of tinkling bells, and sheep bleating, and someone playing a bagpipe. Shepherds! It was lambing time, and down there were the lambing folds. Taking heart, we plucked our heavy feet out of the snow and forced ourselves to stumble on towards the lights.

There was a square enclosure of wattles, partly roofed over, and piled with straw to a depth of three or four feet; into this the sheep were nested with their lambs, and the shepherds too. There were two of them, with one small lantern; they had no fire, but the warmth of their bodies, men and sheep together, kept them snug in the midst of the snow. The men sat burrowed in, packed close against their sheep, hidden up to their heads in the straw; one of them from time to time creeping out to see to a ewe as she gave birth. When nothing was happening they would play the bagpipe to pass the time.

They were kindly men, as they all are, and welcomed us in with great concern for our plight. We soon found ourselves nestled in the warm straw, each of us back to back with a great woolly ewe who was as comforting as a feather-bed. The shepherds had a flask of a most marvellous cordial, made, they said, of eggs, cream, lemons, honey and strong waters.

'Tis called King Arthur's Ambrosia,' they said, as we supped it gratefully. 'They say it will bring the dead to life and make barren women conceive.'

'Whether King Arthur knows of it or not,' said Merlin smiling, 'it's a noble brew, and I never was more glad of anything in my life.' And almost as he spoke he was fast asleep, and in a few minutes so was I.

When we woke it was still dark, so we thought we had only been asleep a couple of hours. The moon shone over the sheepcote, and the shepherds were moving quietly about. Merlin sat up and called to them.

'We must be going now, friends. A thousand thanks for your hospitality. I don't doubt you've saved our lives. We've slept well.'

'Ay, that 'ee have,' said one of the shepherds coming in under the thatch. 'Well and long. Reckon you needed it.'

'And now I think we have strength enough to get to Stonehenge before Candlemass Day.'

'Candlemass Day?' said the shepherd. 'Why, you'll have to make haste, then. This *is* Candlemass Day, or will be when the sun has risen.

'What?' said Merlin wildly. 'But it can't be – man, it's the last day of January still, isn't it?'

'It *was* the last day of January when you came to us,' said the shepherd, grinning in the light of his lantern. 'But you've slept the day round, you see, right through the first of February – Tuesday – and now it's growing towards Wednesday morning, second of February, Candlemass Day as us reckons—'

'Oh, dear God above!' Merlin cried. 'We shall be too late – quick, Melior, quick—'

He staggered out into the snow, and I followed him. While I groped around for the donkey, and collected up our few things, he pressed money into the shepherd's hand.

'Not a penny, sir, not a penny. Why, I might need shelter myself on a cold night. We'll take nothing but your blessing, for I see you're a holy man.' And so Merlin gladly gave him his blessing, and having made sure of the road, we tottered out together through the snow, under the uncertain moon, only half awake, but driven on by a terrible fear lest we should be too late.

And now, as we were out of sight of the shepherds, a cloud came over the moon, and a white mist came up, steaming from the ground, until the air was all white and thick, and we were lost in a blank of whiteness. We stared into nothingness, holding tight to each other and the donkey for fear we should lose touch. We came to a standstill, for we could not tell which way to go.

'Oh Master, we're lost!' I exclaimed, and an uncanny echo threw back at me: 'Lost, lost, lost.'

'Nonsense, we're not lost,' he almost snapped, but the echoes mocked him again, 'Lost, lost, lost.' Then, as we tried to step forward, we were conscious of a strange thing – the mist seemed to become solid like a wall, and to press us back. Something resisted us.

'Well, now it must be magic,' said Merlin, but he said it low, so as not to wake those echoes. 'Turn the donkey loose – he will go back to the shepherds and be safe enough there.' He raised his staff with both hands and touched it to his lips – I knew that that action, and the word he said made it no longer just his walking-staff, but a rod of power – and then with that staff he drew a great circle round us in the snow, and within the circle a pentagram. Then he raised his voice, loud and awesome.

'Who are you, that thrust us back from our way?'

And a voice came out of the solid mist, a voice deep and harsh and horrible.

'I am called Bertilak, and my name is a name of violence.'

'Whence come you?'

'I come from the lowest parts of That Which Is, out of the depths of Annwn, through the lower circles of Abred. I try to rise, from the beast of the slime to the beast of the hills, to the lower man and to the higher man, but always I am drawn back into Annwn.'

'Who draws you back?'

'She whom I obey.'

'Who is she?'

'You know her name, but I may not speak it.'

I could not hear the words that Merlin spoke now, but the white mist grew black around us, and a coldness that was not of the winter air, but something far more dread, crept through my body and raised my hair upright.

Merlin stretched out his right arm with his staff to its fullest extent, and traced out a pentagram in the air, and behold! as he traced it a line of light was visible against the blackening mist.

'I command you,' he cried, and uttered great Names of Power, 'Bertilak, unhappy soul, come forth, and appear before me in the shape you now wear.'

Then I heard heavy, shuffling footsteps, and out of the mist came looming a shape so terrible that I could hardly stand and face it.

It was like a bear, upright on its hind legs, but taller than any bear – perhaps three times the height of a man; black and hairy, with its great paws extended showing the claws tipped with fire. But the head was more hideous than a bear's, for it was horned like a bull, and the jaws and snout were those of a boar with yellow, foam-flecked tusks; and the eyes, slit like a goat's, glared with bestial malice as it shambled down upon us.

Merlin's voice spoke quietly in my ear.

'Show no fear, Melior. You must not move.'

I forced myself to obey, though the thing came on, closer and closer. Words came from it, though it did not seem to speak with its mouth.

'If you come one step nearer I will tear you with my teeth and claws.'

I stood rigid, but turned my eyes from the horror, and looked towards Merlin. He stood unmoved, with his staff still stretched out before him. His hood had fallen back, and his white hair gleamed; and his brow was like an immovable granite cliff, facing towards the beast.

'Bertilak,' he cried, 'unhappy Bertilak, look at me.'

And the tiger-glaring eyes of the beast met his, and were held. Merlin's great invocation rang out, and the echoes took it up.

'In the Name of the Light of Lights, in the Name of the Sun of Suns, in the Name of the Flame Within, Bertilak, I command you to yield to His Compassion and Mercy.'

And behold! the terrible eyes clouded over, and red tears dropped from them; the menacing paws dropped to the beast's sides, and it fell on all fours. Down went the horned head, and laid itself in the snow at Merlin's feet; and the whole great terrible creature lay prostrate and subdued, and I thought I heard a sound like weeping.

'Come,' Merlin said, 'this beast will aid us now, and lend us his strength.' He seemed to have something like a bridle in his hand, and he stooped and placed it over the beast's head and set it in its grisly mouth, gently, and caressing its head as he did so.

'Come, poor creature,' he said, and I have never known his voice so sweet and loving, 'your redemption is begun.'

Terror rose in me, for I saw that Merlin meant me to ride upon that beast.

'You must not be afraid,' he said sternly to me. 'Mount and ride. Do not hesitate, lest we come too late.'

So, trembling in every fibre of me, I mounted that hideous creature behind Merlin, clinging to its coarse black fur – and in a moment, dreamlike, we were borne along through the darkness at incredible speed.

When I could look around me, day had come, grey and sad, and we were approaching Stonehenge. Somehow I had dismounted from the terrifying beast, and Merlin and I were walking up the long avenue of stones – Merlin was almost running, dragging me with him. As we went, suddenly a woman's scream rent the air, and as suddenly was still. Merlin gave an exclamation and rushed on.

As we breasted the slope, there was the great circle, pale against the black clouds, and before it stood the great upright stone; behind the upright stone stood a tall veiled figure in black, with arms upraised as in invocation; and between that figure and the upright stone, on the flat stone, a knight and a lady lay dead, with one long sword piercing through the hearts of both of them.

I could not see the knight's face, for the lady's hair, red-gold, lay spread across it, veiling his eyes; but her face, white in death, was frozen in terror and agony. Her hands were clasped upon the sword that had united while it slew them, and their blood was all about the stone and streaming down to the earth.

I recoiled in horror, but my master strode forward with staff uplifted against that black-robed figure. I had thought it an old man with a red beard – but as Merlin approached it, the figure became that of a tall woman, of bold aspect – and I trembled, for it was the same woman I had seen in my fevered dream, and once again she was laughing. She laughed as Merlin approached her.

'So, my old friend and kinsman Ambrosius, you come too late. The ancient sacrifice is accomplished.'

'So I see,' he said, with his face stony and his eyes dry.

'You should be glad,' she went on, taunting him, 'if you are any true liege of King Arthur. For Arthur's life is saved, and his strength renewed for another seven years.'

'Yes,' he flung the words at her, 'and you could proclaim me to all the world as disloyal if I wished the Old Sacrifice *not* to be made, and Arthur to die this year? That would be treason, would it not? – And for what have you saved Arthur's life? Tell me – for what? You know well enough.'

He was close to her now, and facing her across those two pitiful, blood-soaked bodies.

'I tell you, if Arthur had died this year, the rule of the Table Round would have passed to Galahad, the saintly knight, and England would have had such a king as she shall not have again till the holy Edward comes. Mordred is not yet come to full strength, and the love between Lancelot and Guinevere is not yet become a danger. But in seven years' time Galahad will have achieved the Grail and departed, and sore trouble will have fallen upon Arthur and Guinevere and Lancelot, and Mordred will have grown to be Arthur's bane, and the Table Round will pass and be lost to men – for this Arthur is to be kept alive another seven years.'

'I know,' said that dark woman, tossing her head. 'Arthur shall indeed reign another seven years, while his kingdom breaks up; but I shall be the true Queen of the land – I, Morgan le Fay, the mistress of magic.'

'And for this,' said Merlin, looking down in wrathful sorrow at the two victims, 'for this, these lives have been taken— Do you know what you have done here?'

'Yes, I know,' she said smiling.

'Hear this, Melior,' he said, half turning to me. 'Here has died the root of the best part of Britain's race – the beginnings of that line that would carry the spirit of Arthur through ages yet to come.'

'My line will inherit in their place,' said the dark witch-queen.

'*Your* line, Morgan?'

'Yes, why not my line – Come here, Bertilak.'

And hearing that name I looked behind me in fear; the beast that had carried us was gone, but in its place stood a man, a knight in green armour – a man bluff and burly and grizzled, but certainly no beast. He stood looking at Morgan with eyes of fear, as if he struggled within himself.

'Come here, Bertilak!' she repeated – but he did not move. She shrugged her shoulders.

'No matter for one faithless lover. I shall find another – there will always be some to love the Mistress of the Night— What say you, Merlin? Is this not my victory?'

He gave a deep sigh, as if forced to some decision against his will.

'No. I cannot yield it to you like that. Arthur's destiny must go as the die is cast – the sacrifice is made and his life is prolonged to his sorrow – but I will not accept the death of these.'

'What else can you do, my good Merlin, unless the dead can be raised?'

He looked piercingly at her.

'Even that may be done, if the price is paid.' He waved her aside and strode past her. 'I act now in magic stronger than yours, Queen of Deceits, and you know it. So stand aside and do not hinder me. Melior and Bertilak, carry these bodies inside the Circle, and lay them on the altar-stone.'

*

Then began a strange and solemn thing. Bertilak and I, we took up the bodies, and having washed the blood from them as best we could, and composed their limbs and garments decently, we laid them side by side on the great altar-stone within the Circle, with their feet towards the east.

There was only Merlin, and myself, and that strange heavy-built, humble-eyed man who was called Bertilak and had been the beast; he now moved quietly hither and thither doing as Merlin directed him. The witch-queen made no move to hinder us; she had withdrawn, still proud and scornful, but from the time we entered the Circle we thought no more of her. Merlin stood in the eastern part of the Circle, towards the place of the sun-rising – he seemed to be taller, and the grey mantle in which he had journeyed was now white. On the forefront of his hood gleamed the *tribann*, the jewel of three bars of light descending; and on his breast the snake stone shone resplendent.

The cold light of the morning, by which we had arrived at that bloody scene, crept into the Circle between the tall stones, but now it had become strangely red, and behind us in the west great thunderclouds were mounting up. The air was still, over miles of snowfields – no breath of wind was stirring, and from far, far off I could hear the trivial sounds of life in distant homesteads, as remote from us as in another world. The rising cloud came up, and the silence and tension grew, as if one stretched a bowstring. Merlin beckoned us to him, and in swift quiet words told us what we must do.

So we took up the rhythm of a great ritual; I had known parts of it before, but never the whole great powerful solemnity. Circles of protection we made, and purifications, and invocations of the Four Angelic Powers, and of the Three that are above all; but more than this I may not say. And all the while the thundercloud in the west came nearer and nearer, and the stillness deepened.

Then Merlin began to chant, one single low humming note that did not vary, but vibrated on and on; and Bertilak moved into place behind him, holding that same long bright sword that had been used for the death of those two. He held it point downwards, unsheathed, resting his hands on it; then he raised it, and held it with both hands high above his head. At the same moment Merlin uttered a great cry, and bending forward took the hands of the knight and the lady each into one of his.

Then the lightning split the sky, and the earth shook with the crash – all down the sword in Bertilak's hands the white light ran, and poured over us for a dazzling second.

And then it was gone – and who can tell how long after, with the thunder reverberating away under the earth, I dared to open my eyes.

The two who had lain dead upon the altar were risen, and stood clasped in each other's arms, and looking into each other's eyes with a gaze of unutterable happiness. Merlin stood before them still on his feet, but swaying. I ran and caught him before he fell.

'The sunrise is accomplished,' I heard him say.

I laid him with his back propped against one of the standing stones; he still held his staff, and was powerful for a few moments more.

'They shall live,' he said, though he spoke with difficulty. 'They shall live and fulfil their destiny.'

And as the knight and the lady stepped forward from the altar-stone, I saw with fear and doubt that prone in their path, stretched out before them, lay the form of the witch-queen.

'Look, Master!' I whispered to him, 'Morgan le Fay! What shall be done with her? Will you not bid the knight to slay her and make an end of her wickedness?'

My master turned his great blue eyes on me.

'No Melior. By no means slay her. For she is Dream and Fantasy and Shaping, and without her the world would be poor indeed. She must live, for we shall always need her. But do you, Gawain, set your foot upon her head, and you shall draw power and wisdom from her, so long as she is beneath your feet.'

And Gawain, the tall knight, with his lady's hand still

clinging to his arm, set his foot upon the head of the
conquered witch-queen. And a light, and a power, seemed to
flow upwards from her, through his feet and throughout his
body, and flamed on his forehead, and crowned his head; and
most strangely the thing on which he had set his foot
shrivelled, and shrank to a skull and a few bones, and melted
away into the grass, and sank out of sight in the earth.

I turned my eyes back to my master, for the shadow of
death was over his face.

'I have paid the price, Melior,' he whispered. 'I am going.
Nimue calls me, and I go with her into Broceliande. Some day
I return . . .'

And the light went out of his eyes, and he was gone. So
passed Merlin, the Mage of Britain.

The knight and the lady looked down on him with sorrowful
eyes; and I laid him on the ground, and went back to where
Bertilak lay unheeded. The sword in his hand was burnt and
melted to the hilt, but he was alive. The eyes he opened were
blank and lightless, and he stretched out his hands to me.

'Blind, blind!' he muttered. 'Give me your hand – it's dark.
Take me – anywhere you will.'

'Come, sir,' I said, 'I will take care of you.'

He rose unsteadily to his feet.

'But I have seen,' he said. 'And I shall see her to the end of
my days. Not the Enchantress – I am freed from her at last,
for I have seen my true lady, whom I shall always love. Our
Blessed Lady, with the child in her arms. Whether it was
Blessed Mary, Ever-Virgin, or – or another, I know not; but
she is my love and I am her liege man, through this life and
all lives.'

And so I took his arm and led him; but before we left that
spot, we stood, the four of us, around the body of Merlin as
he lay on the altar-stone; north, south, east and west we stood,
as the Four Archangels stand around Britain; and the clouds
cleared away, and the morning sun shone bright on his face.

The King's Damosel

Note from the Author

Many years ago, Edith Ditmas, who was at Oxford with me, published a novel, *Gareth of Orkney*. This gave me the idea, long in germinating, of treating the Arthurian stories from a more human and modern point of view than Tennyson or William Morris. In particular I became interested in the previous and subsequent adventures of the Damosel Lynett.

If Edith Ditmas reads this, I hope she will remember me (as 'Molly' Fogerty) and accept my thanks, and acquit me of any charge of plagiarism.

V.C. 1976

1 · How Two Brothers Married Two Sisters

The flags on the great towers of Camelot fluttered, the roof-tiles glittered in the sun – every window was garlanded with flowers or spread with carpets and gay draperies – bells pealed, and the shrill note of trumpets wafted up towards the blue skies. For this was a wedding day, a double wedding, two brothers marrying two sisters, as was meet and right, the brides being given by King Arthur himself.

In their tower bedroom the two brides were dressing. The elder sister, whom one might have thought was the younger, all pink and white and golden – in tissue of gold, with her hair loose and flowing to signify her virginity, spread like fine gold thread over her shoulders, crowned only with a circlet of pink roses worked into a light diadem of goldsmith's work. The other bride, in silver, was less happy. Her hair, black as night and straight as rain, was spread out, like her sister's, over the silver dress, and crowned with white roses – but it only made her face seem the browner and plainer (for she disdained to plaster it with red and white paint) and her figure the more gaunt and angular. Her great brown eyes were hidden under her eyelids, and her lips were pressed together.

Leonie, the fair bride, stepped across to her sister with a rustle of silk and clasped a jewel round her neck.

'Be happy, Lynett darling,' she said, and kissed her. Lynett drew a long breath, clenched her fists at her sides, and returned the kiss.

'Oh yes, I'm happy, Leonie dear – of course,' she said.

The attendant maidens gathered round them – it was time to start the procession. Oh, God, thought Lynett, now it begins.

Down the small twisting stair in single file, because you

couldn't go any other way, her train-bearer fussing behind
her and gathering her train in a bundle. Then into a room
large enough to spread themselves and form up, two by two
– Lynett and Leonie hand in hand, their train-bearers behind,
the rest of the ladies following, all with posies and garlands –
and so down the great double staircase, to the thrum of the
lute-player behind them – out into the courtyard, and there
the procession of the two bridegrooms met them.

This was the moment Lynett had dreaded – or the first of
many moments to come. There they stood, the two brothers,
side by side – Gareth and Gaheris. Gareth – her heart turned
over as she looked at him. The man of all men. Gareth, the
gentlest of the Orkney brothers – his tall figure, moving with
the grace of strength, his blue eyes that stole her heart –
Gareth, the adorable, and her sister's bridegroom. And beside
him, Gaheris, to whom she had been given instead. Gaheris,
tall enough, strong enough, fair like Gareth and blue-eyed –
but his blue eyes were dull protuberant pebbles, his skin
coarse, his mouth drooping – as brutal as his brothers, Gawain
and Agravaine, and stupider. This one – for her! And Gareth,
whom she had brought through miles of forest to rescue her
sister – she not liking him at first, and then drawn to him by
a love she had tried hard to deny – now, after all this, taking
her sister as the reward of his exertions, as one would choose
the prize for a game – the first prize, and she the second prize
to be kindly bestowed on his brother.

The two processions met, a rainbow of colour between the
grey walls, and the two couples were brought face to face.
Leonie, dimpling, mincing, from her small stature looking up
confidingly at Gareth, placing her hand in his with an
altogether womanly smile; he taking it, proud and happy.
Lynett and Gaheris confronting each other, stiff and hostile,
drawing back – then, as was required of them, joining cold
hands. And so, Sir Kay the Seneschal in his black velvet and
silver lace marshalling them, they turned together and went
up the steps into the chapel. Lynett was dimly conscious of
all the company there – King Arthur himself, the young king,

not so much older than herself – Lynett was eighteen and her sister nineteen. Arthur was about twenty, and had already been king some five years, since he pulled the Sword from the Stone, and already he was a renowned fighter and leader of men. By his side the Queen, the pale, moonlight-haired Guinevere, not long married to him. There was Merlin, white-bearded and eerie – Merlin knew too much, and at the sight of his frosty blue eyes Lynett's heart missed a beat – but there was no betrayal in those eyes. Merlin showed no uneasiness in a holy building – he had a kind of holiness of his own; but there were three women, withdrawn into the back of the church, who looked too much like witches to be there – the three sisters, Morgan le Fay, Vivian called Nimue, and the Queen of Orkney. Surely the Queen of Orkney looked too young to be the mother of those four young men? But then witches could make themselves look what age they pleased ... The Queen of Orkney was coming forward now, florid, red-haired, overdressed – as of course she must come forward as mother of the two bridegrooms.

Now, Lynett, you must remember where you are and what you are going to do – and oh, my God! Lynett replied to herself, would it were otherwise.

The solemn pageantry of the wedding went forward.

'Wilt thou, Lynett, take Gaheris—'

No, no, no! she was shrieking inwardly. Not Gaheris – not Gaheris, but Gareth, Gareth, Gareth. But Gareth had taken Leonie, and Leonie had taken Gareth – *taken* him, taken him away, carried him off from Lynett for ever. And now Gaheris had taken Lynett, for better or worse, and God knew what that might mean.

The jubilant voices of the choristers shattered the silence, with the flutes and viols and tabors, and the clouds of incense rose against the blue and gold painted ceiling. The priest was joining their hands, winding his stole around them. Now the procession led out. This was the end – or the beginning.

The endless tedium of the wedding feast had at last come to an end. From the gallery that ran around the great hall of the castle, two large rooms opened out, and these had been prepared as the two nuptial chambers. In each one was a vast bed, enveloped in curtains, with a pile of feather mattresses one could drown in – all garlanded with flowers and green leaves, strewn with rose petals and scented herbs. Now for it . . .

The two processions led their two brides to their respective chambers, and undressed the victims with a mixture of ceremony and play. Lynett was at least free from Leonie's embarrassing presence for the moment. Though she could not see Leonie, Lynett was sure that she was reacting with giggles and dimples.

She for her own part tried her best not to wince and shrink too perceptibly from the bridesmaids' playfully rough hands, not to mind when they pinched her cheeks and pulled her hair.

They were all so nice to her, after all, kissing her and patting her head, and singing just the same songs as were being sung to Leonie in the next room. She roused herself to take part with a good grace in their games, threw the garter for them to scramble for, laughed and applauded when some girl, whom she didn't know from Eve and didn't care to know, caught it and held it up. At least they didn't make her get into bed naked, like so many brides; both she and Leonie had insisted on bedgowns, silken and fur-edged, so she wrapped hers round her and lay tense and tight, like a worm in a cocoon, while the girls withdrew to Leonie's room to bring in the first bridegroom.

And now Lynett could lie and think. Gaheris was coming now, and she would have to endure him, and the first thing he would discover would be that she was not a virgin.

2 · Of the Wrong that was Done to Lynett

Five years back it was, when Leonie and she were care-free girls living in their father's great rambling house in Lyonesse. Lynett had never known her mother, and when her father had found himself with two daughters and no wife, he had put his younger daughter into the place of the son he would never have, and brought her up like a boy. He might have done the same with Leonie, the elder, but she had nothing boyish in her temperament – small and dainty, she was all feminine, not at all physically brave, sensitive rather than bold; you couldn't make a tomboy of her. Leave her in the nursery with her dolls and Dame Juliana, her governess; she would be happy trying on trinkets and gaudies. But Lynett was always ready to ride out on a horse too big for her, or shoot arrows at a wildcat, or tickle trout in the stream. Her father was Sir Lionel of Lyonesse – the lion was the emblem of the family and of the land, so the elder daughter was Leonie, the lioness, and the younger was Leonet, the lion's cub, which became Lynett – though some called her Linnet, the name of a silly little bird, which annoyed her very much. Nobody ever called her pretty – her hair was nothing but black wires, and her eyes two burnt holes in a blanket, so she made the best or the worst of it, and grew as brown as a vagabond, her arms and legs scarred with briars and branches, her hair streaming like a witch's, till when she was eleven she had it cut short like a boy's so that she could wear a helmet. Ugly, they said – but she also, as her muscles developed tough and smooth, and her arms and legs moved without constraint, grew up with the grace of a young wild animal. But there were very few to notice it.

It was when she was just turned thirteen, at the beginning of a fine hot summer, that their father came to tell the girls they were to have a guest. 'A very powerful knight,' he said, 'oh yes, very brave. His name is Sir Bagdemagus.'

The girls laughed, with their arms round each other's necks, once their father had gone out of the room 'Bag-de-magus! What a name – Baggy-de-maggy. Old Baggy . . . Wonder what he'll be like. Wonder if he'll be as baggy as he sounds—'

'I'll bet he will be,' said Leonie. 'Baggy and fat and flabby and toothless. Why can't Father ever bring home a nice *young* knight?'

'Father says he's brave,' said Lynett. 'He can't be all that baggy.'

But when he arrived he surprised them. He leapt off his horse, all in a rush, and came striding and clanking into their hall in full armour, not shining but dull from travelling and hard wear. A tall man, tough and lean, his face marked with the lines of long jaw-muscles, broad in the shoulders, narrow in the hips; his hair, his bristling brows, his moustache, his small trimmed beard, all a lively tawny blond; his eyes boldly grey. He and Sir Lionel met with hearty back-slapping greetings; then the daughters were presented. Up to now, when their father's friends had visited, it had been a matter of a courtly exercise, under Dame Juliana's eye; deep curtseys, kissing of hands: 'You are welcome, good sir,' 'Your servant, gracious lady' . . . and after that, to be seen and not heard. Not so now.

'So these are the wenches, Leo? Come on, give us a kiss – come *on*. Oh, yes, this one's a little lady, no less. This one isn't – are you?'

Lynett looked up at him, ran her eyes over him. This man wanted to make her afraid, but she wouldn't be.

'No,' she answered, and looked him in the eye.

'And you don't want to be a lady?'

'No, I don't.'

'That's the spirit! I'll bet you'd rather be a boy, wouldn't you?'

'Yes, I would!'

He turned to Lionel.

'You've got a brave little tomboy there, Leo. Give her to me for six months and I'll make a man of her!'

'Oh, come away and don't talk nonsense,' laughed Lionel, and led him off. From the background, Dame Juliana pounced upon Lynett.

'How *could* you, my lady – answering him back, and looking him in the face as bold as a beggar, and you never even curtsied – oh, you've disgraced us all . . .'

Leonie pursed her lips and rounded her eyes, but Lynett tossed her head and laughed within herself at silly old Dame Juliana. 'Give her to me for six months and I'll make a man of her!' Oh, if it could be so . . .

All the evening she watched him, at supper and when they sat afterwards by the fire in the great hall. He told stories, wonderful stories, of adventures and wars and daring deeds; of marvels he had seen, and desperate perils he had been through. Always he himself had been there, had seen and known and done. He must have travelled all over the world, and he must be brave and clever, and certainly he cared for no man, and nothing in earth, heaven or hell could daunt him. She listened, and said nothing, and he took no notice of her, and she for her part asked nothing better, at the moment, than to listen.

She saw him next morning in the mews, that great, light, dusty room next to the stables, where the hawks were kept. He found her there, dressed in leather hose and a woollen doublet like one of the serving-men, caressing the great peregrine falcon.

'Hello, boy!' he greeted her. She grinned back at him.

'Do you know anything about falconry?' he asked, sarcastic.

'Yes, do you?' she retorted.

'Impudence! – I suppose you know that's a highly danger-ous beast you've got there?'

'What, Jeanne!' She rumpled the great bird's breast-feathers. 'Now, fancy that. I think Jeanne forgets it when she's with me.' The peregrine ruffled up and started to 'bate', or beat the air with its wings, at the sound and smell of a stranger. 'But you'd better keep away – she doesn't like strangers.'

He laughed, shrugging his shoulders.

'Well, let's hear what you *do* know,' he said, and proceeded to put her through a falconer's catechism. He couldn't fault her.

'Oh come on, then, enough of this. Can you ride?'

'Certainly I can. Come, I'll show you.'

'Oh yes,' he said as he followed her into the stables, 'side-saddle on an ambling pad, like an abbess.'

'Abbess indeed! You get your mount and I'll get mine.' And presently she reappeared sitting astride on her father's big Brutus, whom she was forbidden to ride. But Dagobert the dwarf, who was her groom, came with her. He had protested against her taking Brutus, but he couldn't stop her; however, she couldn't prevent him following her on his little shaggy donkey, as he had orders to do whenever she went riding.

That was a thrilling ride. Some of the time she was terrified, galloping so furiously on big Brutus, but she wouldn't let this man know it. Dagobert's scanty white hair stood on end, as he laboured along behind. Bagdemagus led her over jumps, where Dagobert had to go a long way round, and through all sorts of dangerous places. It was terrible, it was wonderful – she had not known she could do it. At first she wished for it to be safely over – and then when they rounded and came back to the castle, and trotted soberly enough into the stableyard, she wished it could have gone on for ever.

She swung to the ground without waiting to be helped.

'I'll call you Robin,' he said. 'Linnet is no kind of bird for you to be named for.'

'Not a bird,' she said frowning. 'It's Leonet really – the lion's cub.'

'And so you are,' and he clapped her on the shoulder as if she had been any stable-boy. 'But I like Robin best. You'll be my friend Robin?'

'For certain I'll be your friend Robin.'

*

She worshipped and adored him, but it never occurred to her that there was anything of sex in her adoration. She looked to him as her father, or as to the brother she had never had. She was his page, his squire, his soldier. He was her captain. Day after day they rode together, and he taught her forest lore, and to shoot with the bow, and all the tricks of horsemanship; and told her stories, wonderful stories about his own adventures. Day by day she felt herself growing into a kind of manhood. This was life – not ninnying in parlours and gardens like Leonie and precious Dame Juliana.

'My lady Lynett,' said Dame Juliana, 'I think it not prudent that you should pass so much of your time with Sir Bagdemagus.'

'Oh nonsense, Dame!' retorted Lynett. 'He's my father's guest, and I can't slight him. My father says I may ride with him every day for my health,' and she tossed her head and swept out of the door. Leonie followed her into their bedchamber.

'She's right, you know, Lynett,' said Leonie. 'Don't you see? You two stick together like lovers, and people will talk.'

'Like lovers?' Lynett turned on her, not blushing, but in a royal rage. 'Why, but that's ridiculous – how you dare to say such a thing! He – I – oh, it's quite, quite different. Can't you *see*? It's nothing of that kind at all. I'm – I'm like a *boy* to him – he teaches me things – I'm his page—'

She stopped, looking at Leonie's smirking face.

'You've got a horrible mind, Leonie! Oh, it's not that sort of thing at all. I shouldn't like him if it was. Why, he's not a bit like those silly young fellows that come running after you – like Father's page that had to be sent away – or that horrible old priest – oh yes, I know – *not* like that at all. And anyhow nobody runs after me that way. I'm ugly. Everyone says so. *He* knows I'm ugly, so that's all right, you see?'

Leonie sighed.

'All very well, Lynett dear, but I still think you're wrong.'

'And I still know you don't understand.'

... Lynett and Bagdemagus rode companionably together and he discoursed to her of woodcraft and of fighting.

'If we could go on knight errantry together, boy Robin!' he said. 'Just you and I, without your dwarf – riding for days through the forest—'

'Oh, if we could!' she agreed. 'And camp at night around a fire in the forest, in the very heart of the forest – I'd cook for you, and fetch water from the spring in my helmet—'

'What if it rained, eh?'

'Oh, if it rained I wouldn't mind – we'd sit in a cave or a hollow tree, and sing songs—'

'But there wouldn't be room for Dagobert,' he said, casting a glance at the dwarf behind them only just out of hearing.

'No, there wouldn't be room for Dagobert.'

So at last, in the heat of the summer, they contrived it. Sir Lionel was away from home, as he often was. Lynett managed to send Dagobert away on an errand to an acquaintance of hers many miles distant – with an adequate bribe to hold his tongue. They could not make it more than a long day – they would have to be back before sundown – but they would have a long, long day together, quite alone.

She stole out in the dewy sunrise, in her doublet and hose to meet him; this time on Mayflower, her cream-coloured mare, for she meant to enjoy this day without worries. They rode, and savoured the fresh morning, and laughed; they took their luncheon of bread and ale under a tree. Far and far they rode, into deep woods. As the afternoon went on, he shot a small deer, and skinned and gralloched it with his hunting knife; she set her teeth and took her part in the operation, not daring to admit that it made her feel slightly sick. Then, having built a fire, he showed her how to skewer the gobbets of venison on sharpened sticks and cook them over the fire. They feasted royally, in a warm nest of beech leaves at the foot of a big beech tree, their horses tethered behind them, shaking their bridles with a quiet sleepy noise. He produced a flask of wine, sweet, pleasant and quite surprisingly strong.

Everything was quiet, warm and pleasant; they relaxed with their backs against the tree. Then he turned to her and said, 'You're my good comrade, aren't you?'

'Oh yes, I'm your good comrade,' and she leant against his shoulder.

'Well now, you'll do what a good comrade always does.'

'What do you mean?'

He told her.

'No – no – no.' Wide-eyed with horror, she shrank back against the tree, trying to get away from him.

The shock to her was beyond description.

'Come now, don't be silly. Don't waste time. You know you've been inviting me ever since I set eyes on you.'

'I don't know what you mean.'

'Oh, yes, you do. Come on.'

'No – no – get away from me – don't touch me . . . I never thought . . .'

'Oh, yes, you did. You're one of that kind, are you? I know – tease a man, lead him on, drive him mad, just for sport, and then – "oh no, don't touch me!" By God's nails, my girl, I'll make you pay for this!'

'Let me go—' She tried to get away, but his hands were each side of her, pinning her against the tree. She managed to get her hand on the little dagger she had been using to eat with – but with a quick movement he snatched it out of her hand.

'None of that, now. There's nothing you can do, my beauty, so make up your mind to it.' With that, he seized her and took what he wanted, roughly and brutally.

And there was indeed nothing she could do but to suffer the shameful violation of her body and the bitter disillusion of her mind. With his hot and sweating face close to hers, he was saying, 'And if you tell anyone of this – anyone at all – I'll come to your bedroom at night and slit your throat from ear to ear. Understand?'

Later, he stood up and threw her like a limp doll against the roots of the tree.

'You can go home now if you want to. I must say you've disappointed me. Not much sport after all.'

'How can I go home?' she said from the ground.

'How? Oh, your horse is there and you can follow my track. It isn't far really, and you can be back before dark. But I tell you again,' and he bent over her, 'if you breathe a word to anyone – your sister, or your father – especially your father – I will, I really will come into your room at night, whatever you do – and first I'll do the same thing to you again, and then I'll cut your throat. The blood will run all down in great gouts all over your shoulders and soak your sheets, and your soul will go right down into hell. I mean it, so remember.'

And without another word he turned away, mounted his horse and rode off into the green.

She lay for a long time in a stupor of shock and misery. Then suddenly she was aware of a strange man standing by her. An old man with a white beard, dressed in a long white robe, with a white linen coif over his head – not a pointed cowl like a monk's, but laid flat over his forehead, and on it a strange jewel. Round his neck hung a small crystal globe, and in his hands was a long carven staff.

She struggled to her feet, clutching at her disordered garments.

'Do not be afraid of me,' said the old man in a gentle voice. 'I know what has happened.'

'Who are you? – What do you want?'

'I? – Oh, I'm Merlin. As to what I want – why should I want anything? I am here to help you.'

'To help me?' she looked up at him, unwelcoming. 'How will you do that? Will you show me a cliff I can leap over, or a river I can jump into? Or perhaps you have a poison on you? My dagger's gone, he took it.'

'No, child.' He spoke firmly. 'You have got to live.'

'To live? What for?'

'For one thing, you might care to live to carry this Bagdemagus's head on your saddle-bow.'

'Ah.' A touch of colour returned to her cheeks. 'I could bear to live for that.'

'And then to forgive him.'

'Forgive him? Not I. Not in the ages of ages – not if the saints and angels begged me. I'll curse him, not forgive him. Look and listen now.' She stood erect and stretched her hand before her, her fingers in a forked shape. 'For the first time, Bagdemagus, I curse you.'

'Don't do that,' said Merlin, his voice deep and quiet. 'Not only because it's against holy charity—'

'I don't care for holy charity. For the second time, Bagdemagus, I curse you.'

'But not the third time! Oh my child, not the third time!'

She paused. 'Why not?'

'Because they come back to you. Look!' He laid his hand lightly upon her head, and suddenly all the lights and shadows in the wood were changed, and through the strange flashing lights she saw two things running away from her – like spiky, bristling black globes, with thin black legs and padding feet like claws, that ran with a smooth and relentless movement – they turned for a moment, and she saw they had eyes and grinding teeth. The first that went was small and ugly, the second, that had just left her, was larger and much uglier.

'They will come back, you see,' Merlin was patiently explaining. 'Do you want the third to come back to you?'

'Oh no!' she exclaimed, and at once the sight vanished. She stood trembling. No, I won't curse him the third time. But – what am I to do now?'

'What are you to do? Why, go home, of course, and go on living.'

'I've lost all that a girl lives for.'

He directed a thoughtful look at her. 'I don't believe it, nor do you. If you really do believe that that particular thing is a woman's whole life, why, yes, I suppose so. Some women – yes, for some women, virginity is the only treasure they have to bargain with, and a place in a man's house the only thing they want to use it to buy. But not you, I think. Am I right?'

She nodded.

'Yes, I knew it,' he said. 'There're things you can do, and things you want to be. Go home and grow to your full stature.'

She stood hesitating, her face crimson now.

'Oh, I know what you're afraid of. No, you won't conceive a child. Stop worrying. How do I know? I just know – No, I don't think you'd better tell your father, or anyone else. We don't want a war just now. Say nothing, but wait. Your time will come. Now tie up your hair, get on your horse, and go home.'

Under his quiet voice she did so. He guided her till she was within sight of the castle, and then turned aside into the woods. She slipped in unobserved. Bagdemagus had arrived back an hour before, they told her, but had received some sort of message, and was gone. She never saw him again . . .

. . . And so she had lost her maidenhead, and now Gaheris would find it out. Gaheris, coarse and stupid and violent. Gareth would have understood, and been patient and sympathetic. She could have told Gareth the whole story. But there *he* was, away in the next room with the bridesmaids and groomsmen singing round him and Leonie – No, they had finished singing, and were bringing her bridegroom to her. She shrank deeper into the bed and clutched the bedgown tightly round her. Here they came, Gaheris also in a long furred gown (thank God he wasn't naked either) supported by two groomsmen, probably more than a little drunk. They thrust him into bed beside her, with plenty of coarse jokes. The maidens tossed flowers at them, and sang:

> Now you're married we wish you joy,
> First a girl and then a boy,
> Each year after, son or daughter,
> Now, young couple, go kiss together.

Then they drew the curtains and left them. Both lay rigid, wrapped in their bedgowns, till the last of the crowd had gone and taken the torches and tapers with them, leaving them in the dark. Then without turning, he said to her over his shoulder. 'I think, madam, this arrangement is as little to your liking as it is to mine.'

3 · *How Sir Ruber Laid Siege to the Lady Leonie*

So once again she was left with time to remember, through that long, tense, sleepless night.

Cruel and violent were the changes that life had had for her, before she was seventeen years old. Leonie, she remembered, was just turned eighteen, when suddenly their father was brought back dying after a hunting accident. And hardly was he buried before the Knight of the Red Laundes moved in and took possession.

The Knight of the Red Laundes was horrible. At least Bagdemagus had had a pleasing appearance. This man ... The Red Laundes, or plains, from which he took his name, were a dismal tract of swamp at a sluggish river's mouth, where trickling rusty water stained the mud and the roots of the reeds, all that would grow there. It flowed out of caves, red with iron, where it was said a tribe of dwarfs worked for him, making swords and armour – but not free dwarfs, as most of them were, working as good craftsmen for their own honour, but miserable slaves of the Red Knight. And he was like his land, a red man – they called him Ruber, the Red Knight – not Rufus, for his hair, short, bristly and scabby, was jet black; but his face was red, flushed, swollen and coarse. His teeth were decayed, and his breath was loathsome.

He came, with a company of twenty men, ostensibly to pay his condolences on the loss of the ladies' father, and so courtesy obliged them to receive him, although they were in mourning. Leonie and Lynett roused themselves from their grief, and gathered such household as they had – Dame Juliana, the old steward, the dwarf Dagobert, the cook and his boy, the two waiting maids, three house-carles – that was about all; and between them they did their best to organize a dinner for this unexpected guest and his twenty followers. Leonie, Lynett and Dame Juliana sat at the high table with him, in their black dresses, and tried to be as polite to him as possible. His conversation was far from polite.

At the end of the dinner, when Sir Ruber had made short work of the best wine they had left, he pushed his chair back and stood up, and rapped on the table with his knife handle for silence.

'Madam Leonie of Lyonesse,' he said, 'without more ado – I'm here to offer for your hand in marriage. You need a man to protect you, now that your father's gone – er – God rest his soul, of course – a man to take charge of you and your lands and your castle. Here I am, and I hope you'll say yes and we'll be married tomorrow. Eh?'

The three women gasped simultaneously, and shrank together; then they all got to their feet, and Leonie faced him. He and his twenty men waited for her reply.

'My lord Sir Ruber,' Leonie said in her high clear voice, 'thank you very much, but – no.'

'No?' he shouted, his face suddenly convulsed. 'You say no? – you *dare* to say no to my good offer?'

'That is so, my lord. I say no.'

'But, God's blood and bones! This won't do – I won't have it. Madam, I say you *must*—'

'There's no *must* about it. Come Lynett, Juliana, quick—' for she saw him about to grab at her. The high arms of her chair checked him for a moment, as she and the other two women quickly dodged out of the door at the back of the dais, the household servants following them.

'Dagobert, push that big bench in front of the door – see that all the bolts are home – now—' and she led them all upstairs to the gallery that overlooked the hall. There, just as the Red Knight began to hammer on the door below, she opened a window above his head. He looked up and growled like an animal at her.

'Do you defy me, madam?'

'Yes, I do. And I am come to bid you goodnight and goodbye, thank you for visiting us, and please leave quietly.'

'Oh no, we don't. We're stopping here, my lady, till I get yes for an answer.'

'Then you will stop in the hall, for the door below is strong enough for a siege, *and* – the kitchen and larder and all the food and drink are on my side of the door.' With that she slammed the gallery window and left him.

Later, Leonie called the household together – the steward, Dagobert, the cook, and all the others, and told them her plan, which was simply to sit tight in her own quarters, the solar chamber and the best bedroom, below which were the kitchen and larders, and leave Ruber and his gang in the great hall with nothing to eat or drink until they went away. Their defences were reasonably good – Dagobert and the house-carles piled so much stuff against the door that it could never be broken through, short of using fire.

'He won't set fire to it,' Leonie reassured them, 'for he doesn't want to damage the house. He covets it, even more than he wants me, so he won't burn it. Listen to the noise he's making, out there with his friends! But we'll starve him out.'

And so they thought till next morning they peeped through the gallery window, and saw a large fire roaring up the wide chimney, and an ox roasting over it – an ox certainly stolen from the castle's own herd. There were hogsheads of wine, too, plundered from somewhere.

'I'm afraid we're not going to starve them out,' said Lynett.

'My lady,' said Dame Juliana, 'do you not think, perhaps – as you have no man to protect you, and a woman alone needs a protector – after all, he has made you an honourable offer—'

'Honourable offer?' Leonie exclaimed, her blue eyes flashing. 'Are you really suggesting, Dame Juliana, that I should
yield to that robber? I will not, not, not – and I'm grieved that
you should think of it. Come now, we're well provisioned for
a siege. What do you say?' She looked round at the servants.
The maids just looked frightened; the steward stood on his
dignity; but Dagobert, the house-carles and the cook
applauded.

'Don't you give in to that brute, my lady. We'll beat him
yet.'

'We shall,' she smiled at them. 'No surrender.'

4 · How Lynett Became a Damosel Errant

So they dug themselves in, and endured the siege. The
days began to pass wearily – and hungrily. The servants
managed to clamber over roofs and along ruinous galleries
and bring them news from time to time.

'They've taken all the horses, ladies. Taken and ridden
them away somewhere – Brutus and Mayflower, and all.'

And next day: 'They've let all the hawks loose,' said
Dagobert.

'What, Jeanne too?'

'Yes, Jeanne too, I fear.'

Oh, damn and blast them!' cried Lynett. 'I spent months on
that hawk, and she had come to understand me, and – and
I'd got fond of her. All my work gone for nothing.'

'At least they haven't eaten them,' said Dame Juliana with
a grimace. She had her gravest suspicions about the last dish
which the cook, most apologetically, had served up to them.

'If only we could get a message to King Arthur,' said
Lynett. 'The young King Arthur. They say his knights go all
about the country rescuing women from brutes like these. If
somebody, somehow, could get to Camelot and tell him—'

'Somebody!' said Leonie. 'But just who? Which of the servants could you send?'

Lynett frowned, and leant her chin on her fist.

Leonie continued, 'We can't spare any of the house-carles – there's only three of them anyway. Dagobert is too well known, they'd spot him at once. Barbon – could you go?'

Barbon the steward spread his hands.

'Pardon, my lady – my old limbs—'

'No, of course not. The cook – we couldn't do without him, and anyway King Arthur wouldn't listen to a cook – and the scullion boys wouldn't even know what message to take. That leaves—'

'Not me, my lady,' said Dame Juliana.

'Well—'

Lynett got up, shaking her head as if coming out of water. 'Of course. It has to be me. Who else could possibly go?'

'But Lady Lynett!' wailed Dame Juliana. 'How can you go? How will you go? How will you get past the watchmen?'

'I'll go on my feet, since they've left us no horses, and I'll go dressed like one of the scullions. They don't trouble much about them, and I'll either slip out unseen or play some sort of trick on them. I'll do it.'

'Oh, but Lady Lynett – the unseemliness of it!'

'It'll be more unseemly if Sir Ruber gets us,' she retorted grimly. 'Oh, I'll go, God help me, I'll find my way to Camelot somehow. It may take me a month, but if you can all – just keep alive till I come back?' Her resolute tone faltered and died away.

So, in a rough suit of hairy wool, none too clean, with her hair cut and her face smeared, she slipped out of the little back gate. It was heavily barricaded, but the house-carles unbuilt the barricade for her, and with prayers and God-speed opened the door and sent her on her way. The door closed behind her, she heard the crashing and rumbling as they rebuilt the barricade, and then she was alone, outside the walls. Alone – not even a horse to lend her courage.

It was pitch black, and she was down in the dry fosse that

surrounded the castle. She shut her eyes for a second to adjust them to the dark; it seemed a little clearer when she opened them, but she felt more vulnerable too. On the high edge of the fosse there was a man pacing to and fro. She waited till he had gone by, and then scrambled up. The man was waiting for her – his arm shot out – she stepped quickly back, dodging his grasp.

'Please, master, let me by. I'm not doing no harm.' She managed a reasonable simulation of one of the vagabond children who used to infest the courtyard. 'I've just been in to get a bite from where the knights are cooking in the hall. You – wouldn't want to buy a couple of silver spoons now?'

'Oh, be off with you, devil's brat!' said the man, and lunged at her with his pike. Lynett gave a lamentable howl and ran off down the path into the forest.

So far so good. When she was far enough away from all human sounds, she stopped running and stood still. And now the excitement of the moment was spent, and it was very quiet indeed. Very quiet and dark, and the trees were overhead and the bushes close round her, and she was deadly afraid.

Nobody went into the forest at night. Nobody hunted at night, save a few desperate bad men. Even when she had been hoydenishly ranging around with Bagdemagus, she had never been in the forest after dark. And now she was alone, alone and on foot, and hardly even knowing her way, except that she must follow the path and keep going away from the castle. If only she could turn about and run back! But this she could not do, no matter how much she wished. Go on – that was the only way.

So, trotting pathetically on the dusty path, looking to left and right, her hand clutching the dagger that was her only means of defence, she set out.

Dark and rustling, the forest closed round her. There was no moon, and the wind came in gusts, and between the gusts everything creaked and cracked. Noises – noises— She ought to know, she told herself, angrily, that that horrible shriek was a hunting owl, and that long wailing cry another owl,

and the things in the bushes could only be small birds, or
voles, or – or— She couldn't follow up the thought – what
did it matter what they might be, when, Oh God, oh God, her
heart was hammering so she could hardly breathe – She kept
trotting along, not allowing herself to break into a run. She
looked behind her, and the path was glimmering and empty.
Again she looked back, and the moon was rising. Then against
the rising moon, as she stood still for a moment, a thing came
rolling. Like a rough black ball, it seemed to come rolling out
of the moon and towards her, with a whirling, growling,
worrying noise. Then it unrolled itself and rose up, a tall black
shape, upright, surmounted by a head like a fox's, and came
on towards her. She shrieked, but could not move. Within a
few yards of her the thing turned suddenly and plunged into
the bushes at the side of the path. But it was not gone. She
heard it rustling along in the dark foliage at her side, as she
turned and ran. And then as she ran she heard something else
rustling on the other side of the path. They, whatever they
were, were pacing her on both sides, running as she ran.

Then the moon came up behind her, and shone on the path
ahead, and there they were – two of them – the tall, black,
fox-headed things with gleaming eyes and teeth. They were
standing each side of the path and waiting for her.

She gave a pitiful cry like a forsaken child, and crouched in
the middle of the path. But in that instant came a whistling
and a thin angry shriek from above – like a hawk's, but how
could a hawk be there at night? And out of the sky dropped a
furious flurry of claws and beak and thrashing wings, launch-
ing itself violently against those black bogies, dodging and
dashing from one to the other – They cringed and shrank and
fled – perhaps they fell to pieces, Lynett could hardly tell –
but they vanished, as if the wind had blown them away, and
the falcon, with a soft whirr of feathers, flew to Lynett's
outstretched arm.

'Jeanne!' she exclaimed. 'Oh, Jeanne! You came to help me
– oh, my darling Jeanne!' and she caressed the hawk's soft
downy neck. Jeanne paced up and down on her wrist, and

put her beak to Lynett's ear. To Lynett's surprise, she heard Jeanne speaking in a soft throaty voice.

'Of course I came. Now you needn't be afraid of anything. I'm with you. When it comes daylight I'll catch a rabbit for you. Let me sit on your shoulder and then you won't have to hold your arm out.' So they went on through the forest, and now indeed Lynett had no fear.

5 · How Lynett was Affronted with a Kitchen Boy

So in three days she came, with her hawk, to the outskirts of great Camelot, where the young King Arthur's banners were flying.

'I must leave you here,' Jeanne whispered, 'for if I go in with you they'll put me in their mews, with all sorts and kinds of birds. But I'll come back again, sometime.' And she lifted off from Lynett's arm and lost herself in the sky, and Lynett went on into the citadel.

She was brown enough and dusty enough, and looked the very picture of a ragamuffin boy.

'Hi, not that way!' a man said, as she reached the great main entrance. 'Round to the back for such as you.'

Bewildered in the crowd of strangers all pushing, jostling and shouting, she followed docilely enough, and found herself at the door of the great kitchen.

Here another rough man pushed her to one side.

'Kitchen boys sit on that bench there,' he shouted above the noise.

'But I'm *not* a kitchen boy,' she protested.

'I know you're not, yet. And you'll have no chance to be, unless you behave yourself till Sir Kay comes along – and *then* you'd better behave yourself.'

There was nothing for it. Lynett was thrust on to a bench, the last in a line of equally ragged boys. At least there was some warmth in the great kitchen, and shelter from the rain outside, and there was an encouraging smell of food – encouraging but tormenting, she was so hungry.

Over by the big fire place she saw him – Gareth. Tall, but with the softness of youth still about him; tow-haired, and with startling blue eyes that looked across to her and seemed as if they would speak. He left the fireplace and came to her side.

'Don't be afraid,' he said. 'It's always like this when you start.' He put a bowl of savoury pottage into her cold hands. 'There, eat it up before anyone comes along.'

He stood by her while she ate the pottage, which was excellent and made her feel very much bolder. He was just concealing the empty bowl, when the man who had first spoken to Lynett came bustling by.

'Now then, you Pretty-Hands,' he said, 'look lively there – Sir Kay's just on his rounds now. You boys, stand up when he comes in, and be sure to call him Sir.'

There was a stir at the door, and Sir Kay, a thickset, black-bearded man, impressively robed, entered with a retinue of cooks and kitchen clerks. He approached the boys on the bench, who all stood up obediently. Not so Lynett.

He halted opposite her.

'What's this, eh? Not another Pretty-Hands? Stand up, boy, when I speak to you.'

Lynett remained sitting, but drew herself up to her full height, and spoke on a high note.

'*Master* Kay – for I will not dignify you with the honourable name of Sir – for if you are a Knight of the Round Table, their famous courtesy is a long way to seek.'

Everyone around stopped talking, stopped whatever they were doing, and listened.

'*Master* Kay – I am no kitchen boy. I am a lady. I am a damosel in distress, come to ask a boon of King Arthur, and you and your minions have treated me like a scullion. Like a

vagabond. Like a common kitchen knave. Because I have
come among you dressed as I am – because I have escaped
barely with my life from my castle, and journeyed on foot
through perils that would daunt any one of your fat hangers-
on – and therefore I come in my necessary disguise, and
travel-stained – therefore you have let me be thrust into your
kitchen, and let your kitchen-officer here treat me as if I were
the wretchedest vagabond churl seeking employment – seek
employment here? I'd sooner seek it on the hobs of hell—'

She drew breath for a moment, and realized with a pleasur-
able shock that these men were afraid of her. She went on, 'I
am a noble lady, the daughter of a great house, and I have
come a long and perilous journey to ask King Arthur's help
for my noble sister, shut up by a churl in her castle – though
it seems there are churls everywhere. I had heard that the
Knights of the Round Table were courteous and ready to help
ladies in distress. It seems they are no better than other
mannerless churls . . .'

She warmed to her theme. She tongue-lashed them, in a
royal rage. Words came to her, red-hot. Sir Kay and his
retinue stood fidgeting. At last, 'Lady, lady, enough!' he cried.
'Lady, lady, lady – oh, I beg you – I ask your pardon – but
enough, enough. Come with me and all shall be put right.
King Arthur shall see you at once.'   'Not so,' she said. 'Is the
churlish fool going to thrust me into King Arthur's presence
as I am, foul and travel-stained? No – you shall find me
decent apparel, and a bath—'

'Oh, certainly. Only come this way, madam.'

And he led her out of the kitchen, with all the crowd
gawping. Pretty-Hands was lost and forgotten among the rest.

So the greatly chastened Sir Kay took her up many flights
of steps, into a luxuriously furnished ladies' bower, where
some very surprised court ladies bathed her, and combed her
hair, and dressed her becomingly, with gasps and cries of
astonishment for her adventures and her bravery. And at last
she was led before King Arthur.

*

He was young, was King Arthur, not much older than herself, but full of power and dignity, as he sat dominating his Round Table. It was a simpler thing than it later became – as Lynett saw it that day it was just a vast, bare, circular board, with neither carving nor painting – all that came later. The knights sat round it in their appointed places, each with his shield behind him, over the back of his chair, showing his device. At the King's right sat his newly wedded Queen, Guinevere the White Spectre; and at his left was Merlin, and at the sight of Merlin, Lynett's heart missed a beat. She had not expected to see him there.

Briefly she told her tale, and the King answered her courteously.

'Fair damosel, you are welcome, and your wrong shall be righted. We have heard of this Knight of the Red Laundes. We shall send a knight with you to rescue your lady sister. Now who—'

He broke off, for behind Lynett there was a commotion at the door, and someone had entered. She heard a fresh young voice say, 'My lord King, I claim this adventure for my own. This is the second boon I was to claim from you, of three you swore to grant me; and the third is that you make me a knight forthwith, that I may go with this damosel.'

'Who is it?' asked the King, and Merlin whispered to him. Then he said, 'So be it. Young man, this adventure is yours. You shall be made a knight in due form as soon as may be. Lady, behold your champion.'

And she turned and saw the kitchen-boy Pretty-Hands.

It was like a blow over the heart to her – she reeled with the shock, and grew pale and then furiously red.

'My lord King,' she said in a choked voice, 'is this a jest? If so, it is a sorry jest at my expense ... What? Cannot I come among you disguised as a kitchen-knave for safety on my perilous journey, but you must cast the same in my teeth, by giving me a kitchen-knave instead of a champion? My lord King, this was unmannerly done.' And she broke into tears, and turned and fled from the hall.

She ran away down long stairways and corridors, alone and bewildered. She did not know where she should run, only that she must get away. And at last she sank down on the stone seat of a quiet cloister; and there Merlin found her.

'It's you again,' she said. 'What do you want?'

'As before,' he said, sitting down by her, 'I don't want anything. I've come to turn you into the right road again. Don't despise your champion.'

'Champion! They gave me a kitchen-boy – just because I had to get here in disguise, and that upstart Kay had to take me for what I looked like – they mock me, they mock me – their Round Table, their flower of chivalry, pah! – I spit on them . . . By the Mass, I think their kitchen-boy might be more courteous than they are.'

'Listen, my child,' said Merlin very patiently, 'there was no thought of discourtesy in the King's mind when he allotted young Beaumains as your champion – I swear he did not know of your disguise. No discourtesy was intended. As for the boy, don't despise him – as Sir Kay despised you. Don't you know that you can't judge the man by the apparel? You should know,'

'Who is he then – this Beaumains?'

'No, I'm not telling you that. Try him and prove him for yourself. I'll only tell you that he is fated to be your champion, and the adventure is his. So go back now, and beg the King's pardon—'

'Beg his pardon – I?'

'He is the King. And take your champion and go. Your sister is waiting.'

So she went back, saying very little, and the next day, horsed and accoutred as was fitting, she and Gareth set out on their journey together, as has often enough been told.

. . . And so now as she lay by Gaheris's side, she tormented herself by recalling the taunts, the snubs, the bitter insults she had heaped on Gareth as they journeyed, and how patiently and bravely he had borne it all, and how her growing love had fought with her pride, and overcome it – and all to this end, that she should hand him over to her sister – to live, as they would say, happily ever after.

6 · *How Lynett Became the King's Damosel*

She must have dropped off to sleep, for she woke to hear Gaheris getting out of bed. It was still dark. She heard him putting on his clothes outside the curtains. Then he parted the curtains and looked in.

'Madam,' he said, 'I think it best we should part here and now. I am going, and I bid God-be-wi'-you. I hope we shalt not meet again.'

And he dropped the curtain – she heard the door creak and bump as he swung it to, and his footsteps echoed down the stone passage. He was gone.

For a moment she lay stunned, then angry tears flooded her eyes. A slap in the face, nothing less. Granted she did not love him, that she had dreaded her bridal night with him, that she had felt relief when he had not touched her – yes, but to be left like this! The humiliation, the ignominy. With a sinking heart she thought of the next day, and many days after – the honeymoon of feasting and revelry. First would come the aubade, with the crowd of young men and girls waking them, as if the couple hadn't had enough songs, with songs of the dawn – with ribald cheerful inquiries as to how the night had passed – with ritual assurance that the bride had been found a virgin, and was so no longer – with the spicy caudle to restore their strength after the exertions of the night—

Leonie would enjoy it all, niminy-piminy though she might be, she was eager enough for her bridegroom, and she would enjoy blushing at the rude jokes. But she, Lynett – no bridegroom beside her. Alone, neglected, rejected. Tongues would clack like the great castle bell. He had found her too loathsome. He had found her not a maid – dear heavens, too true if he had known it. For whatever reason, he wouldn't have her. And there she was left like an unsavoury morsel, chewed and spat out ... Then there would be the feasts and revels to follow. Must she sit at table with her sister and Gareth, unpartnered, the odd one out, with all around her singing of joy and love, and pledging them in loving-cups of hydromel? Neither maid, wife nor widow, not even an honourable old maid.

The burning words came tumbling to her mind, words she would say if there were anyone to say them to. Bitterly, she talked to an absent Gaheris in her head, on and on and on, till she felt herself bursting with unuttered anger, and her eyes were burning and her mouth dry and her stomach tied in a knot ...

At last she rose from the bed, and lit a candle – in a chest by her bedside were some of her clothes, with her money and jewels. She found the riding-clothes in which she, with Leonie, had ridden up from Lyonesse. Leonie had ridden side-saddle in a richly quilted kirtle, but Lynett had refused to go so long a journey in such inefficient equipment, and had worn breeches and ridden like a man. Here were her breeches, and a sufficiently rich doublet, and a useful cloak and hood. She put them on.

Then quietly stepping over the trampled flower-strewings with almost a shudder, she went down through the stony corridor and out. The summer dawn was colouring the sky, and she crossed a courtyard, breathing deeply of the fresh air. She slipped into the stables and passed through into the mews. This was very like the mews in the Castle of Lyonesse, and she felt more at home here – its peculiar smell was right, and spoke to her of comfort. And there, on a spare perch, was Jeanne.

Jeanne must have slipped in somehow during the night, and was standing, unhooded and without jesses or bells, between two hooded goshawks. Jeanne had been gone into the wild for more than a year, and a hawk who does that is spoilt beyond redemption – it never comes back. But Jeanne had come back. She made a soft whirring noise and flew from her perch to Lynett's outstretched arm.

Lynett gave a little cry of delight, and then, sinking her cheek against the bird's soft feathered breast, gave way to a flood of tears.

She wondered if Jeanne could still talk. Jeanne said nothing, but deep down under the feathers Lynnet thought she could hear, as she sobbed, a kind of remote ticking, clicking noise as of something saying, 'There – there – there – there—'

A small sound made her look up, and there was Merlin standing over her.

'You!' she exclaimed. 'You again – you're always there when – when I hate—'

'Yes,' he said calmly. 'You do not often cry.'

'No, I *don't* often cry.'

'Then don't cry now. You're a woman grown, and a step nearer your destiny.'

'How you do talk!' she said crossly.

'Now – there's no need to be discourteous, or petulant, or childish. You are of full age now. You should know that a man's need – or a woman's – is not for happiness, but to fulfil his destiny.'

'My destiny!' she mocked, lifting her red wet face. 'What destiny have I – neither wife, maid or widow? What destiny?'

'That needs thought,' he said. He paced away from her, the length of the mews, and back again. Then he said, 'To be, I think, a carrier – a bearer.'

'A bearer of what? Of children?' she cried bitterly.

'No, not, I think, of children. Not your wish – you have very little of the mother's milk in your humours. No, there are other things to bear and carry.'

'Such as Bagdemagus's head?' she burst out.

He turned and looked at her rather sadly.

'So you still think of that?'

'You promised me!' she cried.

'I never promised. I held the hope before you, once, to stand between you and self-destruction. But there are better things to carry than a burden of vengeance. Things that you might indeed bear—'

'Such as what?'

'I will try to show you,' he said. 'I think you will be able to see.'

He guided her to a low stool and made her sit, quietly taking Jeanne from her shoulder and replacing her on the perch – the big hawk submitting to his handling as if she knew him. Then he took from his neck the jewel that hung there. It was a glass globe about the size of a pullet's egg, full of strange cloudy threads of many colours, writhing through the crystal. He placed it in the palm of her hand and told her to look at it steadily; then he laid his right hand lightly on her head.

At first she only saw the reflections of the windows on the crystal; then for a long time, nothing at all. Then at last a picture began to form. A curtain, a dim curtain with a light behind it, and outlined against the folds the shadow of something. A cup, a large chalice like the cup of the Holy Mass. Behind the curtain were many people – she could hear the sound of their voices and their movements, but confusedly – and there was singing too. But something seemed to come to her from the dimly-seen shape of that cup – some great, great holiness. The holiness of the blessed Mass, that she knew – but this was even more. The Chalice of Chalices. In the Holy Mass, she must struggle and aspire, and try hard to attain the grace and blessedness of the Presence – but if she could be near This, without a veil, all would be clear, all would be granted – without striving, without doubt, without distraction. It would all be there, the presence of All Goodness, All Holiness, All Compassion, All Beauty. And those that were within the veil with that holy thing sang softly, day and night for ever and ever, moving sweetly in their bliss as the stars move . . .

Then the picture changed, and she saw the figure of a woman coming out of a door, as in some other place, and she carried in her hands that holy cup, but covered with a white cloth. She came pacing slowly forward, her eyes on the thing she carried, and then she lifted her face for a moment, and Lynett saw it was her own face.

She cried out in surprise, and the vision vanished; Merlin put his hand over the crystal ball and gently took it from her. He seemed to know what she had seen.

'Not for me,' she said, her voice shaking. 'It's too holy for me.'

'But you are not too unholy for It,' he replied quietly.

'That is a work for – a virgin – a woman of virtue.' She looked up at him, angrily again. 'I've lost my virtue and you know it.'

'Child,' he said, very calmly putting the jewel back on his neck, 'some people seem to have taught you that there is only one virtue, at least for a woman, and that is chastity. Or virginity, which is not always the same. Believe me, there are other virtues. There is charity – and charity is forgiveness.'

'Forgiveness!' she cried. 'You're always talking about forgiveness.'

'Well, yes,' he agreed, 'perhaps I am. But everyone who prays the Christian man's prayer is always talking about forgiveness. Many people say I am not a Christian man – there are those who say I am the son of the Devil. None the less, I know that prayer, and I know what it means. And so should you.'

She sat with downcast head, still looking at her empty hands.

'Then I'm afraid I do not have the virtue of charity.'

'Then you must learn it.'

'But how?'

'That is to be seen. But this is plain: there is work for you to do.'

She thought of that veiled figure.

'Does it mean that I have to become a nun? Oh no – not – *not* to cover up my head for the rest of my life!' and she ran her fingers through her long black hair.

He laughed. 'A very sound reason to know you have no

vocation to a convent! No, my girl, you'll not have to cover up your head for the rest of your life. You might have to wear a hood or a leather casque or even a helmet. You are to be King Arthur's Messenger to his knights. Come now, the King is on his way here. I'll present you to him.'

Suddenly she thought with longing of the road, over the downs or through the woods, a-horseback or afoot – as she had gone, carefree and bold, on her quest to fetch Gareth – yes, for the moment she could think of Gareth without a pang. She was eager to be gone.

'It'll save your face too,' said Merlin. 'You can be away before the castle is astir, and you won't be found alone. They'll all suppose you've gone with your bridegroom.'

She pulled a comic face at the word – she could even smile now. Life was better already.

There was a footstep at the end of the mews, and the King entered. Merlin went down to meet him, and they talked together for some time; and then they came back slowly to where Lynett stood.

He was – the King. No other word for it. Young though he was, the air of command sat upon him, and the magnetism of his power could be felt. He moved with easy grace that gave him dignity beyond his years; his grey eyes and his firm lips had strength and authority, and sweetness also. Lynett felt something pluck at her heart. Her father, in the days when he had taught her skill and courage – all those heroes of her romantic imaginings – even that wicked Bagdemagus as she had first thought him to be – something of her beloved Gareth – the leader who could call out her powers, make her grow, liberate her to be more than a woman, a complete being, a 'man' – this was the King to follow. She sank on her knees before him.

'My lord King,' she said, 'make me your messenger. Send me forth.'

He laid a hand on her shoulder, and a tremor ran through her at the touch.

'What do you say, Merlin – I cannot dub her a knight? No – but I'll do this. Lady—' and again the hand on her shoulder was raised a little and lowered – 'I here create and dub you the King's Damosel.'

Speechless, she held up her hands joined, to place between his. Merlin dictated the words:

∴ 'I do become thy vassal of life and limb, to live and die in thy' service, and in God's service, so help me God the Father, God the Son, and God the Holy Ghost.'

... They walked slowly behind the King through the corridors to a small retired room, where the light shone through horn windows on rich hangings and carven wood.

'My messenger must eat and drink,' said the King, and saw that she did ... 'And now, Merlin,' he said, 'the *mappa*.'

Merlin took from a chest, and unfolded on the table, such a thing as Lynett had never seen before – As she had understood the word, a *'mappa'* was a linen napkin or tablecloth, such as the very rich and fine sometimes used. This was a large tablecloth, but painted on its surface, in coloured dyes, was a sort of picture, so it seemed to her, of the King's dominions, with rivers, woods, hills, roads, castles. Here and there little men were pictured going to and fro, the wild animals peeped out of the forests, or strange and terrible beasts hovered over hilltops. And each place had its name written beside it. She gasped at the wonder of it, and would have liked to spend a long time examining and admiring it; but the King recalled her to the business in hand.

'See – here is the great Road, that the Romans made. All along it, look, are castles, and in each of those castles are knights who owe allegiance to me. I want you to go to each one, and bid them meet me here in two years' time, at the Feast of Whitsun. Oh yes, we'll have a tournament, a very grand tournament – but I want them here, and I want them to pledge their allegiance. I have messages for certain ones, also – some deserve praise, and some I must question, and rebuke some. I'll tell you each one in turn, presently – each one's name and what you are to say to him. But you are to go as a messenger of peace in every case. That is why I send a damosel – you will go, first, attended only by your father's dwarf, Dagobert, who is here with me.'

He turned from the *mappa*, rather suddenly.

'Have you a horse?'

'I – yes, my lord King, I have – just the palfrey that brought me here, a lady's little palfrey – but—' She drew a breath, and spoke on an impulse. 'My lord King – I'd like one of *your* horses. One of your great horses, such as your knights ride.'

The king gave a shout of laughter, throwing back his head.

'Oh, Merlin, didn't you tell me she was a bold lady! – My dear Damosel, do you know what you are asking? My great horses, that my knights ride – my black horses – why, they're monsters! Four hands higher than your British horses. They are bred from the kind the Romans left in Britain – coal black, and as fierce as the devil. Do you really ask me for one like that? Four hands higher than a common horse?'

She looked up at him, not abashed.

'My father's Brutus was no smaller, and I mastered him. Let me try, my lord King!'

He laughed again. 'Oh, bold lady – we shall see. Now – this castle, and this, and this, to be visited. And so you go northwards. And the last I want you to visit, up here, almost by the Wall – is King Bagdemagus.'

She started and turned pale – her eyes met Merlin's, then she snatched her gaze away, and fought to recover her composure.

'*King* Bagdemagus?' she queried, carefully keeping her voice from shaking. 'But how comes it that you call him King?'

'Oh, he calls himself King now! He's set himself up as a sort of king in defiance of me, and keeps his state there with his warriors – making a kingdom of violence and cruelty, where the only right is brute force. You will take him my demand for submission to my rule and the rule of God and the law.'

'My lord King,' she said, and her voice was still not quite

under her control, 'forgive me, but is this not a matter for an armed band of knights—'

'No, my lady, it is not. At least not this time. I am sending him an embassage of peace, for a first step. True, the armed band may come later – But first, I do not offer him war but peace, if he will take it. Besides, there are men among his band who are of a better kind than he, and who were my vassals once – I should like to win them back. Make it known to them that I will welcome and forgive any such. The embassage of peace must be by a damosel. Are you afraid of this man?'

God knows, she thought, I *am* afraid. But I mustn't show it. Aloud she said, 'No, my lord King, I'm not afraid.'

'Good, good. My knights will follow hard behind you in case of trouble, but they must not be within sight of you. You'll deal with this Bagdemagus for me, I know. You'll bring me either his submission, or' – he turned to Merlin with a smile, as if he did not really mean it – 'or his head.'

7 · *How Lynett Came to Castle Hardy*

She came in sight of the looming, ugly battlements of Castle Hardy and stopped for a moment to gaze at it, sitting on her tall black horse. Above the winding road towered the castle, on a spur of the bare threatening hills – she had seen many castles on her travels, but nearly all shining, beflagged, with a welcoming look – none like this.

Dagobert, on his trotting donkey, drew rein behind her, and handed her an odd-looking thing he carried at his saddle-bow, which proved to be a lady's tall conical headdress, a 'hennin', in black satin with a floating veil of white, and a white scarf to go under the chin and hold it. Lynett took off the leather cap she was wearing and carefully put on the hennin. She was wearing leather breeches and doublet, but

over them was a coat of rich black velvet, trim in the waist
and spreading in the skirts. Her long black hair hung loose
over her shoulders, whether under the leather cap or the
hennin. It had been by the King's instructions that she wore
the coat, and her hair long, and put on the hennin when she
neared a castle. She would have preferred her boyish attire,
but he was anxious that she should always be recogized as a
woman. She still insisted to herself that she was ugly, and
made no attempt to be otherwise – her hair scraped back from
her face, her sombre choice of colour, with nothing to adorn
it. Often the ladies in the castles which she had visited had
offered her prettier things to wear, and tried to make her alter
her hairstyle, but she would have none of it. Yet anyone with
eyes to see could have perceived a strange intense kind of
beauty in her ivory-brown face, the clear skin warmed with
sunburning, and her deep-set brown eyes.

She had a company that rode with her – four knights, four
squires and four men-at-arms, making twelve in all – thirteen
with herself, which was a sacred number and well omened as
long as the thirteenth was a woman. There was also old
Dagobert, who made it fourteen, but he didn't count, any
more than did Jeanne, who always rode on her lady's wrist.
The four knights – Sir Percival, Sir Gwalchmei, Sir Lancelot
and Sir Bors – all knew 'the Falcon', which was the name they
gave Lynett no less than Jeanne, and swore by her, regarding
her as their luck.

More than two years they had now spent on the road
together, going along the length of Britain from south to
north. When they came to castles that were known to be
friendly to Arthur's rule, they would advance in a body; but
when it was doubtful – this was by Arthur's express command – Lynett would advance alone, followed only by
Dagobert on his donkey, and would make herself known as a
solitary damosel, travelling in peace and asking a peaceful
reception. If the reception were not peaceful the knights
would follow her shortly. All were in possession of King

Arthur's secret password, and their camp was always closely guarded against any not having this.

They had met with innumerable adventures. Once they had been forced to take shelter in the cottage of a witch, who had tried to poison them – but Lynett's keen sense of smell had detected the poison in the broth the witch had offered them. Lynett had prevented the knights and their men from stringing up the witch on the spot, or forcing her to drink her own poisoned broth – but she had then tongue-lashed the witch till the men almost felt sorry for her.

Another time a band of forest robbers swooped down on them and carried her off. After a week, her distracted escort tracked her down to the robbers' hideout, a log cabin within a maze of thorn hedges – and burst in upon them, to find her treating the robber chief for a broken arm and a fever. This time it was her own people who got the rough edge of her tongue, for she was just in the act of persuading the robber chief to take the medicine she had prepared for him. Of course she was glad to see her own knights again, and to be rescued by them – all the same, she had to tell them—

She was beginning to be known for a particular kind of eloquence. She found it paid.

8 · How Lynett Met Bagdemagus Again

So now at last she was within sight of Castle Hardy – she was about to meet that man Bagdemagus. The man who had taken her maidenhead. The man who had disillusioned her, disenchanted her, struck the cruellest blow to her ideals, her dreams and her pride— the only man who knew she was not a virgin.

All these months she had gradually travelled towards him in a fine flame of indignation and vengeance; now she suddenly felt not so much afraid, as embarrassed. No, she would not meet him first in the presence of these her four knights, who respected her. As by her usual custom, she would first approach him alone, as a messenger of peace, and then the knights would follow, but this time not too speedily. She must have time to make her own impression on him in her own way. So she gave the knights orders not to follow her till she sent Dagobert back for them. They protested, saying it would be too dangerous for her, but she overruled them.

And now she stood before the drawbridge, and Dagobert blew on the horn that he carried.

'Who comes here?'

'A damosel bearing a message.'

This was usual, and as a rule the next was, 'Enter and welcome, fair damosel—' But instead she heard a rude shout of laughter.

'We'll not go in,' she said aside to Dagobert, but it was too late. Men-at-arms, roughly dressed, hairy and untidy, pulled them forcibly inside the great door of creaking logs and impelled them, in the centre of a crowd, up the sloping, turning pathway between the high earth walls, to the door of a log-built hall; here they pulled Lynett from her horse and dragged her inside the door.

The place was indescribably squalid – Lynett was by this time used to all the hardships and austerities of the less fortunate castles, as well as the splendour and state of the better ones – but never had she met with a castle quite like this. The smell of it rose up and affronted her. Everywhere was neglect, carelessness, waste and riot. Everything was dirty, casual, slovenly. The great hall bore evidence of riotous feasts, night after night, never cleaned up after. The hangings on the wall were rich, but torn and splashed with wine and grease – all the long tables had silver cups, but all were tarnished and battered. A smoke-hole over the central hearth took the smoke in a sort of fashion, instead of the newer fireplace and chimney. The smoke itself was heavy and polluted with the refuse flung into the fire. And the company was of the same kind. Among barbarous invading Saxons one might have expected such, but these men were Britons, and many of them wore the trappings of knighthood. But Lynett, as they pressed and hustled her, could call them nothing else but a gang of ruffians. There were no women present, not even serving-wenches; but at the high table there sat some three or four adolescent boys, with long hair and painted faces, bedizened with satins and trinkets, giggling together in shrill voices.

There he was, at the head of his table – Bagdemagus himself, the man she had come to see. He had aged very quickly – he was fatter and flabbier, his skin was blotched and flushed, his cheeks were beginning to sag, his eyes were bloodshot, his fine spare frame was grown paunchy. Lynett looked at him and felt – no, not pity, but a kind of impersonal regret for a fine thing gone to ruin. Then, all her old resentment and indignation arose in her like a tidal wave, and filled her with the courage to disregard her rude escort.

'Get away from me,' she spat at them, and in some surprise they obeyed, leaving a clear space around her, with Dagobert two paces behind, and Jeanne, unhooded as always, threatening on her wrist. She confronted Bagdemagus on the platform above her, and was quite certain he did not recognize her.

'My lord Bagdemagus,' she began in her clear penetrating voice, 'I come as a messenger of peace from King Arthur, the true overlord of all Britain, who bids me say thus—' and she unrolled the scroll she had taken from her scrip, and began to read.

Bagdemagus, bold and truculent as ever, loomed over her and listened, with an air of scorn, only waiting for her to have said enough; around her his rough and hostile men stood waiting in attitudes of menace, or of enmity, or of boredom. But she read steadily on, trying to disregard their mutterings and spittings.

'The best thing about the woman,' she heard one man say to another, 'is that big hawk she carries. We'll have that.'

'Yes, we'll have that,' agreed his fellow.

While she went on reading her scroll, Lynett quietly transferred it to her left hand, and with her right hand she loosened Jeanne's jesses, so that Jeanne could fly free. No, they would not have Jeanne.

The message from King Arthur called upon Bagdemagus to submit himself, as in duty bound, to King Arthur, and acknowledge his rule, and the rule of the Laws of Britain; and to that end, to appear and make obeisance before King Arthur at Camelot that coming Whitsun, on forfeit of his life and honour. It further called upon any of his knights who had aforetime been vassals of the King, to return to their old allegiance, without penalty or pain, and with assurance of the King's pardon.

'And to this end,' it concluded, 'that we might not seem to use force or coercion, we send in the first place these letters by our messenger of peace, our trusted damosel, whom receive with all honour. For be assured that, an ye do not, nor make due submission to us our next messenger will not be so peaceable.'

She concluded the reading, and as if held back till that moment, a thunderous shout of derision broke upon her. She stood compressing her lips, screwing up her eyes, clenching her hands. And Bagdemagus gave words to the rest.

'Your King Arthur! We spit on your King Arthur! Submit myself? I'll see him frying in hell's flames. Boys, what'll we do with King Arthur? – and what'll we do with his charming messenger?'

A shout from the hall answered the question in the coarsest possible way. Lynett's face first reddened, then blanched bone-white with rage. She sprang up the steps to the platform.

'Hear me, you men!' she cried, making her voice heard across the tumult. 'Here me while I tell you what I know of this man, your leader. Oh yes, he doesn't know me yet, but he will – oh, he will. Knights, listen. This man deceived, betrayed and raped me, when I was a virgin, thirteen years old, and he a guest in my father's house. Cruelly and deceitfully – not by any persuasive seduction, look you, but practising on my innocence – I who trusted him as a father. Oh men and knights, the hardest of you would respect a child, below the age of consent, ignorant of all evil, trusting her father's guest. Not only the treasure of my body he took from me, but the innocence of my mind, the trust and confidence of my heart. As a father I trusted him, as a father, and lo what he did to me . . .'

Bagdemagus stood aghast, recognizing her now, and his men drew a little away from him, muttering, swayed for the moment, moved with sympathy for her. If she had rested her case there, she might have had them on her side, but some devil of foolishness made her overplay her hand. She went on,

'Do I blush? It is he, whose brazen brows have never blushed, that should blush with shame now. Call this a knight, a noble, a paladin, a King to command your allegiance . . .'

She went on and on. She warmed to her theme, and worked upon it. She harangued high and low. The mood turned again, and the crowd surged. Bagdemagus clapped his hands over his ears, and cried, 'Silence the scolding bitch!'

And another yelled, 'To the ducking-stool with her!'

'A common scold!' cried another.

'Put a bridle in her mouth!'

And the crowd rushed upon her.

Dagobert flung himself forward.

'Sir, sirs,' he cried, 'respect my lady—'

To Lynett's horror, a hand in the crowd whirled up with a heavy mace and brought it crashing down on the old man's head. He fell, and was trampled underfoot. Lynett stood for a moment stupefied. Then she gave Jeanne a quick and gentle shake from her wrist – the big bird took off, fluttering above the heads of the crowd, up into the smoke-hole. As she went, however, a bow twanged, and Lynett cried out again as a feather floated down. She could not see whether Jeanne had been hit. But she turned on her persecutors in a frenzy, and struggled while they pinioned her arms and dragged her

away again – through corridors, stony and grim – up stairways – at last to a little bare cell, high up, cold, lonely and
hopeless.

9 · How Bagdemagus Dealt with Lynett

'So it's you,' said Bagdemagus, lounging in. 'I might have
known it.'

A day had elapsed since Lynett's capture. Her prison was
no dungeon – an attic, high up among the roofs of the castle,
dry on the whole and not too cold, with a bed and various
other provision for her comfort, and a window through which
she could see how impossible escape would be. An old serving-
man, probably dumb, had brought her bread, meat and small
ale. On the whole her captivity was not barbarous, but deadly
tedious, and not without an ominous undercurrent of worse
to come. There was poor old Dagobert, ruthlessly murdered,
and Jeanne probably shot too. What better was she to expect?

She looked up as he entered, but did not move from the
edge of the bed where she sat, upright and tense.

'Yes, it's me,' she said. 'And now your men have murdered
my servant, and shut me up here, when you ought to have
respected the King's messenger.'

'King's messenger my foot! Oh yes, it's you, boy Robin.
Impudent enough for that or any job. Come here and kiss
me.' He dragged her to her feet, and clutched her to him –
she struggled, fiery with hate. He held her a moment, and
then threw her aside.

'No – on the whole, no. Not attractive. You've not worn
well. Skin's gone coarse, hair's a mess, and your figure's gone
bony and scraggy. I don't want you.'

'Nobody asked you,' she flung at him. 'Come to that, my
lord, you've not worn so well yourself. Coarse skin – just look

at you! And red nose too – and as for figure, no one could call you scraggy – baggy, I'd say—'

He laughed, but with anger. 'You dare! Impudent as ever. Bold Scold, that's what you are. Oh well, I don't want your ugly body now, don't fear. But I'll have a use for you all the same.'

He turned to the door and whistled. A man came in with a leather apron and some metal things in a bag.

'You've got some useful knowledge I'd like to have. For instance – King Arthur's secret password?'

Grim terror struck her. This was it. This would be the test. Torture.

'No,' she said, very pale.

'No? I think yes. There's things we could do to you, I and my friend here, not so pleasant, after all, as what I did under that beech tree. Things that would alter your mind quite a bit. I think you'll tell me.'

'No,'

'All right, the thumbscrews first. Begin with one hand. Just a first taste—'

The pain was atrocious. She screamed at the full stretch of her lungs, because she couldn't help it. The pain stopped – and then began again. At the third touch she fainted, but a strong aromatic smell jerked her back to consciousness; and she heard Bagdemagus saying; 'You won't escape that way.'

She would go out of her mind, she knew only too well. The pain would send her mad, and she would tell them anything, anything – It came again ... Then a desperate plan formed itself. If she told him something – something he would think was the secret password – and his men would try to use it, but she could make it something that would warn them, that would bring them to her aid ...

She opened her eyes, and passed her tongue over her lips.

'I'll tell. All right, stop doing that and I'll tell.'

'Why, good girl!' he said. 'I knew you would. All right, Sarkos – take it off. Well?'

'It's this. "The falcon's feather cries out."'

'The falcon's feather cries out,' he repeated. 'Is this the true word? On your oath?'

'On my oath, yes.'

'Look me in the eyes.'

She did so, but the blaze of hatred in her eyes hid any trace of hesitation.

'Do you swear it on your eternal salvation?'

'I swear it.' she said. (Oh God, oh God, she thought, You'll surely forgive this – it's under duress – oh, You know it's under duress.)

'Now think – say after me: If this is not the truth—'

'If this is not the truth—'

'May the thing I fear most—'

'May the thing I fear most—'

'Pursue me and overtake me—'

'Pursue me and overtake me—'

'And may the Black Ones that follow me—'

(Now how on earth did he know that? But she must go on and say it – and if her voice faltered, it must seem only from the pain of the thumbscrew—'

'And may the Black Ones that follow me—'

'Overtake me and have my heart and my soul—'

'Overtake me and have my heart and my soul—'

'Amen.'

'Amen.'

She drew a long sigh, and collapsed on the floor with her face hidden.

'Will you let me go now?'

'Let you go? Oh no. My dear woman, what d'you think? No, you'll stay here, and if your password proves to be a deceit, we'll think of something to do to you. So, you see—?'

He left her, without lamp or candle, as the dusk crept over her chilly little room. Crouched on the small hard bed, she nursed her mangled thumb.

What had she done? The false password she had given would certainly bring her bodyguard to her rescue, if Bagdemagus or any of his men tried to use it to get into their camp

– but would they come in time, when her enemies had
discovered the deceit? Her deceit – oh yes, all was fair in war,
but what, what had she done? Not only had she perjured
herself, but what were those frightful words he had made her
say? 'May the Black Ones that follow me, overtake me and
have my heart and my soul—' How did *he* know about those
Black Ones? Did he, perhaps, have Black Ones that followed
him? And if so, what and how great must be the black devils
that followed such a man ... Almost she felt – no, not pity,
but a sort of awestruck horror at the burden of his guilt. But
this man had done her a fresh wrong now. He had made her
forswear herself, so that her immortal soul was forfeit; and he
had made her put herself in the power of those Black Ones—
She shivered, drawn into herself with hatred, sucking her
aching thumb. The corners of the room filled up with darkness. They were full of black bristling things – round spiny
black balls with legs, that would presently roll out, and
stretch into tall fox-headed figures— Also there were wings
fluttering at the window.

When at last she dropped off to sleep, she was plagued
with horrible dreams – plodding over miles of desert, clutching something – what was it? a sword, a pair of shoes, a
basket, a book – whatever it was, she had to hold it tighter
and tighter, though it turned red-hot and burned her. And
behind her came the Black Ones. Once she stopped and
turned on them, and said, 'I know what you are. I made you.
Go away!' but they grinned horribly at her, and would not go
away. They came nearer, and grew larger and more hideous
... She awoke with a shriek.

The pale light of morning was coming faintly in – but
something blocked the light of the window – wings fluttered
– it was just an ultimate terror ... Then she looked again and
the terror was turned to joy. It was Jeanne, clinging to the
grating of the window.

'Oh, my darling!' she exclaimed. She thrust a finger through
the grating – there was no glass – and ruffled the peregrine's
breast feathers. Then she saw, tied to its foot like a jess, a strip

of cloth – blue cloth, such as the young Lancelot wore. Oh yes, help was on the way. She sobbed with relief.

There was nothing she could do but wait. Jeanne seemed to have no speech now, though she clicked and chuckled and made whirring noises in her throat. The hours were long in passing. The mute serving-man brought in food – Jeanne, sensing a stranger, hovered away from the window while he was there. When he was gone, Lynett shared her meat with Jeanne. The day passed.

10 · How Lynett Dealt with Bagdemagus

Then suddenly there was noise, and the smell and sound of burning. Not the encouraging smell of a household fire, but the panic smell of things that ought not to be burning. Voices shouting, heavy feet running, the grinding of metal on metal, the crash of objects falling. Lynett tried to lean out of her window and see what was going on, but her window was placed so that she could see nothing. Jeanne gave a hoarse cry, and soared up out of sight.

Somewhere in the castle was burning, and Lynett would burn with it. Was that the last malice of that man – to leave her to burn in a cage, so that her rescuers would find only her bones? She tried to pray – but how should she pray? Wasn't her soul damned already?

Then her door burst open, and there was Bagdemagus, struggling in the grasp of young Lancelot, who held him by the hair while two squires pinioned his arms.

'Have no fear, lady,' said Lancelot. 'Here is your enemy.'

He held his sword over Bagdemagus's neck.

'Shall I cut off his head, lady?' he asked her.

Bagdemagus's face was yellowish-grey, and the sweat was tracing runnels in the dust from brow to chin. His hair fell forward over his eyes; he struggled, and fell limp, and then struggled again. Great dry sobs broke from him.

'Have mercy,' he moaned. 'Oh sweet lady, have mercy. Don't tell him to kill me. Don't tell him to kill me. Have mercy. I'm sorry for all I ever did to you. Oh lady, lady, spare me.'

'No,' she said.

'I implore you – I beg you – have pity, just a little pity—'

'All you ever did to me? You did more than anyone will ever know. You blemished my body and my soul. First you took my virginity, and then you made me forswear myself and damn my own soul. I do not forgive you.'

He grovelled between his captors, sinking on the ground. He was beside himself with fear.

'You!' she said. 'You taught me boldness – and now you haven't even the courage to face death decently.'

'I am beaten, lady. I yield myself. Remember I loved you once—'

'Call that love? Your beastly appetite, that was all.'

'Boy Robin—'

'Don't you dare to call me that. All right, kill him.'

And Lancelot swung his bright sharp sword downward. It shore through everything – the man's head rolled on the ground, setting free a torrent of blood under Lynett's feet. She stood looking, spellbound. A horrible feeling came over her that she was going to be sick.

'Give me a drink of strong waters, quickly,' she muttered. One of the squires handed her a flask of aqua-vitae – she gulped a mouthful of it. It scorched her throat, but the one shock overcame the other, and the nausea passed; she drew a long breath, and leant against the wall, white and shaking.

'How is it with you, lady?' said Lancelot. 'You are not well—'

'I'm well enough,' she said in a choked voice. 'Just a fever, I think. I'll carry this head to King Arthur.'

'Come with me,' he said, and gave her his arm. He led her down through the castle, now strangely silent, only echoing here and there to slow footfalls, where they dragged the dead men away. The serving-men had made the best chamber ready for her, such as it was, and they left her quiet, on a warm soft bed – shaking, and unable to get any warmth into her body.

After three days the young Lancelot stood at her door. In his hand he held something round, black, hairy and bristling. She shrieked.

Always those round, black, hairy things – in all her dreams now. Rolling after her, or tracking her on their horrible thin legs – more of them and more of them – and now this . . .

'Take it away,' she screamed. 'For God's sake take it away . . . What is it?'

'The head of your enemy, lady,' Lancelot said in gentle tones. 'You said you would carry it to King Arthur, as is your right and privilege. We have had it cunningly embalmed – it will not stink – and it is laid up in this goatskin bag—'

She forced herself to look at it.

'Oh, is that what it is? Well, put it in some other bag. Leather, or cloth, or basket, or what you will – only – not black and hairy.' She shuddered.

'Why, with all goodwill, lady – nothing easier.' He retired, shaking his head at her fancy, and went off to find a calfskin satchel.

So later they rode away together from that castle, and Lynett carried the head on her saddlebow, in a seemly smooth calf-skin bag. And she wondered – should she not feel like Judith of old? She had avenged her virginity, and removed her King's enemy. The world was a better place without that Bagdemagus. His centre of lawlessness and crime was dispersed. King Arthur would be glad, and his dream of a better Britain, united, law-abiding, safe for honest men, was that much nearer. Her personal quest, her own long-desired revenge, was accomplished, and she ought to find it sweet. And yet – and yet she looked at the thing that hung on her saddlebow, and felt not so much like Judith as like Salome.

Oh, nonsense, she told herself. Just the disgust of seeing the thing done – no more than a squeamishness of the flesh. If these knights could kill men and sleep no worse, why should she shrink from it? And yet . . .

11 · *Of a Vision in the Forest*

They had a long journey before them, no less than the length of Britain from Northumberland to the Thames.

Mostly they went from castle to castle, and claimed hospitality as they went; but sometimes it was an anxious and weary moment towards the end of the day, when they had to hope they had not missed the way to the next castle . . . They were a smaller party now, only the knights and Lynett, for their work was accomplished for this time, and the squires and serving-men had remained behind to hold Castle Hardy till a castellan could be set there.

Yet as the summer advanced, the boughs were leafy and they rode at ease, the bare moors soon giving way to pleasant greenwoods. On warm nights they saw no reason to seek shelter under a roof, but camped in the greenwood; the knights raised a tent for Lynett. This was supported on their four lances, and the cloth of which it was made was carried in their saddlebags; in this tent they would make a narrow pallet for her, like any soldier's, and there she would sleep well enough, while they lay around the campfire outside, their heads resting on their saddles.

It was one of these calm and warm evenings, and they sat late round the campfire before sleeping. There were the four knights – Sir Bors, red-faced and slow, but infinitely reliable; Sir Gwalchmei, tall and dark and with a certain look of the great Gawain, for he was kin to the Orkney family; Sir Perceval, a strange man, straw-pale both in hair and skin, with great luminous blue eyes – it was said that his mother had brought him up in the seclusion of a forest till he was eighteen years old, without any knowledge of the world, and especially without any knowledge of women. He had been very reluctant to go on an adventure with Lynett because she was a woman, but the King had overruled his objections; and in their journeyings he had lost his fear of her, and accepted her as a sister; but he was never at his ease with the ladies in the castles. And the fourth was Lancelot, so young, so vulnerable, but always so ready with hand or sword. Long back in their journey he had ridden alone with Lynett, and from his over-burdened heart told her of his unlucky love for Guinevere. Up to now it had been no more than distant worship, but he knew its force, and what must come of it in the end.

There they sat in the flickering firelight.

'Soon we shall be back in Camelot,' said Lancelot, musing.

'And then, what shall we do?' said Gwalchmei.

'Have a good long rest, I hope,' Bors pronounced so positively that they all laughed.

'Oh, agreed, agreed!' said Lynett. 'But what after that?'

They sat silent for some time, and then Perceval spoke.

'We will go and find— It.'

'Yes,' they said one by one after him, 'we will go and find— It.'

Lynett looked from one to the other, with a sad feeling of being left out of a secret.

'What is— It?' she asked. 'May I be told?'

The four looked from one to the other, dubiously.

'May a woman be told?' said Perceval, shaking his head.

'Well, why not?' said Bors.

'Yes, why not?' said Lancelot, and brushing aside the others, went on, '*It* is the Holy Grail.'

'Ah!' sighed Lynett and bowed her head, and the rest sighed too.

'Lady,' Lancelot continued, 'we saw it once, but veiled, at Arthur's table. They say that once in seven years it is shown to men, but veiled, and then some must go in search of it to see it plainly. Once we saw it, we four. It was on Good Friday, in Camelot, as we sat round our fasting meal at the Round Table, in the Chamber of the Round Table. At noon – you remember?' He looked round at the others, who nodded as a chorus. 'First the sky was darkened like midnight, and it thundered; then from the high window above, it came on a beam of light.'

'How did it come? How did it seem?' whispered Lynett. Bors took up the tale.

'It was as if a cup or a chalice was covered with a veil – none carried it, it moved down of itself—'

'No,' said Gwalchmei, 'there was a hand that carried it. I saw the hand.'

'Not so neither,' broke in Perceval. 'There was a damosel carried it, but veiled, heavily veiled from head to foot – not even her hands could be seen.'

'But when it was amongst us, we were – how were we then, Perceval?'

'We were blessed,' said Perceval simply, staring before him with his pale eyes.

'We were – oh, it was like this,' Bors went on, almost stammering in his eagerness. 'It was as if the dry bread and salt fish and the water in our cups was turned into the food we liked best in the world. Oh, it wasn't that really, but the same pleasure as if it were ... Oh, long ago, when I was a child, and had had a fever, and had tasted no meat for days, when I was recovered my mother cooked me a dish, and it was the best thing I had ever eaten in my life – a roast chicken with herbs – it was like that. Was it not?' and he looked round at the others.

'For me,' said Perceval, 'it was like peaches warmed in the sun, that angels might eat in Paradise when man was not yet fallen.'

'For me,' said Gwalchmei, 'Yes, it was like I remember once when I was hunting with my father, and we were starving hungry, and he cooked a deer over a campfire and we ate it

in haste – so hungry we were. The food one had longed for
. . . And what to you, Lancelot?'

Lancelot's face was red in the firelight.

'I cannot say,' he said. 'I think the bread and fish were still
bread and fish, but I tasted nothing, for – my lady was there.'
Then he sunk his head on his knees.

'They say,' Bors went on, 'that it can cure every sickness,
and every grief, if a man seeks it truly and finds it. We all
saw its veiled shape, for a moment, and felt its blessing; and
then it was gone. We would have departed that moment to
seek it – though God alone knows which way we should have
gone – but Arthur forbade it, saying the time was not yet
come.'

'But when we return,' said Lynett, 'might it be the time?'

'God only knows the time,' said Perceval.

She thought deeply, staring into the crackling fire, and then
said, 'Might a woman go in search of the Grail?'

They all looked up, startled at the idea.

'Surely,' said Lancelot.

'A woman – never!' exclaimed Perceval.

'Why not?' said Bors.

'Perhaps if she were a virgin—' said Gwalchmei, and then
seeing Lynett's face redden, 'Oh, pardon, lady. I only meant –
you are, of course, a married lady, the wife of Sir Gaheris. I
meant no disrespect.'

—But he doesn't know, thought Lynett unhappily.

They sat in silence, then suddenly across the soft forest
rustlings came the sound of a bell, struck once. A clear silver
bell – it came again, not tinkling, but sounding slow and
regular, sweet as crystal. And with it there came to their
nostrils the smell of incense, true holy incense of myrrh and
galbanum. And far away from where they sat, between the
trees, along some unknown pathway, a light glowed.

They sprang to their feet and stood gazing out between the
dark tree trunks. The light grew – and at last there came in

sight an awesome procession, lit with its own strange gleam, and singing as it came.

First came slowly pacing a noble white hart – taller than a red deer, and spotless white, with his great spread of horns held proudly aloft, and between the horns as it were a carven crucifix, from which a white light radiated. Then behind the white hart came six maidens all in white, veiled so that their faces could not be seen, but with golden circlets over their veils – they moved with bowed heads, and sang softly. Then came thurifers and acolytes and priests, all in their due vestments, but with their faces hidden in white hoods. Then four tall men, walking side by side, each of which carried some sacred thing covered with a rich cloth, so that none could see what it was. And then behind them, guarded by four young boys, came slowly pacing a damosel, whose soft white veil fell over her, wrought with golden flowers, and covered the thing she carried, preciously in both hands. The veil covered it as it covered her, but from that hidden thing a light rayed out, a light that was every colour, and whose colours were so pure that they carried bliss to the eyes and the heart.

The five watchers fell on their knees while the procession went by. The silver bell sounded, slow and sweet; the soft voices chanted; the incense drifted across in blue clouds. And then at last all was gone, and there was nothing but the quiet forest.

Of the five, not one could speak a word, nor look at one another. They turned away and with one accord lay down to sleep.

12 · Of a Glamour and a Trial

They continued on their way, through the dense forests and then again through open downlands. There came a day when they had set out cheerfully enough in the morning – a fine day in the late summer – and yet about noon as they stopped and dismounted and sat on a green bank together to eat their luncheon, they looked up and found mist all round them. A gentle mist at first, and then a dense white fog – a white blindness, where all sense of direction was lost. They mounted their horses and rode slowly on, watching the edges of the road. But after a time this direction failed them. The dark came down.

'We can't go on in this,' said Lancelot.

'If we've followed the road, we should be nearing a castle now,' said Gwalchmei.

'There should be a light – yes, look—'

The fog seemed to lift a little, and far off a small point of light appeared.

'Could it be the castle? No, look, it's moving—'

'A man with a lantern!' cried Perceval, 'Come on, he'll guide us—'

'No, no!' Lynett cried, and clutched his arm. 'Not a man with a lantern! Don't you see – it's *the* Man with the Lantern—'

'The *ignis fatuus*. God shield us!' the knights muttered, and crossed themselves. Far off, three, four, five points of light danced and jumped in the dark distance.

'What can we do?' They gathered together. 'We can't go on in this – God knows what sloughs and quagmires are round us. This is evil country.'

In the end they could do nothing but stay where they were, crouched on the ground in the close circle made by their horses, all the cold, damp, miserable night. They drank what they had in their flasks, and ate hard bread – they had endured hardships together before this. But when the daylight

came there was still no break in the fog, and they were
perished with cold and had no more provisions. They tried to
move on step by step, but every direction was unsafe, and no
trace of road could be found.

Darkness fell again, and they were all exhausted, weary,
famished. The horses cropped the scanty grass of the waste-
land, but they shivered also. It was no summer mist – it was
bleak, chilly, penetrating. And another night of this misery
lay before them.

Then, strangely, as the light dimmed, the mist seemed to
clear, and to their surprise they found they were not on the
bare plain, but in a wood – a clear high wood of arching trees.
It seemed they must have strayed into it as they moved in the
fog. There was a wide, well-marked path before them through
the wood, and walking along it, away from them, were three
women.

'Why, this must be the way!' exclaimed Lynett, and they all
mounted their horses and went on at a footpace into the
wood, endeavouring to overtake the three women. But fast as
they went (short of breaking into a trot, which they felt
unwilling to do) the three still kept ahead of them.

There seemed to be more light between the trees; the fog
had receded. Coming closer behind the three women now
(who heeded no calls) they could see them a little more
plainly. All were in undistinguishable black robes, but their
heads were unveiled. The one on the left had jet-black hair
flowing almost to her feet; she in the middle had florid yellow
curls, dressed high and sumptuously on her head; and she on
the right had golden-red hair that floated around her. They
seemed to come to a place where their ways divided – the
black and the golden one went on towards the left, but the
redhead parted from them and went to the right. And there,
coming down to meet her with the light on his face, was
Merlin.

Lynett cried out.

'Oh, there's Merlin! This *must* be the right road – come on!'
and urged her horse that way. But somehow she could not

pass. There seemed to be an invisible barrier that thrust her back to the other path, and ahead of her, Merlin and the red-haired woman were suddenly gone. She looked back, and the fair-haired one was gone also – there remained only the dark-haired one, and she had turned to face them, and behind her was a fair and stately house, with lights glowing in every window.

A grand place it seemed – no fortified castle, but a palace, with broad steps leading up to a wide open door. The dark-haired woman was smiling, with outstretched arms.

'Come in, come in, all of you,' she exclaimed. 'Be welcome, weary travellers.'

Serving-men were suddenly there to take their horses as they dismounted; they passed up the steps, and through the doors into the light and warmth. Music of harps came out to meet them, and perfume, and even more welcome, the smell of good meats roasting. A noble hall, its floor tiled in bright patterns and strewn with scented herbs; long tables laid, and bright cressets burning against burnished shields all along richly draped walls. All was welcome and comfort. Fair pages and gentle maids led them away to exchange their worn garments for rich and easy robes; then they found themselves seated at the table and feasting royally. One and all, the knights and Lynett too, gave themselves up unquestioning to the heavenly comfort, sank into it with nothing but thankfulness.

Then the handsome dark-haired lady took Lynett by the hand and led her away to her bower. From the stately style of the hall, Lynett expected a rich enough chamber – tapestries on the walls, perhaps, and a table covered with a carpet – but not this. Here were carpets richly piled on the floor, so that one's feet made no noise, and silken cushions lying in heaps. Above, from a carved and painted ceiling, a lamp of many-coloured glass diffused a soft light. From every corner of the little room, fantastic images looked down, and jewelled pendants glittered. Lynett had heard of such rooms, in palaces among the Saracens and Paynims, but never thought to see one.

The black-haired lady sat down upon a pile of cushions, and beckoned Lynett to do the same; then she poured her a cup of sweet wine.

'My dear,' she said, 'we are not strangers. I met you at your wedding, don't you remember? I and my two sisters—'

Lynett stammered some uncomprehending words.

'Yes,' the lady went on, 'I am your aunt by marriage. Queen Morgause of Orkney, your bridegroom's mother, is my sister – the third of us is Vivian, who is betrothed to Merlin. But King Arthur is also our mother's son. So we are all kinsfolk.' She smiled and drew Lynett closer to her.

'Oh, I know, child, you have no joy of your marriage. There's little I don't know ... And so you have become messenger to my brother Arthur? – Oh, but he is making a great mistake, this Arthur. He intends to make himself king over all this land. And I do not intend that he should ... Oh, you may look surprised. You will of course not understand why he should not. You think him a great king and a good king – but there are things you don't know, things you can't understand ... Listen now. What does this Arthur give you for the hard service you do for him?'

'Give me?' said Lynett, staring rather stupidly.

'Yes – every servant deserves his wage. What do you get in his service?'

'Get? Why, I had never thought ... Why, I'm like one of his knights. What should we get? He gives us armour, and he gave me clothing, and one of his own great horses—'

'Nothing more? Even knights must eat.'

'Oh, we have *bouche de court* when we're there – and he gives me enough gold pieces to pay for lodgings on the road when I need them – oh, and he gave me this beautiful ring—'

'In other words, you serve him for bare board and lodging? Why, child, that's a villein's fee! He should do better for you than that!'

Lynett's face reddened. 'We his knights – I – I mean, I don't want for anything. Why should I desire anything more?'

'Oh, you're simple!' The lady smiled. 'Why, child – those other knights, each has his manor, his own house and his lands to which he can return when his errand is over. But what have you? Your house in Lyonesse is not your own, now your sister is married and dwells there with Gareth. Your Gaheris has made no provision for you since you left him. What home have you to return to, when your errantry is over? What has this Arthur given you? Had you thought of that?'

'I hadn't thought of that,' said Lynett, her eyes downcast.

'Now I,' said the lady, 'I could do better for you than this. I also need a messenger. I would reward you well, with gold and houses and lands.'

'I could not leave my service with the King.'

'You need not. All I should ask is that you continue as you are, but carry a message from me also from time to time, and send word back to me of where you are, and where the king is going to send you.'

Lynett looked up inquiringly, a long straight look.

'And that you change your mind a little about certain things.'

'No,' said Lynett.

'Ah, but think— Not, perhaps, a palace like this, though I could give you that if you really wanted it – but a comfortable moated grange, with orchards and beehives and dairies, and the rich fields around it, and a lovely little garden of herbs – like your old home in Lyonesse.'

'No, no, no !' said Lynett, and thrust her fist into the soft cushion before her.

'No? Oh well, perhaps not. But another offer – Why not go home? – oh yes, give Arthur due notice, that having done this errand, you work for him no more – say you have had enough of roaming. Go home to Lyonesse, where your sister lives with Gareth. She is with child, and – a man's fancy sometimes strays at such times. I will promise you, if you will pledge yourself to me, that he, your Gareth, will turn to you—'

A sudden fierce longing gripped Lynett's heart, and she averted her face. The lady could hear the sharp intake of breath.

'Oh yes, I know, that would be your heart's desire. I will promise you this, without fail. You will have nothing to do but to be there, and remember me and what I shall tell you. And there will be his son, and you will teach him what I shall tell you as he grows up. It would be easy enough for you – why should you not go home?'

'No again,' said Lynett, but this time her hands were gripped tightly together.

'I am sorry then,' said the lady, frowning, 'for I cannot be your friend as I should have wished. Promise me one thing, though – that you will never forgive this Bagdemagus, though he is dead.'

'Oh, I can promise you that!' she exclaimed, looking up and meeting those hot dark eyes.

'That's right. Never, never for your own honour and the dignity of your womanhood. Never, never forgive him!'

'That I never will!'

'Then there is one point on which we can shake hands,' and the dark woman stretched out her hand to take Lynett's. Lynett clasped her hand, and at once the dark woman seized her hand and pulled it, so that Lynett fell forward on the carpet – but it was no longer a carpet, but hard, gritty ground, and Lynett was being dragged over it, roughly, by someone gripping her hand – the rocks raked her body and her knees – another hand pulled her hair—'

Gone was the coloured bower and the lady. There was only a barren plain, in a pale clouded light, and two rough men in the livery of Bagdemagus were dragging Lynett along the ground. She shrieked and struggled.

'Now we've got you,' said one of the men. 'A fine body-guard you have, all fast asleep. We've not left much of them.'

As she twisted her head, struggling, she could glimpse dark forms, flung down – dead horses or dead men.

'You had your vengeance of Bagdemagus, our chief,' said the other man, 'and now we'll have our vengeance on you.'

'And so will King Arthur avenge me,' she spat back at them.

'So? And then we'll take vengeance on King Arthur, and so it goes merrily on.'

She spoke no more while they hauled her up, flung her over a saddle, and carried her away. The prison where they left her at last was far underground and pitch dark.

13 · Of the Terrible Head

As she lay in the darkness, on filthy straw, a man thrust open the heavy creaking door, and came in bearing a torch. It was one of Bagdemagus's followers, a rough, bearded, uncouth man as they all were, clad in the coarse russet that was his livery. He carried something with him.

'Here, you scolding hellcat,' he said. 'You can have some company. Here's our Chief's head, that your leman cut off at your orders – you can have it with you to think about. Scold it if you want to – *he* won't hear you.' And holding the torch up with his left hand, he hung on a nail in the stony wall opposite her the calfskin bag whose contents she knew only too well. 'There. Now you can contemplate that, my lady, while we take our time, and decide what we shall do with you. It won't be quick or easy, you can be sure.' And he went out, clanking the great door to, and shutting out the light of even his smoky torch.

There in the dark she sat, knowing nothing, but that *that* horrible thing was there on the wall above her, to set the seal on all the other horrors of darkness . . .

Then presently a faint and repulsive light began to glow

from the bag where that head was – a pale glow like rotting fungus in a tree-stump, or decaying fish in a dark cellar. Her hair rose, and a deadly coldness gripped her. The horrible light grew and grew – and then she seemed to see the dead face through all the leather and wrappings – it was plain to see, and it grew and grew, larger and larger till it loomed over her, covered the vault above her, filled the whole cell – She shrieked, but there was none to hear her. For a moment her brain was numbed, almost in a swoon. Then slowly the terrible face receded, shrank again, down and down, till it was not much more than lifesize. And now it hovered on the wall before her, and was no longer a vast Sphinx, but Bagdemagus's face, dead and ghastly. But in its ghastliness there was a terrible grief. Not only the collapse of decay, but that the whole face drooped. The brows drooped, the eyelids were pressed together – the nostrils were pinched, the lips pressed together also, the corners of the mouth dragged down in a dolorous curve – It was like the face on a crucifix.

Then those compressed eyelids opened a glimmering crack, and the thin lips parted, and the head spoke, hoarsely and quavering.

'Forgive me.'

She gave a cry, clasping her hands to her breast.

The head spoke again.

'Forgive me ... For God's sake ... Lynett ... grant me pardon and let me go.'

She answered, speaking in a whisper.

'How can you speak to me? Where are you? Are you in Hell?'

'I do not know,' replied the spectral head. 'I do not know if this is Hell. But I know that I suffer, and I know this is not Purgatory, for in Purgatory there is hope, and here there is none. In Purgatory there is progress, and there is no progress, no going on for me. Oh, that I could enter into Purgatory and begin my purgation! But I cannot, till you forgive me.'

'You pleaded with me before, and I said no,' she replied. 'Why do you think I should forgive you now?'

'I pleaded with you then, because I was in fear of death. But now I am dead, and things are different. I see now what I could not see before, and I ask your forgiveness because I am sorry for what I did.'

She sat silent.

He went on.

'I understand so many things differently, after being dead for a few days – or is it a few months, or a few years? It's hard to tell.

'But now I know what I did. The thing that I never understood was your innocence. How could I, when I had never met that kind of innocence before? A plain touch-me-not chastity like your sister's, I could understand – but your frank friendship, with no thoughts of evil – that was strange to me. I mistook it for bold wanton invitation. It never crossed my mind that you had no thought of lust. I had never met a girl like you before, and I truly thought that your desire was like my own. And so, in my stupidity, I destroyed that innocence. It's true that I loved you, in my way, but I did not know what it was I loved, and I trampled on it. And now I know what it was I did – and I weep for it.'

'Is this true?' she said softly and breathlessly.

'In the name of God, before Whom I stand,' he said, 'it is true. We who are dead can no longer dissemble.'

And tears, difficult reluctant tears, forced themselves between the tightened eyelids, and spilled slowly down the furrowed cheeks.

Answering tears sprang into Lynett's eyes, and something seemed to break from round her heart.

'Oh, you poor man,' she whispered.

'Forgive me – now?'

'I forgive you,' she said.

'Give me a sign. Kiss me on the brow. Come, do not be afraid of me. I have no body now to harm you.'

Quivering, and with her teeth clenched against the horror, she took two steps across the cell, and reached up, and kissed that livid, gleaming brow. It was colder than stone.

At once the ghastly face relaxed, and Lynett felt her whole body relax also. A strange kind of warmth came over her, and for a moment she felt an inexplicable sensation of light and relief.

'Thank you,' the dead face said, and the eyes opened, and were lucid and mild. 'And thank God – oh, thank God! Now I can go. Leave me here when you escape.'

'When I escape? But how, and when?'

'Quite soon – now. I will help you. Get ready—'

Footsteps were approaching along the stony corridor outside. The door creaked as the guard unlocked it and pushed it open. He carried a pewter platter with food – but at the moment when he opened the door, the head shone out with a livid blue light, tinged with green, the lips drawn back in a gleaming grin. The man dropped the platter, and staggered – Lynett snatched the platter up, and brought the edge of it with a swinging blow against the man's head. He went down like a log. The door was open behind him.

Lynett could hear a totally unexpected sound – the head was laughing.

'Oh, well done, Boy Robin! Go on now, go on—'

And she slipped through the door, and was out into the inky-black tunnel beyond.

14 · Of a Dweller in Darkness

She ran on into the darkness. There were two ways only, up and down, and she ran down, with some dim feeling that her captors must be above, and therefore downwards must be away from them. There was no gleam of light – she just ran on blindly, feeling her way along the walls of the narrow passage. Yet somehow, in that terrifying darkness, for the moment she was upheld by a strange unreasoning euphoria. Not only that she was out of her prison, and had a chance to escape – but from the minute she had forgiven Bagdemagus, she had a sense of being set free. She knew that those black bogies were gone – the round bristling things with the running legs and the hidden teeth – gone, and never would return. Though she might be walking into death, she rejoiced. Neither would that dream come again, of trudging through the wilderness clutching a burden, clutching, clutching— Whatever it was, she had let it go. Now she had nothing in her hands at all, and walked with them outstretched, touching the sides of the passage. But the passage went on and on, down and down, and the glow of rejoicing died away. Now she was cold, and trembling in the dark. Deeper and deeper. Where would this dark way lead her? Should she turn back? But no, that way she would walk into the hands of her enemies. Death either way. No longer running, she groped her way along. She was afraid even to stand still.

Presently she began to hear the rushing of water. Carefully now. She felt every step before her, holding to the sides of the passage, which was becoming more irregular and broken. Then suddenly there was no hand-hold either to right or left of her, and in front of her was the deep roar of a torrent. Left without her support, she lost her balance, fell, and plunged into icy, rapid water.

Drowning in the dark, she struggled helplessly. She came to the surface, gulped a breath of air, and felt something gash her head as she came up – not stunning her but cutting her cruelly. She went down again, the water tearing in through her gullet and her nose – death clutching her—

Then she was seized from beneath and carried upwards – her mouth reached the surface and she could breathe, but a hand was over her head, covering her forehead, eyes and nose, keeping her from lifting her head further. A voice said close to her ear, above the rush of the water, 'Keep quite still. You are safe with me, but you are in more danger than you know. The roof of the cavern is scarcely a handsbreadth above your face.'

A man was supporting her in the water – she was lying

supine over his breast; his right arm was firmly round her, and his left hand was protecting her face. So much she could feel, also that he seemed to be naked in the water. She lay still, though trembling, and it seemed to her, very strangely, that she felt no revulsion or fear at so close a contact with this man's body. Rather did she feel confidence and safety, even in that terrifying dark water and under that menacing roof of cruel rocks.

He spoke again.

'Now take a deep breath and hold it while you count fifty. We are going under the water.'

Obediently she did so, and they went down into the dark again. She could not count fifty – she had no wits to count at all. But suddenly they were up in the breathable air again, and she heard him say 'Fifty'. But still there was no light.

Then there was gravel under them, and he picked her up and carried her, and laid her, as far as she could feel, on a sandy beach. But still all in pitch dark. She lay a long time just breathing, trying to gather a little strength. Perhaps she even slept. There was no difference between eyes open and eyes shut.

'Are you a little recovered?' the unknown man said. His voice was very gentle and musical. 'That is a dangerous way – nobody knows it but I. How did you come to be there?'

'I was escaping from enemies,' she said.

'Ah, yes, of course. What else?'

He was moving about in the dark.

'Rest here,' he said. 'I will go and get fire for you.' She heard his steps go a little way off, and a sound of stones and pebbles being disturbed; then, to her astonishment, a spark of light, as the unknown man struck flint on steel, and brought up a little flame – a small fire of dry sticks grew up, and for the first time for a very long while, Lynett could see.

She was in a vast cavern, so vast that she could not make out its limits at all; she could only see that where she was lying was a beach of sand and stones, on the edge of a dark expanse of water. All the rest was lost in the darkness. Her rescuer, who was crouched over the little fire, was a tall young man, finely proportioned, but with a strange pale skin and a mane of ash-coloured hair. He was naked, except for a leather loincloth which he seemed to wear more as a shield than a garment. As he turned from the fire, she saw his face, and it was as beautiful a face as she had ever seen.

'Come to the fire,' he said, without looking up.

There was something strange about the way he was handling the fire. He carefully felt each twig, and then pushed it forward by one end; then his hands hovered round and over the flames, always at a certain distance, as if they felt for an exact degree of heat. He ringed the fire carefully with a little bank of sand, so that it could not spread. He seemed to have a cache of firewood, flint and steel, and other things, in a corner under some rocks.

The fire burned up and made a comforting glow. Lynett was dreadfully cold, and her garments dripped and weighed her down.

'Now,' said her rescuer. 'You must take off your clothes, and dry them at the fire. Oh—' as he caught the sound of her protesting gasp, 'don't be afraid of me. I am quite blind.'

15 · How Lynett was Brought Back to Light

The strange blind man had a flask of some rare cordial, which he fetched from a crevice in the rocks – moving unerringly there, guided by his feet and hands, and some inexplicable sixth sense. The cordial was rich and creamy, and wonderfully reviving – food as well as drink; and Lynett, crouched naked over the fire, and still a little self-conscious in spite of the young man's assurance, began to feel a little better. He talked to her, in rather uneasy halting sentences, as if unused to talking much.

'I am called Lucius,' he said.

'Lucius? – That means— Of the Light?'

'Yes, although I have long lived here in the dark. My mother named me Lucius when we first – came into the dark. She named me for the light she hoped we would both see again.' He sighed and paused, and then went on. 'I was not born in the dark. I think I once had another name. I can remember when I could see, and I can remember when we had light. I don't know how old I was. There was a wicked man, somewhere up there—' and he waved his hand uncertainly upwards, 'who shut up my mother and myself, because she would not yield to him. A long, long time we were shut up in darkness.'

'Was his name Bagdemagus?' asked Lynett.

'Oh no – this much I do remember. His name was Breuse Saunce Pitié.'

Lynett sighed with relief. To have to un-forgive Bagdemagus again was a thing she could not have borne.

He continued.

'He proved himself without pity to myself and my beautiful mother. A long, long time we were there in the dark – until what with the dark and what with famine, my sight faded, and my mother died.'

'Oh, dear God!' exclaimed Lynett. 'And how long was this?'

'I do not know. We had no means of knowing, down there, how the days, weeks, months, years passed. I know my mother kept some kind of reckoning, scratched on the stones of our prison; but I did not know how to read it, even when they let us have a rushlight, as they did at first. I only know I grew. And when I found she was dead, I escaped down the dark passages, for the jailers left the door open thinking that I must be dead too – so I fled down the dark passages, being then completely blind as I am now, and found my way into a world of caves and tunnels and streams. I learnt to fend for myself and make my way in the dark. Here I have no need of eyes, for I can feel, and hear, and smell, and – well, I can feel without touching. I did not, of course, come by way of the rushing water, or I never would have lived. There are other ways. And I learnt that way later. I know all the ways now. But in the end I found my way to the end of the caves, and there I found my nurse.'

'Your – nurse?'

'Yes, my nurse is a good woman. I will take you to her very soon, and she will look after you as she has looked after me. She lives between the dark and the light. She brought me out into the light, and let the sunshine strengthen me. I can feel it though I never see it – and I sit in my nurse's garden and smell the flowers, and hear the birds, and feel the butterflies alight on my hands. But I do not go much into the lighted world. It is – difficult for me. Here in the dark I know everything, and it is my own; but out in the light world, once I am beyond my nurse's garden, there are strange people, and dogs and other beasts and I find them – difficult. But here – here's my kingdom.'

He laughed, and stood upright, and launched himself into a leaping run, into the dark, at the same time giving a shrill whistle, and seeming to guide himself by the echo, like a bat. He vanished into the depths, and then came back and seated himself beside her.

'But come now – if you are rested and your clothes are a little dry, I will take you to my nurse.'

'What is your nurse's name?'

'She says she has no name, but is just to be called the Servant of the White One; but some call her White, or Candida; others say she is the Witch of the Cave, but I know she is no witch. Others call her Sibylla. To me, she is my nurse.'

Lynett got herself painfully into her partly-dried clothes – sticky leather and sodden wool – and followed the blind man.

'You had better have a torch,' he said, giving her a stick dipped in tar, from a sheaf of them which he kept in his hoard. 'I keep a few here, in case my nurse comes to visit me. She needs to see, just as you do.' He lit the torch at the fire, then put away his things in marked places under stones, and carefully extinguished the fire with sand. Then he took up a

long thin wand, and swung it before him, but not gropingly –
he was indeed, as he said, at home in his dark kingdom.
Lynett's little torch showed her his fine, lithe figure stepping
out before her, and dimly lit up the bewildering arches and
tunnels through which he led her.

After many long wanderings, he stopped and held up his
hand.

'We must stop here,' he said. 'Look where I shall point.
There is the shrine of the White One, whom my nurse serves.
There is her image. They say she has a strange beauty.'

Lynett held up her torch in the direction where he pointed.
Then she screamed – for what she saw was horrible and
obscene.

A vast stalagmite had formed itself, perhaps aided by
men's hands, into the shape of a woman – 'naked like a beast'
was the thought that occurred to Lynett. A naked woman,
but with no beauty to clothe her nakedness. The breasts and
genitals were grossly, crudely exaggerated. The woman was
old, flesh-fallen, hideous. The face, if there were face at all,
was turned away. The lewd, sagging shape gleamed ghostly
in the torchlight.

'Oh, but it's hideous!' Lynett cried. The blind man turned
to her, his pale sightless eyes reproachful.

'Do not say so. I have never felt her shape, for she may not
be touched by anyone – but my nurse has told me. This is the
Mother of All. She has many shapes, and this is how the
people of old saw her. Her woman-parts are shown, that other
women keep hidden, because it is for that we honour her. She
gave birth to us all, and still gives birth, and she nourishes us
all from her breasts. And she is old, because she *is* old – from
the Beginning, next to the Father. She keeps us all in life,
under the Father's power.'

In the stillness it seemed that he could feel the shudder that
Lynett gave.

'You must not be afraid of her. My nurse has told me much
about her. She has many faces, they say, and I shall never see

any of them – but they say that her voice and her touch, when she manifests herself, are sweet and gentle.'

Round the foot of the figure was a ring of flat stones, and on those stones, Lynett saw, were little offerings – small bunches of flowers, some withered, some fresh; milk and honey in earthenware saucers, a few flat cakes of bread, a handful of sweet berries. The blind man, as he passed, raised his fingers to his lips. throwing a kiss to the image. But Lynett turned her head aside, and covertly crossed herself.

As he led her further, round an angle of rock, to Lynett's surprise she saw a gleam of light ahead of them. It seemed to come nearer, and she realized they were reaching the exit from the caves. They came out through an archway into a deep gully, with the sky far overhead. It was a long time since Lynett had seen the daylight. Blinking in the dazzle, she put out her torch; the blind man went on, swinging his wand before him, making no difference.

A rough arch, possibly made by man out of huge stones, spanned the gully; they emerged from it into warm sunshine, birdsong and the humming of bees.

This was a deep gorge, but wide enough to let in the sun; the sides were thickly grown with brambles and ferns, and with small bushes and patches of grass. And here, built into the hillside with the rock for its back wall, was a small hut, part of stone, part of wood and thatch, with smoke going up through a smoke-hole, and a little garden round it. Vegetables stood in neat rows, an apple tree showed its early fruit, the flowers of summer glowed in the borders, and three straw-thatched beehives vibrated to the humming of the bees; somewhere behind the apple tree, hens clucked.

A woman came out of the cottage.

'Are you there, my son?' she called in a pleasant voice. 'Oh, but who is this you have brought with you?'

She was a tall woman, and extraordinarily graceful; a long flowing robe of fine white linen clothed her from head to foot. It folded smoothly round the pure oval of her face, and fell to her brown bare feet. Her face was sunburnt brown, and worked all over with small wrinkles – but these wrinkles were a fine network, not marring the smooth lines of the face, but running over all, like the crackles in some kinds of pottery. Her mouth was generous, wide lips opening over perfect teeth, and her eyes, deep-set, were large and light blue. Without doubt she had once been a beautiful woman, and was still a handsome one, but remote and withdrawn. She moved and spoke quietly and without haste.

The blind man answered, 'Nurse, I found her in the cave. She is a gentlewoman, and she is fleeing from an enemy, just as I was. Nurse, we must take her in.'

'Why, of course we must,' said the woman in the white robe. 'Come, my dear.'

16 · Of the Sibyl, and That Which She Served

So Lynett found herself sheltered and tended in the little cottage of the Sibyl, that some called the Witch of the Cave. Quiet nights followed quiet days. There seemed to be no hurry. Indeed, Lynett was worn out with all she had gone through, and needed to be fed and warmed and rested.

Sitting at the door of the cottage, where the sunshine gathered between the high walls of the gorge, Lynett asked the Sibyl her history.

'I was a country wife like other country wives,' the Sibyl said, 'only perhaps that I knew a little more, and cared to learn a little more, than my neighbours, about plants and herbs, and the seasons, and the sun, moon and stars. Also sometimes I had glimpses of something – of that which men call the Sight. Not a comfortable gift, and let you pray that you never have it. I was married fifteen years ago, but never had a child; and then my husband died, and I was left alone. Soon after this, a woman came one day to my door, looked at me, and said, "You are she." So then I had to leave everything, and come here. For I was she.'

'I do not understand,' said Lynett.

'I was the one chosen to be the Servant of the White One. There has always been a woman here who tends the shrine within the cave, and keeps the words and the secrets, and never lets the power of the White One be forgotten. She must guard the Old Wisdom, and remember it. People come here for help, in sickness or in perplexity, and the Servant of the White One must help them.

'The old Sibyl brought me here, and showed me the holy figure of the White Lady, and gave me the secret words, and other secrets – and then she lay down in front of the holy image, and folded her hands, and died. I laid her to rest in the same little cave where the bones of her predecessors are laid, and built up the wall again. Some day I shall know the time, and I shall go in search of the next Sibyl, and then I shall do as she did.'

There was silence between them for some minutes. Then Lynett broke the silence.

'And Lucius—?'

'Ah, Lucius. One day, just so suddenly, he crawled out of the cave like a lost wild animal – dirty, hairy, starved so that his bones nearly broke through his skin – running on all fours, staring with his great pale eyes, but never blinking, so I knew at once that he was blind. How old was he? God knows – possibly seven or eight – hard to tell. He told me how he and his mother had been imprisoned in the darkness by some accursed ruffian, till he had gone blind and she had died. To think a man could do such things, dear God ... How long had they been imprisoned for? Again, hard to tell, for in the dark one loses count of days and nights. But she had taught him gentle ways – may the Mother cherish her soul! – he knew the manners of a Christian, and he remembered old hymns and prayers, and stories and songs wherewith she had beguiled the time. After he had found the poor lady dead, and escaped somehow – no one knows how – from his prison,

into the world of the caves, he lived somehow in the dark –
God alone knows how. Perhaps the gnomes of the caves
helped him – there are such beings, and I have seen them. But
he learnt to run about those caves like a bat, and swim in the
dark waters too, and never feels the need of eyes when he is
down there in the dark. He can walk in the sunlight with his
staff, and I see to it that he does so, but it's strange to him. In
the dark he is at home, and he feels his way, I think, as the
bats do, by the echoes.'

She broke off, as Lucius came up to the little garden, and
put his arms round her.

'Here, Nurse,' he said, 'I've been walking in the lanes – see
what I have found for you! How sweet they smell,' and he
put into her hand a sheaf of bluebells and pink campions.
'And here's some for you,' and he laid another bunch on
Lynett's lap. 'Blue and pink, they must be. I can remember
blue and pink.' He fingered the flowers delicately. Lynett felt
the tears spring to her eyes.

So the days passed, in the Sibyl's cottage. May ran on into
June and July, and the little apples grew big on the apple tree.

Sometimes people would come and consult the Sibyl –
country people from the villages and farms, mostly women.
They would whisper with her on the bench outside the
cottage. Some would bring small gifts of farm produce, or
little bunches of flowers, but many brought nothing, and
Lynett never saw anyone bring money. The Sibyl would
sometimes give a bunch of herbs, or a flask of cordial, or a
box of salve, and always with a blessing. One day Lynett
heard her voice raised.

'No,' she was saying, 'no and no again. If that is what you
want, go elsewhere. I serve the Mother of life, not of death.'

Lynett spent much time with Lucius. Sitting under the apple
tree in the warm sunshine, she contemplated him, as he
stretched out on the dry grass. He was a tall man and well
shaped; his skin was sun tanned, for he seldom wore much

clothing, but under the tan was the peculiar opaque pallor found in men who have been long in prison, so that he seemed as if made of old ivory. His big blank eyes were bright, and so clear that one could hardly believe there was no sight in them; they followed the direction of what he heard, as if indeed he could see.

A strange man, and she felt strangely towards him. Not like any other man she had met. All those knights, of whom she had met so many, and to whom she was a sister and a comrade-in-arms – they were for the most part thick-limbed, red-faced, hairy, muscle-bound in their carapaces of leather and metal. Apart from them there were priests, pale soft creatures as a rule, anaemic from much fasting, or dried up and acid. Or there were hermits, lean and ancient, remote and holy, not unlike the Sibyl. And there were farmers and villeins – but this man, this Lucius, was not like any of these. She thought of other men she had cared for – her father, and King Arthur, and yes, even Bagdemagus before he had wronged her, and as she had first imagined him to be, and could bear to think of him now. She had not felt for any of them as she felt for Lucius. They had been leaders; but Lucius was one whom she longed to protect. Gareth? – ah, the beloved gentle Gareth – but he had exasperated her by his persistent meek-ness – raised a devil of contradiction in her, that moved her to try him and bait him to see if she could get a reaction out of him – no, he was not like Gareth. Yet, although she desired to protect him, she could not forget how he had held her life in his hands, down there in the awesome underground torrent. He was no weakling, no child. He was the master in his own element.

Sometimes he would take her for walks on dark nights through the woods, striding on before her, swinging his wand when she could hardly grope her way through the dark coverts. He would stop and interpret for her every rustle, every scent in the darkness. 'Moles at work there – they turn up the fresh soil . . . Fox away out to the left – oh, a long way

out – gone to meet his vixen . . . that's a robin on the branch
. . . owl in the pasture, yes, he's caught something . . . the
hay's been cut in the valley . . .'

There was one night when, to her terror, a dark furry mass
came rolling out of a hollow – 'Stand still,' he said, 'it's only a
bear.' The creature rumbled throatily, and Lucius made its
own rumbling sounds back at it. 'All's well, oldfellow. You
know me. We're friends. Go your way, and goodnight to you.'
And the bear turned its back on them and lurched away into
the bushes.

She thought of all this, as he lay stretched out at her feet.
He got up and came closer to her.

'Will you let me feel your face?' he said.

'Why, yes,' she said, and sat still while he ran his finger
delicately over every inch of her face. A quite inexplicable
thrill wakened in her body at that touch.

'Oh,' he exclaimed, 'I think you must be beautiful.'

'I'm not,' she said. 'I'm ugly – I always have been ugly. My
colour is pale and yellowish, my hair is black as night and
straight as candles, my lips are thin and have no redness,
there's no beauty about me at all.'

'But my hands tell me you are beautiful,' he persisted. 'I
know. I know. I wish I could see you – but what's this? You're
crying.'

Sitting by the small fire in the cottage, on a rainy summer
afternoon, the Sibyl drew the long thread from her spindle.
Lucius was away by himself in the caves. Lynett sat by, with
her hands idle, she had no skill in spinning.

'Child,' said the Sibyl, 'something troubles you.'

Lynett hesitated, and then, breaking the silence with a rush,
she said, 'Mother Sibyl – tell me this – why did you tell that
poor boy that the – the White One in the cave was beautiful?
She's foul and frightful.'

The Sibyl thought for a long time before replying – Lynett
was afraid she had given her offence, but for her life she

could not have said otherwise. Presently, after looking long into the fire, the Sibyl said, 'You must understand this. There are many ways of seeing the White One. Lucius must not ever see her with his eyes, because he is a man, and no man may see her and live. That is the law. But I have taught him to see her inwardly.

'Those who first found the White One, and perhaps fashioned her – they must have been women, or if any man helped them he must have been put to death afterwards. It is the Law. Those who first knew her, oh, far, far back – they recognized her for what she is. She is the Mother – oldest of all things except the Father of all. She brings us to conception and birth, she feeds us, she receives us back into her womb when we die, she sends us forth again. It is she that brings the female to the male, the hind to the hart, the ewe to the ram. Without her there is no life. They saw her thus – the breasts that nourish, the gates of birth through which we all must pass. Do you think they knew aught of comeliness or seemliness? I am told that in other countries and in later times, the people made images of her according to their sight and their thought, and some of them were beautiful. But this, my holy image in which her power dwells, is far, far older. To those who first knew it, there was neither beauty nor foulness, but only That Which Is. The parts of woman which mortal women hide, not from loathing, but from reverence. And old – indeed, how should she not be old? And yet some have seen her in visions, walking the hills in eternal youth.

'There are many who are afraid of her – there are men who have hated her, to their destruction. But women should not be afraid of her. *You* should not be afraid of her.'

17 · *How Lynett Found Love too Close to Death*

'Come and see my kingdom,' Lucius said.

'*See* it?' she questioned gently.

'Yes – you can take torches, as my nurse sometimes does. She says it is a wonderful sight, and I know it is a wonderful place. Come and let me show you!'

So they went in, she carrying a satchel full of the little pine splinters, dipped in pitch, that were always kept ready by the Sibyl. Inside the first precinct of the caves, the lamps burned before the White One, but the Sibyl had covered the figure with a veil. Lynett said nothing to Lucius as they passed it, but he, sensing where it was, made his customary reverence.

It was a miraculous region he showed her. Some of it she had passed through before, but then she had been distressed, apprehensive and exhausted; now she was able to give heed to the eerie beauty of it. Grotto beyond grotto, cavern beyond cavern, gleaming with stalactites, golden and rosy, silver, black and white – like ivory and flesh and flowers, and sudden snow, and falls of black velvet. On and on he led her. They visited the edge of the torrent from which he had rescued her, and listened to its awesome noise.

'It's dangerous,' he said, 'but I know how to master it. I like it, because it's dangerous. I swim there for pleasure, and that was how I found you. But I can only go down it – no one can go up. There is another way round, you see, to the beginning – the place where it comes out of a narrow crack in the rock. I go up there and shoot all the way down. That was how I chanced to be there and felt you in the water – before I touched you . . . No, we'll not swim here. I know a pleasanter place.'

They passed a place where the water was hot, and steamed in the light of Lynett's torch. 'Oh, heavens, sulphur!' she exclaimed. 'This must be the gates of Hell!'

'No, no,' he laughed. 'I know the sulphur vapours. There is

a kingdom of fire down here, and fiery spirits, as my nurse has taught me, but they are not spirits of evil. There would be a different feeling if they were. No, it's no power of the Evil One. All this part is under the realm of the Mother. Have no fear.'

He led her onwards following the course of the warm stream; soon the passage opened into a large vaulted expanse, and Lynett's torch showed a clear lake, of a strange jewel-like blue, extending before them. 'Feel the water now,' he said. She stooped and dipped her hand in. It was just between warm and cold, a delightful temperature. All the edge of the lake was clean white sand, fine and soft, gleaming blue in the torchlight reflected off the water.

'See me now,' he cried, and sprang from her side into the – water, as confidently as an otter into the pool. There he swam and plunged, dived and surfaced like a fish. By the glimmering light of her torch she watched him in wonderment. The torch burnt down, and she lit another and yet another.

'There's a place in the wall where you can set the torch,' he said, and found it with his fingers. 'Place it there, and come and swim with me.'

She fixed the torch where he showed her and then – reassuring herself that he could not see her – slipped off her clothes and plunged into the water to join him. She could swim a little, enough to enjoy it. There was hardly any current, and the mild, warm water caressed her skin. He swam towards her, laughing for pleasure, waking musical echoes, and caught her hands. Then his arms went round her in the water, and she felt with surprise that her body welcomed his touch.

Then later they lay side by side on the soft sand, and the torch glimmered down and left them in darkness. They spoke no word, but drew towards each other. And there at last Lynett knew the pleasure of a man's love.

Now began for Lynett a time of happiness such as she had never known before. She loved and was beloved, and there was nothing any more to be afraid of. With her perfect companion she wandered in a dream, whether in the warm September woods, or in his own glittering caverns, or sitting quietly by the Sibyl's fireside, or lying in his arms on beech leaves or on sand.

No longer need she fear bad dreams. All the terrors and tensions, all the hatreds and graspings and gripings, were smoothed away, and she was relaxed and washed as if by a new birth.

'You are happy, child,' said the Sibyl, as they plucked the apples together under the apple tree. The wall of the gorge closed them round, and the far side was in deep shadow, but the sun gathered all its rays on the side where the cottage stood and glowed back from the cliff behind them. The dry grass around them buzzed with insects, and the autumn flowers were bright; not a breath of wind disturbed the orchard. Lynett and the Sibyl were filling osier baskets with the apples; Lucius was away in the woods, walking with his staff – the Sibyl had told him he must store up the sunshine while he could.

'You are happy, child.'

'Yes, I am happy.'

'I know. Your happiness wraps you round like a garment. Child, I know that you and my Lucius are lovers.'

'You – know?' Lynett put down her basket, and stood leaning against the tree, looking anxiously in the Sibyl's face.

'Yes, indeed I know. How could I not know? Oh, I'm glad for you, and glad for him – oh, glad, glad, glad!' She put her hands on Lynett's shoulders. 'Now he has attained manhood, and you have attained womanhood. The Lady has blessed you.' She sighed deeply.

'Then,' said Lynett, 'why do you sigh? Why are there tears in your eyes?'

The Sibyl drew away gently from her, and turned her face, letting her white veil fall forward. For a long time she was silent, then at last she said, 'Why must I drop bitterness in your sweetness? But you must be told. Some day you must be told.'

'Told what?' cried Lynett in an agony.

'This, dear child. He hasn't a year of life left in him.'

'What?'

'It is so. No child could endure the years of darkness and privation and remain whole. He is a dying man.'

'Oh, but surely, surely . . .' Stricken, Lynett saw her happiness fall away to nothing before her. 'I can't believe – his body is so strong, and so beautiful—'

'Yes – the Lady has done the best she could for him in the short time he has. I have often seen it. While he was growing, she built him in spite of all, but now that he is full grown, now his bones are crumbling within, and he begins to dry up and wither. Sometimes he coughs, and his cheeks are flushed. That is not the rose of health but the rose of death.'

'Oh, could you not – You are a healer, and know leechcraft – could you not cure him?'

'Do you think I haven't tried? Every herb, every medicine, every magic – I've tried all. I have tried every saint, every hallow, every relic. Pilgrimages I cannot go on, for I cannot leave him, and to take him from here would hasten the end. But everything else I've tried. Some good I have done him, by wholesome food and sunshine and – and love – ' Her voice was choked with tears. Lynett put her arms round her, caressing her thin bony shoulders beneath the linen.

'How long?' she asked her in a whisper.

'About a year, I think, with care.'

'And there's nothing, nothing—'

A thought flashed into Lynett's mind.

'There is one Hallow that would surely heal him.'

'Yes?' The old woman lifted her sad face.

'The Holy Grail.'

'Ah – the Holy Grail. If one could find it—'

'The knights with whom I travelled – the knights of King Arthur – were resolved to go in quest of it. They had had a brief Sight of it at Camelot, once. Once in the woods as we journeyed together, we saw its procession in the distance, with the Holy Stag. Far, far off it was. But they spoke then of how they would some day seek it.'

'And you? Would you seek it?'

'I said then that I would like to seek it, but they said it was not for a woman – or at least not for a woman who was not a virgin.'

'And you believed them?'

'Of course.'

'Oh, child, there are things you do not know.'

'Do you mean that I – I, a sinful woman—'

'Think less of being a sinful woman. Your great sin is absolved, don't you know that?'

'My great sin? But I'm – an unfaithful wife, and no virgin—'

'The man who had your virginity is dead, and your marriage was in name only – you've told me. No, your great sin was that of unforgiving, and that is repented, and absolved, and forgotten. You have felt that it is so. Let no man say that you are not fit to seek the Grail.'

'But—' a dreadful recollection came back upon her, 'You remember I told you – he made me perjure myself. I had to damn my own soul.'

'My dear, do you still believe in a God who would exact payment of such a debt? In fear of your life, in duress if ever there was duress? No. Forgive us our debts as we forgive our debtors. Think no more of it.'

She picked up the basket of apples and turned towards the cottage.

'Yes,' said Lynett. 'I think I shall have to go in search of the Grail, for Lucius's sake. And now I remember, I am Arthur's Damosel. Oh, dear mother, I should not have stayed here so long ... In any case I must go ... Does he know his condition?'

'Yes, he knows. He lives much on the border of the other world, and I think the prospect of death means little to him – only of late, since he found you—'

'I will go. I will go, and I will find the Grail, and come back to him, with health and length of days in my hand.'

She told him, lying on the warm sand of the cavern, which had become to them as dear and familiar as a conjugal bed.

'So I must go, my love. But I'll come back to you, and I'll bring you your certain cure.'

'Perhaps you will also bring my sight?' he said. 'I should so love to see you.'

She suppressed a little gasp of dismay.

'Surely, my dear, if I can. But you – might not like me if you saw me. I tell you, I am not beautiful.'

'I know you are,' he persisted. 'And I know how a beautiful woman should look. I remember my mother, before the trouble – yes, and all her lovely ladies. Oh yes, I know that you are beautiful. Oh, my dear, ask the Holy Thing for my sight!'

She gazed past him into the depths of the cavern, into the glitter of the stalactites in the dim torch which was all she now needed. To have him see her! No, it would be unbearable. To see the disappointment in his look, to have him turn away from her when he knew the truth – oh no. And yet, and yet, it was not only herself he should desire to see. Flowers and trees, sunrise and sunset, the whole wide sky – could she deny him those, because she dreaded what he would see in herself?

She kissed him on his closed eyelids. 'I will go and bring back your eyesight if I can,' she said.

18 · Of the Setting Out of the Grail Company

They met her at the outskirts of Camelot, just where the road turns to give a distant view of the towers – Lancelot, Perceval and Bors, on their great horses; Lynett, plodding along the road barefoot in a brown smock, ran towards them.

In a moment they were off their horses, surrounding her eagerly.

'Brothers, oh brothers—'

'Our Lynett – our Falcon's Feather – where have you been all this while?'

'We thought you were dead, and we mourned you,' said Bors.

'Until this morning, and then we knew you were coming,' said Lancelot.

'You knew I was coming? How did you know?'

'It was Jeanne,' said Bors. 'Ever since daybreak she was bating on her perch and crying out. We couldn't bring her, for none of us dare hold her, even hooded – she'd have broken away from us. But she's there awaiting you.'

'Also I had a dream,' said Perceval.

'And I knew,' said Lancelot.

She looked from the one to the other. 'But Gwalchmei – where is he?'

'Ah, poor Gwalchmei,' said Bors. 'He fell in the fight, when we lost you. We seemed to be seized by an enchantment – dreaming of a palace and a lady, and then suddenly we woke, and Bagdemagus's ruffians were upon us, and you were dragged away – we fought them, but they beat us off, and – Gwalchmei was slain.'

The colour drained from Lynett's face.

'Oh, not Gwalchmei?— Oh, Gwalchmei—' and she sank down by the roadside with her hands over her face.

Gwalchmei – he had given his life for her. And bitterest regret and remorse of all, she knew that for all of that time she had forgotten him. She had forgotten all of them, and one of them had died for her.

'Sister, no tears,' said Perceval, with a hard look in his pale eyes.

'We are knights, sister, and death is our trade. You have looked on death before, and not wept. Gwalchmei died as a knight should die, and as he would have wished.'

She looked up at him, her hair and her tears all over her cheeks.

'He was our brother in arms. He was – Gwalchmei, and we knew him. He gave his life trying to save me.'

'I had thought you had more fortitude,' said Perceval. 'But a woman still—'

'Oh, enough, Perceval!' exclaimed Bors, with a look that silenced him. Lancelot said nothing, but stretched out his hands to Lynett and drew her gently to her feet; then he took her head on his shoulder; and let her cry as she wished. Presently he whispered to her, 'You are changed, lady.'

'Yes, I am changed.'

She looked round at them bleakly.

'You were four once, a complete square, the pillars of the house. Now you are only three, and the square is broken.'

'No, we are still four,' said Bors, 'now that you have come back to us. As four we will go together on the Quest.'

No need to ask what Quest.

'Oh, yes, brothers – I'll come with you on the Quest – if – *if* you will have me?'

'A woman?' said Perceval, and still his pale eyes were cold. 'Our gallant sister, and dear to us, but still a woman?'

'Why not?' said Lancelot.

'We will ask Merlin,' said Bors, 'and as he decides so let it be.'

Arthur gave his consent with reluctance. The quest of the Grail was a thing to which certain knights, from time to time, felt a call, rather like a holy vocation, and no man might or ought to hinder them. But few of them returned.

They stood outside the door of Merlin's chamber, he had a turret room in the castle, very high and private. The four of them stood together, and Lancelot knocked.

'Enter!' said Merlin's voice within, and solemnly as in a ritual, they opened the door and entered. Merlin, in his robes, stood to receive them; the room was dark, and lit by a large fire, and its light illumined him, but scarcely showed them the strange things the dark corners of the room contained.

'We are four,' said Lancelot, speaking for the rest, 'who have Arthur's leave to follow the quest of the Holy Grail.'

'Four knights?' said Merlin, as they ranged themselves before him.

'Three knights, and – one is a damosel.'

'Ha, a damosel?' exclaimed Merlin, startled. He peered at them in the uncertain firelight. 'Come here, damosel. Oh yes, it's you. I might have known.'

Putting out a long white-draped arm, he drew Lynett to him. She came unresisting. He laid his hand on her shoulder and looked searchingly into her face.

'Yes,' he said at last, in a low voice for her alone. 'You're ready. All is well. Go and have no fear. You understand now, do you not?'

She nodded. 'Yes, I understand.'

Perceval, close behind her, said, 'Master Merlin – tell us – may a woman truly be numbered among us?'

Merlin lifted his eyes from his contemplation of Lynett's bowed head, and speaking across her, said, 'Yes, Sir Perceval. A woman may truly be numbered among you. As you know, knights in search of the Holy Grail must set out in a company of four, no more and no less. I name the Damosel Lynett here amongst you as the fourth of your company. So be it.

'Now listen to your road-learning.

'From here you must travel all together, towards the west, the direction of those who seek. Then each will receive a sign according to his nature, and that sign he must follow. For you, Sir Perceval, the sign of water; for you, Sir Bors, the sign of fire; for you, Sir Lancelot, the sign of earth; and for you, Lady Lynett, the sign of air. These will lead you on your four several ways, and not one of these will be at all like another, for each has his way set out for him that only God and his heart know. But in the end you will all meet together, and the place where you meet will be Carbonek – Are you all shriven and houselled?'

'Yes,' they all replied, and Lynett marvelled, having always thought of Merlin as no Christian at all, to hear him anxious that they should have received the Holy Sacrament.

'Then go, and the Lord be with you,' he said.

So they went, and followed the road west from Camelot. And on the second day their road led them through a thin country of small dry bushes; and the light of midday shone upon something bright gold in colour – a great golden beast, prowling ahead of them through the bushes – a lion.

'I didn't know there were lions in this land,' said Lynett in a startled whisper to Lancelot.

Lancelot and Perceval put hands to their lances. But Bors said,

'This is my sign, the sign of fire—' and he urged his unwilling horse forward towards the beast. The lion looked over its shoulder and walked on, as if inviting him to follow; and the horse seemed to lose its fear, and went forward; and they lost sight of Bors among the small trees.

'He follows his sign,' said Perceval, sighing.

And the next day they came to the sea coast, and to a causeway made along the edge of the sea, and they rode along the causeway. And when the tide came up, and brimmed to the edge beside them, they saw two dolphins sporting and leaping in the waves. And Perceval threw off his armour, crying 'This is my sign, the sign of Water,' and plunged in after them. Lynett shrieked, and would have dived in after him, but Lancelot held her back with force.

'No, my dear,' he said, holding her in spite of her struggles. 'All is well with him. He's in no danger, he'll not drown. This is his sign, as the lion was Bors'. We shall see him again.'

But Lynett wept and shook, and Perceval's horse trembled and for a long time would not leave the spot. That night, when they took shelter in a monastery, they left Perceval's horse behind with the monks.

So now it was Lynett and Lancelot who rode alone, and as

they rode they opened their hearts to each other on many things. Lancelot told her of his heartbreaking love for Guinevere, and how his loyalty and duty to Arthur pulled him one way and his love pulled him another, till he was nigh tortured to death between them, and how he had chosen the adventure of the Grail so that he might put distance between him and his torment; but for all that, he feared he could never attain the Grail, because he knew the imperfection of his own heart. And Lynett told him her own story, and did not keep back even her love of Lucius.

'And who am I,' she said, 'who can claim no purity of heart or body, to seek the Holy Thing? And yet I must do it for love's sake. Oh, surely you, Lancelot, are no worse than I am? Let's take heart, both of us—'

'I will, surely,' said he, 'for I think that is my sign yonder.' And they looked, and along the road, and leading away to the right, was a noble white bull. 'The sign of earth,' he said. 'But, Lady Lynett, must I leave you all alone?'

'I shall be well enough,' she said. 'Have no fear for me. For, after all, I must soon get my sign too. A bull for earth, but what is the sign for air?'

'Why, the Twins,' he said, 'or the Water-carrier. And so – are you sure you will be well? – and so good-bye, dear Lady Lynett—' and he rode away after the white bull.

19 · Of the Finding of the Grail

So now Lynett went on alone. The road now led her away from the sea, and through sandhills, and it was high noon, and though it was winter, all seemed dry and hot, and the sun beat down. The belt of sand between the road and the sea widened, all bristling with coarse rough bent-grass. Nothing else was visible. The heat grew intolerable, and both Lynett and her horse drooped and could hardly stagger along.

Then far off a small object, like some sort of statue, broke the monotonous roll of the sandhills. As she drew nearer, it showed itself to be no statue, but a young man, only lightly draped, holding a large earthenware vessel on his shoulder. As she came up to him he tipped the vessel forward and began to pour a stream of water out of it. Water! Both Lynett and her horse plunged desperately towards it – she jumped from the horse and ran to place herself in that cool stream, and then . . .

Then a gust of wind, out of the windless sky, so violent that it wrenched her neck and shoulders, hit her and spun her round – water and sand whirled together – the horse's reins, over her arm, snapped, and she tried to look round for the horse, but there was nothing, nothing but that whirling— Away and away, the relentless wind howling through her very brain – driven before it, walking, running, flying—?

She lost all count of time – then, after what seemed an endless period, the wind slackened, and awareness came back to her, and she knew herself to be walking along a bare open road, still carried by the wind, but no longer whirled about, and able to look around her. Now it was no longer a waste of sandhills that surrounded her, but stony ground covered with trees, but such trees! White bleached skeletons, all stretched one way with the pressure of the wind, shining here and there with encrusted salt. Large trees and small, relics of little low shrubs and of what had once been fine spreading shade-trees – and yes, there were traces of walls, and now the ruins of houses – a town, but as desolate as the trees – in the deserted street, the skeleton of a horse, of a dog – yes, of a man. Of many men and women. And as she went on, there were those with flesh still on them – with clothes still on them – and oh heavens, some that still seemed to be alive . . .

It was then that the wind increased again, and with it a mist that wrapped her round, and voices in the mist.

'You haven't forgiven him really – you still hate him – how could you forgive him?'

She was back in that wood under the beech tree, enduring what she had endured then – she heard his contemptuous laugh as he flung her from him. She was back in his hall of Castle Hardy, and he was saying, 'Oh, a scold's bridle! To the ducking-stool with the bold scold!' and then in his prison-room under the roof, his look of disgust – 'No, not attractive!'

Then he was putting the thumbscrew on her. Then he was making her swear that frightful oath—

And then those Black Things were rolling towards her, and uncoiling and rising up tall with foxes' heads—

Shrieking she ran before the howling wind, and the voices went on, 'You've not forgiven him – you've not forgiven him – and you'll not be forgiven yourself, never, never, never – now's the time the Black Things will have you—'

Then in desperation her thought reached out to Lucius, and something of warmth and tenderness came through the driving wind. And then a great feeling of pity, a pity that covered her enemy also. An impulse of compassion like a sob burst from her.

'Oh, God forgive us all!' she cried, and then she turned and faced into the wind. 'I'm done with you, Black Things!' she said steadily, speaking into the tempest. 'I have forgiven him, and you will go and pursue me no longer. I am not afraid of you. All that is past, and I am free.'

And suddenly the wind dropped, and all was still. The desolate land lay calm before her, in the light of sunset. And there across the stony plain rose a castle, pinnacle on pinnacle, black against the westering sun, and she knew it was the Castle Carbonek.

Long, long she walked across that dreary plain, and at last reached the gateway. A man, clothed in black and with his face hidden in a cowl, stood by the door.

'I bid you enter if you can,' he said. 'This is indeed the Castle Carbonek in the Waste Land. If you can read the riddle of what is within, and attain the healing of the Fisher King, then you may bring back life to the Waste Land and attain your heart's desire. But not if your heart's desire be unworthy.

'Earth and water have long ago proved you; air you have lately endured; but now fire.'

And at that moment the castle portal, through which Lynett was about to go, sprang all into a blazing fire.

'Go through the fire,' said the hooded man.

But Lynett faltered and hung back.

'Go through the fire,' he repeated. 'Have no fear – if you have truly forgiven your enemy, and if you desire nothing for yourself, the fire will not hurt you.'

'Then God be my helper!' cried Lynett, and strode straight into the fiery doorway. She shrieked with the pain, one moment only, and then she was through the fire, and into the castle.

Her hair still crackled where the flames had touched it, and her clothing smelt of fire, but she was through it. The great stony vaults of the Castle Carbonek stretched before her, and suddenly with a deep and heavy clang, the door swung shut behind her.

All was gloom and silence. A dim light came from some-where, only enabling her to see the awesome dark arches, and another door, a strong oaken door, ahead of her. No human face or voice. No human thing at all – not a bench, nor a shelf, nor a weapon, nor a vessel, nor trace of a window, nor any sign of human occupation. She went towards the door, with her footsteps sounding loud on the stone floor. As she approached the door, it opened silently and let her through, closing equally silently behind her. Again her footsteps echoed, alone and dreadfully solitary, through another bare vault, and to another door – this also opened, but behind it was a dimmer light, and some sort of soft carpet under her feet, for now her footsteps made no noise. Quieter and quieter – no sound anywhere but her own breathing and the beating of her heart. Enough light, faint and greyish, to show her which way to walk, but no more. She wanted to scream aloud to break the terrifying silence, but she did not. She went on, gasping now because she was conscious of her breathing –

and reached, not a door, but a heavy black curtain. It gave to her handling, and she was in a dimly lighted room.

Tapers burned, quietly in air that was not stirred by any breath. In the midst of the room a great bed, a bed of state, with curtains drawn back, and in that bed lay a dead man. His calm noble face was turned upwards in peace, and his hands folded on his breast above a rich pall of black velvet embroidered with silver. An old man, but comely. His hair was white but thick and smooth, and his beard was white but trim; his neck and shoulders were bare above the velvet pall.

She stood looking at him, calming her thudding heart and entering into the solemn and sad peace that lay around the dead man; and then she screamed – for the fine marble face was dissolving before her eyes, dropping away, shrivelling – the neck and shoulders, the arms and hands, drying, perishing, becoming a tissue of sinews – the whole body was crumbling into bones and dust – there was the face, that a moment before had been so beautiful, now a hollow skull, crossed with a few stretched webs of skin and wisps of lanky hair—

In spite of all her self-control she screamed – and then people whom she could not see came up behind her and seized her fast, and laid her in the bed beside the dead man. She could feel his bony arm and shoulder touching her own. Someone drew the black cover over her face, and she thought to herself, 'This must be death . . . Well, if it is death, let it be so. It is hardly as bad as I thought' – and she yielded herself to being dead.

And in a moment she was lifted up, and bright lights shone about her – she was carried away and set on her feet.

She was in a great room, or hall, like a brightly lighted church. Candles glowed against painted and gilded walls, and the smell of incense came wafting up. There she was standing behind something like an altar rail, and to her astonishment, her three companions were by her side – Perceval, Bors and Lancelot.

Before them a deep apse stretched away to the eastward,

and above it a window glowed with such colours as were never seen on earth; but a rich parclose screen hid the apse from their view, and before the screen lay a narrow couch, and on that couch a man lay propped on pillows. He wore a crown, and a purple tunic, but from the waist downwards he was swathed in linen bandages. And with awe and terror, Lynett recognized his face – it was the same face as the dead man's, that had crumbled into a skull. But this man was alive, though his face was fine-drawn with pain, and his deep-set eyes held an awesome light.

He spoke courteously.

'Welcome, knights and damosel,' he said. 'You should know me – I am called the Fisher King. Long ago I was sore wounded in the thigh, and never can be healed but by that one who shall achieve the Grail. You four have passed through your probations, and now you are near the final step. Behold.'

And as he spoke, they heard the single note of the silver bell, as long ago they had heard it in the forest. Then, from the far end of the great dim hall, came the procession. Not led by the white hart this time, but by a tall man, bareheaded, who carried high a crucifix of gold and ivory. For now all those whose faces had been hidden before were unhooded and unveiled – the chanting maidens, the thurifers, the solemn musicians, the white-robed men and boys – and each of the four Grail-seekers thought he (or she) saw among them at least one remembered face of one long dead. Solemnly and with great stateliness the procession moved on. The four men were there, and the four holy things they carried were unveiled now – a sword, a lance whose point dripped blood, a cup that received it, and a silver platter. And finally came the maiden who carried the Grail, but she alone was veiled. She carried the Holy Vessel high before her, and it was covered with a veil also, but it seemed to Lynett like a fine bowl or dish, closed with a curiously wrought cover, as if the very precious food of some great lord was being carried to him. The procession passed by the Fisher King, and she expected it would stop and serve him from the Holy Vessel; but no, it passed on, and none turned a head towards him. They went on, at their slow and steady pace, behind the parclose and into the apse, where none could see them; and the maiden carrying the Grail vanished with them.

When long ago they had seen the procession in the forest, a light of bliss had radiated from the Grail and filled them with happiness; but nothing reached them now. It was there, the power and the loveliness, but not for them. And if not for the Fisher King, then for whom?

Silence fell, as the last of the procession disappeared. The Fisher King said nothing; the almost invisible attendants said nothing. They waited. The four waited, wondering what should come next. Something was required of them. Lynett looked at each one in turn – they were eager, enraptured, but had no words. The pressure of the silence deepened, and the Fisher King's head drooped, as if he lost hope. Then prompted by some strange impulse, Lynett spoke into the silence, terrified at her own voice.

'To whom do they serve of the Grail?'

And at once it was as if a great company sighed deeply; the Fisher King lifted his head, and stretched out his hand to her, beckoning.

'Well have you asked, daughter. Come, and your question shall be answered.'

He drew her towards him, clasping her hand, and with his mouth to her ear, whispered a name.

But that name was so secret, so sacred and mysterious, that it may be spoken by none save those to whom it is given in the rightful way and at the rightful time; least of all may it be told here. For that name is Holy, and that name is Wonderful.

So then the unseen people behind her led her away with a gentle pressure, and she looked behind to see if her three companion knights were to follow her, but a barrier of crossed spears held them back. Bors had hidden his face; Perceval stood gazing anxiously; but Lancelot was stretching his arms out across the spears, as if he would struggle to follow her. But none of them might follow.

She was led through the parclose screen, into the apse, where the procession had gone; and there the Grail was revealed to her.

Afterwards – how long she could not say – she was taken back into the great hall, and saw her three comrades kneeling round the couch of the Fisher King. In her hands she held a bowl, which sometimes seemed to her like a plain bronze bowl, the size of her two cupped hands, unadorned save for the roundels at the rim – and sometimes seemed to be that rich and glorious thing she had seen behind the parclose screen. In it lay two wafers, like consecrated Hosts.

On bended knee she presented the Holy Vessel to the Fisher King. She saw him stretch out his emaciated hand and take one of the wafers – the three knights, kneeling, watched with awe. And, as the Fisher King put the wafer to his lips, suddenly the colour came into his face, and a softly glowing light radiated from him. With one smooth movement he rose from his couch, and the bandages dropped from his legs, showing him fully clothed and nobly armed. His face was hale and firm, and the hand that had been wasted and tremulous was well-fleshed and powerful. He lifted above his head the jewelled sceptre that had lain beside him, and cried with a great voice, 'Deo gratias!'

And the voices of unseen presences took up the chant.

The three knights had been led away – Lynett never knew how or where, nor had she any chance to bid them farewell. All she knew was that she now stood at the great gateway of Carbonek, and the Fisher King was beside her, and in her hands she still held the sacred bowl.

'Now you have your answer to your prayer,' he said, 'and now you must go. Take the Holy Thing in your hands, and go on foot, with such speed as you may, back to where you are awaited.'

She looked before her – it was the fall of evening; she had long lost all count of days and hours. It seemed to be about sunset, on an evening in spring. The bloom of the sunset was in the sky, and the bloom of growth on the hedgerows and coppices; the evening star hung like a jewel.

'Go straight before you,' he said. 'Look – over there, straight ahead, is a hill where burns a beacon. Keep that in sight. When you reach its summit, you will see a round mere below you, and beyond it another hill. Go on towards that hill, walking always so that the mere and the beacon are in a line – thus you will be on a straight track, with no quagmires or chasms. So on again, mere and hill, and hill and mere. And by daybreak you will reach the Cave of the Sibyl, and you will give that which is in the Holy Vessel to the man for whom you sought it.'

'But am I so near, then?'

'Nearer than you thought. When you were led here, some of the way was through the Country of the Mind, and as you go back, some of it will be through the Country of the Mind again. But you will know when you come to the land of living men.

'Speak to none, salute no man by the way. You will not be tired, nor hungry nor thirsty, for the Holy Thing you carry will sustain you.

'But remember this: when you reach your beloved, and give the Holy Thing into his hands, he may have one boon granted to him, one boon and no more. Either his life, or his sight. He may not have both, and – you may not choose for him. He alone must choose, and as he makes his choice, so must it be.'

'Is this – is this indeed the Holy Grail that I carry?' she asked, for now it seemed to her only the simple bowl of bronze.

'Have faith – have you not seen?' For suddenly it blazed again with gold and gems and a light beyond anything earthly – then the glory was gone. The Fisher King covered it with a dark cloth.

'Now go,' he said, and kissed her on the brow. 'In the Name of God!'

And she went steadily down the path and away from the Castle Carbonek – never looking behind her, for she knew it would no longer be visible to her if she did. Fixing her eyes on the beacon ahead of her, she began her long walk.

20 · *Of the Boon that was Granted*

It was a serene evening as she set out – an evening that waited for something. No wind breathed – the soft misty bloom of the horizon seemed to hold a tension of waiting – for what? For moonrise, for spring, for Easter? Dimly she wondered what day it was. Could it be Good Friday?

How different from the time – how long ago? – when she had approached the castle. Then she had been driven by a tyrannous wind. Now, no wind. Only silence, and waiting. Something she remembered of the way she had come – it had been through a desolate land, a desert place, with skeleton trees, and beasts, and men ... Now she began to recognize the waste places, but a change was coming over them. A soft light, greenish as the red afterglow of sunset faded, was raying out from the Holy Vessel she carried, and where its light fell, the green grass sprang up in the twilight, and the wave of life rippled outwards. The gaunt trees put on the soft colours of living bark, and buds were swelling on the twigs, ready to break at the first touch of sunlight. Buds of crocus and daffodil pierced the soil. A stir of sleepy birds was heard in the trees, and here and there some little furry beast looked out from its burrow with bright eyes. As the evening darkened, it was not sleep that came upon the countryside so much as a breathing readiness for waking. Life flowed into all the land, life that only waited for the morrow's sun. In cottages lights shone softly. A dog in a doorway (surely she had seen a white skeleton there?) sighed deeply and happily in its dream; and a horse stood relaxed in sleep in its pasture. By the roadside – where she had seen huddled corpses before – a man, a woman and a child lay embraced, and she saw the woman raise herself on her elbow, and touch the man's face, and heard her say softly to him, 'Tomorrow . . . hope, hope, hope!' before she fell asleep again.

At the summit of the hill, where the beacon flared, she paused. Yes, there was the round mere, gleaming dully under the deepening sky, and there was the next hill, with a cairn of stones visible on it, and there, too, a beacon. Remembering what she had been told, she went on, keeping the mere and the beacon in line, walking fearlessly through the dark as the night fell, and never looking down at her feet. And over the next hill she knew she was in the world of earthly men.

But still it was a night of spring, and the full moon rose, and she saw the dormant leaves and flowers all around her. The virtue of the Grail still radiated forth, for sometimes she passed a cottage where a light shone in a window, and in some way she knew that some sick one within had received healing.

But now her own thoughts came back upon her. Soon she would be back – she would be with Lucius, and she would bring him the answer to prayer – but to his prayer, not hers. He might have one boon, and one only – life, or sight. She had gone to bring him life – what if he chose sight?

If he chose sight, how he would enjoy the world of light and colour around him – for a short time. And then he would die. But perhaps he would think it worth while to have a short time to enjoy the world's full beauty. Beauty! Oh, he would look at her, and see her, and know that she was not beautiful. No deceiving herself – no deceiving him. He would see her as she was – ugly. She had always known it. Oh, yes, he would not be deceived. He remembered his mother, and her lovely ladies. Lovely ladies! With a true woman's reaction, Lynett realized that she would not have time so much as to smooth her tousled hair or wash her dusty face, for she must go straight to him with the Holy Vessel. Oh, he would look at her, and turn away – he would not know how to dissemble his disappointment. He might try, afterwards – how pitiful that would be! – but she would have seen his first look. And that would be all she would have to remember – afterwards, when he was gone.

But if only he would choose life – just as he was, without sight! How gladly she would devote the years of her life, as many as might remain, to caring for him, nursing him, being his eyes. Perhaps – oh, perhaps there might be children ... She would give him everything, everything but sight ...

But it was he who must choose.

Why, why had this thing come upon her? Could she not have left things as they were? Perhaps – perhaps if she did not tell him there was a choice? If she told him that she brought him life, but could not bring him sight? – The eyes of the Fisher King were suddenly before her, and the Holy Vessel shook in her hand. No, not that – But if it were not there at all? If she had achieved no Holy Grail? If she had never gone on the quest? – Then, of course, he would die, and soon, very soon. But at least he would die still loving her, still believing her to be beautiful. Supposing – down there in the valley she saw the spire of a little lonely church. Supposing she stole in there, and left the Holy Vessel on the altar, and went away back to him empty-handed – saying she had failed to achieve the Grail, as so many had failed before— Or if she dropped it into the depths of the last of those guiding meres? All would be as before—

The temptation was sharp, and she stood still, trembling all over, as her hands which held the bowl – now the simple bronze bowl – shook as with a palsy.

No – how could she tell herself that all would be as before? Never as before. No – with a deep sigh, she cast her eyes up to the vault of stars above her – itself another great bowl – and went on. Love could do no less.

*

The path led her at last into a way that she knew. The day was breaking – the soft gradual light of an April dawn – surely it was Easter? – was all around her, and the colours of all things began to show, and the long shadows were all lying the wrong way. She was at the entrance to the long coombe that led into the cleft where lay the Sibyl's cave. She hastened on.

There he was, coming to meet her – tall, pale, almost naked, glimmering against the dark shadows of the gorge. A ghostly beauty was his, as he walked from the cavern in the sunrise.

'My love,' he said. 'I felt you coming long before I heard you. In my dreams I felt every step of the way you took. And I know you have it with you – the Holy Thing itself.'

He fell on his knees before her. Trembling, she laid one hand on his head, the other hand holding the cup.

'Beloved,' she said, 'I have It here, and I have the answer to your prayer. But It will give you one boon only.' She strove to keep her voice steady. 'Either you may choose life, or – you may choose sight. You may not have both. And only you may choose. So – choose, my dear, and may God guide you to choose aright.'

She knelt facing him now, with the Holy Cup between them; and to her eyes it seemed that it was once more the Great Grail, glowing with gold and sparkling with gems, and a soft light radiated out from it. Lucius put a hand on her shoulder, and fixed his sightless eyes intently upon her face. There was no escape for her now.

'I do not hesitate,' he said. 'I choose sight. Lord, let me receive my sight, though it were but for a day.'

Under his steady gaze, she withdrew the veil from the Holy Cup, and took the single wafer it contained, and like a priest, placed it in his mouth.

A flash of light seemed to fall between them – and then as she saw clearly, Lucius's eyes, with a full light of perception in them, were looking into hers.

'Oh,' he cried, 'you are beautiful! You are beautiful! You are beautiful!'

Her hands were empty – but now he had clasped her in his arms, and was kissing her, and then drawing back to look at her face – then looking around at the brightening landscape of morning – and always coming back to look at her face, and her body, and her face again.

She moved her hands, seeking the Holy Cup. It was gone.

'Where is – It?'

'I saw nothing. I see only you. You're beautiful – oh my love, you're beautiful!'

At the door of the cottage, the Sibyl watched silently. Tears were streaming down her face, but she lifted her arms in thanksgiving.

21 · *Of the End*

The time of happiness lasted about the space of a month. From April into May – and all that time was sunshine and warm winds, days and nights of beauty. Together they enjoyed all the loveliness of the countryside, and each other most of all. They made love among the primroses, and among the bluebells, and in the beechwoods, and on the tops of high hills. He could never have enough of looking at her.

For she was beautiful, in very truth. She had, indeed, long been beautiful, for any who had eyes to see. Her face, once pale, was now brown and warm-tinted as a gypsy's, with a bloom of health on her cheeks; her brown eyes were long-lashed and brilliant; her lips were red, and her teeth flashed between them when she smiled. Her long black hair, which she now brushed and combed carefully, or braided with flowers, was sometimes like a silken curtain, and sometimes gleamed with blue like a starling's back. And her body, which in that secret and secure place could often be naked, was brown and smooth and shapely as our mother Eve's. And all over was the glow of love and happiness.

Sometimes they went back into the cavern with torches, and explored it – she was the one, now, who could show him the underground river, and the warm bathing pool under the stalactites, and the white sand beside it. He had to shut his eyes to recapture his old skill, and he was less fond of his dark kingdom now than he had been. Neither could he enjoy swimming, even in the warm pool, as he used to. He was weaker, and often feverish. Passionately he craved for every moment of light above ground – discovering sunrise and sunset, moonlight and starlight, and his nurse's quiet and loving face, but always coming back to Lynett. And his nurse – if she sometimes wept quietly, she hid it from the happy lovers.

And after about a month, the end came, quickly and quietly and without pain.

They did not lay him in the grotto with the bones of the Sibyls but dug a grave for him under the apple tree. And there they stood, looking at the green turves and the flowers they had set above him.

'I took him from you,' Lynett said to the Sibyl.

'No, my dear. I could not have kept him, nor could you. A man belongs to himself and to God.'

They were silent for a time.

'There is a thing I don't understand,' said Lynett. 'What became of it – It – the Holy Grail that I carried?'

'It went back. It always goes back when its work is done. I never saw it, nor did he. Only you could see it. It has gone back to its own place, but it will be shown again to Arthur and his knights when the time comes for the last great quest. Perceval will go out when that time comes, and Gawain of Orkney, and Lancelot – and Lancelot's son, who will achieve the Quest.'

'And I – what am I to do now?'

'Let me think, and I will tell you.' The Sibyl left her side and paced away among the shadows of the gorge. A terrible foreboding fell upon Lynett. She thought of how a woman had come to the Sibyl's door as she sat mourning her husband,

and had said to her, 'You are she.' Could she bear to be named as the Sibyl's successor? Cold sinking fear gripped her at the thought.

The Sibyl ceased her pacing and came back to her.

'No, my dear,' she said. 'I know what you are fearing. No, not that. I am not going to name you as the next Sibyl. Time is coming soon that I must go, and another come, but it will not be you.' She smiled, she almost laughed. 'I know you're relieved. No, that's not your destiny. Yours is another path, the one you least expect. First you must go back to King Arthur, and tell him all that has befallen. You must not forget that you are still his messenger. And then – you must go home.'

'Home? What home have I?'

'You must go back to Lyonesse, where your sister Leonie lives with Sir Gareth.'

'Ah—' Her heart seemed to contract suddenly.

'Yes. You are fit to go back now. You are cured of your love for Gareth – are you not? – and you will no more have any jealousy or craving. Your sister Leonie has borne Gareth a son, Gawain the younger, and you will have much to teach him, and maybe his son after him.'

'To teach him!' she burst out, with something of her old bitterness. 'Who am I to teach a man? An aunt, an old aunt! A nursemaid!'

'No, my dear. Not a nursemaid. Your father taught you the arts of chivalry, though you were a woman. And you, a woman, will teach his grandson the arts of chivalry. Perhaps before the end you will have a greater part to play than anyone knows.'

So later, on a cold morning when the sunshine of May had turned to rain, Lynett, alone and on foot, set out again from the Sibyl's cave. And from a branch above her, with a soft whirr of wings, Jeanne flew down and settled on her wrist. And from the road ahead of her, Bors, Perceval and Lancelot, leading her tall black horse, came to meet her.

King Arthur's Daughter

Note from the Author

The chronology of King Arthur is at the foot of the rainbow. The more we try to approach him by scholarly research, the further away he recedes. He was, we are told, perhaps a Bronze Age warrior; perhaps the last leader of the Romano-British resistance against the Saxons; perhaps an old god of the British, or the eidolon, ikon or egregore of the British people and land, later projected as Saint George. Or perhaps he never existed at all, but was a pious invention of such writers as Geoffrey of Monmouth and Gerald of Wales, to fill a political need.

Yet there were ages when he was devoutly believed in; generation after generation has built up the shining figure, and from Malory onwards he, and all his company and environment, have become as solid and detailed as our admired Professor Tolkien's 'Middle Earth'. Milton considered 'The Matter of Britain' as a serious subject, Tennyson and many others, culminating in the late T. H. White, have made Arthur and his Round Table more real to us than much of history. But no one can say, of course, what is or is not 'true' about Arthur. The old romancers took the story as free for all, to retell it, elaborate it or add to it. I have therefore ventured to do no more than any jongleur would have done.

Nobody can say that Arthur did *not* have a daughter. Kings' daughters, unless they make dynastic marriages, are apt to slip out of history and be ignored. So I present my invention of Ursulet, daughter of Arthur and Guinevere – Ursa Minor.

As to period, I have followed Malory's lead, with something from Geoffrey of Monmouth; that is, a civilization more or less that of the twelfth century (with pardonable overtones from the fourteenth) but with the political situation as about the sixth century – the Romans not long gone, the Jutes and

Angles settled here and there, the old Celtic kingdom broken up and struggling for survival, and the Saxons about to descend in an avalanche.

So I present my tale, with no more pretensions to historical accuracy than were made by that good knight Sir Thomas Malory, on whose soul be peace.

V.C. 1976

1 · *The Heiress and the Witch*

The stars of the summer night, with the Great Bear, constellation of Arthur, conspicuous among them, shone down on the walls and battlements of Camelot, and into the great hall where King Arthur sat lonely upon his dais.

There were two winding staircases in the extreme corners of the hall, and a screen masked the entrances to both. One led up to Arthur's own chamber, and the other to the Queen's. In the stillness, he could hear footsteps going up one of the stairways. Lancelot, going up to Guinevere's room. Well, let him go, then.

Pain squeezed Arthur's heart. That it should come to this! Lancelot, his friend, and Guinevere, his beloved. But he would not break in upon them. Better to swallow his bitter jealousy, and hide his humiliation, as long as he could – as long as Mordred would let him.

Mordred! That coarse-grained, swaggering youth, with the loud mouth and the dirty mind – his bastard son by the woman Morgause, the Queen of Orkney, his own half-sister. Why, oh God, why had he ever let her have her way with him? It *must* have been enchantment – and God wot, he hadn't known at the time that she was his half-sister. Why should he be punished with a son like that? Never, oh never let the rule of Britain fall into Mordred's hands. Mordred's only care for any people he ruled would be to get all he could out of them for his own pleasures, to oppress and persecute them so that he could enjoy the sense of power. He, Arthur, 'the Bear of Britain', had built up and unified his country in the face of the encroaching barbarians; churches and monasteries and the arts of peace had flourished under him; the common men had lived in safety and happiness; and his chosen knights had learnt to aspire to such holiness as to reach out to the Holy Grail. But Mordred would ruin all this. Mordred, if it suited his plan, would let the heathen in. Even now, he knew, Mordred was only waiting to force his hand about Guinevere, and precipitate the break-up of the kingdom in scandal and faction and civil war. Rather than that, he would shut his ears, for many nights yet, to those footsteps going up to Guinevere's room.

If only he and Guinevere had had a son – but there was only their little daughter – his beloved little daughter Ursulet, his 'little bear', with her hair as white as Guinevere's. A woman could not rule in her own right – or could she? Some of the older races of the land held that the true inheritance was through the mother, not the father – and even that he himself held their allegiance by right of marrying Guinevere, the descendant of a long line of queens.

He roused himself. 'Bedivere!'

'My lord?' He was not quite alone in the great hall; Sir Bedivere, who seldom was far from him these days, had been sitting quietly beside the fire.

'Bedivere, is my scribe there?'

Bedivere called quietly for the scribe, a monk, who came with deep obeisance and stood ready to write.

'Good scribe, I want you to write this, and to have seven copies made, and send six to Chester, York, Winchester, London, Lincoln and Canterbury. Thus: I, Arthur, King of the Britons, do desire that at my death the crown shall pass to the Lady Ursulet, who is my lawful issue by Guinevere my Queen, and let no man deny this. Mordred my natural son is unlawfully born, being the son of Morgause, the Queen of Orkney, she being my mother's daughter. Let him not succeed to the throne of Britain, nor any of his issue. Let him be an Earl, and hold the feoff of Maiden Castle in Dorset, but let him after my death hold the same in homage to Ursulet my aforementioned daughter, or else depart this realm. And let all men know that though I die, *I shall come again* – write that last in large letters, scribe: I SHALL COME AGAIN!'

The scribe carefully wrote the words down.

'Now have copies made,' said Arthur, 'and when all are made, bring me wax and my great seal, and I will seal them. You, Bedivere, shall keep the chief copy.'

In one of the bedchambers of the castle, Mordred lay tossing on his bed, biting his nails, eaten up with desire. Not desire for any woman – he could have such as he desired easily enough – but worse, far worse. Desire for a crown and a throne. Desire for wealth. Desire for power. Desire for the name of a King.

So great was the power of his passion that it hung in the air around him like a cloud. It bristled and crackled with sudden spurts of hatred and cruelty. It reached out claws. And it called, called, called across the darkness for such powers as were of like kind with itself. Impossible that something should not hear and answer.

Out across marshes and plains, white vapours streaming from below the ground sent up a spurt of more solid vapour that hovered, took direction, and sailed across the sky, like smoke drawn by the draught of a chimney. In the white cloud of vapour was something that laughed to itself, exulted in its own freedom and sense of power, rejoiced to break free from the earth where it had been hidden, and to feel its substance hardening again into the fine shapely limbs of a woman. The draught that had pulled it up from the ground pulled it straight towards the narrow window of Mordred's room and inside.

He had not been quite asleep, but he jumped into full wake-fulness to see a tall, pale, handsome lady, with jet-black hair and cat-like eyes, standing by his bedside.

'Who are you?' he exclaimed. 'I don't remember having sent for you.'

'You didn't.' She smiled, a cold and rather eerie smile. 'I'm not for your bed, my lad. I'm your aunt.'

'My aunt?'

'Yes, your mother's sister. Morgause, Nimue and I were

three sisters, and Arthur was our brother. You know? Then you know that I am Morgan le Fay.'

'My aunt Morgan – but they told me you were dead.'

'Such as I don't die so easily. Now, now, my lad, no ceremony of welcome. I know what you want, and maybe I want the same. Oh yes, it was the power of your desire that drew me here. You want many things, but one thing more than all – you want to be King.'

'Oh, I do, dear lady, I do.'

'Why then, we may work together. I believe. But are you prepared to swear allegiance to me?'

'By all means, if you'll give me what I desire. I'll swear anything to any man—'

'I know you will,' said she, again smiling coldly, 'and be forsworn again as readily. But this oath you will not forswear. Look in my eyes and you will see why you dare not.'

And he looked in her eyes and knew.

So, trembling (although he was a bold man), he placed his hands between hers, and repeated.

'I, Mordred, swear to thee, Morgan le Fay, to be your liege man in word and deed, to my life's end and in the world to come.'

Then she kissed him on his forehead, and it was like a red-hot coal.

'You will hear from me,' she said, and went quietly out through the door, walking on golden sandals with her white robe swirling around her feet.

In another castle, miles away, a four-year-old boy, whose name was Ambris, started up from his sleep and screamed, 'The Princess! The Princess! Save her! Save her!'

His mother stood beside him, tall and white in the dark, with her red hair over her shoulders.

'Hush, my love – no, wake up, there's nothing to be afraid of.' She gathered him into her arms, and by degrees his terror subsided, he stopped trembling and opened his eyes.

'You were dreaming, my dear. There now, it's gone.'

He drew a long breath, looking up at her. 'But I saw it,' he said. 'A battle, and there's the Princess. I had to save her.'

His mother made the sign of the Cross over him. 'So you shall in due time, my little one,' she said. 'So you shall. But go to sleep now.'

After a minute's thought, she traced a pentagram in the air around him, the point upwards; and seeing that he was quiet now, she tiptoed away.

Her aunt-in-law, the stiff-backed, leather-faced Lynett, met her in the stony corridor.

'That child knows too much,' she said.

Playing in the sunshine around the castle grounds, Ambris soon forgot the terrors of the night. It was a very pleasant castle, in sea-girt Lyonesse – the south wall had a grassy slope outside, where his mother's little garden stood, full of flowers. The castle gates were never shut by day, for there were no enemies here in Lyonesse – no matter what might be in other parts of the world not so happy. King Arthur had put down the robbers, and kept the heathen Angles and Saxons at a distance. The grand glittering knights of Arthur's court, of whom Ambris was born to be one, rode to and fro about the country, redressing all wrongs. His father, Gawain the Younger, was one of these, and so were his grandfather Gareth and his great-uncles Gawain the Elder, Gaheris and Agravaine. They all rode out on adventures by the King's command, but Gawain his father was very often at home, with his mother Vivian, and his grandmother, the proud and dainty Leonie of Lyonesse, and his great-aunt, the tough old eccentric Lynett.

But the next night the dream came again, though differently.

He was standing by her bedside, where a small taper, like his own, gave a soft light; she was asleep and he could not see her face clearly, but she seemed only a little older than he was. A tall dark-haired woman came into the room and opened a little box; and from the box a spider crawled out, such as he had never seen – huge, as big as a man's hand, black and hairy. The woman let it drop on the floor, and it crawled towards the Princess's bed.

It crawled rapidly, leg by horrible leg, over the rushes and the skin rug at the side of the bed, up the bedhanging towards the sleeping child. A black cat crouched by the child's pillow, as if to protect her, but though its green eyes were fixed on the crawling spider, and its hair was stiff on its back, it seemed powerless to move. Ambris could not move either. He tried to cry out a warning, to rush forward, but his body would not answer him. Then his terror for the helpless Princess, and his determination to save her, broke through whatever it was that held him, and he thrust out his hand with a huge effort, and pushed one of the tall unlit candlesticks that stood by the bed – it fell, missing the spider, but shaking it down on the floor – in the same instant the cat, as if released, sprang and crunched the spider's horny back in its teeth. He heard the cat's hoarse snarl as the dream broke, and he found himself awake in his own bed, sweating with remembered terror. But this time he did not cry out.

In Camelot at that same hour, Guinevere started up in bed, in her lover's arms. He too started.

'What was that? I heard a noise—'

'It's the turret room above – shall I go?'

'No, no—'

'Who sleeps above?'

'Ursulet and her nurse. It was the cat I heard. The cat guards her. If the nurse wakes she might come in here. Keep quiet – no, stay here, and I'll go.' The very white lady slipped softly out of bed and threw a robe round her; so, carefully closing the door behind her, she went up the winding stair to the next room of the turret.

All was quiet and safe; Ursulet, her little daughter, slept undisturbed, only one of the great candlesticks had fallen over and in the corner the black cat was devouring something. Guinevere looked at her sleeping child – Arthur's 'little bear'

– and for a moment her heart misgave her. She had such a look of Arthur as she slept. Poor Arthur . . . The white lady stooped and kissed the child's soft cheek. Then she went back to Lancelot.

'All's well,' she said. 'Black Gib caught a mouse, I think.'

2 · *The Convent*

'Ursulet,' said the novice mistress, 'Ursulet, you're dreaming. Get on with your work.'

Ursulet, fourteen years old, gave a sigh, and picked up her needlework. She had indeed been dreaming. There was little else for her busy mind to do, now that most of her friends had left the convent. They had left, it was said, because the country was disturbed; but more than that she did not understand. There had been more than a dozen of them once; now there was only herself and Jeanne. So she had little company but dreams, and her dreams were mostly sad ones.

No sooner had she picked up the tambour frame and re-threaded her needle, however, than another nun came across the smooth lawns of the cloister garden.

'Ursulet, you're to go to the Lady Abbess at once.'

She rose, as she had been taught to do, promptly but without unseemly haste, folded and put away her work, and went through the cloister arches and up the stone stairs with even step and downcast eye – but her heart was hammering. Being summoned to the presence of the Lady Abbess was always momentous, and sometimes frightening. She remembered the last time – when she had been called in to meet a tall grey man in a monk's habit, who yet didn't look like a monk – a man so thin, so wasted, she had never seen such a thin man, like a walking skeleton inside the sagging grey robe, with his hair and his beard like thistledown – she could not think that this had been Sir Lancelot, the gay gallant who

used to be always with her mother. Very gently, with his big
blue eyes running over with tears, he had told her that her
mother was dead; and he had held her in his arms – his body,
as she felt it through the threadbare habit, was almost nothing,
a bundle of frail sticks – and they had cried together. Then
the novice mistress had led her away dazed with shock, and
as she went down the corridor she could still hear him sobbing
in the room behind her.

So now she entered the same room full of apprehension.
But there was no one with the Lady Abbess this time.

'Sit down, my child.'

Ursulet, having curtsied, sat down on a low stool, with her
back very straight and her hands folded. She was a very quiet
little girl, for events had left their mark on her. She had long
hair almost as lint-white as her mother's, who had been called
'the White Apparition'. But her eyes were like her father's,
grey and with boldly marked brows.

'Yes, Reverend Mother?'

'You are fourteen years old. It is time that we thought of
your future.'

'Yes, Reverend Mother.'

'You should consider preparing to take the vows.'

Ursulet lifted her eyes for a moment.

'Reverend Mother – I am not sure that I have the vocation
– that is – I am almost sure I have not.'

The Abbess clicked her tongue.

'Child – I think you do not understand your position. You
would no doubt think of a life in the world – of marriage?'

Ursulet dropped her eyes again. There were so many
thoughts in her mind – to be sought in marriage, to have a
lover – of course she had thoughts. Not to be all her life
among old beldames!

She and her friends – while there were still a dozen girls
like herself in the convent – had talked, and played the usual
fortune-telling games. Last St Agnes' Eve they had gone
through the whole ritual, pinning bay leaves to the corners of
each one's pillow, and all had had dreams of one kind and

another. But Jeanne had woken up screaming with the horrors, saying she was being devoured by a great horrible bear. They had laughed at her, and made jokes about Ursulet being the only little bear there – but Jeanne said it wasn't funny. It was horrible – something like a bear but worse— And then the novice mistress had heard the noise and come in, and given them all penance for taking part in heathenish practices. But Ursulet's own dream? Ah, that was something she told nobody.

She spoke now, with her eyes on her folded hands.

'Reverend Mother, I think my disposition might be towards being a wife in due time.'

'Yes, my dear child. But be wise, and consider. These are ill times we live in, and who is to make a marriage for you? There is no peace and no safety in the country now. Do you know who you are?'

As if repeating a lesson, she replied.

'I am the Princess Ursulet, only daughter of Arthur the King and his Queen Guinevere.'

'Even so, child. And being so, you stand in great danger.' She turned back to the polished table that stood behind her, where was a chessboard and pieces. 'Look, you know the game.' She held up a delicate ivory pawn. 'You are this pawn. There is only one left on the board, and if it can be moved up to the last square – here – it becomes a Queen. You understand? Many dangers lie in wait for that pawn.

'Your father's kingdom is gone, divided, broken – the Saxons overrun it, and warring factions split it up – there are many who will try to seize Arthur's daughter, to make good a claim to Arthur's throne. There were many in days of old, and there are still some, who consider that the lawful royal descent is from mother to daughter, not from father to son – the king reigns by right of marriage to the queen or the queen's daughter, as Arthur made good his claim to the Round Table by his marriage to Guinevere. There is one now, who I know would lay hands on you alive or dead. His name is Mordred. You know?'

Ursulet nodded.

'Arthur's son, but not lawful. I know he would try to have you for his own, to make good his claim to the kingdom.'

Ursulet shuddered and her face crimsoned.

'But – my half-brother!'

'He would not care for that. He is a wicked man, and knows no law but his own will. If he could not get you with your consent, I think he would bring you to dishonour, so that your claim to the throne could no longer stand. He is capable of any villainy. So far, we have kept you hidden from him, but I do not know how long we can do so. Therefore, for your own safety, it were better that you should take the veil.'

'But if he is so wicked and determined, Reverend Mother, would the veil be any protection?'

'We are in God's hands, child. Perhaps he would not respect even the veil – but it would be some barrier, some safeguard. It would be easier to hide you, or even to deny you if he traced you. Your name, your dangerous name and your lineage, would be forgotten, and you could serve God, live a quiet life here, and end your days in peace, safe from wicked and cruel men.' The Abbess's calm smooth face was moved with emotion, and Ursulet almost saw tears in the fine hazel eyes. 'Think of it,' child, think of it.'

'I will indeed think of it, Reverend Mother, but I cannot decide now.'

'Of course not. Nothing can be decided hastily. Go now, dear child – fear nothing, but consider carefully what I have said.'

She spoke a blessing over her and dismissed her. When the girl had gone, she sounded her small silver bell. A nun answered it.

'Sister Mary Salome, the situation is serious, they say. How near have the Saxons come?'

'As near as Poole, Reverend Mother.'

'I had not thought them so near. Did the messenger reach Camelot?'

'He did, Reverend Mother, but the only answer was that

they would send knights if they had any to spare – they did not say, *when* they had any to spare, but only *if*. I fear they will not come.'

'Then we must do what we can in the time we have left. Call in the house-carles and all the men from the farms – such as there are. Set them to pile up logs against the doors and windows. Put the treasures in the hiding-place prepared for them.' She sighed. 'I am concerned for the young pupils. What can we do for them? There is nowhere we can send them in the time. They will be no safer anywhere else. Well, if none will help us we must help ourselves, and commend us to God.'

3 · *Run for Life*

But all was too late.

That very night, Ursulet and Jeanne, in their big half-deserted dortoir, heard the thundering of a great log against the main outer door, and the crash, and the cries of the house-carles in the outer yard.

'It's the Saxons!' Ursulet cried. 'Get up—'

Their clothes were simple – the smock over which the gown and bodice went was like the one they slept in, indeed only a delicately brought-up girl would change into a different one for sleeping. This was Jeanne's undoing, for she threw off her night smock and reached for her day one, while Ursulet kept her night smock on but quickly put on her shoes. So that Ursulet was at least in smock and shoes, but Jeanne was naked when the door splintered and fell in, and a great creature burst into the room. It was all covered with tawny hair, like a bear – Ursulet thought with terror of Jeanne's dream of a bear, but this was a man. He seized Jeanne, smothering her in horrible hair, and fell to the floor with her.

Ursulet did not wait to see more. Afterwards, long afterwards, she reproached herself for having fled away and left her friend to her fate, but she could not have saved her. She slipped through the door that the raider had broken down and rushed down the stairs, out into the courtyard. Everywhere she went was terror, confusion and ghastliness. Numbers of great hairy men were everywhere. They were carrying off the altar candlesticks, the chalices, the lamps. One of the nuns stood desperately in front of the aumbry where the sacred Host was kept; a Saxon thrust her aside and wrenched the aumbry, which was silver-gilt, out of the wall with his sword while the next behind him seized the nun and began tearing the clothes off her. Two Saxons held the Abbess, her cropped head unveiled – a third swung his sword under her chin. Ursulet, in a moment of awed fascination, saw the head fall and roll away, and the blood gush down over the white habit – Everywhere were pools of blood and splashes of blood on the walls, and bodies whom Ursulet had known as living people lying like bundles of soiled clothes – And from somewhere came the smell of fire and the crackle of mounting flames.

Ursulet ran across the courtyard, not stopping to heed what she saw, and made for the gateway – the great door was lying in fragments, shattered by a log used as a battering ram; four house-carles lay dead around it, but it had no living guardian – the Saxons were all further inside the convent, looting, killing and raping. With terror behind her, Ursulet ran through the gateway, and on and on, along the road that led from the convent. At first she heard pursuing feet behind her, then they fell away, but still she ran on. For far too long she could hear the savage shouts, the screams, the crashes, and smell the smoke of the burning. It was dark still, before daybreak; but the skies soon paled towards morning; and when at last she stopped running, the first light was in the sky. She stopped through sheer exhaustion and threw herself down on the grass by the side of the track.

She had no idea where she was, still less where she was to

go; one thing only was certain, she could not go back to the convent. And there she was, in the cold daybreak, in her shift and her shoes, without a roof or a bed, without a penny, without a friend. Nothing, nothing, nothing.

Worse than nothing – the world was full of ogres.

While she lay there the rain began to fall, and this was the last misery. She crouched in the ditch, her fair hair plastered to her head, the raindrops mingling with the tears on her cheeks, her only garment sodden and clotted with mud.

Then she heard the whistle. It was far off, but clear and somehow significant – somehow alluring. Like a bird's note but much sweeter. It sounded again and again. It changed, bit by bit, into a kind of barbaric, up-and-down warbling tune, that seemed to call her to follow it; and as all directions were the same to her now, she got up and followed where it led. It seemed to come from the depths of the forest that bordered the road; the trees were heavy with late summer leaves and dripping with the rain, but they smelled sweet. Deeper and deeper into the wood the piping led her; one could hardly say there was a path, but there were openings between the trees where it was possible to penetrate. And at last the music led her to a clearing, and in the clearing was a neat little hut, that might have been a hermit's. But it was much prettier than any hermit would own; it was decorated with shells laid out in patterns, and creeping flowers climbed all over it; there was a bright flower-garden in front of it, and each of its four little glazed windows had its window-box of flowers. It was a reassuring and heartening sight, and Ursulet hastened towards it, sure that nothing but good could live in such a pretty house.

The door opened, and there came out a handsome woman, about forty years old, very tall and full of life; her hair was jet-black, and her complexion pale and yet rich, like thick cream. She wore a flowing dress of white silk, with a very beautiful gold girdle and gold border, and many other gar-

ments of gold, and golden sandals. And she opened the door
to poor forlorn Ursulet as if she had expected her.

'Oh, come in, come in!' she exclaimed. 'My poor child, what
a state you're in. But I was looking out for you. I know who
you are, you see.'

This seemed strange to Ursulet, but the lady put an arm
round her and drew her into the house. And once inside the
house, everything was different – this was no cottage, but a
rich palace, a vast palace – how was it that Ursulet had
thought of it as a cottage? It was such a place as she had
heard of in romances but never seen. The walls were panelled
with marble, polished and gleaming; carpets covered the
shining floors; soft light shone from concealed lamps, and
braziers warmed the air with the scent of perfumed gums.
Quiet smiling maidservants removed Ursulet's wet shift, and
clothed her in a beautiful dress of sky-blue and gold, and
replaced her soaking sandals with soft warm slippers. Then
they led her to a table, where the lady in white served her
with delicious food and drink. The maid-servants said no
word, but vanished. After a while Ursulet began to find
words.

'Who are you, kind lady?'

'That you will find out in time,' her benefactress said. 'Let
it suffice that I know who you are. I am very interested in you
and I am watching over you to help you recover your
kingdom.'

'My kingdom?' Ursulet looked up sharply.

'Yes, of course, for you are King Arthur's daughter. But we
must be careful. You are set in the midst of many and great
dangers – you know that, don't you?'

'I do indeed,' she said, remembering what the Abbess had
said to her – and then when she recalled how she had last
seen the Abbess, she shuddered and felt sick.

'But never fear,' said the strange lady, and put a glass of
sweet cordial to her lips. 'I am your friend. Come now, do
you like my palace? Come and walk through it – there are

gardens beyond and fountains with floating lilies, and groves of oranges.' And she led her on through fresh delights.

'I think it's wonderful, wonderful!' cried Ursulet. 'And you're so kind—'

'All this can be yours,' said the strange lady. 'All this, and your own rightful kingdom too. Only you should swear fealty to me. Will you?' And she looked into Ursulet's eyes with what seemed like pure friendship. 'Simply put your hands between mine,' and she stretched out her hands, 'and say: I swear to be your liege vassal, to do your bidding, to live or die, here or hereafter, till the world shall end.' She stood expectant, but Ursulet drew back.

'I don't think so – yet,' she said. 'Not till I know who you are, and what you want me to do.'

'You must trust me,' said the lady. 'Cannot you do that?'

'No – I'm sorry,' said Ursulet, in some confusion. 'I don't want to be rude to you, in any way – you've been so kind but so big a promise, without knowing anything . . .'

The lady frowned. 'You disappoint me. Well, in that case I shall have to send you back whence you came – and that wasn't very pleasant, remember? – Still, my offer remains open, if you should think better of your decision. Wear my token, and you will certainly see me again,' and she placed around Ursulet's neck a silver chain on which was a little charm in the shape of a pentagram, with the middle point downwards. And then, suddenly, everything was gone – the lady, her palace, Ursulet's new clothes and all. She was back by the roadside, in the rain, with her streaming hair and her wet shift. Whether she had indeed eaten and drunk, and been rested and warmed, she could not tell – she was certainly very cold and hungry. But round her neck was the chain with the reversed pentagram. And it was only then that she remembered that it took the place of a little gold cross that her father had hung about her neck long years ago, and which had never left her till she had dropped it, she supposed, in her flight.

4 · *The Jutes*

And now she was more desolate than ever. There seemed to be nowhere to go but along the road, so she plodded forward. And then suddenly a man sprang at her from the roadside. Like an animal, she ran without looking round to see him clearly, and just evaded his grasp; but she got the impression of a thickset, heavy man in a sheepskin cap, with a sheepskin over his back that was about all the clothing he had, and a wide, red, stupid face. Not a Saxon, but what of that? Every bit as bad, and pelting after her, uttering cries of imbecile desire. She ran and ran, and eventually distanced him, but she could still hear him pursuing. And now in front of her was the first sign of human habitation she had seen since she ran from the convent – not, of course, counting vision and glamoury. This seemed to be a rough homestead, a group of four or five untidy thatched huts enclosed within a thorn fence. She made for this – there might be refuge here. There was a gap left in the fence, and she ran through and approached the huts. They were connected by rough paths of large stones, making a causeway through what was otherwise a sea of mud.

As Ursulet approached one of the huts, a woman came out right in front of her – a big ugly woman, immensely fat and rotund. She was carrying a brimming bowl in both hands, probably full of curds, and as she was within arm's reach of Ursulet she stumbled and fell forward. With an instinctive movement like catching a thrown ball, Ursulet caught the bowl from her and held it safely, as the woman measured her length on the muddy ground. Ursulet stepped quickly inside the hut – it was cluttered and filthy – and with some difficulty found a place to put the bowl down; then she went back to the woman, who was still lying on the ground and moaning. Ursulet examined her carefully, but could not see any injury

– and then it suddenly dawned on her with a shock that the woman was about to give birth to a baby.

Living as she had in the convent, Ursulet had never even seen a pregnant woman before; but once, very daring and in great secrecy, with the connivance of a kitchen-maid, she and Jeanne had watched a cat have kittens. She knew very little indeed about birth, and worst of all, she did not understand a word of the woman's language. She appeared to be a Jute – there were settlements of Jutes towards the sea-coast, and they were said to be not quite as bad as the Angles, nor anything like as terrible as the Saxons, in fact almost human but that they didn't speak the Celtic tongue. The woman, rolling over on the ground, jabbered away in her own language, and with gestures and looks implored Ursulet not to leave her. It seemed to Ursulet that certain things needed doing, such as to get the woman into a hut and if possible to bed; so she helped her to her feet – the woman was remarkably heavy and inert – and supported her into the nearest hut, and got her into the kind of shallow box full of straw that was evidently the proper lying-in bed.

The Jutish woman made a great many things clear enough by signs – she herself knew all about childbirth anyhow, having had six children (so she indicated on her fingers), of which four had died. Her need, it appeared, was not so much for expert help as just for someone to fetch things for her, to put water on to boil, to get in more straw, to unpack the swaddling clothes from a wooden chest – and also to give her moral support and hold her hand in the crisis of the pains. She gave Ursulet to understand that it would be quite a time before the baby was born, and indicated in the meantime that she might help herself to milk, bread, cheese and bacon, and dry her garment at the fire, which she gratefully did. Ursulet sat comfortably enough on a stool between the straw bed and the fire, leaning against the wall, and rested at last. Then suddenly the door creaked open and the woman's husband came in and Ursulet sprang to her feet – it was her pursuer. He gave a long chuckling 'O-ho-o-o!' and shot out his arm for

her; but his wife jerked herself upright in the straw and threw
a volley of harsh guttural words at him – rising step by step
to a shriek – then for good measure she reached out and
seized a large log of firewood, and before sinking back in
another pain, flung it at him. He went out of the hut quicker
than he had come in. The patient fell back in the straw, and
between moans made a long and impassioned speech clearly
about the said husband. It hardly needed translating.

When the birth took place, the woman herself seemed to
know exactly what to do, and showed Ursulet what needed
to be done. Presently the husband reappeared, and with him
the midwife, a gnarled and witchlike old woman. But the
baby was already born and yelling heartily. It was a boy, and
quite successfully brought into the world, as the midwife was
the first to admit. To Ursulet's delight, the midwife spoke the
Celtic tongue as well as the Saxon.

'You a midwife?' she said to Ursulet. 'You're too young.'

'Oh no – I just happened to be here. I ran away – the Saxons
burnt the convent.'

'The Saxons? Ha, yes. You'd do better to stay here and
work for Hertha and Burl. They're all right. Yes, Burl is a
randy beast, but Hertha won't let him touch you, she's as
jealous as the devil. You'll get food and a roof over your head,
and be safe from the Saxons.' Her eyes strayed to the charm
about Ursulet's neck. 'Here, what's this? Are you one of
them?'

'I don't know what you mean.'

'Oh, of course you wouldn't say so, but you needn't be
afraid to tell me – I'm on good terms with plenty of them,
though I'm not one myself – lots of people would say I am,
for they'll say that of anyone who knows anything. You're
young, but I'd say you were an apprentice.'

'I'm not a witch, if that's what you mean,' said Ursulet.

'Then why do you wear the Witches' Star?'

'Is it? I didn't know – somebody gave it to me—'

'Did they so? Then I'd counsel you to hide it if you don't
want to be taken for a witch. Oh, one more bit of advice. Keep

close inside this hut tonight, and as near as possible to Hertha. Old Burl will have all his friends in to drink to the child, and if you don't know what that will mean, you soon will. But no matter how drunk he is, he's afraid of Hertha. She makes him hold his wassail in the other hut, so they won't touch you if you stay where Hertha can see you.'

So at last Ursulet lay down to rest on a heap of straw in the corner of the hut, amidst indescribable muddle and squalor; and she hoped to sleep at last, but was too jangled and strung up by all that she had been through. For hours she listened to the Jutes yelling over their drink in the other hut, the baby crying at intervals, and Hertha snoring. So began the first of many, many nights, and many days, as unpaid drudge among the Jutes, without a name or any to recall her identity.

5 · The Knighting of Ambris

When Ambris's father, Gawain le Jeune, was slain in Arthur's last great battle, the light of the sun went out for Ambris, and for his mother, and for many besides. There were so many that died there – not only Young Gawain, but Ambris's grandfather, the gentle Gareth, and his three great-uncles, Gawain the Elder, Gaheris and Agravaine. Some said that Gawain and Gaheris had been killed earlier, almost accidentally, in the mêlée that went on when Guinevere was rescued by Lancelot from execution by burning; but no one quite knew the rights of it. Least of all Ambris, who was not much more than seven years old. But he knew that they were gone, with Arthur the King and all the Round Table, and he was all the comfort left to the red-haired Lady Vivian. His grandmother Leonie of Lyonesse was so broken by the grief of losing both her husband and her son that she died soon after. But none witnessed the grief of the Lady Lynett.

The Lady Lynett was not like anyone else at all. From fifty

years old she had not changed much. She rode about the country on one of King Arthur's own black horses (which men said were cross-bred from the tall Eastern horses which the Romans brought over), sometimes with an attendant dwarf, sometimes all alone, as a kind of special messenger between King Arthur and his knights. She had been doing this ever since she was young. She it was who, when her sister Leonie, the Lady of Lyonesse, had been besieged by the Knight of the Red Laundes, had ridden to Camelot to ask the King for a champion for her sister, and had brought back Gareth. All the world knows how unmercifully she treated him on that journey – for she was deeply in love with him. Of course he married Leonie, as Lynett had foreseen he would; and King Arthur had ever so kindly bestowed Lynett's hand on Gareth's brother Gaheris. What wonder that the marriage was not successful? It was as well she had not been given to Gawain, for he was subject to sudden rages, and might quite well have lopped off her head in one of them. Gaheris had left her on their wedding night and carefully avoided meeting her again; and Lynett could have gone back to live with her sister – and Gareth, and their son Gawain the Younger; but this she would not do. So it was at this time she became Arthur's 'Damosel Errant', riding about the country for months together, carrying letters, taking confidential messages to outlying rulers, turning up at the most unexpected moments. There was a bag on her saddle-bow, which might contain letters, or golden coins, or now and then the decapitated head of a man, with a demand for vengeance, or a story of vengeance accomplished. In appearance she was an impressive woman even into her sixties, having a well-shaped face and a clear skin, though very sunburnt, and bright brown eyes. She was taller than many men, and sat her horse with a back as straight as a soldier's; she rode about wearing a soldier's old leather hauberk plated with metal, and a wide skirt of coarse grey frieze, and great boots up to her knees. She wore her grey hair streaming down her back, with a red kerchief tied over it and caught back behind the ears – so that people should see she was a woman, she said, and accord her the privileges of her sex. In King Arthur's time she rode fearlessly up and down the country; now the land was not so safe, but still she rode up and down, and took her chance on what she met. Robbers and outlaws all knew her as a remarkable healer of wounds and sickness – this in itself would sometimes have been enough to brand a woman as a witch, but the outlaws valued her, and perhaps feared her acid tongue. What errands she rode on now that the King was dead were her own business.

Ambris heard her come in, after one of her long absences – she strode through the open hall, and into the panelled solar where he was sitting disconsolate and idle by the fire. She slapped her big leather gloves down on the table.

'Come,' she said. 'We're going on a journey, you and I. Tomorrow morning.'

Nobody gainsaid Aunt Lynett, least of all her grand-nephew, though he was now eighteen. The next morning, after a leave-taking with his mother that Lynett mercilessly cut short, they were out on the roads together – he on his good bay hackney, she on the great black horse of Arthur's stable. It was said she had outlived three of them.

They rode all day with but short pauses for rest, and in the evening (it was late sad January) came to a place which seemed to be more than half underwater, for all along the side of the road, sometimes on both sides, stretched pale, still meres, bordered with thick beds of reeds. No hills or trees anywhere, only the flat sheets of water, and the reeds, and the road winding on a narrow causeway. In some places there were bays among the reeds, where wildfowl of all kinds gave life to the scene – ducks playing in the waters, moorhens, swans, and once a white spectral pelican. But in other places, and increasingly as they went on, the water was deserted, quiet, broken only by a rising fish or a frog. The sun had disappeared into clouds, and set without glow or colour, and the meres gleamed as coldly as mirrors in an empty room.

Then, while there was still faint light in the sky, Lynett

reined in her horse and they halted. She pointed, where far away a solitary hill rose, a towering pointed hill with a strange turret on its top.

Then, she said: 'There is Avalon, the holy Ynys Witrin.'

'Do we go there?' he asked, almost in a whisper, for the name and the sight had struck awe into him.

'No. We stay here. Dismount now.'

And as he dismounted he saw, almost as if it had previously been invisible, a group of low dark buildings beside him. One was a chapel – it had the pointed shape, the belfry above, and a subdued, flickering light coming from the candles that burnt on the altar within. Another was a rough reed-thatched hut, and from it came firelight; and a man stepped out and greeted Lynett with courtly formality. The words and gestures suited oddly with the wild, cold, barbaric scene by the bleak waters at the fall of night.

The man did not seem like an ordinary hermit – he wore no monastic cowl or habit, but the rough leather garments that a knight would wear under his armour. His head was not shaven, but bald with age, except for the white locks that hung behind his ears and on his neck; his brows were bushy, and a thin, straggling, forked beard fell down over his breast. His face was mild and calm, and his eyes such as Ambris felt he would trust entirely. The old man was girt with a leather belt, studded with bronze, that held a long sword in a threadbare scabbard; and behind him, in his hut, the full armour of a Knight of the Round Table hung in order on the wall.

They stepped inside the hut, a small enough place but neat, and lighted by the fire; and Lynett put her hand on Ambris's shoulder.

'This is the boy,' she said. 'Ambris, my young kinsman, this is Sir Bedivere, the last of the true Knights of the Round Table.'

With tears in his eyes, Ambris knelt and kissed the old man's hand.

Sir Bedivere smiled, and drew him to his feet.

'He'll do,' he said. 'Tall and has a look of the Orkneymen. Is he old enough?'

'He's eighteen.'

'It will suffice. *She* must be nearly two years older, of course, and we must not wait too long. I think it is time.'

'That is why I have brought him to you.'

'Yes, I think it is time, or nearly so. See here,' and from the back of the hut he brought what looked like a long garland of leaves, some parched dry, some only wilting as if newly plucked. There were bunches of different kinds of leaves, tied at regular intervals along a piece of cord. Lynett sat down on a stool and examined each bunch in detail.

'Let me see – birch, ash, willow – that's Belinus. Hawthorn, holly, hazel – Hauteric. Vine, ivy, willow – Margansius. Elder reed, rowan – Ringel. And each one with an acorn on a twig, to show they stand pledged to Arthur's heir.' She went on counting over the leaves. Every combination of leaves and twigs spelled out a name to her, and there were maybe thirty bunches of leaves in the garland. Over some she chuckled with pleasure – others, she looked sharply up at Bedivere and questioned him, but always she was satisfied.

'Have they all been here?' she said.

'They have all been here, and made their vow, to support the lawful house of Arthur, if his true heir can be found.'

'Not Mordred and his brood?'

'I said his lawful heir. We know who that is – the true-born daughter by Guinevere his queen. The Princess Ursulet – if she can be found.'

At the mention of the Princess, Ambris lifted his head and gave a smothered exclamation. The other two turned, looked at him, looked back at each other with raised eyebrows, but said nothing. The firelight flickered on the bare walls of the hut. Sir Bedivere rose and made a simple meal for them – rye bread, cheese, cresses and small ale, served in wooden vessels and platters. Hungry though Ambris was, he was too oppressed by the solemnity and gravity of his companions to eat much; but he drank the thin tasteless ale gratefully, for his mouth was dry.

When they had fed and rested, Sir Bedivere broke the silence.

'Ambris, my son – are you prepared for the honour of knighthood?'

'What, me? – I mean – here and now, sir?'

'Here and now. We need you to go on the quest for Arthur's lost daughter, and for that, you must be knighted. I alone am left of the true Company of the Round Table, and so I alone have the right to confer knighthood on you. I wish indeed it could be done as in the old days – with all the knights here, and the ladies, and the monks chanting, the tapers and the banners, and Arthur himself to lay the sword on your shoulder – but since that cannot be, I must do the best I can for you.'

'I am not shriven,' the boy said, his eyes on the ground. 'Will you shrive me?'

'No, I cannot do that, for I am not a priest. Tomorrow the priest will come over from Avalon, as he does every morning, and you shall be shriven and houselled. But for now, you will be purified in another way. Go out now, and down to the side of the mere, and bathe yourself in the water.'

'What, now? In the dark—'

'It is not so very dark. There is a moon behind the clouds.'

'Must I – must I go alone?'

'Of course – who should go with you? Look, you must stand in the water by the bank – it is not very deep – naked, mind you – and plunge right in, over your head and all. Every hair of you. You understand?'

The boy nodded mutely.

'Here is a linen cloth to dry your body, and you will not put your clothes on again, but clothe yourself in this tunic of white wool. It's warm enough. And then come back here to me.'

Ambris said 'Yes, sir,' very quietly and shakily, and went out into the dark. In spite of the moon behind the clouds, it seemed very dark to him, very cold and frightening. At the edge of the gleaming mere, trembling, he took off his clothes, and as he did so, the glittering eyes of a toad came into his sight, on a corner of the bank – a very large toad, and it seemed to be watching him. He didn't like that toad one bit.

He laid his clothes on the wet grass of the bank, carefully placing the towel and the white wool tunic on the top of the pile. Then, shrinking and bare, he stepped into the muddy water. It was intensely cold, and slippery underfoot, with sharp stones and submerged snags lacerating his feet. Gritting his teeth, he plunged under the water and then scrambled quickly out. The woollen tunic felt gratefully warm as he put it on, and slipped his shoes on his scratched feet. In a few minutes he was at the door of the hut, where Bedivere awaited him.

'Not your shoes,' said Bedivere. 'Take those off again.'

Now he led him, cold as he was and with his hair still dripping, to the little chapel adjoining the cell. It was a bare little room of stone, with an opening to the westward that had no door to close it, and a small unglazed window high up to the eastward, under which was a rough stone altar, covered with a cloth, with a bronze cross and candlesticks. The two candles burned steadily. In front of the altar was a faldstool. On the altar lay a sword, and below was piled a knight's full suit of armour.

'Here,' said Bedivere, 'you are to keep your vigil of knighthood. Kneel here at the faldstool, and fix your eyes on the altar. You will stay there until you hear me ring the bell at daybreak, and you must *not* look round. You must not turn your head even once. Not even once you understand, no matter what you may see or hear. Now let us pray for your dedication.'

So Bedivere left him, in the dark little cell, kneeling, resting his arms on the faldstool, staring at the dull gleam of the bronze cross lit by the candles. He heard Bedivere's footsteps die away beyond the open doorway.

As he settled to his vigil he recalled what his father had told him about the time when he kept his own vigil of knighthood at Camelot – how first of all Mordred and his ribald friends had tried to frighten him by making shadow-pictures on the wall in front of him, and had run away laughing, but he had to keep from looking round; and then how dreadful thoughts assailed him, and took the visible forms of demons, a hideous old man, a beautiful woman with the body of a serpent.

But he, Ambris, must not ask for trouble by thinking about such things. He would say his Pater and Ave, and another Pater and Ave, and not fall asleep . . .

A soft footfall behind him startled him into full attention. Very soft and light – not old Bedivere's, and certainly not his great-aunt's. Someone came in through the doorway behind him – without moving his head he tried to turn his eyes as far as he could first to right and then to left. By the corner of his left eye he could almost see the intruder – something white-robed, soft, glimmering, female. She passed behind him again, and he could glimpse her from the corner of his right eye. A very faint breath of perfume came to him.

He brought his eyes back to the centre of the bronze cross, and spoke to the presence.

'Whoever you are, come out here in front, and let me see you.'

There was a rustle of soft draperies, and she came round him and stood between him and the altar. She was strangely beautiful, tall, pale, robed in white, with intensely black hair.

'Since you ask me to stand in the holy place I am able to do so,' she said, smiling. 'That is courteous of you. But I don't think you need go on kneeling there very much longer. You are tired. I am sent to bid you take a rest.'

He drew a long breath and prepared to rise from the faldstool – then he checked.

'Thank you,' he said, 'but I am not to rise till I hear the bell. I do not think it is time yet.'

'Oh, have it your own way,' she laughed. 'If you want to

cling to these old-fashioned forms ... You want to find the
Princess, and restore her to Arthur's throne, do you not? Well,
let me tell you, your dear old godsibs in there, Sir Bedivere
and the lady, your great-aunt Lynett – they don't know where
she is. But I know! Oh yes, I know!'

'Do you indeed?' He leant forward, gripping the rail of the
faldstool. 'Then tell me where to find her.'

'Fair and softly!' The red lips laughed at him. 'Yes, I know
where she is. And I will tell you, nay, I will lead you to her
and help you to set her on Arthur's throne – for a price.'

'What is your price?' he whispered.

'Come with me and I will show you,' and she sidled round
again to his left, and up till she stood by his left shoulder.
'Come with me. It will do you more good than all this ancient
formality. Get up off your knees, and turn round, and come
with me, and I will tell you what my price is.'

'No,' he said, keeping his eyes firmly on the altar. 'I don't
believe you, and I'm not going to be persuaded to leave here.
Please leave me alone.'

'Indeed? But you must believe that I know where the
Princess is. You will not find her without me.'

'I don't trust you, and I don't believe you.'

'Young sir,' she said, coming round to his right again (so
she had made two circles widdershins around him), 'you are
not as courteous as a knight ought to be.'

'I'm sorry,' he said. 'But I have my orders.' But his voice
was beginning to weaken. She crossed in front of him, and as
she passed he could see her golden ornaments, and how her
feet moved in golden sandals. Then she went to his left and
stood again behind him.

'Ambris, Ambris,' she said, very low, so that he only just
heard her. 'Look at me, Ambris.' She came closer, and
breathed on his neck, so that his hair bristled upright. 'Ambris
– look at me. I am very beautiful, Ambris. You may not get
the chance to see me again. Turn and look at me – Ambris,
Ambris ...'

And now indeed it was hard for him to resist – just to look round once, just once—

And then the cock crew – and reminded him of many things.

He clung to the faldstool, crying wildly, 'Oh, no betrayal! no betrayal!' – and then the footsteps suddenly ceased, and the sense of presence and the warmth and perfume were gone. Yet he did not venture to turn round. Instead, he lay against his folded arms on the faldstool, as if swooning. Then in the little belfry above him he heard the bell ring, and Sir Bedivere came in and laid his hand on his shoulder. He looked behind now, and saw that the daylight was coming in through the door of the chapel.

Bedivere said no word to him, but turned the faldstool round so that Ambris could sit and rest himself against it. Then came Lynett, and laid a rich embroidered cloth on the altar, and set up six silver candlesticks and a silver cross in place of the bronze one, and brought holy water and a smoking censer. First she took the holy water, and Bedivere the censer, and they made purification, and censed and sprinkled the armour and the sword; then Bedivere put the armour on Ambris – the breastplate, the belt, the spurs, the helmet, the shield, and lastly the sword. And he made Ambris kneel, and repeat the vows of knighthood; and finally Bedivere drew his own great sword, and held it point upward, so that the rays of the morning sun ran along its blade – then lowered it till the blade rested on Ambris's shoulder.

'In the Name of God, and of King Arthur who does not die,' he said, 'I make you, now and for ever, a knight of the Round Table.' Then he raised him by the right hand, saying, 'Rise, Sir Ambrosius.'

And so Ambris became a knight.

And as he walked from the chapel with unsteady steps, Lynett stood before him.

'Since there is no man to do this for you,' she said, 'I must. Greetings, Sir Ambrosius, and be thou a good knight' – and her great leathery hand lashed out and caught him a stinging blow on the cheek.

He stood bewildered, his hand to his cheek.

'I'm sorry,' he said. 'What was that for?'

Now she caught both hands in her own, and kissed him, and he saw that there were tears in her eyes.

'That is the knightly buffet, my son. It is a dear privilege, and carries all my blessing with it.'

And he remembered how he had heard that the old Gawain, his great-uncle, had done the like to his father, the young Gawain, at his knighting, and knocked him down, so that he swooned; and he smiled, and pressed Lynett's arm that was linked in his.

'Rather you than my great-uncle, dear aunt,' he said, and they both laughed for the first time in those two days.

6 · *The New Knight*

The priest arrived from Avalon, and Mass was said in the little chapel, as was right and proper; and then Ambris was allowed to sleep. When he woke, Bedivere and Lynett had prepared as festive a breakfast for him as a hermit might – frumenty and cream, and eggs, and honeycomb – and afterwards just a small glass of sweet red wine for each of them, to drink to the new-made knight. And after the solemnity and strain of the ceremony, in the light cheerful morning with the birds singing, they relaxed and were cheerful, and Ambris discovered that these two, immensely old as they seemed to him, could be merry company. And after a while, he ventured to tell them of what he had seen and heard during his vigil – and at once they were grave again.

'I thought she was dead,' Lynett said.

'No, beings such as she are not slain so easily,' said

Bedivere. 'They say that Merlin bade the young Gawain spare her life, but banish her from the land of living men.'

'But who *is* she?' Ambris asked.

'She is Morgan le Fay, the mistress of all illusion and glamoury, skilled above all others in making that seem which is not. She was mighty for evil in King Arthur's day. She is also some sort of kin to you,' said Lynett, 'for she is the sister of Vivian-Nimue, who was your mother's grandmother, Merlin himself being your mother's grandfather. Morgan is also the sister of Morgause, the Queen of Orkney, who was the mother of Gawain, Gaheris, Agravaine, and Gareth your grandfather.'

'And of Mordred also,' said Bedivere.

'And of Mordred also . . . She will try every possible means to destroy the daughter of Arthur. It seems she seeks to destroy you also. She wishes to rule Britain herself, or through her creatures – such as Mordred. If she can, she will place Mordred or one of his sons, on the throne. But we, Ambris – Sir Bedivere and I, we know the knights, barons and earls too, that are ready to rise in support of Arthur's daughter, if she can be found. And that is for you to do.'

'I will, of course, if I can,' he said, 'but why me?'

'Bedivere must remain here, as a centre upon which the well-wishers may rally – he is the hub of the wheel. And I,' said Lynett, 'it is too well known that I was Arthur's messenger. If I sought her out now, I would be followed, and would lead the enemy to her. You, I think, will not be suspected yet, unless the spirit of the witch-woman has means to lead Mordred to you. You may escape Mordred's vigilance. But there is no one else. *You* must find her, and bring her here, whence we will go to Avalon, where our friends will muster their armies. The true men, whose names I know, are recorded in my garland of the tree-Ogham. Will you do this?'

'Certainly I will, God helping me. But where do I start looking for her?'

'You could go first to Amesbury, where lives Melior, a

priest, the last man that knew Merlin. He was present when Guinevere died, and from him you may learn something.'

Bedivere turned abruptly. A man stood in the door of the hut.

'What is it, Wulf?'

'He's coming, sir – a great lord on a horse, with two serving-men behind – it could be the Earl Mordred. Three miles off as the road winds – I cut across the bog before them—'

Lynett was already stripping down the garland from where it hung, and cramming it under her wide skirt.

'Hide the boy,' she said. 'Ambris, you mustn't be seen. Get in here,' and she uncovered a hole under a heap of firewood at the furthest recess of the hut— 'Don't, whatever you see or hear – *whatever happens* – don't come out. Bedivere will meet him. I'll take the horses and hide in the reeds – I know how to, well enough. They won't find *this*,' and she touched the garland that rustled under her skirt.

Bedivere had taken Ambris's armour off him, all but the belt and sword; Ambris was now dressed in his leather jerkin and hose, which would not rattle. He drew himself into the hole under the firewood and Bedivere piled the faggots in front of him. He could hear, but could see nothing. Tensely listening, he heard horses outside the hut, and the heavy footsteps of three men.

A heavy voice, between unctuous and brutal, greeted Bedivere.

'Well, if it isn't our old friend Bedivere! A long time since we met, old knight. You'd hardly believe the difficulty I've had in finding you— Oh, sit down, sit down. A snug little hermitage you have here – and a lot of interesting things in it.' The heavy steps went round the hut as if searching. 'Not many books – no parchments now? Or letters? No scrolls of names, for instance? No?'

Ambris heard a metallic clank, as if the newcomer was handling the old knight's armour.

'Ah, you keep your old Round Table equipment. I see. Very

touching sentiment. But what's this? A *new* suit of armour?
Well now, who might this be for?'

'My lord Mordred,' came Bedivere's voice, 'since you ask
me, it's for the nephew of my priest that comes over from
Avalon – his fancies dwell much on the old days—'

'Do you know, I'm not much inclined to believe in your
priest or his nephew?— Men, seize him.' There was the sound
of a scuffle. Then the voice went on. 'Now, don't you think
you'd better admit what I know already – that you're conspir-
ing, together with that old witch Lynett, to set a pretender on
Arthur's throne? Oh, you needn't shut your mouth and roll
your eyes. I know it all, you see, and can wait here till I catch
all your fellow-conspirators. Only I'd rather know their
names, and also who this armour is for – and I think you'll
tell me very shortly.'

There was a tense silence in the hut. Ambris wished he
could only see what was happening.

'Will you tell now?'

No answer, but a hiss of breath drawn in sharply, and then
a long shuddering sigh, and a horrible smell of burning flesh.

Ambris could bear it no longer. He broke from his hiding-
place, sword in hand, scattering the firewood – the men-at-
arms, taken by surprise, but their hands up to ward off the
shower of twigs. All on the spring of the one impulse, without
stopping, Ambris thrust his sword into the back of the man who
was stooping over Bedivere, scooped up the half-unconscious
Bedivere in his left arm as if he had been a child, was out of
the hut, on to the back of one of the three horses tethered
there, and away, thundering down the causeway.

A man rose out of the reeds and ran beside him – he
recognized Wulf, Bedivere's man. 'Come this way, sir,' he
said. 'Follow me, I know the secret tracks.' Ambris listened
for pursuit behind him, but for the moment there was none.
He followed Wulf into the narrow tracks among the reeds,
supporting Bedivere on his saddle-bow against his breast.
What a mercy the old man was so thin and light, he thought.

Presently they reached a little island closed round with

willows, into which the narrow causeway led. In the middle of the willows was Lynett with her horse and his.

She cried out when she saw Ambris and Bedivere.

'What has happened? Why are you both here?'

'The young fool broke out of covert,' Bedivere growled, slipping to the ground and unsteadily finding his feet.

'Sir Bedivere was being tortured,' exclaimed Ambris. 'I couldn't sit by and hear it – I *couldn't*.'

'But my son,' cried Lynett, 'all depended upon Mordred not seeing you. We are undone! He knows you now – are you not pursued?'

'Oh – I seem to have done the wrong thing. I'm sorry,' said Ambris, red-faced and looking at the ground. 'I just couldn't let them torture him.'

'I was enduring Mordred's rough questioning as best I might,' grumbled Bedivere, 'when our young jack-hare here breaks covert and runs for it, taking me with him. And now his face is known and all's marred.'

'But sir,' said Ambris, 'I don't think he ever saw my face – I doubt if his men did either. You see, before I caught you up, I thrust my sword in his back, and as he fell forward his men ran to catch him – and perhaps that is why they have not pursued us yet.'

Lynett's face cleared. 'You did? You thrust your sword through Mordred's back? God send you killed him!'

'I fear not. It wasn't a very knightly blow, for my first. I don't think I put it through his heart – only through his thick buttock!'

Bedivere and Lynett shouted with laughter together.

'Oh, well done, lad! Pity it wasn't higher, but no matter! He won't sit his horse for many months – and how he'll curse—' Lynett slapped her knee and rocked to and fro. 'No, with any luck they'll not have noticed your face, and we've got a start of them. But we won't stay here. Come, whether or no, you must make for Amesbury, but go roundabout. Bedivere and I will go to Avalon, but you mustn't show yourself there yet.'

Ambris turned to Bedivere, who was leaning heavily on his arm.

'Let me help you to my own horse, sir,' he said. 'Did the villain hurt you much? What did he do to you?'

'We won't speak of it. But – thank you, son, thank you. You came in time, when all's said and done. And your aunt has the names safe and sound – under that petticoat of hers. Come, let's be going.'

7 · The Slave of the Jutes

'**W**ife,' said Burl the Jute, as they snorted and shuffled together in their straw bed, 'I'm going to sell that girl Urz'l. Grimfrith the Saxon will give me a cow for her.'

'You're not! She's a good girl, and useful.'

'She's no use. Willibrod is weaned long ago, and you'll have no more children. What, do you think you should have a body-woman to run after you and comb your hair, as if you were a lady?'

'Indeed! And who's to carry water, and feed the swine, and herd the geese, and tend the hens, and wash your filthy shirts when you'll part up with them, and mend Willibrod's clothes when he tears them, and sweep out the byre, and—'

'Oh, peace! Look you, scolding shrew that you are, the cow we shall get for her will have a calf, which is more than this Urz'l will ever do—'

'Not for want of your trying, you wicked old man.'

'Never mind that – but what's the good of a girl who won't take a man at all? Twenty years old and still a maid! It's not in nature – it's all wrong. She's losing her looks, too – she's too thin. Well, if Grimfrith fancies her, let him try, that's all. And this cow, I tell you, she will have a calf, and we can trade that for another girl, younger and even more use to you.'

'More use to you, you mean, you filthy old lecher. That's

what it is – you're tired of this one saying no to you, and she's past her best, and you'll have one young and willing. I know you, you old Nithing.'

'You be silent, or I'll take my strap to you. I say she shall go to Grimfrith, and go she shall. Mind you, these Saxons don't keep their slaves long.'

'So I've heard. I'm sorry for the maid, then.'

'Saxons have no patience – a word and a blow, and often the blow's a heavy one. They can't be bothered with them. That's why they don't often take prisoners in battle – they don't find them worth the trouble of keeping. Especially the clever ones – they die the first.'

'Then I say it's a pity to let the maid go to such as they. She's been a good girl to me these six years.'

'Oh yes, you're getting soft now, are you? I tell you, I mean to have that cow – it's in calf already, did you know? I mean to have it, and get rid of that Urz'l, so shut up, you.'

In the morning, a wet and discouraging spring morning, Ursulet stood by the doorposts looking out on the muddy yard of the farmstead, dimly wondering if there was anything in the world but mud. She was twenty, and very tall and thin – too thin, for her master fed her but poorly and worked her far too hard, and her mistress was much the same, in spite of occasional feeble attempts at kindness that mostly came to nothing. Ursulet wore a cast-off dress of Hertha's, of loosely woven brown linen stuff – a texture not unlike sacking. It was far too big for her, of course, and hung shapelessly on her angular bones; she had tied it up with the straw cord they used to bind the hay-bales. If there were time, she often told herself, she would plait a straw belt – but whenever there was a little bit of time to spare, she was too tired. Her long pale hair was without colour or lustre, and was screwed to the back of her head in a tight bun. Her face was a brickdust brown, in the midst of which her luminous light-grey eyes looked out startlingly. Her feet were as tough as leather, and as brown.

Now she was watching Burl and his neighbour Grimfrith the Saxon walking slowly towards the house.

'Well, there she is,' said Burl. 'We'll walk over to your place together, and then I'll take the cow back.'

'Right,' said the Saxon, and seized hold of Ursulet's arm. 'Come along now – you belong to me.'

Ursulet jibbed, pulling against the unpleasant hand that held her.

'What's this?' she said. 'You can't do this to me.'

'What, we can't do this to you?' guffawed Burl, and the other man joined in.

'You can't sell me. I'm a free woman. I'm not your slave.'

'Not your slave, she says?' roared Burl. 'Not your slave – these six years, eh? Not your slave! Why you no-good bundle of bones, who in the devil's name do you think you are, then?'

And who was she? *Who* was she? Ursulet could hardly think, could hardly remember, after six years of no other life but this – only that she was no slave. Then, like a lesson learnt long ago, it came back to her. She drew herself up.

'I am the Princess Ursulet, lawful and only daughter of King Arthur of Britain and his queen Guinevere.'

For a moment the two men, and Hertha in the background, stood round-eyed and round-mouthed at her sudden stateliness, then they all roared with laughter.

'Princess, she says! Daughter of King Arthur, she says! Oh, beg your pardon, your royal ladyship! 'And Burl swept her a mock bow, and followed it with an obscene gesture. 'Wife, we thought she was mad, but we never thought she was as mad as this.'

'See what a bargain I'm getting!' shouted Grimfrith. 'A royal princess for the price of one cow! Thank you, good neighbour, I'm sure. And now I can call myself King of Britain – that's a good one!'

'Come along, king's daughter,' said Burl, and grabbed her at one side while Grimfrith closed up on the other. 'See the royal neck-ring we've got for you,' and between them, in spite of her struggles, they fastened an iron slave-ring round her neck. There was a chain attached to it, and Grimfrith held the end of the chain. She was as helpless as a puppy on a leash. She fought and struggled with all the strength in her spare wiry body, but the horrible ring bit into her neck and choked her. No use to scream, though she rent the air with her screams. If there were any people within miles, they were only too used to the sound of screams coming from that quarter. She dug her feet into the mud of the path, but her captor dragged her to the ground and she was pulled along by the collar, strangling. In the end, exhausted, she gave up, and trudged along where she was led, her captors still laughing.

She knew exactly what the Saxon would want, as soon as he got her to his house. Which house was the usual one-room hut, even more dirty and untidy than the Jute's, for Grimfrith's wife was dead, and his last woman slave also. There was the box of straw that served for a bed, and he tried to drag her to it as soon as Burl had left with his cow. Having got his cow, Burl was no longer interested in Ursulet. But the moment Grimfrith loosed his hold on Ursulet's chain, having her behind a barred door, Ursulet snatched up a knife from the table, and held it point upwards towards him. He gave back a little at first, but would still have overpowered her, but that he snatched away the upper part of her garment, and there round her neck was the reversed pentagram.

'Oh, good God!' he exclaimed, for he was a Christian of sorts when he remembered it. 'The woman's a witch! Burl never told me that.' He backed over to the other side of the hut making first the sign of the Cross, and then that of the Hammer of Thor to make sure.

'Are you a witch, girl?' he asked in rather less than his usual loud tone. She saw her chance and took it.

'Yes, I'm a witch, and if you lay a hand upon me the creeping palsy will take you. The man who lies with me will never be a man again.' She pointed two fingers at him, and he shrank back against the wall.

'The Lord between us and all harm! I'll not meddle with a

witch. Get out of here. Get out, do you hear?' He groped to the door and unbarred it, then he grabbed a pitchfork, and with the tines each side of her neck thrust her out, slammed the door, and bolted it. She stumbled and slipped in the filthy mud outside the door, but quickly picked herself up, and ran with all her might away from the homestead – anywhere to get away from both the Saxon and the Jute. So far she had escaped; no doubt the two would get together after a while, and Grimfrith would accuse Burl of having sold him a witch, and Hertha would say she had never shown any signs of witchcraft, and then they'd start looking for her again. Grimfrith wouldn't lightly give up the price of a perfectly good cow. But for the moment she was free, so she ran on further into the forest.

8 · Fugitive Again

She was a very different fugitive from the one who had fled from the sack of the nunnery, six years past. Then, she had been tenderly reared, soft of flesh, as innocent of the world as one of the Abbess's white rabbits. Now she was hard in every muscle, and the feet that had been so bruised, even in sandals, had never worn sandals since, and were harder bare than many feet in shoes. There was no form of work that was hard, dirty, unpleasant, filthy or tedious to which she was not hardened.

And as to her mind – it might have been expected that the numbing routine of work, exhaustion, sleep – work, exhaustion, sleep – would have atrophied her mind, and made her incapable of either thinking or feeling. But the intellect with which she was born was not so easily killed. When she had recovered from the shock of her violent uprooting, her mind had adapted itself, and made the best of what it had. She had quickly learnt the language of the people around her – that of the Angles, Saxons and Jutes – but she continued to say her prayers in Latin, and sometimes sang the Latin hymns of the convent when Burl was not there to hear her – Hertha and little Willibrod listened to them with wonder. And she talked to herself inside her head in her own Celtic language. Sometimes she spoke it with the midwife, so as not to forget it altogether. There was very little company at the Jutish 'Ham', only Burl and Hertha and Willibrod, and sometimes Willibrod's brother and sister, who were grown up and had settlements of their own; sometimes the midwife, and very occasionally a neighbour or two – otherwise, nobody.

There were things that Ursulet could not bear to remember, so much of her convent life was blotted out, together with much that was behind a still earlier barrier – her beautiful mother and her heroic father, and everything before she was six. But some of her convent training remained with her, and set her apart from the grossness of the people around her; and she had a feeling for personal cleanliness which the Jutes ridiculed; she clung to fastidious table manners, which they ridiculed still more. And now and again, something – a smell of flowers or of aromatic wood burning, or the recollection of a song – would cause some strange thing to flash into her memory.

But here she was, an outcast and a fugitive once again, going deeper into the forest, on a wet, raw afternoon now rapidly falling towards night. She thought she could make shift, now, to sleep rough, knowing much more about how to manage than when she had first run away; but on the other hand she knew the limitations of wild living. She knew that all the beds of beech-leaves in the forest would now be soaking wet, and that at this time of year there was very little wild food to be found – no berries, no nuts, roots were hard to find, mushrooms not found at all in that kind of country. She had no means of catching any kind of animal or bird. No, even for a skilled woodcraftsman, it was a bad time of year. Her clothes were wet and torn, and she was very tired and hungry, and still had that frightful slave-ring on her neck, and

the chain weighing her down. Altogether it was a poor
prospect. And then, she had heard that there were wolves. So
it was hardly to be wondered at that she sank down on the
ground and cried.

Presently she recollected something. The silver pentagram,
which had made Grimfrith call her a witch. The midwife had
called it a witch's token, too, and bade her hide it. There was
a lady who had given it to her – well, perhaps it would do
something, if she tried.

So she clasped both hands over it, on her neck, and wished,
but nothing happened. Then she took it from her neck and
laid it on the palm of her hand, and fixed her eyes firmly
upon it, keeping her gaze steady and her mind on the lady,
and trying to remember what she looked like. And the white
reversed pentagram grew larger and larger, and a door
opened in the middle of it, and she went through.

'I was wondering when you would come to me,' said the
Lady. She was just the same, and so was her beautiful house;
there were the quiet gentle maidservants, the beautiful dress
of sky blue, the food and drink, the warmth and rest. And at
the Lady's first touch, the slave-ring had fallen off and
disappeared. Ursulet lay back and enjoyed the comfort, the
safety, the reassurance.

'So now you have considered, and decided to accept my
help?' said the Lady at last.

'Oh, madame, my state is desperate!' said Ursulet simply.
It was strange how she slipped back into the convent's manner
of speech.

'I know it – and you a princess born. Arthur's heir, and due
by right to sit on Arthur's throne. You are not destined to
starve in a forest and be eaten by wolves. Many, many people
are seeking you, the time is moving, and your crown hovers
in the air over your head. But not all seek you for your own
good. The man who can win you can win Britain, and many
know it. Therefore, my child, let me make sure that you meet
with the right man. Will you do as I say? Oh, dear child, I'm

not asking you to pledge your fealty to me now. Pledges of fealty are frightening, and I have no wish to frighten you. But I will direct you for your own good. Will you let me?'

'Oh, yes, madame,' she sighed.

'Well then – do not go to Camelot or to Avalon. They are held by your enemies. Go south and west – there is a place called Mai-Dun – the Saxons call it Maiden Castle, for they think the name sounds so – but we call it Mai-Dun, the Great Fortress. Go there, and ask for the Lord of Mai-Dun. He will be your helper and protector.'

'And how will I get there, madame?'

'Look, I will draw you a map. We are *here* a good way south of Wimborne, where your convent was. You go further south again, and cross a river to the westward here, and then, when you are in sight of the sea, you will find a road going west; keep the sea on your left hand, and go always westwards, till you reach the town of Dorchester, and there is Mai-Dun. It will take you many days, but there are villages and small settlements along the way, and the folk will help you.'

They seemed to be sitting in a garden, with a floor of white sand, and the lady drew in the sand with an ivory rod. 'There you will see me again.'

'I see,' said Ursulet, and pondered the matter. Then she said,

'My kind benefactress – may I ask one question?'

'Ask one.'

'This token that you gave me – is it really the token of a witch?'

The lady laughed.

'Now, there's a thing to concern yourself with! Why should you be afraid of the name of witch? You told the Saxon, yourself, that you were a witch, and he believed you, and that saved you. Think of it as you please.'

'No, but tell me, for I must be sure. Will you swear to me, by God Almighty, and our Lord Jesus Christ, and His Blessed Mother, that there is no witchcraft in this?'

And suddenly it was as if a mirror was broken – for an

instant she saw the lady's face disfigured as with sudden rage and fear, and there was a smell as of hot metal – and then all was gone, lady and house and garden, and Ursulet was sitting alone in the dark wet forest, shaking with fright. She moved her hand, thinking the silver pentagram was still in it, but somehow it was back on her neck, but the slave-ring and chain were gone. Had she perhaps not taken the pentagram off at all? But then how had the slave-ring disappeared? Her first impulse was to snatch the pentagram off her neck and throw it from her – and then she hesitated, and left it.

And now she was in a desperate state indeed, for the forest was dark and terrible, and far off she thought she could hear a wolf.

'Without doubt she is a witch, that Lady,' she said to herself, and she fell to praying, the old Latin prayers of the convent.

Then before her through the trees she saw a sight that made her hold her breath. A light began to glimmer, and in the midst of the light walked a unicorn. It was the loveliest thing she had ever seen – like a noble white horse, but both larger and shapelier than any horse, with silver cloven hoofs, and a silver beard like a goat's, and the long tapering horn above the eyes. She had heard of the unicorn – and although this also might be glamoury, it surely could be nothing unholy.

So she raised her hand and traced a great cross in the air, and said aloud, 'O thou creature, in the name of God the Father, God the Son, and God the Holy Ghost—'

And she waited to see if this also would disappear. But it did not. The unicorn came on steadily towards her, stopped, and sank on its knees, laying its head on her lap. And now such a feeling of security and holy safety surrounded her that she nestled down beside the unicorn, twining her arms round its neck, and fell happily asleep. And no wolves or any evil thing troubled her at all that night.

When she awoke it was full bright morning and the sun was shining as it should shine in the spring. The unicorn was gone, but so were all the terrors of the night, and she could see that she was out of the forest and on the edge of open country, with villages in sight and a clear road. But she pondered carefully over the visions of the past night.

'One thing is certain,' she said to herself, 'whatever else I do, I must not go where that witch lady told me. I will *not* go to the Lord of Mai-Dun – but I'll remember his name. That road, there, leads south towards the sea, as she said – but from here I can see a turning that goes back north again. That is the way I will take.'

And so she went boldly down into the valley, with her eyes on the far-off church tower, where surely she would find people and help.

9 · *The Snake-stone*

Close to the convent walls of Amesbury, there was a little enclosure of stone walls; inside was fifty feet or so of well-kept grass, with a bed of herbs and a few early spring flowers showing, and a neat stone cell with a chimney. Here, sitting on a bench in the sunshine of a March morning Ambris found Melior, and an old man sitting beside him.

Melior was a man of fifty, but looked much older; he wore a long white robe, and a white hood over his head, to which was pinned a burnished copper jewel, representing three bars of light coming down from above. His companion, who wore a monk's habit, was a big, muscular man, but bent and slouched with age and infirmity – in his youth he must have been powerful, almost a giant. He turned blank white eyeballs towards Ambris as he heard him come through the wicket-gate, and groped towards him as soon as he heard his voice greeting Melior.

'Oh, I know you, young knight. Come here, stand still and let me feel you.'

'Don't be afraid,' Melior said aside to Ambris. 'Let him feel your face. He is blind.'

Ambris stood still, though he shuddered – it was eerie to feel the blind man's fingers running over every inch of his hair his face, his neck, his breast, his arms.

'Good, good,' the blind man muttered. 'He's a good lad. I know him – this is the son of the young Gawain and Vivian, as was destined. Young man, the last sight my eyes saw upon earth was when Merlin raised those two from the dead.'

Ambris felt the hair on his neck creep with awe, and turned to Melior.

'Could Merlin raise the dead?' he almost whispered.

'Yes – once, and paid for it with his life. I was there too.'

'And was it as he says – my parents?'

'Yes, indeed it was, else you had never been begotten.'

The blind man moved away from them, to where a little image of Our Lady stood over by the wall among the flowers, and Ambris heard his deep rumbling voice intoning the 'Ave Maris Stella', and then breaking into it, 'Lady, Lady – beauty beyond belief. Lady, star of the evening. Lady, star of my eyes – I see thee, always I see thee.'

Melior led Ambris into his cell and closed the door.

'That is Sir Bertilak. He was a knight once, though not of the Round Table. As you see, he is stone blind. He was for many years enthralled to Morgan le Fay, and she worked her evil magic on him and changed his shape, many times – horribly. I saw it once.'

'What shape did she give him?'

'I will not tell you. It was horrible. But he was also the Green Knight, whom your father Gawain the Younger withstood. Some day the story shall be told. But long ago he was released from le Fay, and serves Our Lady with great devotion, as you saw – but sometimes he invokes her by strange names— But come, you have an errand to me?'

Briefly, Ambris told his quest.

'Arthur's daughter? Yes, I know there was a daughter, who Merlin said should be the hope of Britain. But I do not know at all where she went, or where she is now. Guinevere spoke of her before she died, but she said she had hidden her from the world, for she did not want her to suffer as she had suffered. By that, I understood the Princess was in a nunnery, but not here in Amesbury. The Queen would not tell me more – I think she was unwilling to have her discovered.'

'Yes, but reverend sir,' said Ambris, 'the country needs her. Britain is divided up and torn into pieces – every baron sets up as king, and there is no law, and Mordred is the worst of all. Britain needs its lawful Queen.'

'I know, young sir, I know, and therefore we must try to find her.'

'Were you the Queen's confessor, reverend sir?'

'I? Why no, I am not a priest – and yet I am a priest. I am a Druid, as Merlin was.'

He was silent for a moment, and then said, 'See here, young knight. I will try if we can find where the Princess is, by Merlin's own craft.' He began to move back stools and tables so as to clear the floor of the cell, and then drew a circle on the floor with chalk.

'What would you do? Are you going to raise the spirit of Guinevere to tell us?'

'God forbid. I will not draw back the spirit of that poor lady from the peace she has found. No, I will look in the Snake-stone, and see what it can tell us.'

From a little casket that stood in a niche of the wall, he brought out a jewel of transparent crystal, like a reliquary.

'Look – this is a very precious thing, and more precious to Bertilak and me than anything but the Body of the Lord. It is a lock of Guinevere's hair.'

Ambris looked with reverence into the little round crystal and saw the hair coiled within – whiter than silver,

'Was her hair always white?'

'After her great sorrow it became white as ashes, and so it was when they clipped this from her head . . .' He controlled his voice with an effort. 'But when she was young it was straw-white, lint-white, with a gleam of sun in it.'

He arranged a kind of small altar in the middle of the circle; Bertilak came quietly to the door, seeming to know what was happening, and the two men, with Ambris looking on, made purification with water and fire. Then Melior sat down on a low stool in front of the altar, whereon was the reliquary containing Guinevere's hair, one lighted candle, and a red rose. There was no other light in the room but from the fire on the hearth.

Then, when all was quiet and tranquil, Melior took the Snake-stone from his neck and held it in his right hand. The Snake-stone, which he had been wearing on a thong round his neck, was a perfectly round crystal about the size of a pullet's egg, clear and colourless as water, but with swirling lines of blue and green inside its transparency. Melior looked at it a long time, then reached out and took the reliquary from the altar, and held it in his left hand. After another long wait he raised his left hand with the reliquary to his forehead, and rested it above his eyes. Then he began to speak.

'The child is in a nunnery – a long way from here, but not overseas. Over a river, but not overseas. Mark this, Ambris. Green hills, not wooded – the road passes a giant – a naked giant cut into the chalk of the hill. There is a harbour, a long deep harbour – follow the river up, up towards its source. The winding bourn – I have it – wim ... wim ... yes, wim ... bourn ... Wimborne. That was the place.'

He looked up from the Snake-stone.

'Wimborne in Dorset. I have heard of it. There was a nunnery there, but that's years ago. It could be there still – Come, we must make an ending.' And he and Bertilak very carefully and deliberately finished the rite for consulting the Snake-stone, and put everything away, and opened the cell door to let the daylight in. Only when everything was completed did Melior address Ambris again.

'So, my young good knight, I advise you to go to Wimborne, and inquire for the nunnery there. There is a road that passes the naked giant at Cerne – the people there think it is devilish,

but I know it is harmless now. Thence turn inland again, and
go by Wool and Wareham, and so you come to Wimborne.'

'Shall I find her still there?' asked Ambris.

'Who can tell, after these years? But at least it is the first
link of the chain. Go on your way, and God speed your
search.'

10 · *The Pentagram*

$\mathcal{H}$e had passed the naked giant and traced his way up
through Wool and Wareham and now came where
Wimborne should be. But no signs of habitation greeted him
as he came over the high downs and into the valley. Mounds
of brambles and nettles here and there, and broken walls, as
if cottages and farms might have stood there – nothing else.
No town at the crossing of the little river – a few tumbled
stones that might once have been a bridge, otherwise only a
neglected ford where his horse stumbled through. There was
the outline of a tower standing up against the sky, by which
he knew it must be the place; but the tower was crumbling
and ruinous. There was the remains of a cobbled street,
overgrown with grass, where his horse's hoofs broke the eerie
silence – burnt-out houses lay to right and left of him. There
was the convent gateway still standing, but no gate. He rode
slowly in. The place was a burnt-out ruin, overgrown with
many years' weeds. Here and there a wall or a pillar showed
where buildings had stood. The church lifted its blackened
walls, and the tottering tower leant over the deserted scene.
There was a thick bush of brambles close to where he stood –
a bunch of rotting rags fluttered from it. It drew his eye, and
as he peered into the bush the eyeholes of a skull peered back
at him . . .

He turned his horse and clattered noisily out of the ruined

gateway – down the ghostly road, through the ford – away from that frightful place.

Beyond doubt the Saxons had been there. Been and gone, leaving their horrible signature behind. So that was where the end had been? This was all? Here the trail ran out?

He sat still on his horse and tried to think. Of course, the Saxons had raided here, as they so often did with no one to stop them now. The nunnery had been burnt to the ground, and all the nuns and their pupils had been killed. So she had been killed too, and there was an end of it. He could go back now and tell that to Lynett and old Bedivere, and watch their faces as their hearts broke. As his was breaking.

Yet some kind of ridiculous optimism made him refuse to admit defeat. Supposing, just supposing, she had escaped? She wouldn't have been a baby. It was hard to tell just when the destruction had happened, but she surely would have been old enough to make a run for it – just supposing? Well, then, which way? Which way more likely than the way he himself had run, straight along the road over the ford – there had been a bridge then. Due south. Well, one road was as good as another to him now – he might as well go and see if there was any place where a fugitive might have been harboured. He shook his reins, turned the horse away from the ruins of Wimborne, and went south.

Plodding onwards straight before him, he found himself first in thick woods, and there made a small camp-fire and spent the night. He slept as best he might, and in the moment of waking he thought he saw a man he knew was Merlin, who said, 'Beware of *this* – but trust *this*.'

The first 'this' was a pentagram with two points upwards and one downwards; the second 'this' was also a pentagram, but with one point upwards. He remembered how his mother (who knew more than anyone might think about magic) had told him that the 'right' pentagram was the one with the point upwards.

Pondering over this, he was quenching the ashes of his fire, when his eye was caught by a metallic gleam on the ground. There lay a little silver pentagram. But which way up is a pentagram when it is lying on the ground?

He considered it a long time, and then he picked it up and examined it carefully. It was made with loops at the back of each point, so that it could be worn any way – either hanging from one point or from two; and there was nothing to show which way it had last been worn.

He found a piece of thin leather thonging among his things, and attached the pentagram carefully by one point and hung it about his neck. And the thought occurred to him that this might be a sign that his quest was not quite so hopeless.

11 · *The Gold Cross*

Following the same road, about noon he smelt wood-smoke, and came to a clearing. There were huts and byres, a couple of cows, and a smoking chimney; and a rough-looking man was sitting on a log and fondling a fat girl with long plaits. The man would be a Jute, Ambris supposed.

'Give you greeting, neighbour,' he called, dismounting from his horse. 'Can you give me a cup of milk, and perhaps a bite of bread? I've money to pay you.'

'Huh?' Burl, for of course it was he, shoved the girl off his lap. 'Money? See it?'

Very cautiously Ambris let him see the glint of a silver piece between his finger and thumb.

That seemed to be the extent of the man's vocabulary in the Celtic, but Ambris had learnt a little of the Saxon, which was always useful, and so he turned over to it.

'Good money here – and thanks.'

'Go fetch bread and milk,' Burl ordered the girl. She

slouched off towards the byre. Ambris tried to engage Burl in conversation, which was far from easy in any language.

'You are a Jute, good man?'

'Jute, yes. Jutes good – Angles not so good. Britons bad. Romans bad.'

'Saxons?'

'Saxons – some good, some – pah!' He spat.

'You have Saxons here?'

'Yes, yes – Grimfrith, my neighbour.'

'But others who come to raid?'

'Yes, yes – six, seven years ago. Very bad. Come up from Poole, over there.'

'Was it the Saxons that burnt Wimborne?'

'Ja, ja – those Saxons, they burnt Wimborne. But not my friend Grimfrith. He good man – Christian, I think.'

At this moment the girl came back with the milk and bread, and with her were Hertha and the midwife. Hertha no longer required the midwife professionally, but liked her occasional company, and found her a rich source of gossip. They greeted the stranger rather more pleasantly than Burl had done.

'He's asking about those damned Saxon raiders,' said Burl.

'Did any escape from Wimborne?' Ambris asked.

'Not a soul,' asserted Burl. 'Killed the lot, they did – nuns, priests, monks, singing-boys, little girls, babies, old beldames – the lot. Burnt the whole place to the ground. No one escapes from the Saxons.'

'Eh?' said the midwife, looking up sideways like a shabby old bird. 'You forget your maid – that girl Urz'l. She escaped from the Saxons at Wimborne, she said.'

'Oh, did she so?' said Burl. 'I'd forgotten.'

Ambris's heart gave a leap.

'What was it you called her?'

'Urz'l.'

'She escaped from the Saxons, and came here? And where is she now?'

'Oh, devil take her,' said Burl. 'I sold her two moons ago; She wasn't any use. She was mad.'

Desperately anxious to find out what the man was saying, Ambris found that it was beyond his capacity to understand his thick Saxon speech. But the midwife translated.

She said in Celtic, 'He says he sold her two moons ago, because she was mad.'

Ambris gave a groan of despair.

'Ask him who he sold her to, and where.'

The midwife turned to Burl.

'The young lord seems mighty concerned about her. He wants to know who you sold her to.'

A look of cunning came into Burl's small eyes. Ambris knew well enough what it meant. Again he showed a coin between finger and thumb, this time a gold one.

Burl roared with laughter. 'Here's a to-do about an ugly bony slave! Well, tell him I sold her to Grimfrith the Saxon, over at Grim's Ley. That madwoman! I'll die of laughing!'

'What does he say, good woman?' Ambris pressed the money into Burl's hand, and Burl went on whooping with laughter.

'He says he sold her to Grimfrith the Saxon, at Grim's Ley, which is west from here along the river.'

'Thanks, thanks – but why do they laugh?' (For Hertha and the girl had joined in the roaring.)

'They laugh, my lord, because that madwoman said she was a Princess, the daughter of King Arthur and his Queen.'

It took Ambris all of that day and most of the next, beating up and down the forest, to find Grim's Ley and the dwelling of Grimfrith. And when he found it, he thought it best to approach it with care. Jutes were all very well, they had been living peaceably under King Arthur for some while, and only wanted to be left alone in their mucky little farmsteads; but Saxons were always out for a fight, even when they were settlers and not raiders. They had seized their lands by violence, and held them by violence; they begrudged the time spent in cultivating them, leaving it to the women as much as they could, and regarding warfare as the only proper occupation for a man.

There was no one outside the house, so Ambris dismounted, hitched his horse, and walked up to the door. He paused a minute, and then knocked.

Instantly the door burst open and Grimfrith hurled himself out, red-faced, dishevelled and drunk. Giving Ambris no time to state his business, he whirled a club over Ambris's head, shouting, 'Damned Welshman!'

Ambris caught his wrist, and the shock made the Saxon drop the club; but he grappled with Ambris now, and they reeled all over the yard together, struggling furiously.

Ambris tried to make him listen.

'You fool, I'm a friend – you fool, stop it – you fool, I want to ask you—' To try and remember the Saxon words while struggling for one's life was just too much. But Ambris had a great deal more science than his adversary, and was also sober; so in a few minutes the Saxon's arm was twisted painfully behind him, and Ambris was holding him firmly down.

'Now – listen,' said Ambris in such Saxon as he could muster. 'You are a fool. I am a friend. I will give you money if you will tell me a thing.'

'Eh?' said the man. 'Why the devil didn't you say so before?'

He relaxed, and very cautiously Ambris let him go. The Saxon staggered back against the wall of his hut.

'Well?' he said. 'Give me the money.'

'First the question,' said Ambris. 'Where is your slave-girl?'

'Oh—' the man shrugged his shoulders. 'Which one?'

'She you – bought – from Burl.' (Yes, he had just enough words to get that across.)

'Oh, her! I sent her away – she was a witch. You understand – a witch.'

'A witch! Oh, great heavens, not a witch!'

'She wore the witch's sign.'

'Where did she go?'

'How the devil do I know? Witches are dangerous. I sent her away. She ran into the woods, I think. Perhaps the wolves ate her.'

'But which way did she go?'

'Which way? Any way. I don't know. Why do you want her? Are you a witch too?'

'Oh, take your money,' said Ambris, altogether disheartened. He tossed the man a gold piece, and mounted his horse.

For many days he ranged round about the woods, searching every corner, pushing long sticks into every drift of leaves; hoping and yet dreading to find something that would tell him of her fate. In particular he tried to find the spot where he had picked up the silver pentagram, but he could not be sure of it – in any case he found nothing anywhere. At last, having convinced himself that he had done all that was humanly possible, and that this time the trail had indeed run out, he turned back. But first he thought he would look once more at the ruins of Wimborne. Not that he hoped to find any further clue there, but that a kind of fascination drew him back. At least it might be a suitable place to say a prayer for her soul.

So he rode up the deserted street, and tethered his horse at the wrecked gateway, and walked once more among the tumbled blocks of stone, the charred beams, the heaps of weeds, now bursting into green growth. There were wild flowers now, pushing up through the decay. The poor little bones in the corners would have their maiden garlands.

Under a bush a gleam of metal caught his eye – a little gold cross was hanging low down on the bush. He stooped down and put out his hand to take it – and at the same instant another hand, smaller than his but browner, reached out to it from the other side of the bush. Amazed, he drew back and stood up – to find himself looking into the light-grey eyes of a girl.

She stood facing him, almost the same height, thin and brown, with dusty, tangled, straw-coloured hair streaming round her face. She was as lean and tough as a young colt. And she, for her part, was looking up at a well-shaped face, the eyes green, the hair dark chestnut and cut straight across the brow, the mouth boyish and impulsive.

She gasped.

'That's mine. Don't you dare take it. My father gave it me.'

Without quite knowing why, he said, 'Who was your father?'

'My father was Arthur, King of Britain,' she answered.

To her astonishment, the strange young man cried out, and running to her side of the bush, fell at her feet, and kissed the hem of her ragged garment.

'You are the Princess,' he said. 'Oh, take your father's jewel from my hands,' and he held the little gold cross up to her. She almost snatched it from him.

'Who are you, and what do you want?' she said.

'I'm a knight of King Arthur – I'm Ambris, son of Gawain – that is, I'm Sir Ambrosius—' he found himself stammering and blundering. 'But what I want – I mean – I want to make you Queen. Many of us do. I've been sent to find you – but we couldn't find you – till now.'

For a moment she stood as if minded to accept him; then a suspicious look came over her face, and she skipped quickly back out of his reach. As she moved, he noticed how light and shapely her feet were, and how gracefully her legs moved under the sackcloth garment.

'How do I know I can trust you?' she said. 'Who sent you?'

'Sir Bedivere sent me, he who last saw Arthur – and my aunt the Lady Lynett, and Melior, the follower of Merlin—'

She shook her head. He could see that his Princess had turned out to be a very wild bird, who would fly from him if she could. He must not lose her now. So, with a little bit of woodman's cunning, he took care to edge her, as she moved backwards away from him, into a corner of the ruins.

'I still don't know if I can trust you. I was warned that men would seek me out because I was the heiress, and that they would wish me harm.'

'Who warned you, and against whom, then?'

'The Abbess warned me, oh, many years ago. She warned me against Mordred, my father's son.'

'I know,' agreed Ambris. 'Mordred is my enemy.'

'But I was warned that there were others – I was told to trust none but the Lord of Mai-Dun.'

'But the Lord of Mai-Dun *is* Mordred.'

This was a shock to her.

'Who told you to trust the Lord of Mai-Dun?' Ambris continued.

'Oh, the lady – a lady I met in the wood.'

'Did she give you any token?'

'Yes, she gave me – Ah! – as she caught sight of the charm on Ambris's neck. 'She gave me *that* – but you're wearing it upside down—'

'I'm wearing it the right way up,' said Ambris. 'The other way is the sign of a witch. I fear your lady was a witch, and I think I know her.'

'Oh—' Ursulet looked to and fro wildly. 'Now I don't know whom to trust, or where I stand. First I'm to beware of Mordred, and trust the Lord of Mai-Dun – and then the Lord of Mai-Dun *is* Mordred – then the lady is a witch, and all she told me must be false – and you wear the witch's star, but it's reversed and you say it's not the witch's star – and as for you, I don't know you— Oh, let me go!' She tried to run past him, but he had her in a corner, and she would not come within an arm's reach of him. 'Oh, let me go back to begging at the farms. At least when they set the dogs on me I know what they mean.'

'Oh, please, please,' he exclaimed, driven to exasperation, 'don't be such a *silly* lady!'

She gasped, and then a smile relaxed the corners of her mouth. This couldn't be the speech of a deceiver. 'Why,' she said to herself, 'he's nothing but a boy. Just a young boy – he could be younger than I am.'

'I think I will trust you,' she said, and put out her brown

hand to him. He took it in his own, and lifted it to his lips, which made her give a little 'Oh!' of surprise.

'Where will you take me?' she said.

'I think we will go first to Shaston – it's not far, and there's a nunnery there, where you can be refreshed and rested, and dressed as you ought to be.'

So he led her out of the ruins and mounted his horse, and showed her how to get up behind him – she had ridden pillion far back in her childhood, but almost too far back to remember. And when she clasped her arms round his body, he was astonished at the way his heart beat, and kept his face sternly forward so that she could not see how it reddened.

12 · A Royal Progress

At Shaston, he told the nuns that this was a noble lady who had been held prisoner by the Jutes and Saxons, and that he was taking her home to her kindred, but for the present he must not tell her name.

To Ursulet, it felt like slipping back into a familiar world long lost, and the nuns were quick to notice that though she looked so wild, she had the convent manners, that came back to her as she looked around her. They bathed her, long and luxuriously, and rubbed her poor weary body with healing oils, exclaiming over the welts and scars left by six years of beatings. They washed her hair, and combed it out, and braided it into two long plaits. The Abbess had a treasure-chest of her own, where were kept the beautiful dresses that the professed nuns had worn, once only, on the day when each one became the Bride of the Lord. Out of these she picked the best one, which was her own – a lovely white gown, made in a fashion of twenty years past, all embroidered with gold and colours; and the nuns arrayed Ursulet in this. So, from a dishevelled bundle of hay and sacking, she stepped out in her full royalty, tall, white-robed, glimmering, flaxen-haired and grey-eyed – Guinevere's daughter.

Ambris saw her, coming slowly down the broad stairway into the refectory – and he fell on his knees before her.

'Oh my lady!' he said. 'You lack nothing now but a royal crown of gold – and that, I swear I will win for you.'

They rested at Shaston for a week, and then set out for Avalon. The nuns provided Ursulet with a neat dress of dark blue wool, and a cloak and hood of the same, and boots of the finest soft leather. They would have given her a palfrey, but Ursulet could not ride. She could milk goats and cows, and was unafraid of a bull or a buck goat, but saddle-horses had never come her way. So she was content to ride pillion behind Ambris, and he was more than content. It seemed to him, as they set out on a fine April morning, with everything bursting into bloom around them, that his cup of joy was full and running over. He was bringing home his Princess – and what a Princess! And there she rode behind him, pressed close against his back, her arms clasped tight around his waist, her soft sunburnt cheek, like a ripening peach, almost touching his as they rode . . .

Their way from Shaston to Avalon should not have been far, and it led mostly up over dry ridgeways, grassy and warm in the spring sunshine. They rested at noon on a green hillside, with the larks singing above them. Nothing could have been fairer or happier. In the valleys below them the endless bushland of hawthorn was still all shadowy grey twigs, but a haze of green was spreading upon it, and in places there were banks of blackthorn showing drifts of snow-white blossoms.

Yet, as they rode, there grew upon Ambris an uneasy sense as of eyes watching. Nothing to see, but . . . He began glancing over his shoulder, but saw nothing – yet. Ursulet noticed this, and glanced back too – and he felt her shudder.

'What is it, lady?' he asked. 'Did you see anything behind us?'

'No – nothing behind us. I wondered if you did – only –

something made me shiver. They say it's when a man walks over your grave.' She laughed nervously.

'Come, we'll go faster. Hold tight.' They galloped for a bit, and in the excitement lost the fear; but when Ambris slackened the pace and let his horse walk, there was that sense again of someone watching, someone following. They were passing through dry heathy country, golden with gorse, and they went down into a dell; at the bottom of the dell he looked back, and could have sworn that a head moved on the lip of the dell above him. He looked to right and left, and almost thought he saw another at each side. He said nothing, but shook the reins and spurred his horse up the slope, and then looked round and over the border of the dell. Nothing – only open heath and gorse as far as the eye could see. But a noise began, a strange disturbing noise. Too early in the year for grasshoppers or crickets, surely? A noise like crackling, like whispering, like laughing. Not pleasant laughter, either. He wondered if Ursulet heard it, but would not ask her. But she put her lips close to his ear, and said, 'Do you hear it?'

'I do indeed.'

'What is it?'

'God knows. But as God knows, I trust He won't let it hurt us. We must go on.'

They went on, but as they went the watchers, whatever they were, grew bolder and more insistent. The chattering grew louder. No shapes could be seen yet, but tufts of heather moved, and gorsebushes shook, and not with the wind.

Now they left the high heath country, and began to go down into woodlands. The road was no more than a beaten track, but it was as much as men expected in those parts where the Roman roads were no longer kept up, or where they had not been. This was at least the indication of a plain way to go; and it led downwards and abruptly plunged into the shade of the untouched forest. The great oaks stood as they had stood from the beginning; and the undergrowth closed up to the track, keeping its secrets.

Undoubtedly there were things that tracked them, that parted the leaves and looked and were gone.

There were side-turnings out of the track here and there, but it seemed obvious that the way was straight on. But presently for no apparent reason, Ambris's horse stopped short in its tracks, and stood shivering. At the same moment, Ambris felt a tremor run over him – not so much cold, as a disturbing vibration – his hair stood on end, something oppressed his breathing. He clenched his hands to try and stop the tremor. He could see on his horse's neck the sweat breaking out. The horse backed, shaking its head from side to side, its nostrils flaring, the whites of its eyes showing.

'We can't go on,' said Ambris over his shoulder.

'I know,' she answered. 'I can feel it. No, we can't go on. We must go another way.'

He turned the horse – the frightening sensation ceased, and the horse was calmer. But as he turned, he glimpsed the strange things in the undergrowth behind him. They gave before him as he turned, and closed in behind. He retraced his steps, and found a side track that promised to lead round and rejoin their road; he took it, but after about a mile it was the same – something forced him to turn. And then again, and again. The unknown things were driving him as a dog drives sheep. The sun began to decline, and the colours of the forest to deepen – and he began to see the creatures. He would not have mentioned them to Ursulet, but she spoke first.

'Did you see what I saw?

'What was it?'

'A man's head – but it hadn't a body to it. Just a head, and it rolled along like a ball. Did you see it?'

'Yes, and I saw a little dwarfish black man with horns.'

'Worse than that – there was one like a child running on all fours, but its four legs were six.'

'There was one like a bird, on long legs with a long neck – but it had a man's face on its long neck.'

'Oh, Ambris, I don't like them a bit, not a bit!'

'Nor do I, my darling.' (In his fear he had no consciousness of calling her that.) 'I'll get you out of here as soon as I can.'

'I know you will. Should we pray, do you think? I've prayed inwardly, but should we pray aloud?'

'Yes, let us do that.' So they halted, and together said the Pater and Ave. The things seemed to give back a little, but were still there. Then Ambris remembered something of what his mother had taught him about pentagrams, and made the pentagram of the right way on all four sides of them. Again the things took a few paces back. But when Ambris moved his horse on again, the things still followed them, though further off. Ambris had no idea of the way now – he simply had to go as the things sent him. Holding the reins in his left hand, he clasped his right hand firmly over Ursulet's two hands, which were cold and tremulous. Turning his head over his shoulder, he laid his cheek against hers, without thinking at all. 'My dearest,' he said, and she made a little sighing noise in reply, and pressed herself hard against his back. He could feel her trembling, and hear how her teeth chattered. And there was nothing he could do but go on, and try not to look round at the things.

The forest was dark now, almost too dark for the horse to see its way – and then at last there was a light, and Ambris and Ursulet both cried out together. A light, and from an open door! It had loomed up upon them before they could see it through the trees – a tall house or castle set upon a hillside, with a causeway over a deep foss, where they were already going – a courtyard over the causeway, and a door standing open.

'Oh, thank God, thank God!'

13 · *To Dance at Whose Wedding?*

They rode in, and as if they had been expected, serving-men ran out, and women too, hospitable voices bade them come in, willing hands helped them to dismount; grooms led the horse away, and they found themselves in the midst of human concern and comfort. This was no place of glamour, but a good earthly dwelling of men.

A tall man in a leather jerkin who seemed to be in command, poured out a cup of good ale for each of them.

'The master bids you welcome,' he said. 'There are rooms provided for you – go and rest till it is time for dinner.'

A quiet maidservant took charge of Ursulet and led her away up a wooden stair to a solar room, above the hall. As the maid hung up Ursulet's cloak and took off her gown, to dress her, as the custom was, in a robe kept in the house for guests, Ursulet asked her, 'What is this castle called?'

'Maiden Castle,' the girl replied.

'Maiden Castle!' Ursulet's head whirled. 'But we *can't* have come that far out of our road. Maiden Castle's far in the south, by Dorchester—'

'Oh, but this is the new one,' said the girl. 'Mai-Dun Newton they call it. My lord finished building it last year.'

'And – who is your lord?' asked Ursulet, her voice faltering. She knew the answer before it was given.

'The Earl Mordred, to be sure, madam.'

'Then I must go!' cried Ursulet wildly. 'Give me my cloak again – send word to my knight – I'll not stop here—'

The girl – tall and strong, with muscles that could have held Ursulet down, and a sly mouth and eyes – stood over her as if she had been a raving fever patient.

'Now, now, now, my lady – what's this? No, I'll not give you your cloak to go rushing off again. Have no fear of my

Lord Mordred. He's a courteous gentleman, be sure, and wishes you nothing but good.'

Ursulet sat helplessly down. It seemed it was no use to fight or try to run.

'Well – and who is the lady of the castle, then?'

'The lady of the castle— Well . . .' The girl turned away and busied herself folding Ursulet's riding-dress. 'Well, at present it's my lady Aestruda – but foot the dance well, my lady, and it might be you.'

'What do you mean?'

But the maid did not answer, she only said, 'What pretty hair you have, my lady. Come, I'll comb and braid it for you.'

Presently she descended by long winding stairs into the great hall. It was many years since Ursulet had known a lordly hall, but some recollection came dimly back to her now. Yes, thus it was – the vast space, rafters above and rushes below, lit by the flickering light of a great central fire; the long tables, without cloths, running down the sides, where the men-at-arms sat; the dais at the far end, with the high table draped with rich cloths and backed with tapestry. And here she found herself face to face with Mordred.

He stood before her, thick legs astride, arms akimbo; a heavily built man, red-faced, coarse-grained; not yet forty, but with his face reddened with drinking and pouches below his blue protuberant eyes. His hair, blonde and inclining to red, was cut square across his brows and fell to his shoulders, and a heavy moustache hung down in the Saxon style over bad-tempered lips. But he was smiling.

'My lady Ursulet,' he said, and she was surprised that he knew her name, 'you are heartily welcome here, by the Mass! You'll be my guest here for a while. Come, sit you down. Serve up the food, you scullions.'

She looked round anxiously for Ambris, and was relieved to see him some distance off, towards one end of the high table. They exchanged glances, but neither of them happy ones.

'Here, meet my two sons,' said Mordred, and two youths came forward. 'This is Morcar, my eldest.' There was a ring of pride in his voice. 'He's as tough a fighter for his sixteen years as you'll find, fears neither man nor devil, and has a dozen bastards about the bailey – hain't you, my big brat?' and he slapped him on the shoulder. Morcar was as tall as his father, a handsome boy with the bold blue eyes of Arthur's race, and a swaggering walk. He kissed Ursulet's hand, and ran his eyes over her as if she had been merchandise for sale.

'And this is Morwen.' There was no attempt to disguise the coldness in Mordred's voice. The boy was about fifteen, his features irregular and without grace – brown eyes looked up at Ursulet, deprecating; he bit his lip and reddened, and kissed her hand quickly and backed away. 'Poor chap,' Mordred commented. 'You must excuse him. I don't know what use he is. Not like this one,' and he drew Morcar forward to sit at Ursulet's left hand, she being on Mordred's left. Morwen was left to find himself a place at the end of the table; he found himself next to Ambris, who cleared a place for him.

Ursulet's recollection of feasts in the high hall, and of course in the refectory, was that they always began with grace; but no grace was said here. Everyone fell to as soon as the dishes were on the table, or even before; and the noise and riot were appalling. On Mordred's right hand was a lady in a bright yellow gown, very bold and brassy, who drank a great deal and talked very loudly; Ursulet supposed this must be the Lady Aestruda. Behind her chair stood an elderly woman in attendance, dressed in black silk and veiled almost to the eyes. Ursulet wondered what the waiting-maid had meant by her hint that she herself might be the lady of the castle. She had no wish to be the lady of such a castle as this.

Ambris, from where he sat, could see both the sons of Mordred, one beside him, the other at his father's side. A page, offering dishes, stumbled as he handed the dish to Morwen, the younger and brown-eyed one – the page tipped the dish, and a stream of gravy went over Morwen's tunic. Morwen exclaimed, but took a towel from the boy, and

without any fuss began to wipe down his own garment. But
Morcar, from where he sat, jumped up and was beside him,
grabbing the unfortunate page by the ear.

'Look, Morwen, this won't do!' he cried. 'This filthy cur's
spoilt your jerkin, and by God's body, you sit there and do
nothing! Here,' and he unhitched a dog-whip from his belt,
'whip the knave. Come on.'

Morwen shook his head, and made no move to take the
whip.

'Come on, I say – father, he must whip him, must he not?
Morwen, you're a pale-faced dastard. Here, take the whip,'
and he thrust it into Morwen's hand, and holding his hand
tried to make him whip the boy. Morwen wrenched his hand
away, so Morcar turned away from him, and slashed the page
across the face – left, right, left, right- The page backed away
from the table, into the middle of the room, Morcar following
him. The rest of the company looked on, laughing and
applauding. Mordred turned to Ursulet. 'That's my brave
boy,' he said. 'The other's a milksop.'

Ursulet watched in horror as the page was driven backwards, step by step, towards the fire. Morcar was lashing and
lashing and lashing, as if unable to stop himself.

Then Ambris sprang from his place, overturning his chair,
and jumped from the dais, reaching a long arm out between
the page and the fire just in time to catch him back. Morcar's
whip fell on Ambris's knuckles, but the company stopped
shouting, and waited. Morcar, his face working with rage,
lifted his whip again, this time towards Ambris. In the hush,
Ursulet made her voice heard.

'My lord earl – we are your guests.'

'Oh, true, true,' grumbled Mordred, subsiding. 'All right,
Morcar, my boy, let them go. Sit down.'

Ambris turned and made formal obeisance.

'I beg pardon, my lord earl – I supposed that you did not
wish to see murder done.'

'Oh, go on, go on. Give us some more ale.'

*

Later, the hall was cleared, and Ursulet wondered if it was for dancing. She dimly remembered such a thing, when she was very little – for things of that kind, long forgotten, began to come back to her now.

But it seemed it was not for dancing, though the men-at-arms carefully cleared a space, and trumpets were sounded – there entered no mummers, but a priest in his vestments with two acolytes. Gravely, and as far as he was able gracefully, Mordred offered Ursulet his arm, as if indeed for dancing, and led her down till she stood in front of the priest, and Morcar closed up on Mordred's other side. Then the priest began his Latin, and Ursulet listened in astonishment. She was familiar enough with the Mass, though she had not heard it now for six years; but this was no office she had ever heard before. And suddenly it dawned on her – this was a marriage! She was being wedded to Morcar, without any consent of hers.

Mordred stepped back and drew Ursulet and Morcar together, and the priest broke into the vernacular.

'Dost thou, Morcar, take this woman Ursulet, to be thy wedded wife?'

'I do,' said the handsome sulky boy, and put out his hand, but Ursulet kept her hand behind her back.

'Dost thou, Ursulet, take this man—'

'No!' cried Ursulet. 'No!' she shrieked as loudly as she had breath in her body. 'No!' she shrieked again, and heard it echo back from the rafters, while all around her confusion broke out.

Mordred took her arms firmly.

'Dear girl, don't be foolish. I know this is a surprise to you, but what the devil – you must have a husband, and where's a better than my young Morcar?'

'I won't,' said Ursulet, gritting her teeth.

'Oh, come – won't's a bad word for a young lady to use. I think we may make you change your mind. Think – you will be Queen of Britain when Morcar is King—'

'I *am* Queen of Britain!' she said, with such force of

conviction that the priest, a red-faced stupid man, looked up in surprise.

'My dear, I think you had better not be obstinate,' said Mordred, and she felt his nails begin to bite into her arm. She looked round wildly for Ambris – he was not there. Shaking off Mordred's arm, she took a step towards the priest and threw herself into his arms.

'Oh, sir priest – I beg you, I beg you – don't wed me to this man!'

'And why not, my daughter?'

'Because – because—' Suddenly she saw where a white lie – well, a bluff – might help her. 'Because I am married already. Sir Ambrosius and I were wedded three days ago at the convent at Shaston.'

A buzz of astonishment broke out.

'Is that so?' said the priest, rather slowly comprehending. 'In that case – why – why, my lord earl, the lady says she's married already.'

'Oh, hell blast the stupid woman!' exclaimed young Morcar, grinding his heel into the rushes. 'Father said I was to take her, and she's fair enough, and I'd have bedded her too – and now I'm made a fool of!'

'Is this true?' Mordred glowered over Ursulet.

'Yes, my lord,' said she, shrinking in terror from his furious face.

'My lord earl,' said the priest, 'it would seem that it would be – well, doubtful – to marry her to the Lord Morcar at present. It would be better to wait.'

All drew back from Ursulet, and Morcar stumped away. Mordred made no move towards her, and the priest steadied her with his hand. She felt she had at least gained a breathing space.

'Oh, let it be, let it be, then!' Mordred exclaimed. 'All right, girl, you can go to your chamber. No wedding tonight.' The company groaned with disappointment. 'But you can all drink just as well without a wedding.' They cheered once more.

Ursulet turned away gladly, looking for her maid. She wondered again where Ambris was, and whether all was well with him. But as she went, she heard over her shoulder Mordred say to the priest, 'As for you, Sir John, don't leave the castle yet. Stay within call. I might need you very soon to re-marry a new-made widow.'

And then she understood what a deadly peril she had brought upon Ambris.

14 · A Dark Old Woman

Ambris, as the commotion subsided that followed his rescue of the page, felt his arm seized and found himself being drawn into one of the wall-recesses that surrounded the main hall. Young Morwen had hold of his hand and seemed unwilling to let it go. The boy looked very young, and his eyes were full of tears that he fought to keep back.

'Oh, sir knight!' he exclaimed, 'I want to thank you – oh, you don't know what it means to me. Look, that's the first act of mercy and kindness I've ever seen done in this place.' He turned his head awkwardly aside, for the tears had spilled over. Ambris avoided looking at him.

'Sir,' the boy went on, 'it's frightful for me here. You don't think, do you, that a man *has* to be a brute, like – like my brother and my father?'

'Surely not,' said Ambris, but felt embarrassed. 'Look, anything I can do to help you—'

'I must go,' said the boy, listening like a nervous dog. 'If Morcar finds me, he'll put the knotted string round my head . . .' and he was gone.

Ambris stood in doubt, and was about to turn to go back to the hall. There was noise and commotion going on, and he felt it was no place for Ursulet. But before he could turn, he felt a tug on his arm. He looked down, and there was the

most repulsive little old woman he had ever seen. She was
bent two-double, and hobbled sideways; a ragged mud-
coloured cloak covered her, from which came a daunting
smell of age, misery and neglect. Her mouth was a black
toothless hole.

He recoiled from her, but she kept her hold on his sleeve.

'Young knight,' she mumbled, 'if you value your lady's life,
come with me.'

'What?' He drew back shuddering.

'No questions. Your own life isn't worth a straw at this
moment, and hers is in worse case. Come, at once and
quietly.'

Nothing could be worse than going back to the hall, he felt,
so, with his hand on his dagger, he followed her. She led him
to a door in a dark entry, unlocked it, and went on into deeper
darkness still. She took a small lantern from under her robe,
and bobbed on before him like a gnome. Down a flight of
steps, along a stony echoing passage, where all one side were
sinister black cells closed with gratings.

'But these are dungeons!' he exclaimed, and heard his voice
echo hollowly. 'Why have you brought me here, old woman?'

She stopped, turned and held the lantern up – she no longer
stooped or crouched, but stood up very tall.

'Why, lad, don't you know me yet?' she chuckled.

'Aunt Lynett!'

'The same, my boy!' She embraced him warmly. 'Oh, I'm
sorry for these stinking rags. They are necessary, you see, for
the disguise.'

He looked at her as she stood in the dim light of the lantern
– brown, leathery as ever, her cheeks smeared with soot.

'Oh my dear aunt—' he said. 'But for heaven's sake, what
have you done to your teeth?'

For where he had been accustomed to see her firm, perfect
if slightly prominent teeth, was an unsightly gap.

'Oh, my teeth are well enough,' she laughed. 'A bit of
apothecary's plaster over them, that's all. Under that they're
as good as ever, and ready to bite you or any man.' Her eyes

twinkled, and he felt that she was enjoying her frightful disguise.

'But why am I here in the dungeons?'

'Why, better here with me, than here with two of Earl Mordred's men. See, lad – I don't need a magic mirror to know it was only a matter of a minute before Mordred gave his men orders to make away with you. So I thought it was better that I take you out of sight first. He'll not have given orders specially to this man or that man, and none will come back to report to him, so that if any questions are asked afterwards he can take no blame – I know him. So – provided you disappear, each man will think another man did it, and he will just count you – lost. You'll be safe enough where I'll hide you.'

'But the Princess?'

'I'll see that she's safe. I go to and fro in the kitchen, you see, and through all the rooms, to do the dirtiest work, and no one thinks of questioning poor Madge the Dishclout.' She cackled. 'I'll watch the Princess, and in due time we'll make good our escape. But come now, I'll show you your quarters. They're none so bad.'

They went down another stair to another deep level, with more dungeons along the gallery; the stonework seemed to be new, as far as Ambris could see in the dim light of the lantern. Then down to a third level; and at the furthest extremity of this, the passage seemed to come to an end; but Lynett went on, and Ambris saw that where a blank wall seemed to be, there was a narrow vertical fissure in the rock, just big enough to squeeze through.

'We're both thin enough,' said Lynett. 'A fat man couldn't get through this – I doubt if my Lord Mordred could.' Ambris felt the dread of the deep underground, the fear of being trapped under rocks far from the daylight, gripping him. But Lynett led on for a few steps, and then halted before a solidly made oaken door, which she opened with a key.

Inside was a reasonable little cell – a dungeon no doubt, but a dungeon with some comforts. A little fireplace with a chimney held a small fire of logs. A thin stream of water flowed out from the wall into a stone basin, from which it escaped into a groove cut across the floor and out through a drainage hole. There were candle sconces on the walls, into which Lynett fixed candles and lighted them. There was a bed with pillows and blankets, and a basket containing food.

'You've all you want here,' she said. 'The smoke from the fire goes into the great kitchen chimney, so it's never noticed, and the water's always clean and good to drink. You can lock the door from the inside, and open only when I knock thus.'

'However did such a place come to be?' he asked.

'Oh, it's hard to say, but it seems it was made in the old time – you see, Mordred built his new Mai-Dun on the shell of an older castle – it may even have been made by the Romans, for look, the floor is made of tiles. Mordred and his company don't know of this cell – they only know the upper ones that he made. You should be safe enough here for a day or two. You've plenty of food here, and I'll bring you more every day, and there's firewood and candles. And to save you going melancholy-mad with being alone, look here.' She placed in his hands a large, ponderous, handwritten book, a collection of chivalrous romances. 'Here's a treasure for you, to pass the time! Now, aren't you glad I taught you your letters, even if I did beat you sometimes? God knows you're slow at reading, but if you sit down and try to worry this out, it'll give you something to do.'

'Oh, aunt, you're very kind to me.'

'Tush, boy, what else? I prepared this for you some time back.'

'You prepared for me – for us? But how did you know we were coming?'

'Oh, where the vultures gather, there the corpse will be found. Morgan le Fay is here – didn't you see her? That woman in black who pretends to be the Lady Aestruda's maid. We learnt she was here – by means we have – and we knew she would fetch you here. Which she did.'

'Yes, we were – what could I say? – driven here by Things.'

'I know. I've heard tell of them. I never see or feel or hear anything that isn't of this world – now – but others do. They say that Morgan's spells are powerful, and you may yet have to guard against them. But God be with you, and you'll be proof against Morgan and all the lot of them. Rest you now, boy, while I go and watch the Princess.'

'You will give her – my regards, and tell her I'm still alive?'

'I'll give her your love, for that's what you mean.'

So he shut the door behind her, locking it, and heard its hollow clang and how her footsteps died away down the long passages – and then he was left alone, so terrifyingly alone, down under fathoms upon fathoms of earth in the utter darkness, with his candles and his little fire for his only company.

15 · *In Mordred's Power*

The chamber assigned to Ursulet was a pleasant enough room, as she reflected when she woke in the morning. She lay in a fine draped bed, and the walls that surrounded her were hung with tapestry, very gay and colourful. The sunshine came in through narrow windows, high up – and that was the one drawback, she felt. It was impossible to see out, and obviously it would be very difficult to escape. And Ursulet was quite sure that she must escape as soon as possible, but not without Ambris.

The same rather sly maid waited on her, bringing her water for washing and an excellent breakfast; she was attended by a rather dirty old woman, not a very nice creature to have about the place. When they had gone away, Ursulet tried the door, but as she expected found it locked. And not long after, the maid, bobbing obsequiously, ushered in Mordred, and bobbing again, withdrew.

'Madam,' he began, 'I've come to offer you condolences, and perhaps congratulations.'

'What do you mean?'

'Well, condolences on your widowhood, and congratulations on the prospect of a second marriage.'

Ursulet closed her eyes and sank back where she sat. A cold faintness swept over her.

'What – what has happened?'

'Why, it's very regrettable, but your husband, the good Sir Ambrosius, has disappeared since last night – no sign of him anywhere – and we fear the worst.'

'Murderer!' she cried. 'If he's dead, it's you that made away with him.'

'I? Why, no, madam. I've laid no hand on him, and that I'll swear. I tell you, I do not know where he is. But the castle is full of staircases, and awkward corners, and deep wells – we fear he is lying at the bottom of some such—'

'You fear? But where *is* he then? Where is his body?'

'My dear lady, I tell you, no one knows.'

'Then find his body,' she cried, 'for until you do, I count myself married to him, and I will *not* – I will *not* – I will *not* marry your son Morcar or anyone else.'

'Is that so?' he said in a quiet and considering voice. 'Why then, my men shall have orders to search more carefully, and bring his body for you to see. Will that content you?'

'No – yes – no!' she cried wildly, seeing now that she had made his danger, if he were still alive, worse than before. 'Oh, whether he's alive or dead, I *won't* marry Morcar.'

'Indeed?' She was sitting on the edge of the bed, and he came and sat beside her. 'But I can think that you might have reason. Now tell me – you and this Sir Ambrosius – you were not many days together. Did he consummate the marriage?'

She looked at him blankly, not knowing what he meant.

'Oh, God's bones, don't you understand? Did you bed together?'

She blushed deeply. 'No, we did not.'

'So you're still a maid?'

'Yes, my lord.'

'Well then, you still have a treasure you would fain not lose. But supposing you lost it – to me? You'd be glad enough to take Morcar then.'

She shrank away from him, but he had both arms firmly round her, and was thrusting her back on the bed.

'Let me go – let me go – you're my brother – my father's son—'

'What of that?' he laughed coarsely. 'So was Arthur my mother's brother. It runs in the family. You'd be glad enough to take Morcar to save the scandal.'

She tried to push him off, but even her muscular arms were not strong enough.

'If you don't let me go,' she cried wildly, 'I'll swallow my tongue and choke myself, and die. I know how to, and I will. Then what use will I be to you?' (And this was a desperate bluff, for though she had heard the Jutish midwife speak of such things, she really did not know how it was done.)

He hesitated, and relaxed his hold – and at that moment a loud knocking sounded on the door.

'Oh, devil take it, who's there?'

No answer, but the knocks continued to thunder. He got up from the bed, and Ursulet sprang away into the furthest corner of the room.

'Who's there? Oh, go to hell, whoever you are—'

No word answered him, only the knocking went on, louder and louder.

'Oh, God's blood and death, what in the name of Satan is it?' and he opened the door, and made to close it again. But incredibly quickly before he could do so, the old serving-woman skipped into the room under his arm, and stood looking stupidly up at him from under her cover of brown rags.

'Beg pardon, my lord, it's only me, come to see to her lady-ship's room. Work must be done whether or no, my lord.'

'Get out, hag!'

'Oh yes, my lord, when I've done me work. But poor old

Madge the Dishclout has her duty to do the same as greater folk, to scrape out the ashes, and empty the washing-water and the—'

'Go to the devil!' Mordred strode past her, banging the door as he went, and turning the key in the lock. The moment he was gone the old woman stood up to twice her apparent height, threw off the dirty cloth from her head, and said in a completely different voice, 'Come quickly – Sir Ambris is waiting for you.'

'But how—' Ursulet looked helplessly at the locked door.

'Oh, this way – come on—' and the old woman hustled her through a little door behind the tapestry, and into stony, winding, twisting darkness.

16 · *Through Darkness and Water*

In Ambris's refuge, he lost all reckoning of time. He supposed that a day could not have gone by for Lynett had not revisited him as she said she would, though he had no lack of food and drink in his cell. He saw candles burn down, and replaced them from time to time, and kept his little fire going; and he tried to read the romance, but found it very difficult. At least it tired him, so that he slept. And waking up out of sleep, with a sudden beating of his heart he saw a woman standing before him.

Not Lynett certainly – no, he remembered this one, the white-robed, golden-sandalled woman who had haunted his vigil of knighthood. He jumped up from his straw pallet.

'Oh, lie down again, dear young knight,' the woman said in the soft voice he remembered. 'You are weary of your own company. What life is this for a young man who should be pursuing the phantom of Beauty?'

He shrank back from her.

'No, have no fear of me, lad. It's not any carnal pleasure I seek with you. I'm a kinswoman of yours on both sides, indeed. I am great-aunt to your mother, and to your father too – for Nimue and Morgause were both my sisters.'

'You must be very old!' he gasped stupidly.

'Old enough as the world goes. As old as the soul of Beauty Look at me, lad.'

Against his will his eyes were drawn to hers – green eyes – his mother's eyes were a clear blue-green, and his own eyes, he knew, were green too, but these were like a cat's, jewel-like, but with the pupils wide, wide and black.

'Look into my eyes – yield yourself to them, fall right into them. For, old as you think me, I am far, far older. I am she to whom the young men of the East gladly sacrificed their manhood – oh, no, lad, never fear me, I'll not put the moon-shaped sickle into your hand. But give yourself into my hands, and I think the love of one woman will trouble you but little, for you shall know the love of Beauty – not this one nor that one. but the Beautiful that you will never touch or kiss, but follow for ever over horizon beyond horizon. Far, far lovelier than any daughter of man – a Grail holier than that which you have called the Holy Grail – terrible and guarded with death and madness, but dear beyond all thought and all dream. I am the White One, of whom all other white ladies are but shadows. Forget all others, and seek the unattainable in the pools of my eyes.'

Helpless and spellbound, he drifted towards her as if towards sleep. Then suddenly a knock sounded on the door – Lynett's agreed signal. He broke from the glamour – and like a burst bubble, the lady was gone. Rubbing his eyes, he stumbled across and opened the door – and there found, not Lynett, but young Morwen, big-eyed in the dim light. Ambris cried out, and made to shut the door again, but the boy laid hold of his arm.

'No, don't shut the door on me – it's all right, I'm a friend. The Lady Lynett sent me. Look, here's her token,' and he put into Ambris's hand one of the massive silver rings that he knew his aunt wore.

'All right, come in.'

'My lord,' said the boy,' she sent me to warn you. She is with the Lady Ursulet now. I was to tell you, get ready to go, and quickly, for it will be a near thing. My father thought you had been put away secretly, and that was well, for he didn't search, but the Lady Ursulet bade him show her your body, else she wouldn't marry my brother Morcar. So he is having search made for you.'

All this was hard for Ambris to take in, dull as he was with his long confinement.

'To marry Morcar?' he said. 'Mordred's son?'

'Yes, my lord. They brought the priest there and all, but she would not marry him, being already married to you.'

'What?' The whole cell seemed to reel round Ambris. 'She said she was married to *me*?'

'Of course, my lord,' said the boy. 'You are married to her, are you not?'

'Why – why, yes,' he stammered. 'Yes, of course we are married.'

'And so, of course,' said Morwen, 'if you were not dead before, my father will make sure you are. Oh, my father's a fell man! Sir – will you let me go with you when you escape? For my father and my brother will kill me.'

'Surely,' said Ambris, looking down on the lad's earnest, white-rimmed eyes. No more than a child – and he, Ambris, was he so very much older? But certainly he must protect this boy.

'The Lady Lynett says you must put out your fire and all the candles,' Morwen said, 'and be dressed and shod, and pack provisions for a journey – she herself will bring weapons.'

So they quickly made their preparations, but Ambris's head was whirling and his heart singing. Ursulet had said that? Not one recollection remained in his mind of the vision of the White Lady – only of Ursulet, one woman, human and to be loved with a man's love.

*

As soon as their preparations were complete, Morwen quenched the fire, and put out the candles one by one, till they stood uneasily in complete darkness. They listened, and each thought the other must surely hear his heart beating. So they listened.

Then there were soft steps, and the agreed knock. Ambris opened the door quickly and quietly; there was Lynett, with her horn-lantern, and behind her Ursulet, muffled in a dark cloak.

No time for words of greeting. 'Come quickly,' said Lynett in a gruff whisper. 'They've got the dogs out. The narrow crack will be no protection. Come with me, and stick together now.' With ears sharpened by fear, Ambris could hear a tumult of men and dogs coming down the echoing passages. 'Not much time,' Lynett went on. 'Follow me, and do as I say. Don't ask questions.'

Lynett leading, Ursulet went next, and Ambris put the boy Morwen in front of him, and brought up the rear. Like a string of blind beggars, they stumbled down the pitch-dark passage, their feet hardly able to keep them on the rough path. The noise was behind them, and ahead all that Ambris could see was the faint glow of Lynett's lantern obscured by those in between. The path went steeply down – they had to steady themselves with their hands against the clammy sides of the passage – and a new sound suddenly came up to them – the rushing of water.

'Now,' said Lynett, halting. 'There's water here, and there's death behind. If anyone's heart fails them they can stay behind for the dogs and Mordred. Otherwise – let yourselves down into the water – draw a long breath, hold your nose with your fingers, shut your mouth, hold your breath, and go under. Let the water carry you while you count fifty – hold your breath all the time. If you raise your head above the water before that, your brains will be dashed out on the rocks above you. Is that clear? It may be death, but there's certain death behind us.'

They could hear the bloodthirsty clamour of the hounds

close to them now. The water was at their feet, dimly seen in the lantern's glimmer, flowing rapidly without a ripple. Ambris reached out and put one arm around Ursulet and one round Morwen, but Lynett prevented him roughly.

'Not like that,' she said. 'The channel's narrow, and you must go in one by one, after me. Come now – blessed God, they're here—' and she flung herself into the water, pulling Ursulet by the hand after her. The lantern hit the water and went out and the long howl of a hound broke out almost at their backs. Morwen and Ambris plunged quickly in.

It was surely like death. The shock, the dark, the cold – the bursting lungs, the rushing current sweeping away all sense of direction – as if asleep in a horrible dream, the eyes tight closed; nothing real but the frightful urgency to breathe – how could one count? ... thirty-two, seventy-five, twenty-one, forty-four, oh, anything ... and then somehow, his head was out of the water, and he was breathing, and thanking God for just breath – but the darkness was so total he might have been blind. He put a hand above his head and touched rock less than a foot above him, though he could feel solid ground under his feet. He felt a terrible fear of the roof closing down on him again – if he went in the wrong direction, he would get pushed into another horrible crack – oh, which way? And then above the rush of the water he heard Lynett's voice: 'This way! This way! Keep over to your right – have no fear, the roof's high enough here—' and struggling in the direction of the voice found his knees scraping on the bottom where the water ended on a sandy beach, and cautiously he stood up. Still all was inky black, but he felt other bodies standing round him, and they clasped each other, dripping, shivering like wet dogs. They were all there, Lynett, Ambris, Ursulet, Morwen – and for a moment they clutched each other's bodies in the dark, indiscriminately, desperate for human contact and reassurance.

'A step or two more this way,' said Lynett. 'The water's behind you. Now you're safe. Now stand still, all of you, while I go and find some light.'

She left them and they could hear her groping round.

'Can she see in the dark?' Morwen whispered.

'I suppose so,' replied Ambris. 'Indeed, I don't know what she can't do.'

Lynett could be heard crunching over pebbles, shuffling, stumbling; then they heard the sound of flint on steel, and in a minute they saw a faint flicker of light glimmering out.

'Come over here, but carefully – the going's rough.'

They groped towards the light. By its gleam they could see they were in a vast cavern – how big, the light was too faint to show them, but they seemed to be in a world of looming rock columns and arches, receding into endless echoing night. Underfoot the ground was rough and ankle twisting – they made their way with difficulty to where Lynett was sitting crouched over the little glimmering torch she had managed to light. She had, they found, uncovered a cache of small pitch torches, with flint and steel, and a stone jar she was uncorking.

'Here's something to save our lives,' she said, and poured each one a drink, in turn, from the stone jar – she had a little silver cup hanging from her girdle. It was a rich, sweet liquor, thick and creamy, and wonderfully heartening. 'They call it King Arthur's Ambrosia,' she chuckled. 'The shepherds make it of eggs and strong mead and cream and lemons, and they drink it when they go lambing in the snow. They say it will raise the dead, or make a barren woman conceive.'

'You had all this prepared for us?' asked Ambris, with wonder.

'Oh, yes, my lad. I've been here before, a time or two, and I knew it would soon be needed. One has to look ahead.'

'But how did you find the place?' (It was comforting and steadying to keep on talking.)

'Oh, a blind man brought me here once or twice. Long, long ago, that was. Blind as a bat, but like a bat he could feel his way in the dark better than with eyes – yes, and swim like a fish too. Oh, but that was years ago. Well, Mordred and his dogs can't reach us here, and I've no doubt he counts us dead. So far so good. Yes, and another blessing – these stinking rags of mine have had a good wash.' She laughed again. They were all feeling the better for 'King Arthur's Ambrosia', and a little light-headed with the sense of escape – although their clothes were drenching wet and their bodies battered.

'You're not too bad, girlie?' Lynett said to Ursulet, putting an arm round her shoulders. 'You don't know who I am – I'm Ambris's great-aunt.'

'Did ever a man have two such great-aunts?' said Ambris, laughing too.

'*Two* great-aunts? What do you mean?' said Lynett, rather sharply.

'You and Morgan.'

'Morgan? Have you seen her again?'

'Why, yes, or dreamt of her. She came to me in the dungeon—'

'All right, lad. I've no doubt she put you to the test, but I've no doubt she'd little success with you. *I* know, even though I can't see your face. But we still have to beware of her. No matter. If you're rested we'd better go on. There's a trace of a path here. Follow me in single file, and hold on to each other. You, Morwen, take the bundle of torches, and Ambris take the bottle. Oh, and one other thing I hid here for you.' She held up a sword and belt, which she fastened upon Ambris, and gave Morwen and Ursulet two useful sheath-knives. 'A man feels better if he has a weapon – so does a woman for that matter. Myself, I always have my dagger on me – now let's march.'

17 · *Encounter with a Sibyl*

How far they trudged and struggled through pitch-black caverns, they never knew. It was a long, hard day's march, so far as they could think it to be a day. Several times Lynett halted them for a rest, and gave them another drink of

'King Arthur's Ambrosia'. But they rested very uneasily, for their garments were still drenched and clammy on them and dried but slowly, being thick wool and leather – they weighed them down, and chilled them to the bone too. Ursulet had lost her cloak and hood – as for Lynett, her shapeless rags flapped and squelched as she walked.

At last, far off, they saw a faint gleam of light coming from fissures in the rock high above them – then more, till their way became clearly visible – it seemed as if they must be nearing the outlet of the cavern. Suddenly they, halted, once again on the brink of a dark, wide, slowly flowing stream.

'Are we to go in the water again?' asked Ursulet, with a sigh, and yet with such an edge of resolution on her voice that Lynett laughed.

'And by the Mass, I believe she would if I gave the word! Look, you boys, do you realize that she's never whimpered once? She's King Arthur's daughter sure enough – yes, and Guinevere's as well, for Guinevere had guts too – No, my pigeon,' and she drew Ursulet to her, 'no need to swim again, I'll have a boat for you this time.'

She raised her voice, and sent a long 'Halloo-oo—' echoing to the other side of the water. A high thin voice answered her from the other side, and a woman came into sight.

In the dim light she was a strange object, very tall and thin, naked to the waist; a skirt of patched goatskins swung round her narrow loins. Strings of crystal beads dangled round her neck and copper bangles gleamed on her stick-like arms; her hair, dusty grey, bristled out from her head. Red-rimmed eyes peered from under shaggy grey eyebrows. She held a torch above her head.

'Hey there!' she hailed them. 'Whose name do you come in?'

'The Radiant Brow,' Lynett called back.

'Of nine kinds of fruit?'

'Of nine kinds of flowers.'

'All's well, you can come over,' piped the old woman. 'I'll fasten the boat to the rope. Pull it over.'

There was a rough arrangement of wheels and pulleys on the bank on the travellers' side, and Lynett turned a wheel; a rope went round the pulley-wheel which presently pulled a boat across the dark water towards them; they all got in, and with Ambris and Morwen pulling the rope, reached the far shore. As they disembarked, they could see a glow of firelight, and far beyond that, a glimpse of daylight.

'Welcome, cummer!' the strange old woman greeted Lynett. 'Nay, I knew it was you, but I had to try you with the questions – there are many deceivers about. Welcome, and your folks too. But I warn you, I've no good news for you. The cat's at the mousehole. You'll not get out *that* way. This morning they all came pouring into the gorge, Mordred and all his fighting men, and they've pight their tents, and sat down like a besieging army round the mouth of my cave. I think *she's* with them, and *she* hears and smells out the very emmets in the hills. No, you'll not get out that way.'

'Then what shall we do?'

'You'll do as the mouse does – bolt out by another hole. There's only one way now, and you know it.'

'What, the long way?'

'Yes – I don't know another.'

'Then we must take that way.'

'So you must, if you can. The Old Cold One is still down there, did you know? He sleeps much, these days, and with luck he'll not wake when you pass.'

'We must risk the Old Cold One,' said Lynett, and Ambris wondered with dread what they meant.

'But come,' the old crone said. 'You'll rest and be refreshed before you start again. I've meat and drink, and what you'll need more – warmth and dryth.'

They followed her round a screen of rocks. First they passed a kind of niche like a chapel, where lamps burned and garlands of wild flowers lay fading in front of a hideous stone figure, whether made by man or chance-formed out of the rock it would be hard to say – a figure something like a woman, with the breasts and other sexual parts grotesquely exaggerated. The old woman hailed it with a strange sign as she passed it. Next was a little cell, evidently the old woman's own dwelling; peering from the doorway the bright eyes of a fox and an owl looked out on them. And then came a large recess where blazed a lavish fire of logs on a hearth of white sand. As they stepped on to the sand a grateful warmth met them, such as their shivering bodies yearned for.

'Now,' said Lynett briskly, 'here's what we need. Strip off your clothes, every shred, and we'll dry them for you here, and warm you too.'

As they hesitated, she went on, 'Let's have no nicety about this. We're all as God made us, and we're soldiers on campaign and make no fuss for modesty. I'll not have you all dying of ague and fever and the lung-rot, which assuredly you'll do otherwise. Come now – the girl can stand behind me here, and you boys face towards the wall over there. Now strip, I say.'

They did so, she throwing off her clothes too; and the warmth of the fire and of the dry white sand was heavenly to their chilled bodies. The old woman ran round picking up their wet garments and hanging them over poles in the glare of the fire. Ambris kept his face turned to the wall, but the thought of Ursulet's slim white nakedness on the other side of Lynett fairly took his breath away.

18 · The Cold-drake

Warmly clothed again, and adequately fed with roast meat and herbs by the old woman, they slept on the sand round the fire; waking once in the night to hear the old woman intoning some kind of chant before the stone image – a waft of incense came across to them, not the kind they ever smelled in church, but hinting of aniseed, valerian and pinewood. And when the light from the mouth of the cave indicated that it was morning, they broke their fast on rye bread and goats' milk and started off again, back down into the darkness of the cavern. The witch, for she seemed to have no other name, gave them a lantern with a lighted candle, and to each one a long staff of ash, tipped with an iron spike, to help them in walking. So they went back into the dark, and Lynett picked out a way for them, not the same as that by which they had come.

'Tell us,' said Ambris, 'what is the name of the kind hostess of that place?'

'She has no name. They call her the Witch of the Hole, for all that the folks know of this place is a hole in the rocks. And yet I think she is not so much a witch as a priestess of the older gods. She and her forbears have always been there, mother to daughter, time out of mind.'

'And how did you come to know her passwords?'

'Ask me no questions, boy. As I overheard you say, "I don't know what she can't do." There's much about me that you don't know.'

And with that they trudged on in silence.

'What a strange smell,' said Ursulet.

In a few minutes more the strange smell had become an overpowering stench. There was a horrible odour of decaying meat and animal filth, but besides that, the smell of some strange animal such as none of them had ever met before. At the same time a feeling of coldness, a freezing horror, began to creep over them.

'What is it?' cried Ambris. 'What are we coming to?'

'The Old Cold One,' said Lynett, lowering her voice.

'What in heaven's name *is* the Old Cold One, then?'

'A cold-drake.'

None of them could help shuddering at the ominous word.

'The fire-drakes are all gone,' Lynett said, 'but here and there a few of the ancient cold-drakes live on. This one has been here for who knows how long – the simple folk outside worship him, and bring him offerings – sheep and cattle now, but once it was men. Sometimes he sleeps for months together in his den, and I'm hoping we may get past his den without waking him. Go quietly now.'

But after about fifty yards more, Lynett halted with a sharp indrawing of breath, and motioned them all back with her staff.

Right in the narrow path where they stood, a thing like a tree-trunk, or a black basalt column laid on its side, lay right across the way. It seemed to be made of stone, till one looked more closely. It was a neck – the body to which it belonged was hidden in the recesses of the rocks, but the head in which it ended lay on the ground, flat and blunt like a snake's, and measuring more than a fathom each way. A bunch of skin and quills on the back of the neck hinted at a crest, now folded; and the eyes were tight shut, the long eyelids lying in leathery folds. And from it came both the horrible smell and the feeling of a cold breath.

'Can we get past?' Ursulet whispered into Lynett's ear.

'I doubt it – I had hoped he'd be inside his cave.'

'Look,' said Ambris, and he too dropped his voice to a whisper, 'I could cut his head off here – '

'Don't you try,' retorted Lynett urgently. 'You'd only bruise him and wake him in a fury. His skin's like horn.'

'Could we step across him?' Ursulet suggested.

'One might get over, but not the rest.'

'Then what are we to do?'

For once, Lynett seemed at the end of her resources – and as they hesitated, the creature's eyes opened in two long gleaming slits and the head raised itself from the ground and like a snake's began to weave to and fro, searching. Then its great body heaved itself out from its hole in the rocks, and it raised its head and its huge crest erect, and its eyes and mouth strained open wide – the eyes enormous, round and fiery-rimmed, the mouth full of teeth. The cold breath steamed from it like a fog. It came lumbering towards them, its head swinging.

With one impulse the four of them scattered and crushed

themselves into crevices of the rocks, as the creature, clumsily gathering speed, crashed past them and down into the tunnel whence they had come. They heard its great footsteps shaking the earth as it receded.

'Come quickly now,' cried Lynett. 'It can't turn in that narrow passageway.' Together they ran forward, across the great trace left by the cold-drake's neck. And then they heard it again.

'Oh God – it's coming back!' cried Lynett.

'What can we do?'

'No use to run—'

'Is it vulnerable anywhere?' Ambris panted, tugging at his sword.

'Only the eyes and the mouth.'

'Then this is what we do,' said Ursulet, suddenly taking the lead. 'This must be done together. We've our staves. Ambris and Lady Lynett, you've the longest reach – make for its eyes, one the right and the other the left. Morwen and I will thrust our staves into its mouth and try to hold it down. It's coming—'

And sure enough, in the dim light – for Lynett's lantern had gone – the beast came up again out of the depths, its ugly head seeming to float in mid-air before it, eyes round and glaring, mouth distended, a bluish light flicking around its dripping teeth. It made no sound but its harsh breathing and the thunder of its heavy hoofs.

It was upon them.

'Now!' cried Ursulet, and the four of them struck home together – Ursulet felt her staff catch and sink and wrench in her hand, as the cold-drake writhed and struggled – Morwen's staff held firm beside hers, and she felt them clash together – she ground hers down firmly, trying to ignore the poisonous teeth that grazed her wrists. She could not see what Ambris and Lynett were doing. But Ambris felt his sword thrust deep into the cold drake's eye. and reach something soft. The cold-drake lashed and shook them, like a bear shaking dogs – and then its resistance slackened – its

jaws clashed together and Ursulet and Morwen sprang back
as the great teeth shore through the ash-staves, but it was its
dying convulsion. The struggles ceased, and the repulsive
head lay on the ground.

The four drew back, and leant against the walls, shaken
and faint. Lynett was the first to speak.

'Well done all. Champions all of you – and my Ursulet,
she's a general. Cheer up, it's over now.'

But Ursulet was convulsively crying, in Ambris's arms, her
head pressed against his shoulder. Behind them Morwen,
crouched on the ground, was shivering like one with the
ague; Lynett put her arm round him.

'All's well, my boy. Yes, here's another one who is of the
true blood of Arthur, whatever men say. Come lad – Look,
we must get away from here – the cold breath of the cold-
drake still hangs about and daunts us. Come away, and leave
the Old Cold One. He'll give you no more trouble. What!
Heads up and look like victors – we've slain a dragon
together.'

She had no torch now, but the cavern was less dark than it
had been – it was all pillars and sheets of clear crystal and
alabaster, and from somewhere above, light, very faint, fil-
tered down. As they gathered themselves to march again,
Lynett said, 'I had always heard that the Old Cold One
guarded something, but I have never known what it is.'

How far they marched after it was hard to say – on and on,
into the dim world of stalactites, sometimes darker, sometimes lighter. The terror of the fight with the cold-drake began
to pass from them, and they walked on more hopefully, but
as they went, more and more quietly, for the floor of the path
where Lynett led them was no longer so rough – the uneven
rock gave way to sand, white, soft and deep, so that their
steps hardly made enough sound to wake the sensitive echoes
of the glassy pendants above them. They felt afraid to speak
even in a whisper. And then they found themselves passing
through stately arches, which could almost have been made

by human hands – arch after arch, and below them screens and curtains of hanging alabaster, till they stepped into a hall of solemnity and wonder.

A high vaulted roof extended above them, shaped by good mason-work – the ribs of the vaulting converging in a carved rose far overhead. A smell of incense floated there, holy incense and no witch's brew. Lamps hung on chains, burning quietly, and tall tapers on sconces, their flames burning without a flicker. And their light showed a circular space, as it were a chapter-house. Round it lay twenty-four couches, and on them twenty-four knights, all in their armour, laid with their feet to the centre. And in the centre, on a stately bed, was Arthur.

The knights lay, deep asleep but breathing. Their breath rose and fell like a scarcely heard music. Bare-headed they lay, but each one's helm was by his right side, and each one's hands were clasped on his breast, and his sword, sheathed, lay girt to his left side. Over each one's head a shield displayed his name. They were all there, the earliest ones of the Round Table – Sir Kay, Sir Griflet, Sir Tristram, Sir Gawain – yes, Lancelot was there, though that seemed strange to Ursulet, who had last seen him as a skeleton-wasted hermit. He lay there fresh-cheeked, smooth-haired, young.

There was one couch empty, awaiting its owner, and that was Sir Bedivere's. And Galahad was not there, for he was in a far holier place.

And Arthur lay golden-haired, golden-bearded and calm; and above him the shield proclaimed:

ARTURUS: REX OLIM: REXQUE FUTURUS

The four stood awestruck, and with one accord sank on their knees, and so remained for long minutes. Then Ursulet rose, and walking reverently, but as one who had a right to be there, approached the couch of Arthur, and the rest followed her.

At once a deep voice, coming as from nowhere, boomed out across the vault,

'Is it time?'

And all the knights stirred in their sleep, with a clink and hiss of metal as each one laid his hand upon his sword. Urgently and in a whisper Lynett made the response.

'No – no – no – Not yet.'

The whisper carried like a grey wave through the still air of the vault. The knights folded their hands back on their breasts. But Arthur had raised his head from the pillow, and his eyes, those unforgettable blue eyes, were open. Ursulet stepped up quickly to his right, and Lynett behind her. Lynett, with a gesture curiously practical in the strange place, picked up a cushion and propped his head with it. Ambris came up to his left, and Morwen behind him. So they waited, till the King's lips framed themselves slowly into speech, and his voice came halting and indistinct as from far away.

'It is not time – but there is a word I must speak.'

He reached out his hand, groping – Ursulet took it in hers, and the cold of it sent a shock up her arm, but she held it, and tried to send the warmth of her own body pulsing down into the cold body of the King. He spoke again, gathering strength.

'Ursulet, my daughter – my little Bear. My crown is yours, but you will not rule in Britain. Not now. Not yet.' He paused, and drew a sighing breath, then reached out his left hand towards Ambris on his other side, and placed Ambris's hand in Ursulet's.

'Ursulet, Ambrosius, I join you,' he said. 'Remember what I have done. For you must carry on the line of those that look for my returning.'

He rested a moment, then spoke with more energy.

'Mark this. Men give their names to their sons, and the mother's name is forgotten. And if the line from father to son is broken, the name is lost. But the mother-line – ah, that runs on, hidden and forgotten, but always there. You, my child – to be the mother of those that believe in me. Thousands of them – millions of them – mother to daughter, without name or record. No Kings – but Queens a few, and commoners without number – here a soldier, there a poet, there a traveller in strange places, a priest, a sage – from their mothers they take it – some pass it to their daughters—'

'What, father?' she whispered, bending her face to his. 'What do they take and pass?'

'The fire,' he answered. 'The fire that is Britain. The spark in the flint, the light in the crystal, the sword in the stone. Yours, and your children's.'

'His eyelids drooped, then opened again, and his look passed to Morwen, kneeling spellbound beside Ambris. He felt the blue eyes upon him, and the cry seemed to be forced from him.

'My lord – grandfather – have you no word for me?'

'Morwen,' the words came slowly. 'Morwen—' he seemed to brood on the name, and then a look of pain crossed his face. 'Ah, pity, pity. I could have made a man of you. I could have made a knight of you. At least do not slay your brother.'

The noble head shook, and again the eyelids fell.

But once more he opened his eyes, and said loudly and clearly, 'I shall come again. Let Britain remember – *I shall come again.*'

Then he fell back into deep sleep. Lynett withdrew the pillow and like a nurse, laid his head back softly on the couch, and placed his hands on his breast as she would a dead man's – but this was not a dead man.

'Come away now,' she whispered, but Ursulet knelt still by the couch, and laid her head on the sleeping arm of her father, and wept deeply. And so the others waited for her in silence at the door of the vault, till presently she joined them, pale, hands clasped and with her eyes on the ground.

19 · Up and Out

They resumed their march, quiet and dazed with awe. The path was a little wider here, and now Ambris and Ursulet walked side by side as with wordless consent, and her hand was firmly clasped in his. No word had passed between them, but it seemed that everything had been said.

The strange glow that emanated from the Chapel of Arthur followed them and lightened their road some way; then it faded from them and died, as the hanging, glittering alabaster gave way to rude rock, and the darkness shut down again. Lynett called a halt, lit another of the small pitch torches from the scrip she carried and shared out a little food, the bread and cheese and ale that the Witch of the Hole had given them. Ambris came a little nearer to her in the dimness.

'Aunt Lynett,' he said, speaking very softly, 'tell me this only – who fills the lamps for Arthur?'

'I do not know, my lad,' she replied. 'There are some who know, but they may not speak.'

'But are they – is the Chapel, and the assembly of Knights and all of it – are they in this world or another?'

'And that I do not know. I might guess, but if I knew I might not tell. One thing I may tell, though – I have no eyes to see the things of the other world, but I saw this ... But to say truth, I did not know that it was *here* ... I'd often heard tell, since he – went away, that he rested somewhere, with his chosen knights, till the time should come – but I never thought that I – that *we* should see the place.'

'And – when will the time come?'

'God in His Wisdom knows. But not yet.'

'Will it not be when – when his true heir is crowned?'

'God in His Wisdom knows.'

As they went on, the path began to climb. Ambris gave his staff to Ursulet, for hers had been broken in the cold-drake's jaws.

'This is hard going,' said Morwen, stumbling and recovering himself with a hand on the wall.

'Harder yet to come,' Lynett threw back at him over her shoulder.

'Whither are we climbing, then?'

'To a high place.'

'And – how do you know the way?'

'I have my waymarks. Now mind the path, or you'll fall.' And she said no more.

There began to be rough steps, cut out of the night-black stone, where Lynett's torch sometimes picked up a faint scintilla of crystal. Then the steps were more than rough – sheer shelves, where they had to climb from shelf to shelf. At the same time the confining roof fell away – as far as they could see, hear or feel, they were no longer going along a tunnel, but ascending the side of a wide shaft. Behind them was a terrifying drop into blackness, whence a cold wind howled up and tore at their hair and clothing. Up, up to the point of exhaustion. Five times at least Lynett's torch blew out, and they had to wait while she worked its red ember back into flame. Each one of them kept their balance precariously – Ursulet with the help of Ambris's staff – and shuddered at the gulf behind.

It seemed as if they were climbing like flies up the side of a room, to where it joined the ceiling. As they squinted up past the light of Lynett's torch, they could see the black roof above their heads, and no way further on. But here Lynett stopped abruptly at a ledge that just allowed room to pass and led Ursulet to the front.

'Now you must go first,' she said, her voice coming back sibilantly from the roof. 'You *must*. It is right that you should.'

'But where? Where?' exclaimed Ursulet.

'Straight up.'

'But – there's no *up*. It comes to an end.'

'You *must* go up. Up to the roof, and press on the roof with your head and your hands.'

Bewildered, Ursulet braced herself to obey – and then she

saw, on the ultimate step above her, brightly luminous against the darkness, the shape of Morgan. Morgan was, as always, white-robed and golden-sandalled, but all over her seemed to be sharp points of ice, bristling outward like sword-blades.

'Go on,' insisted Lynett.

'I – I can't. Look – there!'

'I see nothing. Go on,' said Lynett.

'But she – but *she* is there!' and in that desperate moment Ursulet understood that Lynett indeed could not see the baleful vision – but she knew also that Ambris could.

'Ambris, help me!' she cried.

'I'm here,' he answered, behind Lynett.

The white lady above smiled coldly.

'Come on up,' she said. 'Come here, and let me throw you down backwards.' And the needles of ice changed into needles of fire.

'Go *on*, go *on*,' urged Lynett. 'There's nothing there. Go *on*.'

Ambris, looking up, saw Ursulet, small, helpless but still not daunted, dark against the white figure of the dreadful lady, and a recollection of his mother's lore came back to him.

With all the concentration of his mind he pictured a great white pentagram, drawn from the left hand upwards and with the single point upright, in the air in front of the lady; and then he pictured a long sharp dart of light in his right hand, and with all his might he hurled it at her, through the centre of the pentagram. And Ursulet saw the gleaming, flaming figure of Morgan shake for a minute, as a reflection in water shakes; and bracing her staff behind her, she trod firmly on the step, placing her feet as if she would trample those white feet in their golden sandals, throwing her body forward against the whiteness and the flames. There was nothing there.

'Wrench upwards!' cried Lynett from the step below, and Ursulet thrust against that crushing black roof. It cracked and gave and crumbled – and Ursulet broke through into blazing light, colour, shouting voices and the shrilling of trumpets.

*

Hands were drawing her up the last step, out of the hole, into the air – faint and pale, dusty and dishevelled, she came up out of the ground, and saw the blue sky above her. She looked out through a tall stone archway, and people were all round her – solemn people in white, and gay people in colourful clothes and crowned with flowery garlands. Firm arms supported her, or she would have fallen. Trumpets blew, and a multitude of voices shouted.

'The Queen! The Queen! The Queen of May!'

Ursulet turned, amazed, to Lynett, who, with Ambris and Morwen behind her, was stepping out of the same strange well-like hole in the ground. Lynett smiled, and laid her strong hand on her shoulder.

'Have no fear, dear child. I've brought you where I wanted to bring you, thank God – to Glastonbury Tor on the holy May morning. Here are all your loyal people assembled to see you crowned Queen of May and Queen of Britain.'

20 · Queen of Britain

Quiet, kind-handed women in long white robes led Ursulet away from the crowd through the back of the tower which stood on the Tor, into an encampment of pavilions, and there they bathed and anointed her and combed her hair, and refreshed her with milk, honey and wine, and made her rest on a soft couch, while outside the chorus went on singing sweet songs about the Queen of May who had risen up out of the ground, like life out of death, like spring out of winter, to bring back the good times to her people. Some of them hailed her as Guinevere, Gwynhyfar, 'the white one that rises up' – the white wave, or the white ghost.

Then they robed her in a dress of thinnest silk, all embroidered with the flowers of spring in every colour, and put a veil upon her head so light that it could have drifted away on the air but for the golden spangles that adorned it and the golden pins that fastened it. And on her neck and waist and wrists were garlands of the nine holy flowers – oak blossoms, primrose, corncockle, meadowsweet, broom, bean-flower, nettle-flower, chestnut and whitethorn; and on her feet were white slippers adorned with trefoils. And so they led her out to the people.

In the glare of the brilliant May sunshine, on the top of that high hill in the eye of the sun, the assembly awaited her, all faces upturned towards her. She looked round first for her friends, and found them near her, they too newly dressed as befitted the occasion – Lynett stately in black velvet, with a tall hennin where floated a scarf of scarlet; Morwen in blue, handsome as a prince's son should be; but what Ambris was wearing she could not have said, for she could only fix her eyes on his face. Next she noticed the stately men who stood around her – bishops and abbots in their robes, earls and knights, and strange men in white with hoods, who were not monks, and wore an unknown sign. And then there were the folk, the men and women and children, with garlands and nosegays and posies in their caps, and green branches in their hands, singing, singing for joy of May and its magic Queen.

Two solemn, richly-robed old men led her forward – one, they said, was the Bishop of Wells, and the other the Abbot of Glastonbury – and they said, 'Do you here agree to accept this, the Lady Ursula, daughter of Arthur the King, as lawful Queen of all the Britons and your liege lady?'

And even in that moment she noticed that they did not use the diminutive of her name, but called her the whole name: Ursula, the She-Bear herself.

And with one accord the crowd that packed the hillside shouted 'Ay!'

Then the two great ones of the church waited while Ambris – yes, Ambris – delivered into their hands a great crown of gold, lightly wrought and all interwoven with fresh spring flowers; and the Bishop and the Abbot together set it on her head; and all the people shouted again.

And then came an old man, bearded and in armour of a fashion of twenty years past – and she could hear surprised voices near her call him 'Sir Bedivere.' He carried his long sword before him, point upwards.

'People of Britain,' he cried. 'You all know that Arthur's own sword Caliburn went back into the Lake, whence it came. Now I, Bedivere, the last of the Round Table, bring you this sword to be the visible symbol to you of the sword of Arthur. Lay your hands on it, and swear to remember that Arthur is not dead, and that he will come again, and that till he comes you will keep faith with him and with his line.'

There was a rush forward, as all within reach laid their hands on Bedivere's sword, now held by hilt and point between him and an old man in white, who was Melior of Amesbury; and those who could not touch the sword laid their hands on one another's shoulders, so as to touch those who touched it. But foremost among those that touched the sword, kneeling, was Ambris, and young Morwen close behind him.

And as Ursulet stood above them, the great crown of gold and of flowers on her head, and looked down from the great height of the Tor, with mile upon mile of green Britain swimming below her in the blue haze of the distance, she felt as if upheld on wings in the mid heaven.

21 · *But Whose Bride?*

Ursulet slowly opened her eyes and spread her limbs against softness upon which she lay. Sheets of fine white linen, a featherbed of the softest down – rich curtains, parted a little way in front, showed a window with coloured glass. For one heart-twisting moment she almost expected her mother to come in. For never since those far-off days had she known anything like this. Even in the good times at the convent, the life of a noble's child among the nuns of Wimborne had been austere on principle. But now as the guest, the royal guest, of the Abbot of Glastonbury, nothing was too good. And to come into it all so suddenly! She turned her face into the snowy pillow and smiled as she remembered.

There had been a procession through the streets of Glastonbury, with crowds of people, thousands of people, shouting and cheering. The women and children threw flowers before her; but the most part of the crowd seemed to be armed men. They had escorted her to the Abbot's stately guest-house, and there had been a banquet, and so many important people had bowed to her and kissed her hand and made speeches, and there was talk that had flowed above her head, tired as she was . . .

And then, somehow, she had found herself in a quiet moment in the Abbot's orchard, in the moonlight, under the full-blossoming apple-trees, and she was alone with Ambris.

There was so much he said to her, but certain things remained and would remain.

'You are my lady and my Queen,' he had whispered, on his knees before her. But she had drawn him to his feet again, and replied, 'I am your wife in the sight of God and King Arthur.'

And holding both her hands he rejoined, 'Ah, but what am I in your own sight, my dear?'

And she had said, 'My true-love and my darling,' and they had clasped each other in a long, sweet, blissful embrace.

She was recalled from her happy waking dream by the entry of the two pleasant, pretty girls who had been given her for waiting-maids. They brought her a breakfast of the best frumenty, enriched with raisins and cream, and served in a silver bowl; and they hoped her Royal Ladyship had slept well. Royal Ladyship! – and such a short time ago she had been nothing but Urz'l, the Jutish farmer's drudge, whom he had sold for a cow. The maidens drew back curtains and opened the casements of coloured glass, and let in the light of a heavenly morning.

Then came Lynett, brisk in a dress of green linen with a white wimple and gorget.

'That's my little Queen,' she said, and kissed her with clumsy gentleness. While the maidens brought washing-water sprinkled with sweet herbs and dressed her in a white smock and a scarlet gown and combed and braided her hair, Lynett talked, and explained some of the things that were still a mystery to Ursulet.

'Kingdoms must be fought for, alas,' she said. 'Your father, our great Arthur, held all one Britain from the Roman Wall to the Channel, and kept the Roman peace and the Christian religion there. But now all's divided, and the Saxons and Jutes and Danes crowd in upon us daily. Mordred sets himself up as King, and he now holds London and the East; but we have Constantine the Roman on our side, who reigns as King in York, and Cadwallo of the West, whom the Bishops uphold. And besides those we have earls and knights all over the country.' She rattled a rosary that hung at her girdle. 'Do you see this rosary? Look, the beads are made of acorns, and each acorn means a knight sworn to us with a hundred men, and each gold gaudy is an earl – that's how I keep count of them, and nobody thinks I'm doing anything but saying my Paters and Aves! – Most of them are here, mustered upon this island of Avalon, or Glastonbury, or Ynys Witrin as they call it. Yet Mordred has his troops drawn out to encircle us between here and the place where we found you. He watched us as a cat watches for a mouse, and not a creature could pass between Wimborne and here – but I brought you by hidden ways, so that you rose up in the midst of Ynys Witrin, as we had promised them, Bedivere and I, on the first day of May. And now you are crowned Queen. It remains to hold your kingdom by force of arms, and secure it against Mordred and the

Saxons. For he will even call in the Saxons to suit his own ends.'

Ursulet shuddered.

'He wanted me to marry his son Morcar – but he tried to ravish me himself.'

'I know. I was closer to you than you knew – And so we come, indeed, to the nub of the matter. All men will have it that a woman must have a man to rule for her, that a woman cannot rule alone or lead an army – God knows why not. And so they say you must take a husband. Now in proper times of peace, a woman has always someone to make the marriage for her – her father, or a guardian, who gives her in marriage. You have no one to give you in marriage—'

She paused, and Ursulet broke in quickly.

'But Arthur my father gave me in marriage to Ambris.'

'Ha! I hoped you'd say that, though I might not put the words into your mouth. Bless you, child, and so he did. I was there – yes, it was no glamour. I can never see the sleights and visions conjured up by the Deceiver, or any of the people of the other world, but I saw that, and so you can be sure it was no delusion. But you yourself – in your heart, how do you regard young Ambris?'

Ursulet turned full to face her, regardless of the two maidens. There was no blush on her face, but complete simplicity as she answered.

'I am his and he is mine.'

Lynett clasped her by both shoulders and kissed her heartily; but at that moment there was a knock on the door. One of the maids ran hastily across and returned.

'Oh madam – oh your Royal Ladyship – it's the lay-brother to say the Lord Abbot awaits you below. The embassies have arrived. His lordship bids you make haste.'

'Oh me!' sighed Lynett. 'Now it begins— You must hurry down – but *remember* . . .'

And she hurried out, while the maids put a robe of scarlet velvet over the scarlet gown, with facings of vair, and clasped a thin golden circlet round her head; then they led her out and down the staircase.

The Abbot's Parlour it was called, but it was almost as stately, if not quite as large, as a knight's hall; warmed by a big fire under a chimney, not under a hole in the middle, and hung all round with tapestries. Here the Abbot of Glastonbury, with the Bishop of Wells at his side, led Ursulet to the dais, and placed her in a chair of state. Further back against the tapestries she could see Ambris and Lynett but she could not see Morwen. The walls of the great room were lined with people – men, all of them.

Outside, suddenly a trumpet sounded, and there was the tramp of armed men marching in step and the rhythmic clash of armour. At a loud word of command it ceased as if cut off suddenly; then there was only the occasional faint scrape and rattle of metal that spoke of armed men standing still. The doors behind the screens were opened wide, and King Constantine the Roman entered, with a body of his guards, two and two behind him, moving as one – eight strong warriors, dressed and armed in the Roman manner, with square shields, short swords and plumed helmets. But as each pair entered, they genuflected together to the crucifix that hung behind the dais.

Constantine the Roman, the third of that name in Britain, wore the tunic and toga of peace; he was a short dark man with a clean-cut profile and piercing dark eyes, perhaps about forty, self-confident and decisive.

He saluted Ursulet with great formality, addressing her as Ursula the daughter of Arthur, Queen of the Britons. He spoke in Latin, but Ursulet could recall enough of the convent Latin, now rapidly coming back to her, to understand. But the Abbot of Glastonbury replied in the Celtic language.

'Honoured lady and queen,' – and so on, through a long honorific preamble. Then, coming to the point, 'And so, honoured lady, it is apparent to all, that, for the consolidation of this realm and the better alliance with our friends and helpers the Romans, a happy and auspicious marriage should forthwith be arranged for you, our lady and queen. In these troubled times it is, alas, too evident that you have now no kindred to stand as your sponsor, and give you in marriage; so, as senior cleric here, and as I claim, senior priest of all Britain and all Christendom – since here and nowhere else our Holy Faith was first preached – I therefore take upon myself the happy duty of being your guardian and sponsor. And as such, I am privileged to bestow your hand in marriage upon King Constantine the Roman, now reigning in York, and here present.'

It was not until the Abbot had rounded off his resounding period that Ursulet found her voice.

'Oh, but no – no! I will not marry him!'

The whole company stood aghast – it was like a stone thrown into the smooth surface of a lake, shattering the reflections – A stone? A storm!

'Child, child, you mustn't say that!' fussed the Abbot in an agitated whisper. And the grave, fierce Roman bristled up like a cat.

'Quid dixit – nolet?'

'Nolet, domine.'

The word he spat out, though Latin, was uncanonical.

Everyone's face was red, save only Lynett's and Ambris's. They were pale and tense, but approving. In the shocked silence, Ursulet spoke.

'I won't have it. You take me and give me, as if I were a possession to be bargained for. I'm not a thing, I'm a person – a Christian soul if you like, my Lord Abbot—'

'Yes, yes, my child, but you mustn't – you mustn't – Look, it's very important, don't you understand? We mustn't make the Roman lord angry—'

And he launched off into a long speech in Latin, too quick and complicated for Ursulet to follow – it seemed to soothe the Roman's feelings somewhat, for his hackles, so to speak, went down – his angry face relaxed a little, and he turned about, after a rather perfunctory reverence to Ursulet and the

Abbot, and stalked out, his bodyguard clanking after him. The Abbot turned again to Ursulet. 'I've told him you'll think it over,' he said.

'Let *him* think as much as he likes,' said Ursulet, 'I'll think no different. I will not marry him. Now who is the next embassage?'

The next embassage was Cadwallo of Wales, with the Bishops of St David's and St Asaph's. Cadwallo brought with him an escort of only four rough shaggy-haired Celtic fighters – but two of them led with them young Morwen, round-eyed and frightened. He walked between them like a prisoner being led to execution; and he looked just what he was, an intimidated boy of fifteen, though obviously efforts had been made to make him look older. He was impressively dressed in the finery of a Celtic chief, with a heavy torque of beaten gold spreading across his chest, and a ceremonial golden helmet with horns. Ursulet looked across at him, wondering what he was doing there, and his brown eyes met hers with a desperate appeal she did not understand.

Cadwallo, thick-set and with brown tousled hair cut straight above his brow, made low and elaborate obeisance to Ursulet, and then motioned forward his harper, who had come in behind the little procession. The harper, a white-bearded, bald-headed man, bowed and sat down on a small stool placed for him by his page, who also handed him his great harp. He ran his fingers very sweetly over the strings, and then began a long laudatory ode, about the greatness of Britain, the resistance of Britain to the Romans (Constantine and his men being out of hearing) and to the Saxons; of King Arthur; of his beautiful daughter (Ursulet suppressed a smile) – of the union of the tribes of the West with those of the South, the North and the East, and their freedom for ever from the Saxon invaders. So far so good – and Ursulet, whose attention had certainly wandered a little with the sweet harp accompaniment, realized that the ode had come to its conclusion, and looked to see if she ought to applaud or praise the bard. But before she could do so, Cadwallo came quickly after the musician with his speech This was long and flowery, and rather to the same effect.

'And so,' he concluded, 'having in mind the union of our peoples, under one strong head, or shall we say, two heads, one strong, one gracious, that shall henceforth be one – I come, to my Lord Abbot, to you as guardian of this lady. Were I not already married, you may imagine, I would gladly sue for her hand – but instead I would put forward in my place one of royal descent, to whom I have the honour to stand guardian – our young Prince Morwen, on whose behalf I beseech your lordship for the hand of the noble Queen Ursulet.'

The Abbot, all nervous twitters, turned, hands clasped, to Ursulet. She, staring incredulous at Morwen, saw him shake his head and with his lips frame 'no'. A look of sheer agony was on his face.

'My lord Abbot,' said Ursulet, 'my answer again is no. I said no before, and I say no now. I will not be given to this one or that one.'

Before the others could recover from this further rebuff, Morwen broke from his guard and knelt at Ursulet's feet, holding her hand.

'Oh sweet lady queen!' he cried. 'They made me come here – it's not my wish at all. Believe me, I could not betray you, and Ambris, and King Arthur. Oh, I – honour and worship you, lady, but I'll not be made to marry you against your will. For I know you are already troth-plight to Sir Ambris.'

The Abbot let his crozier fall to the ground with a clatter – the Bishop of Wells groped for the chair behind him and sat down. A wave of dismay swept through the room.

'Madam, is this true?' the Abbot gasped.

'Yes, it is true,' answered Ursulet without faltering. Then quickly she glanced behind her, and spread her hands to draw forward Ambris, and Lynett, and Bedivere. They closed up around her.

The whole room buzzed with a storm of anger and frustration. Wherever she turned Ursulet could see nothing but angry faces, swaying to and fro, and hostile hands shaken towards her; everyone was shouting at once. Only Ambris's hand sought hers, and held it with a steady pressure. In her mind's eye she could see Arthur's calm pale face, and feel his hand laid across their handclasp; and a strange boldness inspired her. She raised her voice and spoke loudly across the noise.

'Listen, all of you. Arthur my father has joined my hand to the hand of Sir Ambrosius here, and from that act I will not yield or move. Tell that to Lord Cadwallo, and Constantine the Roman, and the Lord Mordred himself. I will not marry any other.'

Cadwallo came shouldering up out of the crowd.

'Then, my lady Ursula, you cannot expect me to fight for you. I bid you farewell.' He gestured to his men-at-arms, who held Morwen firmly by the shoulders and dragged him away like a condemned criminal. The Abbot of Glastonbury stood below the dais wringing his hands.

'Lady, lady – don't you understand? You can't do this, you've wrecked everything. Cadwallo will withdraw his army, the Roman has withdrawn his already. How will you win your kingdom from the Saxons?'

'By God's help and King Arthur's,' said Ursulet, feeling uplifted on a tide of supernatural excitement. The Abbot shrugged his shoulders, shook his head, and turned away.

'May God help you then, lady,' he said, 'for you'll get little help from men.'

And the turbulent crowd began to stream out of the far doors, leaving Ursulet and her three friends alone on the dais, the excitement slowly dying out of her and leaving her cold.

'Oh, I hope I did right!' she exclaimed.

22 · *Counsel from the Enemy*

Inside the precincts of Glastonbury Abbey, which was Avalon, was the holiest spot in Britain, the little church of wattle and clay that was the shrine of St Joseph and of Our Blessed Lady; and from this, holiness radiated like the beams of the sun. The nimbus of glory permeated the Abbey church beside it and the Abbey itself with all its demesnes – a great area of ground lay within a ring of consecration, where nothing ill could enter. Even down through the Abbot's orchard, on the side furthest from the town, was holy ground. But at the end of the orchard, beyond trees and shrubs, there was a fence of wrought iron, that marked the limit of the hallows.

Beyond that, the wild country came up to the boundary of the fence, and there the holy powers had no hold. The country around the Isle of Avalon was for the most part bare and open, wet and reedy and treeless save for a few willows, but here on the edge of the Abbey ground there was a wood, old and neglected, of alders and birches, fast falling into the swamp, dark and ominous. Here, in the red light of sunset, Ambris walked by the railings, with the trim orchard and the hallowed ground on his right hand, and the darkling wild wood on his left. And there suddenly, with a rustle of draperies, was Morgan, facing him on the other side of the fence.

This time she was not radiant in white and bejewelled, but clad in a subtle sombre grey that merged into the colours of the wood behind her; her dark hair was covered with a pearly-grey scarf, but round her neck could be seen a glimpse of strange bronze amulets. She spoke in a whisper.

'Hist there, nephew . . .'

He turned upon her.

'Get thee behind me, sorceress! I know you now – I'll not

listen to you.' And he turned to hasten away. But she spoke mildly.

'Now, now! Is that any way to greet kith and kin? Is it kinsmanly, is it kindly – is it any sort of family feeling? Should there be ill-will between near relatives, on both sides of the family? You ought to spare a word for your great-aunt.'

He knew his danger, but could not break away from her. He turned and walked along the fence in the opposite direction; she turned also and walked with him, matching his pace, turning when he turned, as two dogs will run on opposite sides of a fence. Her feet rustled softly, lightly, on the dead leaves.

'I must not listen to you,' he said. 'I know you are the Deceiver.'

'Oh, sweet nephew! Call me deceiver, call me evil, call me a devil in woman's form if you must – but don't disdain a warning, even if it seems to come from your enemy.'

'Warning?' He frowned, alert to something new.

'Yes, warning. Dear trusting boy, you don't know what you're doing. You love this Lady Ursulet, do you not?'

'That is no concern of yours.'

'Ah, no doubt – but believe me, in your love and devotion to her you are serving her very ill.'

'What do you mean?'

'Ha, you'll listen to me now? – Why, yes, don't you understand? She has her kingdom to fight for, she needs all the help she can get – a woman in her position must have strong allies. She should marry so as to gain the help she needs. Now do you understand?'

His heart sank.

'But we love each other—'

'Oh, dear lad, beware of love! Queens may not marry for love as others do. Love has been the ruin of many kings and queens. Think of Guinevere and Lancelot. Will you ruin her for the sake of this love?'

'I tell you Arthur himself plighted our troth to one another in his cave. We are already lawfully wedded.'

'Oh, my dear young man!' She laughed. 'Have you not seen enough of visions and waking dreams to know that they can deceive you? I can call up all sorts of shows, as well you know – and so can others. Even your own mind, and hers, in that dim strange place and after all you had endured – you saw a vision? No doubt you did, but was it of any more reality than the sleights I could show you? But come – kingdoms can't be won with visions and illusions. How is she to lead an army? How is she to defeat the Saxons? And what if she has to face Mordred's army too, and Constantine's, and Cadwallo's? Who is to be her war general? You, dear child? Or old Bedivere, with his rusty armour? Or your crazy old aunt Lynett? Believe me, that old woman is as mad as a March hare, and thinks herself a war commander, riding about the country in her old leather jerkin – do you know, she is your lady's worst enemy, leading her on with notions of military conquest. There is only one effective war leader in this land, and that is Constantine the Roman. And it is he that she must marry, and gain both a general and an army.'

It came over Ambris like a cold wind that she spoke truth.

'What must I do then?'

'You? You must go away from her – now, at once, quietly and without farewell. Otherwise, as long as you are here, she will not marry another. If you love her, as you say you do, you must cease to stand in her way.'

'It will break her heart – it will break mine too.'

'What are broken hearts to kings and queens? If you stay with her, and force her to fight this battle alone, there will be many more broken hearts than hers and yours. Again I say, think of Guinevere.'

He drew a long breath – oh, she was right, of course, and yet . . .

'Listen,' he said, 'why must you compare me to Lancelot? We are free to wed lawfully – there is no bar between us – my love for her is pure and unselfish and without any self-interest—'

'Yes – is it so?' She halted in her pacing to and fro, and

faced him through the coils of the wrought iron, with the dark wood behind her. 'Altogether pure, and wanting nothing for yourself? Tainted with no base desire? Oh, my dear self-deceiving boy – look me in the eyes. You are a man as other men are, and her body is a woman's body of flesh and blood. Are you sure, are you so very sure, that you desire nothing for yourself?'

He raised his eyes to hers, and then his face slowly reddened, and he dropped his eyes again.

'You see,' her soft voice went on, 'your motives are not so pure after all. Can you in honour seek her for yourself, and ruin her? Come, if you have any noble regard for her – break away at once. No goodbyes – no chance to relent. Go any-where, but go now. Be brave – it will hurt less. Go – go—'

'I'll go,' he cried in a choking voice, flinging his arm up over his eyes; and he broke away from that enchanted corner, and ran through the gardens, now grown dark – not towards the Abbot's house, but towards the stables.

And the shadowy lady gave a deep sigh of satisfaction, and melted like a breath on a window pane.

23 · *The New Round Table*

The maid at the door of Ursulet's room let Lynett in, but shrugged her shoulders, spread out her hands – The curtains of Ursulet's bed were still closed, though it was morning. Lynett flung them back, and disclosed Ursulet lying face down on the bed, abandoned to violent weeping. Hardly looking up, she thrust into Lynett's hand a small scroll of parchment, written in the laborious characters of one not very used to writing. Lynett read, 'Farewell, my love and my lady. It has been shown to me that I am a stumbling block in your way, and therefore I take my leave for pure love of you.

Marry the Roman, for Britain's sake and your own. And I, if I live or die, it is for you.'

Lynett stood tense, crushing the scroll between her hands, and swore – slowly, deliberately, and religiously.

'Oh, God's Blood!' she said, 'Oh, God's own Precious Blood—' It was almost more a prayer than an oath.

She paced to and fro for a moment, and then turned to the shaking figure on the bed.

'Look up, child – you know what this means?'

'It means he has forsaken me,' came the smothered reply. 'Oh, dear God, this is the end! Let me die. How could he, after my father had joined our hands?'

'Ay, how could he? Never of his own will. No, my girl, listen. This is the Deceiver's work. To think she should have got at him at the last – now! No, lift your head and stop crying. Do you want to please *her* by despairing? Come now – do you want a dash of cold water on your head? Well then – get up and wash your face.'

She stamped to and fro, while the waiting maids brought water, and Ursulet suffered herself to be washed and dressed.

'But what do we do now?' Ursulet asked at last.

'We'll call a council of the earls. What the devil – we're not alone. We've men to call upon.'

'Must I marry the Roman, then?'

'The Roman? God forbid! Nor either of the sons of Mordred. Poor Morwen, though – I fear it will go hard with him – No, my little Princess, you'll wait till our Ambris comes back, as come back he will. With an army, no doubt, to turn the scale against our enemies.'

Like a nurse soothing a child with promises, she persuaded Ursulet, who at last came slowly pacing down the stairs to meet the council of the earls – pale-faced and great-eyed, now looking like the White Ghost indeed.

It seemed that the council was not to be held in the Abbot's great parlour, but elsewhere. Lynett led Ursulet out of the Abbot's house, and across the green acres where the apple-trees still shed their blossom, to the Abbey Church. It stood tall, though not as tall as it was later to become, when the world was to know it for a marvel. But already it was a stately house, towering over that which was much more holy, the little ancient church of wattle and clay.

On the south side, by the monks' graveyard, was a low doorway; and here they went in, and down a flight of steps. Ursulet shivered as they left the shadow of the garden and plunged down into the shadow of chilly stone. The little winding staircase led her out into the wide crypt under the Abbey church, a dim vaulted place, lit only by small slit windows high up at the ground level above, and by torches set in sconces against the walls. These latter gave a red and flickering light, by which she could see a number of armed men, in the apparel of nobles, standing round the walls, and in the midst a great round table. It was covered by no cloth, but it was richly inlaid and blazoned with colours and gold; and in the midst was the device of a rose, from which radiating lines divided the circle into its proper 'sieges' – twenty-four of the knights, the central one for the King, the Queen on his right and Merlin on his left, thus making up the magical three-times-nine.

Bedivere, approaching in the dimness, said, 'Be seated, gracious lady,' and Ursulet moved to take the Queen's seat, but Lynett urgently whispered, 'No, not there,' and firmly placed her in the King's own throne. Dazed, she sat down, and the others took their places all round the Table. Melior the Druid took Merlin's seat on her left, but the consort's seat on her right was left vacant – with a pang of heart she realized why. Next beyond the empty chair was old Bedivere, the only face in the circle that she knew. A chair was placed for Lynett close behind Ursulet's throne, for only one woman could be in the circle.

One by one the knights stood up, and saluting with their swords, gave their names. Strange names that recalled those so often told in the stories of Arthur's knights, like them but not many the same – Sir Segwarion, Sir Mortimare, Sir

Nondras, Sir Palarion – just a few were veterans from twenty years past, as Sir Ector and Sir Bors. Some were bright-eyed young men not yet out of their teens. The names went round in a hollow echoing ring, each with a grind of steel as the sword was drawn. Then when all were named, and Ursulet's eyes had wandered to the shadows in the dim vault above them, there was a clash of metal – each knight had laid down his steel-plated gauntlets on the table before him, and all joined their bare hands in a ring. Ursulet's hands were grasped by Melior on her left and Bedivere on her right, and behind her, Lynett laid her hand on her shoulder.

'Now listen all here,' came Bedivere's deep grating voice, as rusty as his armour. 'We here are the new Table Round, and the vows which our forerunners took at this Table, we take again, to live and die in faith and truth, to Arthur the King until he comes again, and to Arthur's heir, the lady Queen Ursula, the true Daughter of the Bear. To her we pledge our service and fealty.'

And they all answered, 'We pledge our service and fealty.'

Then Melior's musical voice broke in.

'Swear we all this. King Arthur is not dead. He sleeps, and will come again.'

And the deep murmur echoed against the dark stone roof, 'King Arthur is not dead. He sleeps, and will come again.'

Then all sat down, and for a time there was silence.

Presently, Bedivere looked up and said, 'But we are not complete. Where is Sir Ambrosius?' and all looked to Ursulet for an answer.

'My lords,' she said, her voice coming cold and thin in that strange place, 'he is not here. He – left me a message to say that he was departing – that he would not – stay with me . . .' She could not go on.

There was a stir, and a cry of 'Treachery!'

'Where has he gone?'

'Has he betrayed us?'

'Has he gone to the enemy?'

Ursulet stood white and shaking, with no words to say. It was Lynett that came forward.

'My lords, may I speak?'

'Speak on, Lady Lynett.'

'Then I'll say this, and say sooth – young Sir Ambris is no traitor. I'll answer for him with my head. He has gone, I know, – I'm sure of it as I'm sure that two and two make four – he has gone because he has been ensnared by the lady of deceits, the Enchantress Morgan le Fay. She knows how to turn a man's mind and make him think black is white – she has persuaded him that honour requires him to go and not to stay – oh, my lords, do we not know the power of her subtlety? Sooner or later he will return, but in the meantime we can do little without him. Our Queen is without her right arm. But oh, worthy and noble Knights, never call him traitor!'

There was a murmur of approval. Bedivere spoke for the rest.

'Be it so, lady – let the siege be left at our Queen's right hand for Sir Ambrosius, in trust that he will return. But now we must take counsel for the war.'

There followed a long and wearisome debate, of which Ursulet could hardly follow one word in three. Maps were unrolled on the Round Table, and the knights pointed here and there – numbers of men, numbers of horses, distances from castle to castle, all flowed over her head. From her high throne she looked up to the murky roof, where the faint beams of light slanted down from the little narrow windows through the smoke of the torches. Oh, if only the Holy Grail could come slanting down along those beams, to put an end to all this round-and-round discussion and show them plainly what they ought to do!

For it seemed there was no agreement among them, no clear lead, no real plan. Too many plans were put forward, by too many with ends of their own to gain, and none would fall in with another's. They wandered into digression, quarrelled fiercely over side-issues. Bedivere tried to hold them together, but they swept him aside. As for Ursulet herself, she just could not follow the multitudinous arguments.

At last they adjourned for the noon-meal, and Ursulet walked out into the fresh air and bright sunshine on Lynett's arm.

'Oh, dear God,' she exclaimed, 'what are they supposed to be doing?'

'You may well ask,' replied Lynett bitterly. 'The fools – the fools. We haven't a leader. Not one leader among us. They will follow you, my dear, as a banner of war, but how can you know how to lead them? How can I? Oh, for a leader—'

'The Roman . . .?' Ursulet faltered.

'No! *Not* the Roman – not at the price he wants.'

'No – not at the price he wants.'

The sunshine blazed on the apple-trees, but far to the north a thundercloud was building up. The air was oppressive.

There was a stir across the other side of the wide lawns, under the apple-trees.

'A messenger, lady.'

A breathless man knelt before her.

'Lady – the Earl Mordred advances from the east, and is nearly at Winchester. He bids you yield, or he will shut you up here by siege. Constantine the Roman has declared defiance against you, and marches with all his army – he halted his homeward march at Reading, and the rest of his legions have joined him there from York. The Earl Cadwallo has proclaimed Morwen King in defiance of you, and holds Camelot.'

Ursulet's face was as pale as the messenger's as they led him away.

'Oh God – what shall we do now? And Ambris not here—' She trembled on the edge of tears.

'No terror and no tears,' rasped Lynett, 'or I'll box your ears like a page, though you're Queen.' Ursulet swallowed down her rising panic, glad of the harsh words. The livid cloud was drawing nearer, covering the sun. Not a breath moved. Far across the smooth lawns, she could see a small black cat, its fur on end, dancing madly in circles under the trees.

'One thing we'll not do,' said Lynett. 'We'll not stay here to be shut in. To die of famine and disease, that's a filthy death. Let's break out of here while there's time, and face them in the field.'

Melior, who stood close beside, stepped forward at the words. He was a tall, fresh-faced man, with serene blue eyes under his close white headdress. His voice, from which he took his name, was clear and sweet, the sweetest of any man's.

'One other thing, lady,' he said. 'None of these lords can agree, but there is one whom they will obey. Now is the time when we shall call upon Merlin himself to guide us.'

'Merlin?' Ursulet felt her heart leap with unreasonable hope. 'But Merlin sleeps in Broceliande, under the stone where Nimue enchanted him.'

'Not so, lady. I was the last to know Merlin. The Lady Nimue was his faithful wife, and died before him, so always she waited and called to him from Broceliande, till his time came. I saw his passing, when he wrought his last wonder in the circle of Stonehenge – some day the story will be told. Merlin sleeps in the Otherworld, as many do – but I believe he will wake if we call him.'

'Call him, then, oh, call him! – and if we may call him, why not – my father also? Is it not – Arthur's Time?'

'I do not think so, dear lady. Not unless Merlin himself, maybe, gives us the word. Arthur may only be wakened once again, and woe betide us all if he is waked untimely. I do not think it is the time. But Merlin will tell us.'

'So be it. Let us call Merlin, for it may be that none other can help us now.'

As they went down again into the crypt, the thunder had begun to growl in the heavy, sagging clouds. A strange tenseness plucked at Ursulet's nerves. She had noticed how, when Lynett ran a comb through her wiry grey hair before they rejoined the others, sparks crackled and blazed; even her own fine flaxen hair followed the comb as if pulled by it.

The crypt seemed very dark and oppressive. Little light came in through the high windows now, only the torches illuminated the stony space, red and fitful.

When all were seated in their proper places, Melior stood up. The golden Tribann gleamed on his forehead, and on his bosom the Snake-stone caught the flickering light and seemed to glow from within.

Then entered two women, white-robed and bare-headed; one bore a bowl of water, and the other a smoking censer. Slowly and rhythmically they paced round the circle, sprinkling and censing, to cleanse and hallow it. The wreaths of smoke from the incense hung in the air in great solid swathes. Then Melior himself advanced, and placed in the centre of the Round Table a bronze bowl of ancient pattern, full of water. He resumed his place, and spoke steadily and quietly in his musical voice.

'Now let all earthly thoughts be laid aside. Let each of us look steadily at the bowl, filled with the water of the sacred spring – and with all the power of our minds, let us call upon Merlin to be here with us.'

All fell silent, and in the silence the thunder could be heard, coming nearer. The sun, in its last brilliant glare before the storm, broke the clouds and for a second pierced dazzlingly down from the high window in the south; then it was gone again, and a black wing seemed to sweep over. A wind began to sigh in the rooftops and the treetops.

Still they all kept their eyes on the glimmering surface of the water on the bronze bowl; then Melior began chanting. Then he raised his voice and called loudly.

'Merlin! Merlin! Merlin-n-n-n . . .'

And on the last syllable his voice hummed on and on and on, till they felt rather than heard it. And the smoke-wreaths that hung in the air above the Round Table moved together and grew thicker, and took shape. All saw it – a human shape, veiled and draped in the wreaths of smoke: 'an old man covered with a mantle.'

A voice spoke – slow, halting, as if not used to speech.

'Adsum . . . I am here. What do you ask?'

Melior was on his feet and leaning across the table.

'Speak in the Name of the One Above All. How is the Kingdom of Arthur to be won?'

Slowly came the words, and then faster and louder as the apparition gathered power.

'Not by battle, not by the sword. They that take the sword will perish by the sword. There will be no victory, no triumph of arms. The Kingdom of Arthur, like the kingdom of his Lord, is not of this world, else would his servants fight . . . Not in this generation, nor for many to come, but generation after generation, soul after soul, mind after mind . . . For the Saxons also will bow the knee to Arthur, but not now and not thus. The conquered shall lead the conqueror, and the van-quished shall overcome the victors. Shall the colours of the dyer strive against the cloth . . .?'

'Oh, speak more plainly!' Melior cried. 'Tell us – is it not yet Arthur's hour? Are we to wake him in this extremity?'

'No – no – no. Not yet. Not thus is it written. By Arthur's line, but not by Arthur's name. By blood, but not by blood-shed. By the distaff, not by the sword.'

One of the knights cried out, 'What, then – is there to be no victory? Are we not to fight?'

And another cried, 'How do we know this is Merlin?'

'Be silent,' said Melior, suddenly authoritative, and then addressed the cloudy presence.

'Are you – are you indeed my master Merlin? Give us a sign—'

'I am Merlin Ambrosius,' the voice pronounced, and then suddenly changed from the hieratic to the tenderly familiar.

'Melior, you bad boy, you made the ass run away with my Plato.'

The voice concluded with the dry chuckle of an old man.

Melior gave a sob as from the depths of his heart, and fell

forward with his head on the table, his arms groping towards the feet of the apparition. Then he raised his head and looked round at the others.

'It is he – it is my old master. That was something none knew but he and I.' Then he dropped his head again and they could hear him weeping bitterly. And again the thunder rolled above them.

The hieratic voice began again.

'Hail to the daughter of Arthur, Ursulet the Lesser Bear, daughter of Guinevere, bearer of the distaff. But where is Ambris? Where is Sir Ambrosius? Without him the prophecy cannot be fulfilled. Where is Ambrosius son of Gawain, son of Gareth, son of Lot . . .'

The voice was fading, and the figure began to dissolve – then the crash of thunder shook the roof above them, and the lightning fell. For one moment they all saw each other outlined in blue fire, and the shape of Merlin, not veiled now, but plain and recognizable, and in front of him, also plain to see, the shape of young Morwen, kneeling with his back to Merlin like a runner poised to start – he was naked and shining as if with rain. Merlin seemed to point with his hand and to release the kneeling figure like an arrow from a bow. Then the darkness closed down, and each one for a second seemed to be blinded. Melior's voice intoning: 'Thanks and blessing – depart in peace into the bliss of Gwynfyd,' was all but drowned in the crash that followed the lightning.

They sat dazed and silent in the dark – the torches had blown out. Then, as pages ran to relight the torches, they gradually gathered their wits. The rain was roaring down on the high roof of the church above them, and at first it was hard to hear each other's voices. Ursulet had drawn Lynett to her, and sat trembling with her face pressed against Lynett's hard bosom.

Voices began to make themselves heard.

'What, so we are not to fight?'

'The wizard prophesied no victory?'

'Do you understand it?'

'No, do you?'

'This is no answer.'

'This is no proper augury.'

Ursulet suddenly felt strength and resolution come into her. She sat upright upon her throne again – then she stood and cried as clearly as she could.

'Worthy knights, hear me!'

But her voice failed in the hubbub.

Bedivere drew his sword and beat it against his shield, and the clamour pierced all other sounds.

'Silence for her Grace the Queen.'

Now they were silent – only the rain hissed – and Ursulet said,

'Victory or not, my lords, we must break out of here. We must not be shut up in Avalon. Sir Ector and Sir Bors are my father's oldest veterans, with Sir Bedivere – I choose that they three shall direct the army. So let us go and prepare to march.'

24 · In the Lightning

The guards at Camelot, that great fortress within its circle of earthworks, where Cadwallo had taken the place that had long been Arthur's, had orders to wait upon the young Prince Morwen, protect him and watch him, but nothing had been said about restraining him. It had not occurred to Cadwallo that there would be any need to do so.

The storm that had long been creeping up on the country-side, sharpening everyone's nerves and weighing on every-one's brain, had broken in terrifying force – crash after crash, lightning flash after lightning flash, and the rain coming down in a hissing sheet through the solid dark that broke, every few heartbeats, to show all objects curiously reversed, white for black, before the dark came again. What hour of night it was, no one could tell. Some counted the flashes – others just hid their eyes and waited.

The two sentries in the passage outside the door of Prince Morwen's room had hidden the bright heads of their halberds, and leant against the wall each side of the door, watching the flashes through the little arrow-slit that lighted the passage. In the pause between two roars of thunder the door creaked and opened. They turned and stared silently as into the lightning flash stepped a pale and luminous figure – Morwen quite naked, his eyes shut, his hands groping before him. His short brown hair stood straight out from his head in a wild bristling mop. Although he groped, he walked fast and surely as if someone were leading him. The guards stood spellbound and let him pass.

'Did you see?' the one whispered to the other. 'Fast asleep, and walking—'

'Should we stop him?'

'We daren't. Stark naked, and walking in his sleep. The hand of God is on him.'

'The hand of the gods is on him,' said the other man, who believed in older things. 'No, we daren't stop him.'

Past sentry after sentry, it was the same. None dared lay hands on the naked boy who walked with his eyes shut in the midst of the thunder and lightning. Out into the pouring rain, with the levin-flash all round him – now the rain pouring over his head quenched his bristling hair, and his bare skin, washed all over, gleamed when the lightning flashed – but his eyes never opened and his feet never faltered. Down through all the long banks and winding slopes of the great fortress – at the foot of the long approach was the gatehouse, but the gatehouse keeper, seeing the pale figure pointing to the gate as a crashing bolt seemed to fall from the sky, hastened in panic to open and let the terrifying ghost depart, and then ran to hide, leaving the gate swinging. What earthly foe could trouble them that night, when gods and ghosts were stalking the land?

*

Ambris never knew where or how far he had ridden after he left Glastonbury. Somewhere, maybe at Amesbury, after the morning broke, he had found himself tired out and thirsty, and had snatched a drink of ale at some tavern, and then later had found a corner of a field and slept. Later, waking dazed and dull, he had plodded on, without any plan. He had seen the clouds bank up and the storm grow, but had gone on through it in stolid indifference. Then when he had come out of his misery a little, and considered his situation, there seemed to be nothing to do but press on; for there he was in the middle of a very wet wood, with the light failing, and the rain coming down on him, and the thunder and lightning terrifying his unfortunate horse. Stopping still was no better than going on; so on he went.

Suddenly a flash of lightning lit up a figure standing right in his path – a naked boy, streaming with rain. His horse shied, screaming shrilly, rising with its hoofs above the strange figure – Ambris struggled and pulled on the reins, turning the horse, or its thrashing hoofs would have descended on the naked boy. He fought the horse round in a circle, and at last made it stand still, and quietened it. Then he looked at the boy, who was leaning back against a tree, exhausted and blinking his eyes as if just awakening from sleep. To his astonishment, Ambris recognized Morwen.

In an instant he was off his horse and ran to catch Morwen, who collapsed into his arms. The boy was as wet as if he had come out of the sea, deadly cold and shaking. Ambris took off his cloak and wrapped it round him.

'Morwen! What in God's name are you doing here, like this?'

Morwen was frowning and blinking and shaking his head, and putting up his hand to push the wet hair out of his eyes.

'I was sent to you,' he said, speaking rapidly as if not quite of his own will, 'to say, go back to her at once, she needs you as never man was needed before, in Arthur's name go back to her, so says – so says – Merlin . . .' His voice faltered and came to an end.

'Why, what's this, Morwen? Here, come awake. Drink this, it's as well I've a bottle at my belt. There – now pull yourself together. This is no night to go running about the woods as bare as an egg. What did you do it for?'

As he spoke, he held him close up against the flank of his horse, supporting him; under the thickest covert of a tree, he managed to find some little shelter from the rain. The thunder had begun to slacken off a bit, and the rain to decrease.

'I don't know,' said Morwen. 'Yes, I do – a man came to me – an old man covered with a mantle – and told me to get up at once, just as I was, and run, and run, and run to find you, and tell you – what I told you just now. So I had to ... But I didn't know I was dreaming – I was dreaming, wasn't I?'

'Yes, I think you were,' said Ambris. 'But it could have been a true dream. These things do happen. Tell me again what you had to say.'

'I've forgotten it now, every word of it.'

'Oh – that's a pity. But I think I remember it – was it that I had to go back – that Ursulet – that the Queen needed me? Was that it?'

'It might have been. I said it, and then it went from me.'

'No matter – if I'm to go back – if I'm really needed, and Merlin said so – he did, didn't he? Then I'll go back. Let's go.'

'Wait a minute.' Morwen was recovering his wits. 'Look, we can do better than that. I know the men in Camelot Castle want to fight for Queen Ursulet. Cadwallo and the Bishops brought them here for that, no matter for whether she was to marry me or not ... of course you don't believe I ... oh, but never mind. The thing is, they will fight for her – *not* against her – if we get at them quickly and quietly. I am sure this is the road to Camelot – come back with me now, and we'll take them by surprise. The storm's passing, thank God, and the moon will give us some light. Old Cadwallo will still be in his drunken sleep, if we hurry. I've a plan – come on.'

They rode on through the still dripping woods, Morwen riding behind Ambris, and they were approaching the out- skirts of the forest, when the last flash of lightning suddenly showed Ambris the form of Morgan le Fay, standing full in his path, more radiantly beautiful than he had ever seen her. His horse reared up, for the second time that night, and he struggled to steady it, while Morwen cried out in sudden fear. The lightning passed, but a gleam like the levin played still around the white figure of Morgan.

'Go away from me!' Ambris cried. 'Let me alone, witch-woman!'

'Who are you speaking to?' said Morwen over his shoulder, in a voice shaken with terror.

'To *her* – to *her* – don't you see her?'

Morwen saw nothing, but he felt the hair rise on his neck and the sweat break out on his skin.

'Once more, go back!' said the beautiful terror. 'You cannot win this battle, and that is no deceit.'

'Leave me alone,' Ambris retorted. 'Woman, I know you for a deceiver. You nearly made a traitor of me. How long will you keep troubling me?'

'All your life, Ambris,' she replied smiling. 'For I am deeply rooted in yourself. All your life, unless – unless perhaps you will pay me to go away.'

'To go away for ever?'

'Yes, for ever, if you will give me what I ask.'

'And what is it you ask?'

'Your right hand, or—'

'Or—?'

'Yes, you have guessed it – your right hand, or your manhood.'

'Oh God!' the cry burst from him. 'Take my right hand, then.'

'Agreed. I will send one to take it, and then you will know that I have left you for ever.'

'Be it so. But oh—' as the full agony of it swept over him, 'I have a battle to fight – how shall I defend my lady without my right hand?'

She smiled that dreadful mocking smile.

'You could always choose the – other.'

'God, no!'

'Well then – but never fear. I would not be so unchivalrous as to deprive a man of his right hand *before* a battle ... The bargain stands. Farewell for the last time.'

Another flash of lightning wiped out the vision. Ambris's horse stirred and went forward again.

'Who did you speak to?' said Morwen. 'I saw nobody.'

'Don't speak of it,' said Ambris, and they went on through the slowly clearing night.

The keeper of the gatehouse at Camelot had had frights enough for one night, so that when two men on one horse came clattering out of the darkness and bade him open in the name of King Arthur, and one of them named himself as the Prince Morwen, he let them through and asked himself the questions afterwards. At the citadel gate there was more explaining.

'I am the Prince Morwen. Rouse the next man of the watch, quickly and quietly. I need you to come out *now* to fight for the Lady Ursula and King Arthur's house.' Word was passed from man to man. Some of them went softly, and made prisoners of Cadwallo and the two bishops. And as the dawn broke, silently and without noise of trumpets, a thousand men, one by one, had stolen away out of Camelot, and were heading southwards towards the plains of Glastonbury, under the banners of Morwen, Prince of Britain, and Sir Ambrosius, the liege men of Queen Ursula.

25 · *Towards the Battle*

Of course you ladies will stay here with the baggage-train when we attack,' said Bedivere.

'Of course we'll not,' said Lynett.

'But the safety of our Queen—'

'Not my safety, I note,' Lynett said, smiling sourly. 'No matter. By the Mass, do you think we'll be any safer sitting here in a ring of wagons, waiting for some rascally plunderer to set the place on fire?'

They had marched out of the Island of Glastonbury long before day, as soon as the thunderstorm had abated – the army of earls, twenty-four of whom were also Knights of the new Round Table; ten thousand soldiers, horse and foot, variously armed, followed by baggage-wagons and sumpters and camp-followers, a fantastic crowd. There had been no time for sleep. Ursulet, dazed and tired, had been made to stand high up on a wagon by the gate at Pomparles – the Pons Periculosus – surrounded by a rank of torches and banners, reviewing them as they went by. This was *her* army, she was told. And in a few hours they would be fighting for her.

After they had all gone by, she had been given a reasonably comfortable seat on the same wagon, and carried along in the midst of the army, with Melior, Bedivere and the two maids-in-waiting – these latter were quite frankly terrified, clinging to each other and crying. Lynett disappeared, and then presently came abreast of them riding one of her famous tall black horses and leading another. They rode a long way, to get clear of marsh country and narrow causeways, above all to avoid getting penned in a narrow place; but they went towards where they knew their enemy to be, not away.

After daybreak they halted, having come out into open country; the wagons were formed into a ring, and there they ate, and some of them slept for a short uneasy while. Now, under the cloth cover of Ursulet's wagon, they were gathered round her – Lynett, Bedivere and Melior. Further off they could see where a very ancient chivalric pavilion, its bright colours faded, sheltered Sir Ector and Sir Bors, bending together over a map in a lantern's light. Smoke and drizzle drifted in on Ursulet, her head ached, and she felt the discomfort of having slept in thick heavy clothes. It was all rather grim and discouraging.

'Of course we'll be no safer here,' Lynett pursued her theme. 'You understand that, don't you? – And then again, the Queen must lead her troops into battle.'

'No!' said Bedivere, and 'No!' said Melior.

'But I say yes,' said Lynett. 'Arthur's daughter could do no less, and it's what she herself wants – isn't it?'

'Oh, yes,' said Ursulet, but she felt her heart sinking. What she felt like saying was, 'No, I don't want to fight at all – why didn't you let me stay in the Abbey?' – but she knew she must not say that. Of course she must want to fight . . .

'I don't see why you men should keep all the fun for yourselves,' said Lynett. 'This is my fight, and the Lady Ursulet's too, and I wouldn't miss it for the world, nor would she – isn't that so, child?'

'Oh, yes,' said Ursulet rather faintly.

'But ladies,' said Bedivere, his leather corselet creaking as he turned with a courteous half-bow, 'I think you hardly understand – has either of you ever been in a battle?'

'I have,' said Lynett stoutly. 'Heavens, man, you should know that. I was in all King Arthur's battles, all seven of them – I carried the King's messages, and brought drink to the fighters, and tended the wounded on the field – precious few there were to do it. Bedivere, you saw me yourself at Badon, unless you've forgotten—'

'Then you should know it's no place—'

'Rubbish! She's got the guts for it, haven't you? Arthur's daughter – Besides, where else would she be safe? – Well, then, that's settled. She will ride my other black horse—'

'I can't ride,' said Ursulet.

'What – you can't *ride*?' Lynett's tone was completely incredulous. 'You mean to say you can't *ride*?'

'No, I never learnt.'

'Never learnt to *ride*?'

'No. Where would I learn to ride on a Jutish churl's farm?' Ursulet was beginning to feel more than a little resentment, now that they were no longer scrambling through dark passages, against this tough and masterful woman who was arranging everything for her.

'But you were in the convent before that,' Lynett protested. 'Didn't the nuns teach you *anything*?'

'Not riding. We didn't go outside the grounds – it was unsafe.'

'Unsafe, fiddlesticks! Can't you remember riding before you went to the convent?'

'On a pillion behind a manservant – but the plain fact is that I can't ride, and there isn't much time for me to learn, and I'm not going to start now by going into a battle.' She snapped her mouth shut. If she weakened at all, she felt, she might easily begin to cry.

'Well then,' said Lynett, 'you must have a chariot. It's quite right for a Queen to lead her troops from a chariot – the great Boudicca did so. Have we any chariots?'

'We've one, I believe,' said Bedivere rather dubiously.

'Right – order them to bring it here, and we'll have a look at it.'

The chariot was brought – an old-fashioned affair, which had been kept more for show than for use, but it would work. It was lightly built, with two large wheels; it had a bench seat where the passenger and the driver could sit together, and a back rail, and was drawn by two stocky British ponies. There was a driver, a young man from the western plains, who knew his ponies well. Forbears of his had driven chariots for the Romans before they went away.

'This will do,' said Lynett. 'You'll sit here beside the driver, where the knights and soldiers can all see you, and I'll ride close beside you and bear your standard. They shall see that Arthur's daughter is in the field.'

'Yes,' thought Ursulet to herself, 'and Arthur's daughter isn't afraid. But I am, oh, ghastly afraid. But I have to go on in spite of it. And I will, too, only – oh, dear God, don't let me show it. When we faced the cold-drake in the tunnel, no one was able to see the way I looked – and I didn't have time to think about it first ... and Ambris was there. But if Ambris has left me I might as well get killed – only it's going to be so messy and horrible. All very well for that Lynett – she's made of leather, heart and face and all. But she's not going to see me look frightened. What the devil! She thinks I'm a queen, and I'll go on looking like a queen . . . only . . . oh God . . .'

'What should I wear for the battle?' she said.

26 · *The Hour of the Morrigan*

And so this was it, Ursulet said to herself – this was the battle, that was coming nearer and nearer to her every minute. This long line of little dark figures, strung out before her, all shapes and sizes, but all bristling, dark against the sky. The two shaggy ponies, capably controlled by the young driver, paced forward, dragging the chariot that swayed and pitched so that she had to brace herself hard against the back rail. She was wearing a corselet, knee-length, of fine chain-mail, and a scarlet cloak over it, quite distinctive and conspicuous; Lynett had wanted her to wear her hair hanging loose, but she herself had realized that it would be dangerous, and had it tightly bound up behind her head with a red ribbon, and surmounted by a little gold circlet. She had to be a sign and a portent to her followers, although she might also be rather an easy target for her enemies. As she went along she did her best to remember to shout – it was supposed to inspire the men to follow her. Though she felt more like watching in silent fascination how that line in front came nearer, nearer, nearer.

Sir Bors and Sir Ector had to make the decisions as to where to go and what to do. She had no idea about it, but that this was the battle and they must go straight before them. She had a dagger at her belt, which might do some damage at a pinch, and a round targe on her left arm, an awkward thing, but it might keep off some of the blows. But they had not thought it right to give her a sword.

They were moving faster now – so were the enemy. Gradually, gradually they speeded up the pace. Now, with the rush of air, she began to feel better. Hoofs drummed all round her, men began to yell, an infection of excitement took them all – there was no point in being afraid of anything any more – one could just go, go, go – and then – *crash!*

It was the first blow on her shield – at the same time as the whole world broke up in a furious confusion of crashes all around her – she heard cries that seemed to be directed at her, and there were hands, hands, hands, clutching – the chariot rocked and swayed wildly, and then it was through the first rank, and both she and her driver were still there. Behind her she heard Lynett crying out, 'Oh, well done!' But then there were men running in front of her, and another rank to break through. She realized that she had automatically put up her shield in front of her face, and was beating off the blows that rained randomly upon it. Then she looked past the shield, and the first thing she could see was a sword coming down on the thickness of a man's leg, like a cleaver on a butcher's block – but the blood doesn't flow like that from dead meat – this was spurting out like a red fountain. Another man, she couldn't tell if he were friend or enemy, was right in front of the chariot, his face the colour of clay and helplessly upturned – the chariot wheel went over him and on, and she felt the ribs crack under the wheel.

The horror of it made all seem unreal to her. It did not mean anything – these carcases being so horribly unmade right before her eyes, they were not people – not human beings, surely – just – things? And she, what was she doing there? Remembering for a moment what she had been told she must do, she uncovered her face, waved her shield, and cried, 'Arthur for Britain! Arthur!'

Some quite unknown fighting man, below her, said, 'But you're unarmed, lady,' and handed her a sword. She took it – the hilt was still warm from the hand that had just dropped it

– and somehow the feel of it in her hand made her feel stronger, more assured – she could do something now, not just dodge the blows. She swung it experimentally, and then thrust it full in the face of a fierce man who was bearing down on her. It met his cheek, and the blood flowed – then the man dropped and seemed to vanish. So she thrust again at the next one.

She could not tell how long they had been fighting. It was all a confusion, a struggling, snarling crowd. Then above her she saw two glittering figures, armed and mounted – Mordred and his son Morcar.

Morcar gave a loud laugh.

'Oh, look, father – here's my wife come to meet me in her chariot!'

Two of Mordred's foot-soldiers ran to the ponies and held their heads; they reared up, and the chariot rocked backwards, Ursulet clinging on and only just keeping her feet; and Morcar, with a quick movement, sent his short stabbing spear right through the body of the young driver.

Ursulet cried out, hardly knowing what she was saying, 'You brute, why did you do that? He was a *good* driver—'

'You won't need him now, my love,' laughed Morcar.

Ursulet sprang quickly from the chariot to the ground; her foot soldiers surrounded her at once, lifting their shields to cover her. There did not seem to be as many of them as there were, and when she looked round for her mounted knights, she could hardly see any. Somewhere she could hear the ponies scream.

Then through the surrounding ranks of the foot-soldiers she heard a frightening word passed from one to another.

'The Romans! The Romans are coming!'

And at the same moment there broke out the awful terrifying sound of the great Roman war-trumpet – the Bull's Mouth.

They came cutting through the Britons like a knife through butter – the helmeted, red-cloaked men of Constantine, Britons trained like Romans, moving together at the word of command. Ursulet saw her men begin to waver and turn to run. Vainly she shouted to them: 'Stand, stand! Forward, forward, for Arthur and Ursula!'

She could see Lynett, some way off, still on her towering black horse, swinging her sword, beating the fliers with the flat of it, scolding them like a fishwife, all to no avail.

Then behind her went up a new cry, 'Ursula! Ursula! Arthur for Britain!' and other troops swept up from the rear, like the tide flowing into a river, and carried them forward again. A voice she knew said, 'I'm here, my dearest—' and Ambris's arm went round her, and under his shield he kissed her.

Behind him young Morwen, with a thousand men from Camelot, swept in to turn the tide against Mordred; and even the troops of Constantine were checked by the sudden surprise and broke their ordered ranks.

Ambris lifted Ursulet on to his horse before him; she held to him, but still her hand grasped the sword.

And in the midst of the confusion Morwen met with his father and his brother.

'God's death, you rebel!' thundered Mordred, charging down upon him, but Morcar was nearer in the crowd. Both the brothers had dismounted now, and were face to face.

'So, you milksop,' said Morcar, 'you've decided to try fighting for a change? No doubt because the women are fighting too. Come on – kill me if you can!'

He was within sword's length of him, and Morwen pointed his sword right at his breast – and dropped it again.

'No, Morcar, you know I can't kill you.'

'Then I can kill you, you coward!' and Morcar whirled his sword high in the air, and brought it crashing down on Morwen's head. Ursulet saw it split the boy's head as one would break a plaster image, and she was too stunned to utter more than a choked cry. She saw Mordred laughing heartlessly as his elder son killed his younger son – and then from the towering black horse, Lynett's whirling sword struck down Morcar, and he fell over his brother. And Mordred gave a great cry that pierced through all the noise. 'By a woman!'

he cried, and put his mailed hands over his face, and swayed where he sat on his horse.

There rose before him a kind of mirror, a kind of screen, cutting him off from the sight and sound of the battlefield – and in that mirror he saw Morgan le Fay. But now her dress was blood-red, and dripping with blood; and the rich jewels that adorned her neck and girdle were all made of bones.

She laughed at him.

'Now you may call me The Morrigan,' she said. 'It is one of my names. And you, Mordred – my vassal in soul and body, you are coming with me.'

'But my kingdom!' he cried. 'Woman or spirit or whatever you are – you promised me the kingdom. But now my sons lie dead—'

'I promised you nothing. All I said was that I had power to grant your wishes – and then you pledged yourself to me as my vassal. You should have known better than to trust me.'

He groaned, and could say nothing.

'And now – first I am going to send you to collect a certain pledge, and then, my vassal in this life and the life hereafter, you are coming with me.'

The vision passed, and Mordred sat on his horse bemused in the midst of the battle.

In front of him was Ambris, with Ursulet on the crupper of his horse behind him. Ambris held his long keen sword before him, but he had no gauntlet on his right hand. Mordred whirled up his sword, and as Ambris parried upwards, Mordred brought the keen edge down hard across Ambris's wrist, and struck his hand clean off. A horrifying fountain of blood spurted up. But Ambris, whose left hand was close to Ursulet, snatched the dagger from her belt with his left hand, and as he fell forward, drove it with all his force into the neck joint of Mordred's armour, and Mordred crashed with him to the ground and lay still. Ursulet tumbled from the horse, avoiding its hoofs as it broke free, and knelt beside Ambris. The blood was still pumping from his arm. She looked round for Lynett to help her, but could not see her – so, with her every breath a sob, she quickly untied the ribbon from her hair, and tied it tightly round Ambris's severed wrist, to check that ghastly bleeding. Then she picked up the sword that had fallen from his hand, and stood over him.

Somewhere behind her she heard Lynett shrilling out, 'They break, they give! Mordred's slain – come on, come on, come on!'

But at that moment a more deadly rumour went through friend and foe alike – a rumour that turned to a cry, a shout, a shriek of terror, 'The Saxons! The Saxons!'

Like a landslide they came – hordes upon hordes, sheer weight of numbers overwhelming all before them. No poet chronicled that battle – who can chronicle a moving mountain? Useless now for the Britons to turn and unite against a common foe. Too late, exhausted and leaderless, they broke and were swept away – even Constantine's Roman army was scattered, and forgot the Roman drill – what use was it here? And so the dark came down.

In the last light of day, Ursulet stood on what had been a little hill, but was now a mound of dead bodies, with Ambris at her feet. She swung the long sword in a ring – she had beaten off the foes, one by one, and now she beat off the black crows that flapped nearer and nearer, and the foxes and the rats. There was nothing else to do, but to keep swinging that sword. Her red cloak was in rags and soaked with blood, her hair down over her shoulders, tangled and ash-coloured, but the gold circlet still clung crookedly over her brow as if in mockery. So the night found her.

27 · *The Wälkure*

Two Saxons were crouching over a little fire under a thornbush, on the untidy, filthy field of battle, in the dark, when no man can fight. They looked up at the sound of plodding hoofs.

Two black horses, taller than any British or any Saxon horse, and a woman riding one and a black-cloaked man leading the other. A tall thin woman it was, wearing a leather corselet – an old woman, with wild grey hair streaming out on the wind. She rode slowly, looking at each corpse as she came by it.

The Saxons cried out, and both pointed together.

'Look! the Chooser of the Slain!'

'The Wälkure!'

'But they told us they were young and beautiful, and galloped fast along the sky—'

'How could they find their men if they galloped? And young and beautiful or not, this is the Wälkure. Look at her face—'

'It's a god-touched face. Thor preserve us! May he send a younger one for me—'

Presently the Saxons, watching, saw the two tall black horses coming back, and this time each was ridden by a woman. The grey-haired one carried a man lying across her saddle-bow; but the other woman, sitting stiffly on her horse, and staring before her with eyes that did not see, was young, pale-faced and with streaming flaxen hair, a torn red mantle, and a golden crown, and the black-cowled man led her horse.

Both the Saxons shuddered, one made the sign of the Hammer of Thor; the other said, 'The Lord between us and all harm!' and crossed himself; for he had once been a Christian of sorts.

The horses gathered speed in the darkness, and presently

were heard going away into the distance. Surely there would be company in Valhalla that night.

28 · Rex Futurus

𝔍t was a long while after that Ursulet opened her eyes to the light again. There had been a long, dark, dim time, when she seemed to have been carried in some way – she could faintly recall Lynett giving her a drink, and then only sleep again.

But once she had seen Ambris's face through the mists, and heard his voice, so she was sure that all was well, and slept again.

But now she was full awake, though very weak and stiff and sore. She was in a little whitewashed bedroom, very neat and light, on a soft curtained bed, but in no place that she had seen before; and Lynett was with her, she also very neat, almost like a nun in a white gorget and wimple.

'What's this?' she said. 'Where's Ambris?'

'You'll see him in a minute. Take it easy. Drink this.'

'What place is this? How long have I been here? How long have I slept?'

'Why, one way and another, you've slept a good many days. I gave you a sleep-drink, or it would have gone hard with you – since the battle, and that's the best part of a week ago.'

'The battle?' Ursulet struggled to rise. 'What of the battle?'

'Ah, lie still. No more battles for us now. I'll tell you all that later. You're in a safe place here – this is the heart of the mountains of Gwent, where the Saxons will never follow us. This is to be your home – yours and Ambris's.'

'Ambris! Oh, where is he? Let me see him – I won't rest till I see him.'

'Here he is, then.' Ambris stood by her bedside – pale, but

smiling. His right arm was wrapped in linen and slung in a scarf round his neck, and he laid his left hand on Ursulet's hand.

'I'm here, my love, my princess. Yours in heart and hand – but it will have to be my left hand now. I shan't wield a sword again.'

'Oh, your hand! Your right hand! Oh, Ambris . . .'

'My mother used to tell me,' he said, 'of an old heathen god who put his right hand in a wolf's mouth to save his people.'

He smiled, and all round her the faces were smiling and cheerful – the room was full of sunlight and flowers – and yet there was something . . .

'My mother's here too,' said Ambris, as a handsome woman came to his side. Her eyes were green but soft-lighted, and her hair was white, but held a hint of redness.

'This is the Lady Vivian, come from Lyonesse,' said Lynett. 'She will live here now. They – fear the floods in Lyonesse.'

Vivian stooped and kissed Ursulet, and Ursulet noticed how cold and tremulous her lips and her hands were.

Then they left Ambris and Ursulet for a little while, and they had a great deal to say.

Later, Lynett came and dressed Ursulet in a simple white dress, with a coronal of flowers; and in the little church on the mountain side, so small it might have been a hermitage, the solitary priest pronounced them man and wife – but Arthur had joined their hands long before.

Then they shared a quiet little feast together – the bride and bridegroom, Ambris's mother, and Lynett and Melior, in the kitchen of the farmhouse that was to be their home. A simple meal, and a cup or two of wine. And everyone tried to be light-hearted and happy, but something was amiss. And each time Ursulet asked questions about the battle, they shook their heads, or made excuses, or spoke of something else.

At last they had finished the meal, and drunk the wine, and said a seemly grace – and all drew their chairs in round the fire. Then Ursulet said, 'Now I must know the truth. Tell me about the battle.'

And they looked from one to another.

Then Lynett said, 'Well, you'd best have it straight then. We're beaten, yes, beaten into the ground. The Saxons possess the land.'

Ursulet gave a great cry, and bent her face down on her knees. But she said, her voice smothered by her hands, 'Go on. Tell me all.'

'They swept us off the field by sheer numbers. Friend and foe alike – Mordred's men and even Constantine's Roman-trained legion. They made no odds who fought for whom – they fought for themselves. We were like sheep . . .'

Ursulet wept quietly, and the old woman's voice broke as she went on.

'I should never have counselled fight . . . Oh God, how should I know?'

'Never blame yourself,' said Ambris, his arm round Ursulet.

'They have overspread the country, and hold Winchester now,' Lynett went on. 'Their king has set up his seat there.'

'But Glastonbury?' Ursulet lifted her head. 'They've not profaned the holy Avalon?'

'No – the approach through the swamps was too hard for them, and I think they feared the Tor – they think there is a devil there. So they went on to ravage the Baths of Sul, where they think the Romans have left buried treasure.'

'And we – do we fight again?'

'We cannot. I doubt we could muster five hundred men. The Knights are gone – all slain – Sir Ector and Sir Bors, and our dear old Sir Bedivere – and many, many others—' Lynett's voice, husky with grief, faltered away, and she too hid her face.

'Why did you not let me die then?' exclaimed Ursulet, suddenly fierce. 'Why did you not let us both die, with honour on the field?'

'Listen, child.' The old woman had recovered command of herself and her old manner. 'When I found you and knew how things stood, I had my dagger ready for you both, to give you the kind stroke and let you sleep – but Melior prevented me. He said he must save something more precious than Arthur's throne or Arthur's sword.'

'Yes,' broke in Melior's voice, 'Arthur's true seed. That it is, which we must preserve. Merlin has stood by me in the night, through many nights, and I know what his meaning is. No power can stop the Saxons now – it is written that they are to possess the land.'

'Oh God!' cried Ursulet, 'So all is in vain?'

'No, not in vain. Like a plant that dies down in the winter, and guards its seed to grow again, so you two must raise the lineage from which all Arthur's true followers are to grow – not by a royal dynasty, but by spreading unknown and unnoticed, along the distaff line – mother to daughter, father to daughter, mother to son. Names and titles shall be lost, but the story and the spirit of Arthur shall not be lost. For Arthur is a spirit, and Arthur is the land of Britain. And the time shall come when the Saxons, yes, the Saxons shall pay homage to Arthur too – yes, and other races we do not know yet ... But in the end, Cymry and Saxon, and others from over the sea, will all be one, and all will know the name of Arthur. And there will be those among them, like a thread in the tapestry, who are your descendants, many, many generations to come. Here, in your safe retreat in the mountains of Gwent, you shall be Arthur's Adam and Eve. So shall Arthur conquer, not by one war, nor by one kingship, that soon passes away, but by the carriers of the spirit that does not die. Not by any son of Arthur, born to take the sword and perish by the sword – but by the daughter of Arthur, born to give life to those that come after.'

Ambris looked down at Ursulet, but her face was bent away from him.

'Arthur shall come again,' she whispered, and he felt her tears fall upon his hand. Then she lifted her head, and looked up at him with new radiance in her eyes. 'Oh, yes, yes – Arthur shall come again.'